ABROAD

A Novel of Cross-Cultural Encounters

Greyson Bryan

Magneto Books

NEW YORK, NEW YORK

Magneto Books
POB 230535
New York, NY 10023
magnetobooks.com

Publisher's Note: This is a work of fiction. Names, characters, places, and incidents are a product of the author's imagination. Locales and public names are sometimes used for atmospheric purposes. Any resemblance to actual people, living or dead, or to businesses, companies, events, institutions, or locales is completely coincidental.

Book Layout ©2017 BookDesignTemplates.com
Cover design ©2022 Rebecca Lown Design
Cover Photographs: Top: @Alamy Stock Photo,
Middle: @Shutterstock, Bottom: atlantic-kid @IstockPhoto

Abroad: A Novel of Cross-Cultural Encounters/ Greyson Bryan. – 2nd ed.
ISBN 979-8-9861955-0-6

Contents

Not all those who wander are lost

– J.R.R. TOLKEIN, *The Fellowship of the Ring*

PRAISE FOR *ABROAD*

"Sweet and supremely readable, ABROAD is a celebration of travel and all ways it can lead us to rediscover ourselves and relearn the true meaning of love."

--IMBOLO MBUE, Author of *How Beautiful We Were*

"Grey Bryan's new novel ABROAD is framed, seemingly simply, as a tale told by a recently widowed lawyer, Skip Burton, to his daughter Jenny: a story of youthful travels, with a touch of mystery, about how he and her mother fell in love. Written with a simple direct style that belies a nuanced, complex view of identity, nationality and culture, the novel unfolds as a series of reminiscences of life abroad. The early adventures Skip relates to his daughter—set in Mexico, Taiwan, and Japan—have the moral force of case studies in the dilemmas of international living. They're brought into focus with a psychological clarity that offers a beguiling sense of security, as if Skip were striving to pass along curated pieces of wisdom. But as the principal characters of his tales move through their youth in the 1960s into adulthood in the 1970s, the meanings of the journeys overseas, and our understanding of the direction of Skip's narrative, lose their confident moorings. Moral certainty washes away. The price of self-knowledge becomes steep and emotionally harrowing. And relationships prove to be anything but what they seem. Charged with the emotional blindness and recklessness of youth—and the many varieties of overconfident Americans overseas—ABROAD unfolds and resolves with a touching cumulative force. Its deeply satisfying structural surprises will open readers' eyes to the discomfiting but transformative truths of international life and leave readers shaken and inspired."

--TED BRAUN, Professor of Cinematic Arts at USC

"If you are open to ways of seeing and behaving that challenge your conventions; if you are willing to plunge into romance, friendship, work, or faith unmoored by shared understandings and cultural tropes, and risk being hurt, abandoned, confused but also exhilarated and thrilled, then Grey Bryan's ABROAD is the book for you.

Bryan's characters embed themselves in their new worlds and lives, often with little guidance and no safety net. They suffer disillusionments but also find unexpected joy. Most of all, they are changed. And you will be, too, when you journey into this book."

--RICHARD KLETTER, Film and TV Writer and Long-time Graduate Lecturer at USC's School For Cinematic Arts

"ABROAD is compelling, vivid in imagery and character. In creating a world where the lead character's childhood begins as mine did, leaving the country for parts unknown at the age of six, Greyson Bryan ably captures a child's fear of departing for the unknown on the apparent whim of his parents. I was fascinated by the unease that Bryan creates in the lives of Skip, Maddie, and Rex as they each attempt to reconcile their curiosity about other cultures with their respective blind spots. For those thinking about travel to a new place, whether overseas or in a different region of this country, ABROAD offers a cautionary note on the importance of setting aside our preconceived ideas of culture, tradition, and love. Ultimately hopeful, ABROAD makes a strong case for the importance of cross-cultural experience in coming to understand ourselves."

--JACQUELINE WENDER, Former Executive Director of Overseas Studies at Stanford and lifelong traveler

"In this literary novel centered on travel and the lessons we can learn from crossing borders with an open heart, Bryan, author of the BIG thriller series, weaves an ambitious, globe-crossing narrative of interconnected lives and loves. At its heart is Skip Burton, prompted to reflect on his earlier life and the role that travel played in shaping him. At a young age, Skip proved an extremely reluctant traveler. As he grows and matures, spending time in Asia and Mexico, travel becomes a more permanent fixture in Skip's life, helping him to build confidence as he opens up to new cultural experiences—and new people.

Bryan's story springboards from a grabber of a question. Jenny, Skip's late wife, had told Jen, their daughter, that, despite her years married to a traveler, she herself had never left the United States. A year after Jenny's death, daughter Jen presents Skip with a photo of Jenny and Skip in Japan in 1974. Like Jen, readers will wonder why this was kept secret; the bulk of the novel, covering the journeys and connections made by Skip and his friend Maddie in the long-gone 1960s and 1970s, builds to the urgent, touching answer. Bryan charts his adventures abroad, eventually in the Volunteer Service in Asia, plus those of Skip's Kansan-by-birth but Californian-by-choice VSA rival Rex, whose romantic travails eventually involve death threats in Indonesia. The final chapters, meanwhile, return to the bumptious circumstances of Skip's early relationship to Jenny.

The result is a rich, often finely detailed mosaic of lives and longings, with multiple point-of-view characters and a recurring message of understanding. Some shifts in perspective and place can occasionally jar readers' sense of where they are in the story, but throughout Bryan dramatizes the ways that cultural capital can help build lifelong connections that teach us how we deal with ourselves and those outside our experience."

--BOOKLIFE

PROLOGUE

The door to the study creaked opened. A wide beam of light cut through the dusky room. Skip sat slumped forward in his leather reading chair with his head in his hands.

"Dad?"

Skip ran his fingers through his thinning salt-and-pepper hair and looked up at his daughter with bleary eyes.

"Are you okay?" she asked. "You've been in that chair for hours again today and it's getting dark in here. Should I turn on the light?"

"Oh. I hadn't noticed the time slipping away, but no . . . no, I don't want the light on. Easier to think with it off."

"You mean about Mom?"

His daughter stepped through the door, walked over to him, and set a cardboard box on the floor beside his chair. Her light, citrusy perfume made him suddenly conscious of how close the air was.

"All the time. You know, Jen, in a couple of weeks, it'll be our twenty-second wedding anniversary . . ."

"And almost a year since the cancer diagnosis and three months since she died. I know. I count the days, too. It hurt like hell then and it still does."

Jen stepped behind him and began to massage his shoulders. Her delicate hands were surprisingly strong—like her mother's.

"I was cleaning out the garage to make room for my high school books and way in the back I came across this beaten-up old box. It's taped shut but not the way Mom would do it—you know, perfectly neat and tidy with a description of the contents written on top in her lovely letters. So"—she giggled softly—"I thought it must be your stuff."

"I don't remember packing anything away, but my memory isn't as good as it used to be," Skip said hoarsely. "So who knows." He shrugged.

"Oh, come on." She kissed the top of his head. "You're not even fifty-two! Let's open it and decided if we should toss the contents."

Jen pulled scissors from the back pocket of her jeans, leaned over, and sliced the tape apart. She pulled a chair next to Skip, placed the box on her lap, and opened it. A musty odor wafted up.

"Not much here. Just a rolled-up yellowing poster of some kind. '*À tous les Français. Pour la République avec de Gaulle. Vive la France!*'" she read out loud.

"Is this leaflet yours? You traveled to France?"

Skip stared at the frayed paper, his mind reaching back decades.

"Grandpa and Grandma took me to Paris in 1958," he replied vacantly. "First trip abroad. I was seven, almost eight. I can't believe it's been forty-four years."

"And this . . ." Jen picked up a russet-colored baseball mitt with a black splotch in the middle. "It must be ancient; the fingers are so short and stubby."

Skip reached for the glove and turned it over. The signature was still visible on the back strap. He rubbed his finger gently across the faded ink. How many years have passed?

"Francisco," he breathed.

"Where'd you get this? And who's Francisco?"

"One of the wisest people I've ever known. It was a gift from him. A Mexican friend of Grandpa's and mine. It was his glove when he played baseball in Mexico in the thirties. We met the summer I turned twelve. The last time I saw him—in 1968, before I went to UCLA—he gave it to me."

So long ago, he mused to himself. *I'm as old now as he was when I met him.*

"I knew you spent a few summers in Mexico, but I thought you were on the beach. Tourists. I had no idea Grandpa and you had a close friend there. You are full of surprises today, aren't you?"

Jen shook her head and pulled a book out of the box.

"A 1975 book on Indonesian culture and society? You went to Indonesia, too?"

She leafed through the book and a grimy slip of paper fell to the floor. Jen reached down and silently read the short note.

"Here." She offered it to Skip.

He held up his hand. "I know what it says, sweetheart."

Skip closed his eyes and pictured the brief message that changed his life forever.

"Then who wrote it?"

"A man named Widiyanto. He was a *dukun*. Someone we might call a shaman, but he thought of himself as a healer. Very different from Francisco, but he was also one of the most insightful people I've ever met."

"He mentions Mom. How could he have known about her? She never left the country. Did you tell him about her?"

"No, I didn't tell him anything." Skip exhaled forcefully, as if the weight of the recollection had pushed the air from his lungs. "And all these years later, I still have no idea how he knew about her."

"So you went to France as a child, Mexico as a boy, Indonesia after college, and met two of the most meaningful men in your life overseas. I know you lived in Japan for a time, too. Where else did you travel?"

"Oh, Korea, Taiwan, Hong Kong, Thailand, India . . . a few countries in Europe and North Africa. Before your mom and I got married."

"*What?*" Her voice rose in pitch. "You never said a word about these experiences and yet the people you met were obviously very important to you."

Skip took a deep breath.

"Next to your mom and you," he murmured. "The most important."

"Really? In what way?"

"I loved exploring how people from a different culture think and act . . . but, most of all, how each day taught me things about myself I could never have learned at home."

"There's a lilt in your voice I haven't heard in a long time . . ."

"Thinking about how it felt to go abroad when I was younger, I guess. I . . . I never felt more alive."

"But why am I hearing about this now? We never went overseas as a family—not even to Mexico. *Why?* I begged you to let me go to Japan and Korea last summer with my high school. Mom said I was too young and didn't want me to get hurt. And *you*, you didn't say a word to support me. Why didn't you stick up for me, want me to have the experiences you had? *Why?*"

Skip avoided her gaze and stared out the window at the darkening sky. The answer lay unopened in the box.

"There's one last thing, sweetheart," he whispered and pointed to the box. "The manila envelope . . ."

Jen laid down the note, lifted an envelope out of the box, and opened it with a swipe of her scissors. "Here," she said gruffly and handed it to Skip.

He extracted a photograph of a dozen smiling young Americans. The two kneeling in front held up a sign: *Volunteer Service in Asia – 1974 Japan.* Jen peered over his shoulder at the picture.

"That's you in the back row. Wait . . ."

She fixed her eyes on the photograph, squinted, and gasped.

"Is that *Mom* in the front? But . . . Mom told me she had never been outside the country, felt no need to go, saw no reason for *me* to go. Now I find out *she* was in Japan doing what she prevented me from doing last year! She *lied* to me? And you said *nothing?*"

"It wasn't a big lie, Jen," Skip replied softly. "She was only in Japan for a couple of days and then returned home."

"I don't understand. She flew all the way to Japan for a few days? Did something happen?"

Skip caught his breath for a moment. So here it was. The question he had known ever since her mom died that Jen would ask someday.

"Something devastating, soul-wrenching and . . . when she asked me to help her I . . . well . . ." Skip turned to face his daughter, his eyes welling with tears. "I failed her, Jen. I failed her."

"That's not possible. You *loved* her, Dad. My God, I saw how you loved her. And she adored you."

"Yes, we loved each other very much from the day we first met, but I disappointed her deeply when she needed me most."

"But why?" Jen laid her hand on her father's arm. " *Why?*"

Skip shifted uneasily in his chair. He took his daughter's hand and gazed into her eyes. A vision of his wife appeared. *It's all right, love. You can tell her now.* The tightness in his chest loosened. *Thank you, love.*

"Well, we have to go back to my first trip, when your grandma and grandpa took me to France in 1958. I was so scared to travel overseas that I tried"—Skip chuckled lightly—"in my seven-year-old way, to sabotage the trip before it started."

1 Discovery

Be be be beeep! *Be be be beeep*! The little boy reached out, spread the branches of a huge ficus tree standing inside the fenced-in front yard, and peered down at the canary-yellow taxi pulling into the driveway below. Black and white checkers ran like scales along the side down to its enormous tailfins. His dad helped the driver lift four suitcases into the trunk of the taxi just as his mom swept out the front door. She turned to kiss Grandma on the cheek, stroked the head of Rusty, their aging Golden Retriever, and stepped down the flagstone path to the car. After handing her cosmetic case to the driver, she glanced at the rear seat. Her head jerked back.

"Where's Skippie?" she cried out.

"He was just here," his dad replied as he banged the trunk closed. "Skipper?" he shouted.

"I told you to watch him!" his mom scolded. "You know he's upset about the trip. He wet his bed twice this week. The gate's open for the taxi. Do you think he wandered out?"

"No, I was in the driveway the whole time." His dad shook his head. "Goddammit! We'll miss the train. SKIPPER! SKIPPER!"

The boy held his breath and willed his body to be as rigid as the branch on which he perched. The peanut butter and jelly sandwich he'd eaten for lunch soured in his mouth. His dad turned to the driver.

"Would you honk the horn again?"

Be be be beeep! Be be be beeep! The little boy sighed with relief, leaned back, and allowed the leaves to cover his face. He inhaled their familiar, earthy scent and congratulated himself on his daring plan. His parents wouldn't leave without him. They'd miss the train to New York and the ship to Europe. His mom and dad would be angry for a little while but soon would realize he'd saved them all from a terrible death. They would love him even more.

The tree suddenly began to sway as if a giant animal was trying to shake him to the ground. Large hairy hands parted the branches. His dad's dark blue eyes, crinkled at the corners, looked up at him. His heart sank.

"Skipper? You okay? We have to go, son."

"I don't *want* to go. It's too far away. We'll never make it," he whimpered. His dad smiled and gently squeezed the boy's thigh.

"But you like adventures, don't you? That's why you climb your tree. To see the world from a different place." The little boy felt his lower lip tremble.

"I climb the tree to *pretend*. Besides, the tree is in *our* yard. The trip is real and we're going so far away. You said they don't even speak English in France! How can we understand what they want? How can they understand us?"

A lump grew in the little boy's throat. He felt his eyes water. Nightmares had invaded his sleep during the past week. Horrendous dreams in which their train crashed or their ship sank. Most recently and terrifyingly he dreamed he had wandered a cavernous Paris restaurant desperate to find a bathroom. He asked a crow-faced waiter for help, but the waiter shrugged in incomprehension and hurried on. His groin throbbed in pain. He grabbed his penis but too late. Pee flowed down his leg into a puddle on the floor. Men with thin black moustaches and women with elaborately coiffed hair sniffed the air, pointed at him, and guffawed in a language he did not understand. When he looked up for help, his parents turned away in shame and hid their faces in their menus.

"Yes, this is real and Europe is far away," his dad agreed in his soft voice, the voice he used to read bedtime stories. "And you're right. Most people in Europe don't speak English. But they're people just like us. Do you remember? You were afraid to go up in your tree a year or so ago, but you loved it once you let me lift you up. Before you knew it, you were scampering up by yourself."

"Sort of," the little boy half-admitted, avoiding his father's gaze.

"Well, you're going to love travel too once you give it a chance." His dad's eyes smiled up at him.

"I don't know. I don't *knooooow*." The little boy's voice vanished into a low whine. He felt a knot twist in his stomach. He loved his parents deeply and craved their praise as much as their affection. He had begun to climb the tree by himself less out of a spirit of adventure than a desire to make his parents proud. Still, he had known his tree his whole life and his dad had lifted him up countless times before he scrambled up by himself. Deciding to mount it alone was like doing something new with an old friend at home, not meeting a complete stranger in some faraway place. Fear swelled in his chest, making it hard to breathe. The world abroad was uncharted territory where he might commit some terrible mistake that would disappoint his parents. Would they love him less?

"Say, guess what I have?" his dad said.

"What?" the little boy asked grudgingly.

"I have a book that will help us speak French." His dad held up a book with red, gold, and green horizontal stripes on the cover, the word "Berlitz" emblazoned in gold against the green band, and the word "French" printed in black letters against the gold. A vision suddenly passed through the little boy's mind of his dad reading French from the book to a gray-haired stranger wearing a beret and glasses. The man smiled and nodded his head in complete understanding. When his dad had finished, the stranger replied in nonsensical sounds, gesturing with his hands the way a conductor leads an orchestra. As the man spoke, his dad's eyes studied the book with intense concentration. When the Frenchman had finished, his dad looked up from the book, beamed back at him as if they'd been friends for years, and reached out to shake his hand.

"Come on, Skipper. I'll keep you safe. I promise." His dad tucked the book into his back pocket and held his hands up. "Slide over here and I'll lift you down."

Tears dropped from the little boy's eyes. His throat tightened. "Will you come with me to the bathroom in the restaurants there?" he croaked.

His dad cocked his head and crunched his eyes to examine him. Then he smiled. "Sure I will, if it would make you feel better. Now come on."

The little boy sighed, took a deep breath, and wiped the moisture from his cheek with the back of his hand. He wrapped his arms tightly around his dad's neck and closed his eyes. In a second, he felt himself float away from his tree like a balloon carried by the wind up and out to an unknown land beyond the horizon.

Wu wu wu wuuu. Wu wu wu wuuu. The train lurched forward as its whistle echoed far into the night. Skip opened his eyes. Darkness filled the tiny compartment. He could hear his parents breathing in the bunk beds across from where he lay curled up on the slender couch in his Tom Sawyer pajamas. Turning onto his stomach, he parted the window curtains and gazed out. Dawn was beginning to erase the shadows of the night. The train, which had been stopped at a station, was slowly stirring again like a giant animal rousing itself from sleep.

Suddenly he saw a little girl, about his age, standing beneath a pale white light on a wooden platform. She wore a turquoise blue dress and a pink sweater. Her dad's hands rested on her shoulders. She was waving goodbye to the train with one hand while the other covered her mouth. Her shoulders heaved with sobs. As she passed his window, Skip raised his hand to wave back. He didn't know her name, what games she liked to play, or even whether she liked to play with boys, but he raised his hand and gestured back hoping to forge a silent bond to ease her sorrow, and his own sense of foreboding. He felt her eyes lock briefly on his before she turned away. Skip craned his neck to watch the girl recede into the distance. As the train sped up, she thrashed her hand over her head more and more desperately as if she were trying to warn him. *Don't go any further! Don't go any further!*

"You okay, Skipper?" Dad whispered and sat down beside him. "Trouble sleeping?"

"I saw a girl waving. She looked very sad so I waved back."

"That's nice." Dad rubbed his eyes.

"I wish I knew her name," Skip sighed. "I wish I knew what she was like."

"Well, let's give her a name, then. How about Sally?"

"I like Maddie better."

"Like your friend, Madeline, at school? The tall girl with the short blonde hair? The one who plays games with the boys?"

"Her name is Maddie, Dad." Skip declared in a tone that allowed no disagreement. "She is my *best* friend."

"Oh, well," his dad murmured, suppressing a smile. "I didn't know. Maddie is a nice name. I bet the girl you saw is a lot like Maddie. I bet you could be friends, too." Skip flipped onto his back, folded his hands on his chest, and stared up at the ceiling. He took a deep breath and inhaled the cabin's stuffy, humid air.

"I wish I could stay with her," he whispered.

"Maddie?"

"Yes, Maddie, but also the girl back there."

"Why?"

"Because they're not going anywhere. They're home. Safe."

"Still feeling nervous about the trip?"

Skip pulled the thin, scratchy blanket up under his chin.

"It's such a long way." He exhaled. "Do you still have your book? So we can talk to them? So they can understand us? So I don't make any really bad mistakes?"

"Sure, I do. But, listen, we all make mistakes. That's . . ."

"That's how we learn," Skip chimed in. "I know. You always say that." He yawned and stretched his arms out.

Skip felt his dad tuck the sheet and blanket around his body. A soft kiss on his cheek followed, Dad's whiskers grazing his skin. The comforting smell of Dad's toothpaste filled Skip's nose.

"Try to get a little more sleep. We'll be in New York tonight. It's a huge city with an enormous park in the middle. In late May the flowers will be in full bloom. Say, do you remember the book *Stuart Little,* and the chapter about the sailboat race? The giant pond where Stuart Little raced his sailboat is in that park."

Skip wondered if he would be able to sail a boat on the pond. Then a new worry leapt up in his mind.

"They speak English in New York, don't they?"

"Yes." His dad laughed. "At least a kind of English. Get some more sleep, Skipper."

Ba ba ba baaah. Ba ba ba baaah. Skip covered his ears as the ship's horn blasted above him. Perched on Dad's shoulders, he gazed out at the shore gliding toward them. Seagulls squawked and soared over head. The sharp tang of salt air assaulted his nose and mouth. His mother stood silently by watching the land approach, her hand gently rubbing his back. She had wrapped herself in what she called her black wool swing coat because it swung around her body like a bell when she walked. Dad always said the coat made her look like an actress called Audrey Hepburn.

"Where are we?"

"France, Skipper," his dad replied. "Le Havre. After seven days at sea, we're passing through the breakwater—those boulders on our right and left that protect the port from rough seas. Straight ahead is the harbor where we'll dock. Over there"—Dad pointed to the horizon on the right—"is the mouth of a large river, the Seine. If you follow it east, you'll come to Paris."

"What is on the other side of the river? Is that France, too? Beaches like at home?" Skip could feel his parents stiffen at his question. Why?

"It's a part of France called Normandy," Dad said. Mom abruptly stopped rubbing his back, took a deep breath, and slowly blew the air out through her lips.

"Those are not just *beaches*, Skippie," his mom said.

Skip swiveled to look at his mom. Her eyes had narrowed and the lines around her mouth tightened. "We can't see from here, but the coast over there is where . . ." She paused, then continued in a voice devoid of the music that normally animated it, "Where fourteen years ago, more than six years before you were born, many Americans, English, Canadians, and French landed in ships. They fought and died to rescue Europe from some very bad people."

Mom slumped against the railing as if uttering the words had exhausted her. She stared out toward the faraway shore.

"Was your ship there, Dad?" Skip looked down at the silver hair on his dad's head.

"No. I was in the Pacific Ocean, on the other side of the world," his dad explained in a hushed, hollow tone.

Something *was* wrong. Skip glanced nervously at his mom. Her eyes were riveted on the horizon.

"What are you looking at, Mom?" Skip asked cautiously. He didn't *think* he'd done anything wrong asking about the beach, but he couldn't always tell either, and sometimes Mom or Dad would unexpectedly become angry at him. Mom didn't reply. Skip felt unease swirl around his family like fog.

"Honey, do you want me to tell him?" Dad asked.

Mom continued to peer out over the ocean. She pressed her lips together for a moment and nodded slowly.

"Okay. Skipper," Dad began, "I wasn't there, but a . . . a very good friend of your mom's, someone she grew up with, someone she was very fond of, landed on the beach to fight against the bad people."

"Is he your friend, too, Dad?"

"No!" his mother interjected suddenly and pushed herself from the railing.

Skip could see her face flush and her eyes flare.

"Your dad never met him. He was *my* friend, my dear, dear friend since fifth grade. The best friend I ever had until I met your dad. And he was . . . he was killed that day fighting to save the world from the most evil, vile, brutal people the world has ever known. The *Germans*."

His mother vomited the word from deep within her, cupped her face with her hands, and began to cry in a way Skip had never seen, waves of pain surging up within her as though she had stubbed not just her toe but her whole body. Dad gripped Skip's legs with one arm and put his other arm around Mom's shoulders. Skip felt his stomach begin to churn.

"But, Dad! You said the people here were like us! But they're not! They're *bad*! They killed Mom's friend!"

Dad remained silent for a long time one arm around Mom and the other grasping Skip's leg. He felt his dad's chest rise and fall as if speaking required more strength than he possessed at the moment.

"They are like us, Skipper," he declared quietly. "Maybe not exactly like us but they're human, too. And while most people are good, some are not, even in America. In wartime, sometimes even good people do terrible things to one another, but the war's over now."

"The Germans are *not* like us!" His mother threw his dad's arm off. Her eyes bulged out as she screamed at him. "They are inhuman monsters! How can you excuse the atrocities they committed by saying 'Sometimes even good people do terrible things to one another?' What bullshit! What nauseating *crap*!"

"Honey, I was just . . ."

"Our son has a right to know how barbaric the world can be, why I hug him close to us all the time. He should know that in this awful world love, no matter how strong, even as strong as our love for him, is not always enough to keep people safe."

Skip had heard his parents fight a handful of times, but Mom had never cursed Dad before. He struggled to keep from sobbing, fearful it would only add to the tension that had so unexpectedly boiled up between them.

"All right, honey," Dad whispered finally and reached out to take her hand. "Believe me, I know as well as you do the world can be cruel."

Skip watched his mom stare at his dad, hoping his words would soothe her. After a long time, she wiped her eyes. Her body, which seemed to have been wound as tight as a spring, relaxed. She let out a long, low sound, half sigh, half moan. She reached up to touch the dark red ribbon on Dad's left cheek that Mom called a scar but Dad said was his "beauty mark."

"Yes, I know you do, honey. God, I know you do." She took Dad's hand in hers again and held it up to her cheek for a moment. "I'm sorry, but I . . . I don't feel very well. I'm going down to our cabin to finish packing up."

His mom kissed Dad on the left cheek, leaving a trace of red lipstick over part of the scar. She squeezed Skip's leg before turning to walk back through the door that led to the cabins. Relief that the storm between his parents had passed turned quickly to panic as Skip absorbed what his mom had said.

"Dad," he began to mewl. "I'm scared. What if the bad people are in Paris? Mom said you couldn't protect us. *She* wants us to stay on the boat. *I* want to stay on the boat. Let's go *home*."

Dad reached up to lift Skip from his shoulders. He cradled his son in his arms and pressed him against his shoulder.

"Do you remember how mad your mom was at me the first time I lifted you up to climb your tree?" He held Skip out so he could look directly into his eyes. Skip remembered how Mom had stomped her foot and shook her fist at Dad.

"He's too young! Get him down now!" she'd cried.

"Do you also remember how proud she was when she saw you were good at climbing and loved doing it? I know it's difficult for you to understand, but she can have two different feelings at the same time. She loves you so much, she can be afraid you might hurt yourself and, at the very same time, want you to grow up strong and . . . and adventurous.”

Skip thought hard about what his dad had said. He knew he had mixed up feelings sometimes; he had them now. He was worried about his mom and he was scared for himself.

“Are the bad people all gone now?” he finally asked.

“Yes, Skipper.” Dad exhaled. “They’re all gone.”

Skip believed his dad but wanted to ask his mom the same question, just to be sure. He looked up at Dad.

“Is Mom okay?”

“Yes, she’s okay, but she’s also upset. You said Maddie is your best friend, right? Well, your mom was much closer even than that to her friend. Losing him made her very sad, made her terribly afraid of losing anyone else she loves deeply, especially you.”

“What about you, Dad?”

“Well”—Dad chuckled—“of course, she loves me and I’m sure deep down is afraid of losing me, too. But, I’m not seven . . .”

“. . . going on eight!”

“Yes, going on eight, like you. She knows I can take care of myself. Besides, when she tries to protect me, I just laugh and tell her I love her.” Dad smiled at the thought. “Always remember there’s another side to her, too. She is not a fearful, timid person; she is lively and curious about the world. We’re here not just because your mom wanted to visit Paris, but because she wanted *you* to experience life outside of California. To have memories of this trip abroad to guide you for the rest of your life. She’ll be better once we’ve landed in France. Now . . . let me show you something I think you’ll recognize.”

Dad pivoted around, lifted him on his shoulders again, and pointed toward a town.

“Do you see the buildings and the church steeple? That’s Le Havre. Does it remind you of anything?”

Skip squinted toward the cluster of buildings that was rapidly growing larger and larger. They looked like the pictures in one of his books.

"It looks like where Anatole lives," he ventured.

"You're right! Anatole lived in a small mouse village and would bicycle into Paris each night to look for food. Paris is the capital of France: where we're going tonight."

"On a bicycle?" Skip asked, anxiety cracking his voice. He didn't feel very confident riding his bicycle, except in the parking lot at school on the weekends.

"No." Dad laughed lightly. "On a train. In three or four hours, we'll get off and travel to Paris. I hope you'll sleep on the train. We'll arrive pretty late tonight."

"So, we made it to France? And you still have your book to help us understand what everyone is saying?"

Dad nodded and patted his son's legs gently.

"Yes. We made it. You know, I think you'll like Paris. Maybe we'll even run into Anatole."

"Okay, Dad," Skip said. "I think I'm ready now. Let's go."

"Great, son. Let's see how your mom is doing."

Di di di daaah. Di di di daaah. Skip's eyes snapped open. He peered out into the dark. He couldn't see a thing but he sniffed the familiar sweet-sour aroma of his Tom Sawyer pajamas. He was home! He'd had a long, terrible nightmare!

Di di di daaah. Di di di daaah. Oh, no! He squeezed his eyes shut and clapped his hands over his ears to keep out the sound, willing away the noise that signified something different, danger-ous. He opened his eyes and lowered his hands, slowly praying for silence. The ceiling that appeared through the shadows rose higher than the one in his bedroom. He looked across the room and noticed black curtains covering two long windows. His room at home had three short windows. He reached out and touched the sides of his bed with both hands. His bed at home was much wider. His heart sank. He wasn't home. He wasn't safe, after all.

Di di di daaah. Di di di daaah. The horns blared. Now he remembered. They had disembarked from the ship, rode in a taxi to the train station, and boarded just before the train pulled out. Dad had used his book to guide them and buy sandwiches and a bottle of wine for dinner on the train. He fell asleep with his head on Mom's lap and his legs draped over his dad's waist. He didn't remember arriving in Paris and only vaguely recalled Dad carrying him up to the room in their hotel. He realized now he had been dreaming of the taxi to the train, the train to New York, and the ship to Le Havre, all real only days ago.

A door in the room stood partially open. He rose from the bed and crept on tiptoes toward it. He heard the soft, slow breathing of his mom and the occasional snuffle of his dad.

Di di di daaah. Di di di daaah. He slapped his hands to his ears again. The first three notes were sharp like raps on the window by a stranger who wanted to be let in, short, insistent; the fourth sound was deeper, longer, a stranger pleading for help before it was too late. Too late for what? He knew he couldn't fall asleep again until he had discovered the origin of the strange sounds.

He dropped his hands from his head and stepped to a window. The heavy curtains smelled musty. He slowly parted them, just wide enough to peek out, and stared down at a narrow cobblestone street lined with lamp posts. People crowded the sidewalks, spilling into the street, marching from right to left. Cars, their headlights blazing, moved slowly among the mass of people like floats in the Rose Parade, only at night. And the people weren't cheering like they did in Pasadena. Some shook their fists above their heads. Others swung flashlights to illuminate the road. He could hear the crowd chanting but could not understand the words. He pressed his face to the window.

Di di di daaah. Di di di daaah. "*Vive la France! Vive de Gaulle!*" *Di di di daaah. Di di di daaah!*

A flashlight's beam burst through the glass pane and locked on his face. An old man with a long nose and a crooked grin stared up at him, pointed a gnarled finger, and waved his arm in a sweeping motion, beckoning Skip to come join the throngs below. Terrified, he leapt backwards out of the light, stumbled over a stool, and fell to the floor.

"Skipper?"

The blood in his veins racing, Skip pushed himself to his feet. "What's going on?"

Skip looked up to see Dad standing a few feet away in his robe and slippers, his hand stifling a yawn.

"There are a lot of people outside, and cars, too," Skip spoke breathlessly, words spilling from his mouth. "They're marching along and shouting. They seem angry. I couldn't understand what they were saying so I put my face against the window. All of a sudden, one old man shone his flashlight in my face. He . . . he pointed at me and waved at me to come down! I'm scared, Dad! What if they come up here to get us?"

"Don't worry, son. They won't come into the hotel."

"But the cars are honking the same sound as the taxi, the train, and the ship made. What does it mean?"

"The same sound as the taxi, train, and ship?" Dad tilted his head and rubbed the back of his neck.

"Yes! In my dream. You know, *di di di daaah.*"

Dad frowned. He stepped to the curtains and opened them. He reached out to turn a handle on the window and cracked it open.

Di di di daaah. Di di di daaah. "*Vive la France! Vive de Gaulle!*" *Di di di daaah. Di di di daaah!*

Dad closed the window, shut the curtains, and slowly lowered himself onto a chair near Skip's bed. He ran his hand through his thinning white hair.

"What does it mean?"

"I . . . I don't know, exactly. '*Vive la France*' means 'Long live France.'"

"They want their country to live? Countries don't have lives, do they?"

"No. When they say those words together they mean something different than what they mean normally."

Skip felt queasy, like the floor was swaying beneath him. If French words could have different meanings, they would never be able to understand people here, even if they had Dad's book.

"They're saying they love their country, like our pledging allegiance to the flag. I can't understand the other words they're shouting."

"What?" he barked in utter disbelief. Nausea gave way to a stabbing pain inside. "But you used your book before and it worked in the taxi and on the train. Where is your book? Let's use your book!"

"The book only tells me how to say simple things in French. It doesn't really help me to understand what they're saying except for the most basic words like *oui*, 'yes,' or *non*, 'no.'"

"You mean, you don't understand what the French people outside are saying?"

"No, but I don't think there's anything to worry about."

"Nothing to *worry* about? They're shaking their fists! They're shouting! That's what people do when they're angry. And the old man ordered me to come down! He wanted to take me away from Mom and you!"

Dad smiled wearily at Skip. "I don't think so, son. They seemed to be shaking their fists in rhythm to their chanting to show they're excited, like a physical exclamation point. And the old man . . . well . . . I didn't see him, but perhaps he just wanted to share his excitement with you."

Skip felt as though he'd fallen into Alice's rabbit hole and emerged into a strange, new world.

"So we don't understand their words *and*, even if we did, we might not understand what they mean? And when they're not talking but doing something with their bodies we might not know what they mean either?" Skip wanted to scream. He couldn't believe his parents had brought him into such a perilous world.

"I recognize the sounds, though," Dad said. "They're notes from a famous piece of music by a German composer named Beethoven. The sounds, three short and one long, are the same as those that mean the letter *V* in a kind of alphabet made up of sounds, something called the Morse code."

Panic sharpened the ache in his stomach. Different words, different meanings of the same word, different meanings of the same action, and now an alphabet made up of sounds!

"And the letter *V* stands for 'victory' or . . . '*victoire*' in French. People used it during the war as a sign of hope, hope for victory over the Germans."

"*Germans!* The music was made by a German! Mom said they were the most evil people in the world. Where is she, anyway?"

"She's sleeping. She took some medicine to help her rest, thank God."

"But I don't understand why the French would use German sounds as a sign of hope to beat the Germans? And why are they using them *now*?"

"I don't know, really," Dad admitted with a tired shrug. "Sorry."

Sorry! Skip screamed to himself. *Sorry?* In a flash, he realized what was happening. His whole body slumped.

"I know why," he muttered, fear gripping him, turning his insides out. "The French outside are shouting they want their country to live and making the sound for victory because they are going to be attacked by the Germans. And we're here, so we'll all be killed just like Mom's friend." Skip began to simper. If only he had hid himself better in his tree.

Dad rose from his chair and wrapped his arms around him. "No, no, no, Skipper. The French and the Germans and the Americans and the English are all friends now. I'm so sorry I don't have answers to all your questions. I do know that, while we'll have some problems here, we'll also have a lot of wonderful experiences. You'll see and do things you'll remember for the rest of your life."

Dad stroked his head and kissed his forehead. Skip gulped down his sobs and nestled up against him, inhaling the scent he knew as his dad's peculiar woodsy smell. He wanted with all his heart to believe what Dad had said, but . . .

"Okay," Skip grumbled at last. "But I don't think these people are as much like us as you told me they were."

Dad laughed softly. "Well, here is how I think of it. The French or the Germans or other people from other countries or, for that matter, people from different parts of our own country, do use different words than we use at home, and their words and actions might seem familiar but have different meanings from what we know from our experience. It will take time to learn their words and the meanings of their words and actions. But the feelings *underneath* the different words and actions, the . . . the love, the sorrow, the excitement, the anger, the emotions their words and actions *express,* are the same as our own. And"—Dad took a long, slow breath—"the only way to understand people from other cultures is to live a little of the life they live, because that's what gives their words and actions their meaning. Does that make sense to you?"

Skip stared into his Dad's bloodshot eyes a moment. He burrowed more deeply into his strong arms, a human caterpillar cocooning in his dad's embrace. For a long time, he pondered what his dad said. Then he thought of his tree. He *had* been afraid to climb it at first, and now loved the soaring feeling of freedom that scrambling along its branches gave him.

After a few moments more, he took a deep breath. He unwrapped his dad's arms like a butterfly emerging from its sheath and stepped to the window. He opened the curtain and rested his forehead against the cold glass.

Di di di daaah. Di di di daaah. "*Vive la France! Vive de Gaulle!*" *Di di di daaah. Di di di daaah!*

His whole body stiffened as the sounds shot through him like an electric current. A moment later, he felt his dad's hands on his shoulders, massaging them gently, the way the father of the girl at the train station had rubbed her shoulders. He missed Maddie. He missed being home. But . . .

"What are you thinking, Skipper?"

He turned to look up at his dad and, for the first time, realized how wrinkled his dad's face had become, even where his beauty mark cut across his cheek. He sighed, took a step back to look his dad in the eye, and straightened his shoulders.

"I'm thinking the earth is much, much bigger than I thought. I'm thinking there are really many, many different worlds on earth where before I thought there was only the world we lived in at home in San Rafael. I'm thinking we have a lot to learn and not everything or even most things we have to learn are at home or in books. So"—Skip heaved his shoulders in resignation—"most of what we have to learn is out there." He pointed toward the street below.

"I think you're right, son." Dad smiled. "How does that make you feel?"

Skip shook his head and wiped the last of the tears from his eyes. "Small. Scared," he sighed. "Like I did before I went up into the tree by myself for the first time. But also brave to have come this far and . . . excited to discover all the new worlds. Both feelings. Does that make sense?"

"I think it does. It's just a guess, but maybe the most important things we'll discover will be about ourselves. My travels taught me that going abroad is mostly a window allowing us to view a new world, but . . . have you ever looked out a window when the sunlight hits it at just the right angle and you see yourself reflected?"

"Maybe. What do you mean?"

"I mean that, if we look long enough, we may see what we look like in the eyes of others and learn something about ourselves."

Dad stretched his arms above his head and yawned again.

"In fact"—Dad's voice lightened—"how about going down to the front door of the hotel and stepping outside for just a second? We'll be able to understand a little better what the people outside are feeling. What do you say? I'll carry you down so you can stay in your pajamas. I promise you'll never forget what you see and hear tonight."

Skip stared at his dad for a second. He could still hear through the closed window the crowd chanting and the cars honking. He could see in his mind's eye the old man pointing at him. What if the old man was downstairs waiting for a chance to grab him? His throat tightened for a moment. He looked longingly over at his bed. At last, he shook his head, took a deep breath, and walked away.

"Okay, Skipper," his dad called after him. "I understand. It's late and I know it's scary. Get some sleep and we'll go outside tomorrow."

"No, you don't understand." Skip looked back at his dad. "I *am* scared and I don't *want* to go outside, like how I felt at first about climbing my tree. But I know if I don't, I will wonder what I missed."

"All right," Dad exclaimed. "Let's go! Come on; let me put you on my shoulders."

"No, thanks, Dad. You don't have to carry me down. I'm getting my shoes. I want to walk down. By myself."

2 REFLECTION

Skip felt the ripples of saltwater ebb and flow around his ankles
and inhaled the humid, briny air. He glanced back at the front
deck of the Hotel del Sol across a hundred feet of sand that was
so white the glare from the sun's reflection stung his eyes. Shad-
ing his face with one hand, he waved to his mother with the other.
She was leaning against a wooden railing, staring out to sea
through large, round sunglasses. She smiled and waved back,
pressing down against her straw hat—what Dad called her Jackie
Kennedy sunhat—to prevent the ocean breeze from blowing it
off.

"Don't go any further, Skippie," she yelled and wagged her
finger back and forth.

Cupping his ear with his hand, he shouted, "I can't hear you,
Mom," and turned away in irritation.

Dad told him during their trip to Europe four years before
that Mom had lost a dear friend in combat on D-Day. He later
learned the friend was her first husband. Dad explained she lived
in terror of losing someone else she loved deeply, all the while
wanting her family to share her zest for life and adventure. Dad

described her emotional struggle as "driving with one foot on the gas and the other on the brake."

Skip knew his dad didn't allow her to stop *him* from doing what he loved, even if it was a little risky. He would just laugh, kiss her, and tell her not to worry. Skip, on the other hand, felt his mom stomped on the brakes of his life constantly. No Pop Warner football, no basketball after an elbow bloodied his mouth, and baseball only if he wore sliding pads and a helmet. She took him to the doctor for every sniffle and held him out of school with even the slightest fever. He loved her dearly, but she treated him like he was still seven and he was almost twelve.

Skip lifted his gaze about fifty feet away to where the surf churned toward him. He looked beyond the billows another fifty feet. A gigantic glass wave rose in a curl toward the shore. Just before it heaved and crashed with a boom, he saw his father dive under the trough of the wave. The plunging breaker shot a fountain of water upward that obscured his view for a few seconds. A few more. He took a few steps forward until the white foam swirled around his knees. He strained his eyes but saw nothing. Skip's heart pounded. Something was wrong. Even Dad couldn't stay under water this long. He was about to scream for help when just beyond the break of the wave, his father burst from the water like a breaching orca. He felt relief and pride but also envy and even a little anger roil inside him like the surf around his legs. Skip knew Dad would love nothing more than to teach him to body surf, but Dad was twice his size and the mammoth waves intimidated Skip. So there he stood, feet dug into the sand, halfway between the safety of the beach and the peril of the sea, halfway between the little boy his mom seemed determined to keep by her side and the young man his dad yearned to have by his, irritated and envious and eleven not yet twelve.

"No further, Skippie!"

He didn't bother to look back this time. His eyes were fixed on another huge swell rolling toward his father, who swam toward the mountain of water before it could break on top of him.

Suddenly, rather than ride up and over the towering ridge of water, Dad twisted himself around, torso swiveled toward the shore, head turned back toward the wave. When the wave rolled into him, he began to swim toward the beach. One, two, three furious strokes drove his body forward. His frame rose up the side of the roller and hung at the crest for a moment before sliding across and down the inside of the curl. Racing a few feet ahead of the break, he shot in a diagonal toward Skip. Just before reaching the trough, his father dipped his shoulder and dove headfirst back into the foot of the wave, allowing the breaker to crash over him. Dad disappeared for a few moments behind a huge splash of water before emerging again only about twenty-five feet away.

"Hey, Skipper," he called and waded toward his son. "Didn't quite make it through that last one. Got towed backwards toward the beach."

His father stopped to hop on one leg, his head tilted down to shake water out of his left ear. Gazing at Dad's feathery white hair pasted by seawater to his forehead and his sturdy torso tattooed with brown splotches, Skip twisted his mouth in disbelief. Could it really be the thirteen-year-old boy whose pictures looked so much like Skip did now—thick sandy-brown hair cropped short, fair skin, and a slender frame—had become this middle-aged man?

"Think that's enough for me today, unless, of course, you'd like to come out with me."

Skip saw his father's eyes widen in a familiar expectant expression and took a step back. He didn't want to disappoint him. He didn't want to disappoint himself. But the waves were enormous and he hated the sting of salt in his eyes and the choking feeling he experienced when he would gasp for air and instead get a gulp of sea water.

"That's okay. Mom said I shouldn't go out any further 'cause the waves are so big. Maybe tomorrow?"

"Sure. Let's go see if your mom's feeling any better."

That evening, his mom still wasn't well enough to eat in the hotel restaurant.

"You two go down without me," she said as she lay down on the bed. "The *ceviche* I ate for lunch is still making me feel queasy."

"Sure it wasn't the salsa and the second margarita?" Dad chuckled.

"Ha, ha, ha. Very funny. You had as much of the salsa as I did and a second margarita, too, so it must be the *ceviche*. I'll order *albóndigas* soup and a few corn tortillas from room service to settle my stomach. Skippie?"

"Yeah?"

"You should probably stay away from the fish tacos tonight just in case they're undercooked."

"But I love the fish tacos!"

"Just for tonight, sweetheart. Say 'hi' to Francisco for me."

His father leaned over to kiss his mother lightly on the cheek. "Okay, honey. Hope you feel better. We won't be long."

Skip and his father walked down two flights of red tile stairs to the hotel restaurant and ordered *tacos de asado de puerco*, rice, and beans.

"Mom told me that you weren't going to invite any girls to your birthday party next month. Is that right?" Dad asked as he bit into a tortilla wrapped around a mound of pinto beans. "You had several girls last year. Something change?"

"Yeah, a little," Skip replied warily. "It's my birthday and I'd like to go to a Giants–Dodgers game. Girls don't like sports."

"Maddie Erickson does, doesn't she? She always seems to be playing on some kind of team. Hasn't she been a good friend of yours since kindergarten?"

Skip *had* thought almost every day about inviting Maddie and knew she would love to see the Giants play the Dodgers. She was a huge Giants fan and couldn't understand how Skip could root for a Los Angeles team. Even though she towered over Skip, he liked Maddie, he liked her a lot. Always had in the way he liked Jack or Mitchell or Bob—until recently, that is. At the sixth grade spring Sadie Hawkins sock hop, Maddie had without warning ventured across to the boys' side of the auditorium and asked him to dance. Several of his friends barely suppressed their snickers, but he couldn't refuse. Those were the rules. Luckily, Chubby Checker was singing so they twisted a couple of feet apart. Then, the music changed to Andy Williams singing "Moon River."

"Well, thanks for the dance," Skip said and turned to hurry back to where the boys congregated like a herd of antelopes seeking safety in numbers.

"Where are you going, Skip Burton?" Maddie barked, a hand on her hip. "We've only been dancing for a minute. If you leave now, you'll embarrass me in front of all my friends." She held her arms out and smiled. "Come on. It won't kill you to slow dance with me."

Skip froze for a syncopated beat, took a deep breath, and stepped toward Maddie. He took her right hand in his left, reached around her waist as he'd been taught in cotillion, and felt her arm on his shoulder. As they began to sway to the music, he inhaled her scent, a kind of light, flowery fragrance. The heat radiating from their bodies seemed to swirl around them like a tiny hurricane, making his head spin.

His clearest memory of those dizzying three minutes was that, when the music stopped, Maddie leaned down to allow her cheek to graze against his ever so slightly. Later that night, he felt something for Maddie stirring inside him that was different than friendship, both stronger and stranger, both exhilarating and terrifying. That was the trouble. He worried the other kids—even Maddie—would see a birthday party invitation as proof of the emotions surging inside him.

"No, not really," he answered as evenly as he could, keeping his eyes away from Dad's gaze. "If I did, I don't think she'd come anyway because she'd be the only girl."

Dad cocked his head and examined Skip for a second. "Ah, okay." He shrugged. "It's your birthday."

A few minutes later the head waiter, Francisco, came by their table to say hello and to talk baseball. A short, broad-shouldered man with a black handlebar moustache, Francisco always dressed in an ivory jacket, sky-blue dress shirt, charcoal slacks, and narrow black tie. His clothes made him seem much older than his father even though they were both about forty years old. Francisco had played semipro baseball in Mexico for many years and loved the Dodgers almost as much as Skip did, especially the great left-handed pitcher, Sandy Koufax, and the speedy shortstop, Maury Wills. His eyes flashed and his hands waved as he chatted and joked with Skip. Sheer delight for the game of his summers past transformed the older man into a boy again.

"So, my young friend, do you also play baseball back home in San Rafael?"

Before Skip could answer, his dad interjected, "Skip's been playing Little League for three years. He plays shortstop and bats third."

"Ah, Señor Burton. I wonder. You see, I have a friend who coaches a team of boys about Skip's age. They practice tomorrow. Would Skip and you like to come?"

"What do you think, Skipper?" his father asked. When Skip hesitated, his father added, "Or would you rather swim?"

Skip loved baseball but didn't want to play with a bunch of strangers. He turned his head toward the beach. The surf roared even more loudly than in the afternoon. The sweet, smoky flavor of the pork tacos turned bitter in his mouth. Annoyed at his father for leaving him no choice, he feigned interest in playing but offered an excuse he hoped would get him out of actually doing so.

"Baseball sounds like fun, but I don't have my mitt or bat."

"Oh, do not worry, *mi amigo*. The coach will find a mitt and a bat for you to use. So, the practice is at four. We should leave here at three thirty. Please give my wishes for a speedy recovery to you wife. Sleep well and *hasta mañana*."

Around three the following afternoon, Skip laid out his jeans, a T-shirt, tennis shoes, and one of his Dodgers baseball caps. His head felt light and his stomach was doing somersaults as he dressed in haze of anxiety. A knock on his door and his mom and dad poked their heads in.

"Almost ready?" Dad said.

"Yeah," Skip replied listlessly.

"You okay, Skippie?" Mom asked and stepped into his room. "Worried about something?"

"How can I play baseball with boys I can't even talk to?" Skip blurted out. "And they can't understand me?"

"Hmmm," Dad said. "I'm surprised. I thought you loved trying new things in foreign countries."

"I do, but this is different. I'm not exploring with Mom and you. I'm playing baseball with boys who want to win, just like I do. What if . . . if I can't understand something and make a *big* mistake in front of them?" Skip saw his mom's eyes crinkle with concern.

"Maybe he's right, honey," she said and stepped over to knead Skip's shoulders. "He might get hurt because he can't understand Spanish. We don't know any doctors here. Even a minor injury could become infected, turn into something serious. We'll be back again next year. Why not wait until he's a little older?"

"It's just a practice, sweetheart. If he doesn't understand something, Francisco will translate for him. Besides, he's a good player and baseball is baseball, wherever it's played."

"You're forcing him to go? Even if he might get hurt?" Mom snapped.

"I didn't think I was forcing him to do anything," Dad replied, his lips tight and an edge in his voice. He turned to Skip. "Look, you don't have to come unless you want to, but I'm going in any case. I'd like to see how they practice here and I don't want to disappoint Francisco. What do you say? If you're coming, we need to head out."

Skip looked at his mom and back at his dad. He took a deep breath.

"Okay, Dad. Let's go."

"Skippie . . ."

"It'll be okay, Mom. I'll be fine with Francisco there to help. Like Dad says, it's just a practice and I've never been hurt playing baseball."

"All right, sweetheart. But I want you to stop the *moment* you feel playing might be dangerous. No sliding without pads and no batting without a helmet! Do you understand me?" She waited for Skip to nod before facing Dad. "Do you *both* understand me?"

"Sure, Mom," Skip replied as Dad straightened his shoulders and saluted.

"Yes, ma'am! I will bring him back from enemy territory alive and well, sir, uh, I mean, ma'am!"

"Ha!" Mom snorted and swatted Dad hard on his backside. "You better or *you'll* be court martialed, soldier, and spend the night in the brig!"

At three thirty, Skip and his dad descended the tiled interior staircase to the small lobby. Francisco was waiting for them with a broad smile on his face. He had changed from his formal clothes into slacks and a dark-blue short-sleeved shirt. Skip stared at Francisco's forearms. He had never seen them before; they were thick as a blacksmith's.

"*Buenas tardes,*" Francisco said. "This way, please." They stepped out of the hotel into a blazing afternoon heat broken only now and again by a sea breeze. In front of the hotel stood a dusty, lime-green Rambler Classic with a large dent in the right front bumper. "Ah! I've forgotten my cap. Please get in. I will return promptly," Francisco said.

Skip climbed in the back and noticed the inside door handle and armrest were missing. He reached through the open window and pulled the door closed. He sniffed the air, which smelled of gasoline and air freshener.

"Are we *all right* in this car?"

"Sure," his father replied. "It's old, maybe twenty years or so, but American-made. Besides, I bet we're not going far."

Francisco returned wearing a faded, sweat-stained Dodgers cap. "Good. Now, my friends, let us go to the park."

Francisco drove them away from the well-tended tourist hotels and restaurants that lined the beach and into a part of the city that Skip had never seen. One- and two-story concrete buildings, their white-paint facades chipped and dirt-stained, stood along sidewalks where vendors pushed carts and women strolled carrying large straw purses overflowing with the day's shopping. Every second vehicle on the crowded street seemed to be a banged-up pick-up truck that spewed acrid exhaust. Young men on motorcycles and boys on bicycles darted in and out of the traffic. Skip felt jittery, the way he did when batting against a pitcher he'd never faced before. His hands began to sweat. He unconsciously tightened his grip on the back of the front seat. After about fifteen minutes, the traffic thinned and Francisco pulled up in front of a baseball diamond that stood in the corner of a large park.

"A small moment, please," Francisco said as he slid out of the car and strolled over to the diamond.

Skip's eyes scanned the field. His stomach lurched. The players were teenagers, not boys. They looked twice his size. The pitcher wound up and rocketed the ball toward the plate. The batter swung and missed as the ball hit the catcher's mitt. *THUMP!*

"Dad, these guys are *not* my age," Skip's voice trembled slightly. "Not even *close*. Did you see how hard the pitcher threw the ball? I don't want to play with *them*."

"They do look pretty old, don't they? Let's see what Francisco says. If you don't want to hit, maybe just take a turn in the field? I don't want to hurt Francisco's feelings since he's gone to all this trouble."

Skip listened to his father with open-mouthed incredulity. He didn't want to hurt *Francisco's* feelings? What about subjecting his son to embarrassment? He wasn't so much afraid of being hurt physically as being set up to fail *miserably*. In front of a bunch of *strangers*. Skip slouched down in the backseat.

"So," Francisco announced as he returned to the car, "this is the high school team. The younger boys are practicing on another field today. It is just a few minutes from here."

Skip's shoulders relaxed. He leaned forward. "Francisco? The younger boys are my age, right?"

"Yes, *mi amigo*, I believe so. You are twelve or thirteen, are you not?"

"No, well, almost. I turn twelve next month."

"*Bueno*. Then you will enjoy practicing with these boys."

Francisco directed the Rambler toward the outskirts of the city. In a few moments, he turned left onto a bumpy dirt road bordered on each side by mesquite and thick bush. Dust billowed behind them. After about a half mile, Francisco slowed the car and parked alongside the road behind a faded yellow and white Dodge station wagon covered in dirt. Skip's father waited until the plume of dust had settled, then stepped out and opened Skip's door from the outside. Skip jumped out. As he walked with Francisco and his father, he could hear boys shouting and laughing in the distance.

About a hundred feet ahead, the road ended in a clearing. Four white plastic trash can tops each about a square foot marked off a standard diamond-shaped infield. About fifty feet of earth bordered the infield on all sides before vanishing into a tangle of mesquite, thorn bush, and cactus. Four boys spread around the infield; another three took positions in the shallow outfield just before the dirt ended and the thicket of bush began; and, two players, a lanky boy holding a bat and a chubby boy with a catcher's mitt, stood around home plate. A gnome-like man with short graying hair and a sunburnt face shouted instructions to the players. As Skip approached the field, the boys swiveled toward him. A few of them stared in silence, their jaws pumping up and down as they chewed gum; others looked down and pawed at the ground with their feet.

"*Hola!*" cried the coach. He waved with one hand and held a bat in the other.

"*Hola*, Fernando," replied Francisco. The two men embraced and spoke in rapid Spanish for a few seconds.

"This is Fernando Lopez," Francisco explained to Skip and his father. "We played on the same team for many years. He was an excellent catcher and team captain."

"*Mucho gusto*," Lopez said and shook hands with his dad. Then Fernando gestured at Skip and spoke in rapid Spanish to Francisco.

"What's he saying?" Skip whispered to his dad who shrugged in response.

"Now," Francisco continued, "they will take infield practice. He asks that you play shortstop. Juan has a glove that should be about your size."

"*Darle el guante de béisbol*," Fernando commanded the gangly boy who reached down, picked up a mitt from behind home plate, and in one motion slung it to Skip. Not understanding what Fernando had said, Skip was caught off guard, but managed to catch the glove just before it smacked him in the face. Juan snorted and walked back to home plate. The glove was dark brown, the leather worn and cracked in the pocket. Skip slid the mitt on his left hand and glanced over the field. He saw only backs turned toward him or eyes locked on the ground. He had little doubt Juan and the other boys were as unhappy as he was that he was there.

"*Bueno*," said Francisco. "Not a bad fit. Have fun, *mi amigo*."

Skip glanced back at his dad hoping for a sign of encouragement, but his father had turned to walk toward the sidelines with Francisco. Skip took a deep breath and ran out to the space between second and third base. As the shortstop jogged by Skip on the way to home plate, he abruptly veered toward Skip, bumping his shoulder.

"*Lo siento*." He laughed and tipped his hat.

Skip thought the words meant he was sorry, but the boy's wide grin conveyed no apology. He sensed stares from every side burning into him. Out of the corner of his eye, he could see the second baseman glare at him, hands on his hips, lips tightly pursed. Skip's pulse began to race.

Coach Lopez stepped to the side of home plate and pointed at Skip. The boy who had been at shortstop stood on home plate ready to run. Skip nodded, leaned forward over bent knees, and extended his arms down toward the ground, left foot slightly in front.

Whack! Coach Lopez cracked a grounder. Skip moved left in front of the ball and bent over to catch it on the third hop. Just before the ball reached his glove, it struck a rock and caromed up. Skip jerked his glove up and swung his face away but too late. The ball slammed into his left cheek and dropped to the ground in front of him. Momentarily dazed, he heard laughter and whistles ring out from the other boys. The taunts cleared his mind. The runner raced toward first. Skip hopped over, picked up the ball, and threw it as hard as he could to first base. The ball sailed over the first baseman's head, flew over the dirt road, and rolled underneath the station wagon. The catcalls grew louder.

"*Silencio!*" roared Coach Lopez.

"Are you okay?" His father called out.

His cheekbone throbbed. He felt his eyes water. He wanted to scream back, *No! I'm hurt just like Mom said I would be. They don't want me here anymore than I want to be here. I want to go back to the hotel. Now!* But he swallowed his words. As angry as he was with his father, even with Francisco, for having put him in a situation where he was ridiculed for an error that was not his fault, he resented the boys even more for jeering. A word he had heard used but had never dared to say rose in his mind like black smoke.

"Fuck them. *Fuck* them all," he muttered to himself, vowing not to give them the pleasure of driving him off the field. "I'm okay." He held up his mitt.

He motioned to Coach Lopez to hit him another groundball and leaned over ready to react. This time Juan, the tall, slender boy, stood at home ready to run.

Crack! The ball bounded to Skip's right. Skip pivoted, took three quick steps, and reached down across his body with his glove hand. Just after he felt the ball smack the leather, he grabbed it with his throwing hand, planted his right foot, and rifled the ball to the first baseman who caught the ball chest high a second before Juan crossed the base.

"*Bueno!*" Coach Lopez called out and signaled for Skip to take another grounder. The coach tossed the ball up and chopped down. The ball bounced high to Skip's left. He raced in a diagonal across the diamond in front of second base, reached down to scoop up the ball on a short hop, and without stopping side-armed a throw to first. The ball smacked into the first baseman's mitt again just ahead of the runner. Buoyed by his play, Skip returned to his position with a hop to his step. He took several more ground balls, each time fielding them cleanly and throwing out the runner.

"*Dobleplay!*" shouted the coach as he held up two fingers.

Skip nodded and held up two fingers to indicate that he understood.

Coach Lopez stroked the ball toward the second baseman. Skip broke to take the throw at second. The second baseman gloved the ball, but bobbled and dropped it. He snatched it up, spun around, and fired it to Skip's right. Surprised by the throw, Skip instinctively reached for the ball with his bare hand, plucked it from the air, stepped on second, twirled around, and threw to first just before the panting runner stepped on the base. Skip's eyes watered with the pain in his right hand. He wanted to shake the sting out, but the hoots and whistles from the first grounder still rang in his ears. He clenched his teeth, trotted back to his position, and pounded his hand into his mitt a couple of times to erase the pain.

"Hey, you!" the second baseman shouted at his back.

Skip stopped, his muscles tensed, and he pivoted to glower at the boy.

"*Buen atrapó*," the second baseman called, held out his bare hand, and snatched an imaginary ball from the air.

Skip looked over at Francisco.

"He says, 'good catch,'" Francisco yelled from the sideline.

"Oh." Skip's body relaxed. He faced the second baseman who stood hands on hips and nodded once. "*Gracias.*" Skip tipped his hat.

"*De nuevo, dobleplay,*" Coach Lopez barked. This time the ball bounced toward Skip's left. He fielded it cleanly, but in his haste to get the ball to second, he underhanded it too high.

"*Ay,*" shouted the second baseman who was running to cover the base. Just as the ball reached him, he leapt, speared the ball, landed on second base, and pivoted to throw the runner out at first.

"*Buena atrapada,*" Skip shouted at the second baseman who was walking back to his position. The second baseman turned, a slight smile creasing his lips, and touched the brim of his cap.

"*Gracias,*" he replied.

Before Skip could return to shortstop, Coach Lopez yelled some directions in Spanish and gestured for Skip to come in to bat. He jogged toward home and the shortstop returned to his position, this time without coming close to Skip. Coach Lopez handed Skip a bat. The coach threw several balls out to Juan, who had taken his mitt back and now stood about sixty feet from home plate where a pitcher's mound would have been. Skip looked around for a helmet but didn't see one anywhere. His mother had told him not to bat if he didn't have a helmet, but the jeers of the Mexican players still echoed in his ears. He clenched the bat and walked toward the plastic home plate.

Skip stepped to the side of home, bent his knees, and swung the bat back and forth several times. Juan wound up slowly and tossed the ball toward home in a languid arc. Skip stepped into the pitch and launched a line drive over the shortstop's head that rolled between the left and center fielders and into the brush. The center fielder retrieved the ball and threw it back to Juan, bellowing something in Spanish. Juan grunted and shrugged his shoulders.

Again Juan went into a slow wind up and lobbed the ball toward home plate. Skip wacked the pitch just fair down the left field line. The left fielder howled and chased after the ball, which came to rest under a tall cactus.

"*Que haces, Juan? Lanza la pelota!*" yelled Coach Lopez. Skip looked back at Francisco.

"The pitcher will throw the ball faster now," Francisco shouted.

Juan wound up more quickly this time and uncoiled his length behind the pitch. The ball sped out of his hand on a tightrope toward Skip. Surprised by the speed of the pitch, Skip jumped back but not in time. The ball slammed into his left thigh with a thud and dropped to the ground.

"*Aahh,*" Skip cried out. "Damn it!" He dropped the bat and rubbed the bruise on his thigh.

"*Perdón,*" Juan yelled at Skip, a smirk on his face.

"Are you okay, Skipper?" his father called.

Skip wanted to scream that he was far from okay. The bruise on his leg throbbed. The pitcher was dangerously wild and Skip had no helmet. What if the next pitch hit him in the head? Mom would be furious with them both! But he choked back the words, wiped the water from his eyes, and took a deep breath.

"Yeah. Sure," he mumbled out of the side of his mouth but dared not look at his father lest he lose control of his emotions.

Skip picked up his bat and stepped to the plate. Juan wound up and whistled another fastball. Panic surged through Skip's body. Instead of stepping toward the ball his left leg instinctively swung away and he leaned back realizing too late the ball was headed for the outside corner of the plate. Lunging awkwardly, Skip swung and missed. The ball skidded into the mitt of the pudgy catcher who was standing ten paces behind home plate. Hoots resounded from the field.

"*Dije silencio!*" Fernando bellowed and the noise faded away.

Skip set his jaw and assumed his batting stance. He could feel his left leg shaking as Juan wound up and hurled another fastball. Skip could not help himself. He flinched as the ball zoomed over the plate. Skip reached out at the last moment to flick his bat at the ball and just managed to hit a slow groundball that squirted foul to the right of first base. The first baseman picked up the ball and tossed it to Juan.

"*El último lanzamiento. Si le pegas a la pelota esta vez, corre, por favor,*" Coach Lopez instructed Skip. Skip turned to Francisco.

"This is the last pitch. If you hit it this time, please run," Francisco translated and waved his arm to indicate that Skip should run to first base.

Skip nodded, took his position beside the plate, and waited. Once again, Juan rifled the baseball toward home plate. Skip willed himself to step toward the ball and keep his eyes fixed on the pitch. Though the speed of the pitch surprised him again, he felt the meat of the bat connect against the ball. *Crack!* The ball soared over the first baseman's head. Skip took off. As he ran, he saw the right fielder chasing after the ball, which had skidded into the mesquite bush. Skip sped past first base and churned toward second. Just before reaching second, he glanced over his right shoulder. The right fielder had reached down to pick the ball up. Skip didn't hesitate. He rounded second on his way toward third. As he neared third base, he saw the third baseman's glove reach down to catch the throw from the right fielder. The ball hit the heel of his mitt and bounced away about fifteen feet toward left field. There was no stopping Skip now. The catcalls rang in his ears; the bruise on his thigh pulsed with pain. *Fuck* them! He would show them all.

Skip stepped on third base and shot toward home. He saw Juan push the catcher aside and stand over home plate waiting for the throw from third. Ten feet from home, Skip felt the ball pass close over his head. Five feet from home, Skip saw Juan snare the ball. Juan turned to face Skip, the same smug smile splitting his face as when his pitch had hit Skip. Fury flooded Skip's veins. Determined to knock the smirk off the pitcher's face, Skip sped up and lowered his shoulder. As he barreled toward Juan, he saw the pitcher's eyes swell in astonishment. Juan crouched down to brace himself and held his mitt out to tag Skip. Skip rammed into the pitcher, knocking him over home plate and onto his back.

Juan leapt up and raised his mitt to prove he had not dropped the ball. The boys behind Skip cheered and whistled. The triumphant smile on Juan's face quickly vanished. He pivoted toward Skip, reared back, and fired the ball at his head. Skip ducked. Enraged, he raced toward Juan, tackled him, and drove him to the ground. Juan wrapped his arm around Skip's neck, flipped him over on his back, and climbed astride him. Juan raised his fist to strike Skip, but Fernando grabbed Juan's arm and yanked him off. Skip jumped up and was about to go after Juan again when his father gripped him under his arms and pulled him away.

After Juan and Skip were forced to apologize to each other, the players lined up and Skip went from one boy to the next to shake their hands and exchange a hushed "*Gracias*." Waiting at the end of the line, Coach Lopez shook Skip's hand and clapped him on the shoulder. "*Gracias, amigo.*"

Skip trudged in sullen silence with his father and Francisco to the car. They wound their way back to the Hotel del Sol with Francisco softly humming "Take Me Out to the Ball Game." He pulled up in front of the hotel and shut off the engine.

Skip's dad cleared his throat.

"I want to apologize, Francisco. Skip lost his temper and knocked Juan over. You were kind enough to invite him to play with Coach Lopez's team and it turned into a disaster for everyone. I don't know what got into him. I'm sorry."

"You don't know what got into *me*," Skip blurted out and pounded his fist down on the seat beside him. "You *made* me play. The shortstop ran into me on purpose. The ground ball hit a rock and slammed into my cheek and the boys laughed at me even though it wasn't my fault. You heard them. And then Juan threw a fastball at my leg. On purpose! That's what got into *me*!"

"Just a second, son, you can't . . ." His father twisted around to scold Skip when Francisco coughed twice and held up his hand.

"Excuse me, my friends. Perhaps you would allow me a few words? *Bueno.* Señor Burton, I must respectfully disagree with you. I believe the afternoon was a great success for my boys and, also, for Skip."

"*What?*" Skip and his father erupted at the same time.

"Ah." Francisco chuckled. "You see, my boys had never played with someone from the United States. I do not think it would be wrong to admit they were afraid of Skip and had no desire to practice with him in case they would make an error in front of the strange boy from California. On the other hand, Fernando and I, we believed we should make them face their fears."

"THEY?" Skip boomed. "THEY were afraid of *me*? Why? It was their practice, with their friends, in their country, speaking *their* language. Everything was the same for them. Everything was different for me."

"Yes, of course, many things were different for you." Francisco chortled at Skip's outburst. "Still, give me a moment to explain. First, you were just as unknown, just as strange to them as they were to you. Do you not agree?"

"Okay," Skip conceded after a moment's reflection. "But there were nine of them."

"Yes, but playing baseball with you exposed them to the possibility of—how do you say—slipping up, not just in front of their friends but in front of *you*. This was frightening for them. Even here. Where they live. Remember, you are a *norteamericano*."

"A what?"

"A *norteamericano* is what we call someone from the United States."

"But why does that matter? I'm just a kid."

"Yes, you are. And many, too many *norteamericanos*, even adults, do not take the time to see anything but themselves in those they meet here. But, if you wish to appreciate the boys on Fernando's team as they are, you must try to see yourself from where they stand, to view yourself reflected in their eyes. You are someone who vacations in expensive hotels, who eats in fancy restaurants where a dinner costs a week's salary, who wears nice clothes available to them only in their dreams. You are someone who comes to our country expecting *us* to speak your most difficult language with its incoherent grammar, whose room their mothers clean, whose table their fathers and grandfathers wait on, whose table *I* wait on. They do not wish to admit it, but they fear in their hearts that you *must* be rich and powerful and . . . and perfect. Better than them in all ways. To be sure, their anxiety makes them angry as well. They ask themselves, 'How dare he come to our country and make us feel so inferior?'"

"But I'm *not* perfect," objected Skip. "I dropped the ball and slung it over the first baseman's head. I lost control and got really angry. I slammed into Juan on purpose. I tried to *hurt* him and now I . . . I feel terrible about it."

"No, *mi amigo*, you are not without fault. *Gracias a Dios*. We are all God's children struggling with our imperfections. But your imperfections were, if I may say so, perfect for my purposes. Fernando and I wanted our boys to experience you as you are. I am delighted you dropped the ball once or twice, you made a bad throw once or twice, and you swung and missed once or twice. I am even happier you showed you were hurt and became angry. Yes"—Francisco laughed again—"and I loved that the little Spanish you spoke was, shall we say, not without flaws just like the little English *they* speak is also far from perfect. I am grateful for all these things because my boys experienced you as a human. Just another boy. A boy as they are, and so less unknown, less strange, less frightening, and less powerful than they feared."

Francisco stopped for a moment to gaze out at the surf running toward the shore.

"Not all these boys will have lives that will lead them to meet another *norteamericano*," he continued, "but many will. Now they will be prepared to meet your countrymen with dignity and, I hope, some understanding that the *norteamericano* is another fallible human, not a wealthy superman from a Hollywood film. Does this make sense to you, my friends?"

Skip looked at his father who was rubbing the stubble on his chin.

"Yes, it does, Francisco," Skip's father declared finally. "You are a wise man. And, you're right, the day was a success for Skip. Before we went, he was terrified to be put in a situation where he might make a mistake and be ridiculed for it. Knowing your boys shared the same fear will help him to be less afraid to fail in the future. An invaluable lesson."

"Yes, I believe so," Francisco agreed. He turned to stare out his window at the sea again for what seemed like a long time to Skip. Finally, he turned around and placed his hand on Skip's leg. "You know, yesterday I happened to look out the front windows of the hotel. I saw a boy stand in the surf, too proud to go back, too afraid to swim further out and possibly need help. I believe that boy no longer exists; he has grown into a young man better able to face the fear of not being perfect, to accept with grace his humanity. I also believe he is now aware strangers may fear him just as much as he fears them, as we all are afraid of the unknown. I believe he will be kind enough and confident enough in himself to do what he can to make them feel comfortable, to respect them as they are, to try to see himself and the world as they do."

"I never thought of myself as *different*," Skip said as much to himself as to Francisco. "Certainly not so strange I might scare or upset someone. I'm just . . . just me. Still, I guess in their eyes I was . . . I *am* foreign. I hope . . . I hope we can play together again so we can get to know each other better." Skip's voice brightened. "You know, I liked the second baseman. He was nice."

"Yes, he is a good young man. I am very proud of him. He is my grandson. Now, come. You must be thirsty after the hot afternoon. Please, sit in the bar by the window and let me bring you a Tecate and a ginger ale and a little ice for the bruise on your face. I pray to God the swelling goes down before Mrs. Burton sees you again!"

"Thank you, Francisco. We gratefully accept but on one condition," Skip's father replied.

"What is that, my friend?"

"That you bring a Tecate for yourself, too, let us pour it for you, and let us drink to your grandson, to the rest of his teammates, to Fernando, and, most of all, to you. We have learned so much from you today."

"Thank you, *mis amigos.* I will join you with pleasure."

Skip and his father walked into the hotel and sat in the bar area while Francisco went into the kitchen for their drinks. They sat without speaking for several minutes, each ruminating over the afternoon.

"You know what?" Skip suddenly broke the silence.

"No, what, son?"

"I think I would like to invite Maddie to my birthday party after all."

Skip's father examined his son for a second, smiled broadly, and put his arm around Skip's shoulders.

3 PRESUMPTION

Weird was the only word to describe how Maddie felt. She was sitting in the biggest plane she'd ever been on with her new palm-sized Letts diary closed in her lap. Her rapid tapping on its midnight-blue cover with the top of a shiny, black Parker ballpoint pen betrayed her nervousness. She *really* didn't want to write down her thoughts and feelings like she was talking to herself, the way old people, or crazy people, do sometimes.

Maddie's foot began to drum the floor in time with the beat of her pen against the cover. Her mind drifted back to the day before when her parents had given her the diary and pen.

"Thank you, but . . . you know I've never been the *diary* type of girl," Maddie had murmured.

"I know you've always been more interested in running outside to play sports than sitting at home," Mom said. "I feel the same way. But you're about to embark on an amazing adventure. You've never spent a summer away from home. Think how wonderful it will be to share with me everything that happened in Taiwan and remember how you felt while you were experiencing it."

"I don't know where to begin," Maddie objected.

"You'll be playing a lot of volleyball over there," Dad said. "Talk about *that* in your diary. I'll be interested to hear how they practice in Taiwan. Maybe you'll learn something we can incorporate into our workouts."

"Not everything in life has to be about volleyball!" snapped Maddie's mom. She slid her glasses back to the bridge of her nose as she turned to Maddie. "Describe simple things, like what you want the diary to be about or who you are," she said and then curled her biceps. "It's just like exercising a muscle. The more you do it, the easier it will become."

"Who are you? You're a *great* volleyball player," Dad said and then smirked at her mom. "But, whatever you write, you'll be glad you did when you're my age and you have a record of your first overseas trip."

Maddie couldn't imagine being her dad's age (fifty years old!), but she supposed it might be cool in the year 2000 to read about her trip to Taiwan in the summer of 1968. So, after her plane took off, she stretched her long legs out beneath the seat in front of her and cracked open the journal. A woodsy aroma rose from the blank pages. What did she want the diary to be about? She agreed with her parents. She wanted it to be about her trip—the six weeks she would spend in Taichung, Taiwan, teaching conversational English and working as an assistant coach on a young women's volleyball team at the local YMCA.

Who was she? Mom made answering that question sound so easy, but Maddie knew she was lots of things all jumbled together. She was a tall, blue-eyed eighteen-year-old with bleached-blonde hair cut in a bob, a fiercely competitive athlete who loved playing volleyball, a pretty good student when she could sit still and concentrate, a loyal friend to her teammates, and—at least until they broke up a few months ago—a young woman in love with Skip.

"Hmmm," Maddie murmured to herself as she finished her first paragraph. "Mom was right. That wasn't so bad after all."

She massaged her lips with the end of her pen and considered whether to describe how she felt leaving her parents at the airport. She stared out the window, sighed, and lowered her pen to the paper.

Saying goodbye to Mom and Dad at the gate was the hardest. They kept hugging her and each other and they all cried, even Dad. Seeing them almost happy together gave her some hope that they might stop their constant fighting. She hadn't been getting along with her mom all that great for a couple of years and, though she couldn't know what was really going on with her parents, she wondered if their quarrels had something to do with Dad always taking her side. Could their fights over who did or didn't do what, or who said or didn't say what, actually be a tug-of-war for Maddie's affection? Until recently they had called themselves the Three Musketeers, three buddies on Team Erickson, pulling together to compete against the world—and win! But they weren't acting like a team anymore and the endless sniping scared her. She could share her anxiety with Skip before they broke up. But now . . . Maddie closed her eyes and pressed her lips together. Her eyes welled up. She had been an only child all her life, but had never felt alone—until earlier this year. Now she longed for a sibling to confide in.

Maddie wiped her hand across her eyes, laid her pen down in the crease of the pages where she'd written about her fears, and bit the inside of her lower lip. It was too painful to consider, and impossible to put down in writing, how much a rupture in her family, her *team*, would break her heart, especially if she were somehow responsible.

"Excuse me." A feathery voice startled Maddie. "Sorry to interrupt you, but I wanted to introduce myself. I'm Kimberly."

Maddie had been so absorbed in her thoughts she hadn't noticed the young woman sitting in the aisle seat. She had a lovely oval face covered with what Maddie thought was *way* too much make-up. Kimberly wore a black mini-skirt and cream mid-calf go-go boots. Maddie recognized the stylish Nancy Sinatra look. She knew the same skirt and boots would show off her long legs, but she was at heart an outdoorsy, athletic girl who loved throwing on her comfortable blue and red volleyball warm-ups before she bolted outside.

Glad to be distracted from thinking about her parents, Maddie tucked her diary into her travel bag.

"Nice to meet you. I'm Maddie. Are you going to Taiwan, too?"

"Yes. I'm traveling to Taipei to meet my husband. He has a couple of weeks leave from the army in Vietnam. We were high school sweethearts up in Eugene, Oregon. He was my escort when I was prom queen. We were married when he got drafted right after graduation and haven't seen each other for six months."

"Oh, gosh," Maddie exclaimed. That Kimberly had married at eighteen didn't shock Maddie—a number of her classmates became engaged or started living with their boyfriends right out of high school—but the idea of marrying and not seeing your husband for six months jolted her. "That must be awful."

"It's been real hard. You know, Tom is the nicest, funniest boy I've ever met. His first letters were so sweet, telling me how much he loved me and missed me," Kimberly said and extracted a photo from her purse. "Here's a picture of us at our wedding."

Maddie gazed at the framed four-by-four picture of Kimberly and Tom beaming out at the camera as they raised two flutes of champagne.

"Ah, you look so beautiful and he's a really handsome guy," Maddie said wanting to be polite but feeling uneasy at the amount of personal information Kimberly seemed eager to share with someone she'd just met.

"We were very happy. But, well, the truth is his letters have gotten stranger and stranger, like he's writing because he feels he has to and no longer cares about anything, or anyone."

"Oh, I'm sorry. What did his letters say to make you feel that way?"

"It's not so much what he wrote as what he *didn't*. Nothing about me, nothing about us, nothing about our future together, nothing about what he was doing or even where he was. He wrote, well, he wrote like a zombie would talk, you know, just a few words without any life in them," she said, the words tumbling from her mouth the way they gushed from Maddie's when she became really nervous. "Did you see *The Innocents*? Deborah Kerr takes a babysitting job for kids who are possessed in an old house full of ghosts. The movie makes me worry evil spirits might have taken control of my husband."

Maddie didn't know what to say. She had dated a few boys, mostly Skip, but to be married and think your husband might have lost his soul? Wow!

Kimberly and Maddie continued to chat off and on until the plane stopped to refuel in Honolulu. Maddie excused herself, raced off the plane, and half-jogged around the airport three times to stretch her legs. When they boarded an hour later, Kimberly explained she hadn't slept at all the night before, put her seat back, and fell asleep purring softly like Patch, Maddie's old cat.

Maddie gazed out the window at the Pacific. How could people reveal their deepest feelings to total strangers? On the volleyball court, Maddie didn't care if everyone saw how happy, angry, frustrated, or proud her playing made her. But she couldn't imagine telling her closest friends, let alone a *stranger*, how it felt to kiss Skip or that her parents' marriage might not last. People must realize they'll never see the stranger again so they don't care what they might think. And then Maddie giggled. Wasn't writing in a diary like telling your deepest feelings to a stranger? You won't be judged by your own diary, at least until you read it years later and think, oh my God, how dumb I was!

When the plane traveled across the international dateline and Saturday became Sunday, the hostesses gave each of the passengers a certificate. Maddie tucked hers into her diary for safekeeping. Maybe she would show it to Skip someday as proof of her worldliness. Thinking of Skip, she reached down into her carry-on bag to take out the presents he'd given her. One was an unopened book on life in Taiwan. He had advised her (he could be *so* condescending) to read it to prepare for her visit. He was right in a way—she didn't know much about Taiwan except that it was an island off the coast of Red China. Still, she'd been to Chinatown in San Francisco a hundred times and presumed a YMCA in Taiwan couldn't be so different than the YMCA at home. Why waste time reading about people and places you already knew pretty well?

Skip's other gift was a framed picture from winter break of the two of them standing on the trail to Palomarin Beach north of Bolinas. They had asked a passing hiker to capture the moment with Skip's new Polaroid camera. They grinned happily at the camera with arms wrapped around each other. In the background, the white-capped, sun-splashed Pacific, as sky-blue as Maddie's eyes, stretched out to the horizon. Delight in discovering they were in love with their best friend shone from their faces.

"I still can't believe you like me, you know, as a girl."

Maddie hugged Skip and kissed his cheek.

"I've always liked you," Skip said. "And, if you must know, ever since sixth grade as a girl, whatever that means."

"It means, for one thing, you like kissing me." Maddie laughed, leaned down slightly, and brushed her lips lightly against his.

"Why did you wait five years to ask me out? Was it . . . well, was it because I was so much taller than you?"

"Maybe I was afraid you would turn me down because I was so short. Anyway, I don't mind at all that you're still a little taller. I love kissing you standing up or sitting down." Skip chuckled. "Besides, it's only an inch and a half now. You know, what I really, really like about us is that we were friends before we became boyfriend and girlfriend." Skip cleared his throat. "Do you ever think it's strange we're both only children? Do you wonder if that shared experience drew us together in some way?"

"Skip!" Maddie admonished him gently, her nose crinkling slightly. "Whenever you clear your throat, I know something serious is coming. It's a gorgeous day. Let's enjoy the sun."

"Okay. Okay. And whenever you wrinkle your nose, I know you're slightly annoyed with me!" He reached out to pet Maddie's nose, but she giggled and knocked his hand away. "You know, you were the sister I always wished I had, at least until I fell in love with you and then was glad you weren't." Skip laughed.

"I never felt the need for a brother growing up, but if I had you would have been my choice until . . . well, everything changed."

"I've wondered recently what it would have been like to have an older sibling around growing up. You know, someone to talk to who isn't a parent, someone who has gone through what you're going through. I think Mom would be less anxious if I had an older brother or sister she'd seen grow up before me. Pulling away from her would have been a lot more difficult if my baseball friends in Mexico hadn't partly filled that role, even though I only see them during the summer."

"I've never seen my mom or dad as holding me back. We've always been a threesome . . ." Maddie paused, her voice trailing away. "Though it would be comforting to have a brother or sister,

you know, someone I wouldn't be embarrassed to talk with about family stuff." Maddie pawed the ground with her shoe.

"You're biting the inside of your lip again," Skip said, pointing to her mouth. "Are you upset about something?"

"No! Not really. Anyway," she declared brightly, "enough deep thinking for one day! Race you to the trailhead!"

Maddie liked the picture, but the gift seemed presumptuous since Skip was no longer her boyfriend. She heaved a loud sigh and then panicked for a moment worrying she may have aroused Kimberly, but she just shifted in her seat and stayed asleep.

Two months after the picture was taken, Maddie had led Skip back to the same spot on a blustery afternoon as dark clouds raced overhead.

"I don't understand." Skip shook his head. "You say you love me but you want to break up? That's crazy!"

"I've loved you ever since we danced in sixth grade, but this summer you'll be in Mexico and I'll be in Taiwan. Besides, you're going to UCLA and I'm going to Mills College in the fall."

"So what!" Skip cried. "We may not see as much of each other, but that won't change how we FEEL. And we still have three months of school left. I . . . I thought we were going to the prom together."

"Skip, don't make this any harder. One of the things you said you loved about me was that I was the opposite of your mom, who can be too possessive and protective. That independent part of me thinks we should take a break. Volleyball season is just start-ing, I'll be traveling on the weekends and you're co-captain of the baseball team. Neither one of us will have much time for the other. Be reasonable!"

"We would make time! That's what love is, Maddie. You're the one who's being unreasonable. Please! Please don't do this," he begged with his hands outstretched.

"We're still so young." She reached out to grab his shoulders. "We both have years before we'll be ready to get married. It's because I love you that I want us to split up now. This way we'll have only good memories and keep alive the possibility of getting back together when we're older, when we're ready to get married."

"I . . . I don't know what to say. You want to break up now so we might get married later? You say that's reasonable? I think that's insane. What are you afraid of?"

"What am I afraid of? I'm frightened that we'll drift slowly apart over the next year and end up hating each other. What's crazy is believing high school sweethearts can possibly know enough about themselves or life to spend the next fifty years together and be happily married!"

"Your parents were high school sweethearts," Skip objected.

Maddie pursed her lips and locked eyes on Skip. "Yes, but I'm not sure how happy they are anymore!" she cried out, struggling to hold back tears.

"Maddie, I'm sorry, but . . ."

"Please, Skip. Please try to see it my way!"

"I can't stop you if you want to break up because you're afraid we might turn out like your parents," Skip yelled through clenched teeth, "but I'm telling you now I will NOT have good memories of our time together. I will do everything I can to forget you as quickly as possible!" He sliced the air with his hand as if he were severing the bond between them and stomped away back up the trail.

The pilot's voice interrupted Maddie's reverie.

"Ladies and gentlemen, we will land in Taipei in ninety minutes at approximately eight Sunday evening. If you need to leave your seat to use the restroom, now would be a good time."

Maddie cast her eyes on the picture one last time and tucked it away in the middle of the unread book, a placeholder for the future. Groggy with jet lag, she dozed until the plane bumped down in Taiwan and she awoke with a start.

Exhausted from standing in the long lines at immigration and customs, Maddie shambled into the bustling arrival hall of the airport. She scanned the sea of faces that surrounded her and was stunned to see they were all Chinese, some round, some square, some young, some old, some female, some male, but all Chinese. Taipei was nothing like Chinatown in San Francisco where Caucasian tourists flocked the streets. Disoriented, her heart fluttered until she spotted a Chinese man holding a sign with the Y logo and her name on it. Relieved, she rushed over.

"Hello, nice to meet you, Miss Erickson. My name is Chung. Manager of YMCA and volleyball coach. You look like picture. Welcome to Taiwan."

"Thank you so much for coming to the airport, Mr. Chung!" she sputtered. "I was becoming a little worried we might miss each other. Please call me Maddie."

Mr. Chung seemed about forty years old to Maddie, but she found it really difficult to tell his age. He was about three inches shorter than her—about five-foot, eight-inches she guessed—had a square head and stocky body, short black hair speckled with gray cut in a flattop, and smelled of cigarette smoke. Mr. Chung smiled at her as he talked, but his smile contrasted with his eyes that darted around as if he were concerned someone was watching him.

"Thank you, Maddie. Please call me Mr. Chung or Coach Chung. Here, I help you," Mr. Chung said and reached for her suitcase. "Now, we go. Train to Taichung three hours long."

"No, wait," Maddie objected. "I'm too tired to travel that far tonight."

"Very sorry. Must go now," he dismissed her complaint, then pivoted and waved for her to follow him. "This way, Maddie. Must hurry," he called and started to march through the crowds at a blistering pace.

Maddie had no choice but to throw her carry-on over her shoulder and scurry after him. They rushed out of the air-conditioned, brightly lit airport into the steamy night air. Under flickering fluorescent streetlights, they wove through hordes of passengers waiting to be picked up and stepped around piles of luggage. A swarm of compact cars honking and flashing headlights at one another jockeyed for position by the curb. Passengers waved and shouted at the drivers. As they approached the taxi stand, Maddie gagged on the noisome exhaust from the long line of idling yellow cabs.

"Here. This one." Mr. Chung pointed to a waiting taxi, loaded her suitcase in the trunk, and climbed in beside the driver.

Maddie slid into the back of the boxy Toyota Corona, knocking her knees against the front seat. The taxi sped along crowded, neon-lit city streets to a cavernous train station still jammed at ten o'clock with departing passengers scampering to their trains, arriving passengers rushing out, and food hawkers shouting out their wares. The pungent scents and the pulsating din overwhelmed Maddie's senses. She found it difficult to focus and almost tripped once or twice on the uneven concrete floor.

They boarded the train and found their seats. Mr. Chung directed Maddie to wait and dashed out to buy a couple of bowls of strange-looking soup from a vendor pushing a cart along the platform.

"Please eat, Maddie," he instructed and immediately began to slurp noodles into his mouth using wooden chopsticks. Famished, Maddie lifted the bowl to her mouth and carefully sipped the steaming broth. It tasted like chicken noodle soup, only richer, darker, and with a slightly sour tang. The bowl teamed with long, thick noodles and some odd-looking pieces of chicken with skin and even a few feathers. Maddie suddenly realized it was a neck.

"Yuck!" she gasped.

Mr. Chung looked up from his bowl and grinned, revealing uneven teeth yellowed by cigarette smoke. "So, you like, Maddie?"

She was about to say having a chicken neck in her soup disgusted her, but she was ravenous and the soup *was* delicious, a little like Granny's chicken noodle soup but with the strange cuts of chicken and without the carrots and celery (and, she giggled to herself, the nagging).

"Yes. Very good. Thank you," she murmured, then scooped some noodles into her mouth.

After they finished eating, a train attendant wearing plastic gloves picked up their bowls and threw their chopsticks in a trash bag. When the attendant had left, Maddie leaned forward to be heard over the rattle of the train.

"Mr. Chung, how many other counselors are there? Are any of them from America? Are they all on the volleyball team?" she asked hoping to learn something about her life for the next six weeks.

"Fifteen girls. All Chinese. All counselors and volleyball players for Y. Now, very late. Goodnight," Mr. Chung replied tersely. "Please rest."

Maddie reassured herself that being the only American counselor was lucky. She would have a great chance to become friends with the local girls. Then a thought struck her. What if none of them spoke any English? She was about to ask Mr. Chung, but he had already folded his arms against his chest, leaned back, and closed his eyes.

She would have to wait until tomorrow to get answers to her questions. She reclined the seat as far as it would go, shut her eyes, and slowed her breathing.

Their train pulled into Taichung well after midnight. Mr. Chung hustled Maddie through a small, dark station where the only sounds were the footsteps of arriving passengers echoing against the walls. By contrast to the Taipei train station, where a few English signs had given Maddie some way to orient herself, the signs in Taichung greeted her with a jumble of Chinese characters of every size and color. A vision of wandering at night through an unknown city unable to read or speak the language flashed through her mind. She instinctively moved closer to Mr. Chung.

"This way, please," he commanded as they exited the station and crossed a wide street. Lights shone from a handful of stores, but the sidewalks were deserted. Maddie was surprised to see Taichung was a large, densely inhabited city, more like San Francisco than San Rafael. Mr. Chung escorted her to a tiny hotel a block away, led her into a cramped, brightly lit lobby smelling of cleaning fluid, and checked her in.

"Here is room key. I come back tomorrow at eight. Please be ready. We go to Y," he continued. "You meet other female counselors and teammates. Goodnight, Maddie."

Tired, apprehensive, and grubby down to her toes from the long trip, Maddie trudged up two flights of stairs to a room that was no bigger than her family's kitchen. She threw her suitcase on a bed that was little more than a cot, stripped off her warm-ups, and entered a postage-stamp sized bathroom she could barely turn around in. She stepped into a tub with a shower, pulled the curtain across, and switched on the water. As water sprayed into her mouth, she frantically tried to adjust the showerhead upward to accommodate her height, but it was already as high as it could go. She spat out the liquid because she'd been warned to avoid drinking tap water. She washed, crouching down to allow the hot water to rinse her body. After she dried off, she pulled on the crimson cotton robe she found on the bed, threw the sheets over her, and fell into a deep sleep.

Three and a half hours later, Maddie woke up like it was already morning. She tried to go back to sleep but couldn't. Her stomach growled with hunger. She hoped the Y cafeteria in Taichung served the same bacon and cheese omelet she loved at the Y in San Rafael. *What will today be like?* She knew from the acceptance letter that she was to teach four hours of English conversation in the morning and help Mr. Chung coach two hours of volleyball practice in the late afternoon. She couldn't wait to settle into her dorm room, meet the other counselors, and explore the city with a few of her new friends.

Mr. Chung stood halfway up a metal folding ladder at one end of the volleyball court in the Y's gym. He stared across the net at the sixteen members of the women's volleyball team lined up along the opposite end line. After barking a command in Chinese, he added in English, "Maddie. Again!" Maddie and three other girls started to "run the lines" for the fifth time that night. They raced as fast as they could from the end line to the nearest ten-foot line and back, then to the middle line and back, then to the farthest ten-foot line and back, and finally to the far end line and back to the end line where they had started, bending down to touch each line they reached. When Maddie finished, she bent over gasping for breath and wiped a rivulet of sweat from her forehead.

"You okay?" May Chan asked. She was the only girl on the team who spoke even a little English. Maddie straightened herself and cast a wan smile down at May. She was grateful for the concern in May's hazel eyes, the worry wrinkling her face. Maddie would have done the same for a teammate and May was not only her teammate. Over the past week, she had become a friend.

"Yes. Thanks." Maddie nodded, but inside she seethed at having to practice so hard when Mr. Chung had lied to her about *everything.* What she thought would be a dormitory, where she would have her own room, was the gym on the top floor of the five-story Y building. Maddie and the other fifteen players and counselors had beds of thin foam padding to spread on the hardwood floor and cotton sheets as blankets, which were a foot too short for Maddie. At night they lit mosquito coils between the mats. The chemical smell from the smoke nauseated Maddie, keeping her awake. Worse, the coils didn't work. By dawn, tiny red bites covered her ankles and wrists. Every morning Maddie and the girls dressed, packed up their suitcases and bedding, and stored them in a closet. Every evening after practice, they took the suitcases out and laid them by their mats until morning. Maddie admitted the living arrangement had been kind of fun the first day or two—like camping out on a field trip with friends from school—but soon the lack of privacy, the constant shuffling of luggage, and the stifling fumes grated.

"Maddie! Again you are last! Please try harder," Mr. Chung yelled.

He turned to the rest of the team and shouted an order in Chinese.

"Maddie, side-to-side jumping, four rows."

Maddie lined up with three other girls in the back row, towering over her teammates. She held her hands behind her back and placed her feet shoulder-width apart. When Mr. Chung clapped his hands, the girls started to jump from right foot to left foot, swinging the right foot past the left foot and vice versa. After a few minutes, Mr. Chung clapped his hands again and the girls immediately stopped. Maddie's heart pounded. Sweat soaked her ivory jersey and scarlet shorts. The perspiration, however, did nothing to cool her rage.

Not only had she been misled about her housing, but her work obligations were *completely* different from what the Y's letter had described. She was teaching not four but *eight* hours of English, from eight to noon and one to five, not five but *six* days a week. The grinding schedule allowed her no time to sightsee except on Sunday afternoon after Bible class. Because she also had to wash clothes and do other chores, she had yet to explore the city. When Maddie complained to Mr. Chung, he explained that the Taichung Y's letter to her describing the position had been written before he learned of the unexpectedly high demand for English and other classes. "Change in schedule," he had dismissed her complaint with a shrug.

His failure to apologize or even acknowledge the unfairness of the situation infuriated Maddie further. The tight timetable forced Maddie to eat all her meals in the cafeteria, which served only white rice, cold vegetables and a raw egg for breakfast and greasy noodles drenched in a thick, pungent sauce with vegetables and a little chicken or pork for lunch and dinner. The food was not at all like the great Chinese meals Maddie had eaten at Shanghai Pine Gardens in San Rafael or Mister Chu's in San Francisco.

Even more irritating, women's exercise classes ran in the gym from six to eight thirty every evening. Consequently, Maddie and her teammates weren't able to relax in their so-called "dorm" after dinner, but were forced to hang out in the cafeteria until volleyball practice at nine. After two hours of practice, Maddie was exhausted, wanted to shower quickly, and sleep, but she couldn't. All sixteen girls used the women's bathroom in the gym and there were only three musty shower stalls. It took at least an hour before she could lie down on her pad, trying to rest under a sheet that was too short and beside mosquito coils that seemed to attract rather than repel the pests.

Mr. Chung yelled another order in Chinese and one of Maddie's teammates hurried to carry a bag full of volleyballs to his ladder. Maddie's teammate reached into the bag and handed Mr. Chung a ball.

"Maddie, defense drill." Mr. Chung pointed at Maddie.

She moved to a spot about ten feet in front of the ladder and crouched down in a defensive position. *WHACK!* He smashed the ball to Maddie's left. She leapt with her arm outstretched trying to prevent the ball from hitting the floor but it landed just beyond her reach. Goddamn him! She cursed to herself, scrambled up, and resumed her position. Mr. Chung held another ball up and *WHACK!* He struck it down six feet to Maddie's right. Maddie dove to her right in a vain attempt to dig the ball up. She sprawled on the ground resting for a moment.

"Up, Maddie, up!" Mr. Chung commanded. "Defense, Maddie. Defense!"

When she was ready again, he took another ball and swung as if he would spike it with his right fist. Instead, he dropped the ball from his left hand five feet in front of Maddie.

"*Ugh!*" Maddie grunted and leaped forward with both arms trying to reach the ball. Once again, it fell to the ground just beyond her reach. Maddie lifted herself up and saw Mr. Chung shake his head in disgust. Maddie could barely contain her fury. No American coach would demand players make impossible plays over and over again and then blast them in front of the whole team when they failed.

"Enough this time. Next time do better!" he barked and called May to take Maddie's place. As she passed May, Maddie held her palm out to slap May's as a sign of encouragement. May smiled shyly back and grazed Maddie's hand with her own.

If Mr. Chung hadn't tormented May and all the other girls during practice as much as he did Maddie, she would have walked out after a couple of days. She was, after all, supposed to be the assistant coach, not a human punching bag. But Maddie had grown fond of May and her teammates despite the language barrier. Since they did not complain, Maddie held her tongue.

During the first few practices, Maddie couldn't remember or pronounce most of her teammates' names, except May's, so she called them by the numbers on their jerseys. Some of the girls frowned at first and Maddie wondered briefly if they were offended. Soon, however, her teammates began to call one another by their numbers, too, and laugh and laugh at one another. That she had brought the team closer together delighted Maddie.

Her teammates and co-counselors called her "Maddie," but had difficulty pronouncing it no matter how much she corrected them. They didn't say "MAA-dee" the way her family and friends did; they said "mawDEE," which Maddie thought was cute but also a little annoying because it reminded her of Maudie McGee— her *former* friend—who was dating Skip now and wearing his class ring. Maddie didn't really care, except Skip had asked her first and Maudie was only wearing his ring because Maddie had insisted on breaking up in the spring.

After two weeks in Taiwan, Maddie sorely missed her parents and her friends in San Rafael, but the Y had no international telephone service and the nearest facility was in the post office miles away. Maddie penned letters on Sunday afternoons to her parents and to her two best friends using the wafer-thin aerograms the Y provided for overseas correspondence. She had received four letters in return. Reading about their busy lives in San Rafael only sharpened the pangs of loneliness. While she enjoyed teaching English, and her students seemed eager to talk about American food, clothes, and movies, they were all older— some as old as her parents—and preoccupied with careers and families. They would arrive punctually, take their seats, and rush out as soon as she finished the lesson.

What kept Maddie from becoming *totally* depressed were the impromptu gatherings that sprung up in the cafeteria between dinner and practice. At first it was only a couple of girls but soon all of her teammates would huddle around Maddie in their navy-blue warmups and ask through May about Maddie's family, her school, and her club team. Somehow answering their questions made Maddie feel both less far away from her life in California and closer to her new friends.

"May," Maddie asked one evening, feeling particularly homesick, "do any of the local stations play American music?"

"Yes. Armed Forces Network," May replied and jumped up to tune the Sony transistor radio in the cafeteria to AFN Taiwan. After listening to Tommy James and the Shondells' "Mony Mony," the Beach Boys' "Do It Again," and the Bee Gees' "I've Gotta Get a Message to You," Maddie could restrain herself no longer.

"Will you help me push the tables and chairs against the walls," she asked as she shoved aside a couple of chairs. May translated and the girls soon cleared the floor. Maddie began to show her friends how young Americans danced. She demonstrated the Twist, the Surfer's Stomp, the Swim, and the Mashed Potato. As Maddie twirled, hopped, and gyrated around the floor, the girls giggled and exchanged wide-eyed looks. When she finished, they burst into applause.

"Come on, May!" Maddie called.

Startled, May shook her hands in front of her face and started to back away.

Maddie grabbed her and pulled her out to dance with her. "Join us!" She waved to the others and, in a few minutes, all sixteen girls were twisting to Chubby Checker.

The Monday of the third week, Mr. Chung informed the girls just before practice that he had a meeting that would delay their schedule an hour. When he left, Maddie decided it was a great opportunity for the assistant coach to take over.

"Come on," she gestured with her hand. "Let's play a couple of games." As she began to head up the stairs to the gym, Maddie could see May's eyes widen in alarm. "Look, I'm assistant coach. I promise you Mr. Chung won't mind our warming up before the drills."

"Okay, Maddie," May acquiesced after hesitating a moment. "We follow you." She explained what was happening to the other girls who trailed after Maddie up the stairs.

Maddie quickly divided the girls into two teams of six with the extra three girls rotating in to play. She moved Mr. Chung's ladder to one of the net posts, climbed up, and motioned for the game to begin. *WHACK!* May served. The ball sailed over the net toward a girl in the backcourt who moved to pass the ball forward. *THUMP!* She bounced it wildly off her arms. *WHACK!* May served again at another girl in the backcourt who moved too late. *THUMP!* She swung her arms at the ball. "*AIEEE!*" she screamed as the ball caromed away. Maddie watched each side receive service five or six times and successfully pass the ball on only about half of them.

"Wait!" Maddie shouted and held up her hand, then stepped down the ladder. "May, translate for me, please. The secret to passing is to move your body directly in front of the ball, bend at the waist, and use your hips, legs, and shoulders to guide it. Never swing your arms. Got it?" May translated as Maddie demonstrated the technique. When she saw the girls' heads nod she said, "Okay. Just practice passing the ball to the player in the front middle who will catch it so we can repeat several times." May translated again and served.

WHACK! May served again to one of the girls who had mishit May's service. This time, however, she followed Maddie's instructions. *THUMP!* She lofted the ball beautifully to her teammate. All the girls applauded the passer. About a dozen serves later, the entire team was passing the ball with much better accuracy.

"Okay. Now, pass the ball to the front middle who will set it to one of the players on either side of her for them to hit it."

May explained in Chinese and served again. Another good pass and this time the setter took two steps to get under the ball, but faced the passer and held her hands up stiffly, parallel to each other. *SPLAT!* She slapped at the ball, which spun backwards off her hands and fell to the ground. Why had Mr. Chung focused on conditioning and defense when the team clearly needed help with basic technique?

"Okay!" Maddie called out. "May, would you translate again? To set the ball accurately, you should make a triangle just above your forehead with your thumbs and forefingers, move your forehead under the ball, and turn your hips and shoulders toward where you want the ball to go. Don't forget to bend your arms and knees and make contact with the ball using only the fingertips of both hands simultaneously." As May translated again, Maddie threw a ball up in the air two or three times and demonstrated how to set it correctly. "Okay, everyone?" Maddie asked. The girls murmured and nodded.

"Good. Now, May, ask everyone to find a partner, stand about ten feet apart, and practice passing and setting." After about ten minutes, Maddie glanced around the court and was thrilled to see her teammates passing and setting accurately almost all the time. She swelled with pride in having been able to help her friends improve so quickly.

"Now, I want you to practice passing the ball to the other player who will set the ball back to the passer who will then spike the ball to the setter who will dig it up. May, let's demonstrate."

Maddie and May stood about ten feet apart. Maddie tossed the ball underhand to May, who passed it to Maddie. Maddie set the ball back to May who jumped, swung, and, to Maddie's shock, *WHOOSH!* She missed it entirely. "*AIEEE!*" May cried and stomped her foot.

Maddie delivered directions on the proper technique for spiking the ball and asked May to set for her. The first two times, the ball flew only a couple of feet over Maddie's head.

"Higher, May. Higher," Maddie urged and pointed with her thumb at the ceiling.

Several of the girls chortled through the back of their hands.

"Sorry," May said. "You so tall. I set again."

This time the ball soared ten feet above Maddie who timed her jump as it fell, raised her arms, and slammed the ball down about two feet to May's left. To Maddie's surprise, May slid over quickly on her knees, reached out with her arms, and dug the ball up before it hit the court.

"Great play, May!" Maddie called and ran over to embrace her teammate.

"STOP. STOP! I ask you to wait," Mr. Chung screamed as he strode through the door.

Surprised, Maddie turned to face him. "I apologize. I was trying to help the girls improve their offensive techniques. I thought, as assistant coach . . ."

"I am coach!" he yelled and pounded his chest with his fist. "You must learn Taiwanese way to play before you coach team."

"But, Mr. Chung, the girls are fit already. Why not let me teach what I learned in America about proper ball handling techniques and offensive strategy?" Maddie pointed to her teammates. "I think we all want less time on conditioning and defensive drills and more time practicing skills and playing games so we can work on executing plays. Why won't you let me help you?"

"You good at volleyball only because very tall," he huffed and held his hand up above his head. "For Taiwanese girls, defense is only way to win and tough conditioning is only way to good defense. Team understand this is best way. Now"—Mr. Chung straightened himself—"enough talking. You waste practice time. Taichung City Tournament is less than four weeks from today. No time for new ideas from America. Maddie, go with team for drills at back line," he commanded, shouting instructions at the other girls in Chinese, and clapped his hands impatiently.

Maddie huffed and took two steps toward the door, but May clutched her arm and pulled her to the back line.

"Please," begged May, clinging to Maddie. "Please stay with team."

She looked down at May's pleading eyes. Maddie took a deep breath and joined her friends.

Over the next few days, her resentment toward Mr. Chung simmered barely beneath the surface. She considered going to the post office to call her parents to ask for a plane ticket home now rather than wait for her scheduled flight on the night of the tournament. After a dinner spent poking at her fried noodles, she had decided to do just that when May and the other girls surrounded her table. Grinning broadly, May stepped forward holding a little almond cake with a candle in it.

"We know today is your Independence Day and wish to celebrate with you, our honored guest and assistant coach," she said and dropped her eyes for a moment. "We heard you have a very hard discussion with Mr. Chung several nights ago. We worry you unhappy. We wish harmony between Mr. Chung and you and whole team before Taichung City Tournament."

Maddie looked around and saw sympathy radiating from their eyes, leaving no doubt in her mind that her friends supported her and realized Mr. Chung's autocratic and obstinate behavior would only hurt the team's performance at the tournament.

"I'm surprised you would even know about our Independence Day, but thank you so very much for thinking of me and . . . for your encouragement," Maddie whispered and, overwhelmed by their affection, she began to weep. Soon all the girls were crying and laughing and hugging one another. Maddie did not have the heart to leave now. She vowed that nothing was more important than helping them win the big tournament. She loved them all, especially her dear May.

The next night, two of Maddie's teammates became sick. Mr. Chung not only made them practice, he seemed to relish punishing them. He ordered them to do wind sprints and run the lines with the rest of the team until they collapsed.

"The man's a sadist," Maddie grumbled to herself. She was about to walk out of the practice in protest when an idea flashed into her mind, a way she could help her teammates *and* thwart Chung's bullying.

"I am sorry, Mr. Chung," Maddie said the next day just before practice. "I have a terrible cramp in my stomach and chills running through my body. I apologize but I cannot practice tonight and perhaps not for several days."

"Wait!" Mr. Chung called, but Maddie strolled out of the gym to the girls' bathroom. The next morning, May and some of the other girls brought Maddie a new, longer sheet to cover her at night, a larger mat to sleep on, and some medicine, which had an odd purplish color and pungent odor.

"Thank you so much," Maddie said feeling even more confident in her decision. "I don't need any medicine. But I do need your help."

May cocked her head. "Why my help?"

"I know I would feel one-hundred percent better if Mr. Chung agreed to put us up at a hotel for the four nights before the tournament so we could get some real rest. I would also feel better if he canceled the exercise classes so we could practice in the early evening, and allowed me to coach you at practice." Maddie beamed in triumph.

May looked baffled for a moment before her eyes burst open. She nodded to Maddie and spoke to the rest of the girls in rapid Chinese. They began to talk all at once and wave their hands at each other. After about five minutes, they grew quiet. May approached Maddie.

"I understand," she said.

That evening Mr. Chung and May were nowhere to be seen before practice. When they finally arrived in the gym, Maddie could tell Mr. Chung was fighting to contain his fury. A sly smile creased May's face. Mr. Chung glared at Maddie, but nonetheless informed the team he would implement everything Maddie had requested without admitting it had been her idea. After he walked out of the gym, Maddie couldn't control herself. She went from teammate to teammate embracing them and promising to help them win. There were only three weeks before the tournament. She couldn't wait to start practicing.

For the next two weeks, Maddie and her teammates taught their classes until five and practiced from five until seven thirty. They still had plenty of time to clean up, have dinner, and hang out in the dorm until lights out at eleven. Maddie reveled in her new responsibility as coach and organized practice the same way her dad coached their club team in San Rafael. The session started and ended with twenty minutes or so of light conditioning. In between, the team worked on skills for a good forty minutes and played intra-squad games for another forty minutes, concentrating on game strategy and personnel for special situations. Not surprisingly, Mr. Chung did not attend their practices. To motivate everyone further, Maddie announced she would not play during the tournament, but coach full time in order to give the others as much opportunity as possible to play. Her friends seemed much more relaxed and yet also more energetic than in the past. She saw each player pushing herself to accomplish what Maddie asked them to do. She had no idea what kind of competition they would face, but the effort put out by her teammates convinced Maddie that winning the tournament would be momentous for May and her friends. Maddie wanted more than anything to help them become champions before she flew back to California.

On the Monday morning five days before the tournament, Maddie saw her team gathered around a bulletin board outside Mr. Chung's office. She walked up and stared at a sheet of paper containing two sets of names. Her name was the only English name and it appeared last in the second group.

"What's this?" Maddie asked May.

"Players for two Y teams," she replied.

"TWO teams? What do you mean TWO teams?" Maddie roared. May tilted her head to one side and scrunched her eyes in confusion.

"Yes," May responded evenly. "Two teams for Y. You are here as coach of B team." She pointed to Maddie's name at the bottom of the second group of eight names. "And I am here to help with translation," she indicated her name in Chinese characters just above Maddie's name.

"Who else is on our team?" Maddie demanded. When May read off the names of those on Maddie's team and on the A team, Maddie's heart sank. Goddamn Mr. Chung! All the best players were on the A team except May. He had set her up to fail in front of the entire city.

"I . . . I can't believe it," Maddie stammered.

May looked up at her friend with a furrowed brow. "Y has two teams every tournament. Of course, Mr. Chung selects players. He is coach. You are surprised?"

"Yes," Maddie muttered, feeling betrayed and embarrassingly naive. "Wait, will both teams practice here?"

"No. Mr. Chung team practice at high school."

Maddie knew Mr. Chung's team would crush Maddie's—and the jerk would take smug delight in showing her up. If she had known two weeks ago there would be another team, she would have insisted the two teams practice separately. She had been tricked again, this time into devoting herself to preparing players who would now play against *her*. They would destroy her team, proving she was a terrible coach and Mr. Chung a great one. But Maddie Erickson would not go down without a fight! That afternoon she gathered May and the other six girls on her team together in the cafeteria.

"I have decided we will practice an extra two and a half hours, from five to ten, this evening and every evening from tonight through Thursday. Would you translate, May?"

May's jaw dropped briefly, but she took a deep breath and conveyed what Maddie had just said. Several girls shook their heads and grimaced. A few girls grumbled in Chinese but Maddie continued, "And, at the tournament, everyone on the team will rotate in and out of the lineup, except May and me. We will play *every* minute of *every* game, *especially* against the A team. May?"

May looked down for a moment and paused before glancing up at Maddie. "But you say you not play at tournament," she whispered out of the side of her mouth.

"That was before Mr. Chung took all the best players for his team except you," Maddie replied. "Look, I know how much you want to beat the A team and to win the tournament. Practicing extra hours and keeping our best players on the court is the only way to do it. So please tell them you and I will play every minute of each game. And also explain that practicing long and late means we won't be able to stay at the hotel like the players on the A team. We'll just have to sleep on our mats on the gym floor. See you at five!"

"Wait," May pleaded. "I not understand. You give back everything we request for you from Mr. Chung?"

"I . . . I know, May, and I'm sorry. But Mr. Chung fooled us and beating him at the tournament is the best way to teach him a lesson. To do that, we need to make some sacrifices. Now, please translate. I have to think through exactly how we will use the practice time we have."

Maddie jumped up and marched away so quickly she didn't hear the clamor that rose up from the girls as May translated Maddie's orders.

After practice on Thursday night, Maddie leaned back on her mat, cradled her head with her hands, and smiled broadly. Though thoroughly spent, she felt nothing but pride. Her team had toiled to improve every minute of every hour of every practice the last four nights, all without a whisper of complaint. Even when two of her players became sick on Tuesday and Maddie asked them whether they wanted to sit out, they refused. They continued to drill and play at full speed though they were dry heaving every five minutes. Maddie saw the fire in every one of her teammates' eyes matched the competitive zeal she felt blazing inside her.

The tournament was scheduled to start at eight the next morning on courts inside the Tunghai University sports arena. Twelve university teams and twelve club teams from the surrounding region were competing before hundreds of spectators. Maddie's team was on the opposite side of the bracket from Mr. Chung's team; they wouldn't play against each other unless they both reached the finals. Wouldn't it be sweet, she mused just before drifting to sleep, to meet Chung's team in the finals and take them down in front of the whole city to win the tournament?

Both Y teams won all of their matches the next day and moved into the best two out of three finals. During the first game, Maddie continued to play like a demon, spiking the ball down harder than ever, blocking the A teams' hitters across almost the entire net, serving top-spin winners down the line, and even stepping in front of her teammates from time to time to receive serves she knew she could handle better. She felt sure she would be voted a tournament All-Star for her play, an accolade that would stick in Mr. Chung's throat for weeks. *You good at volleyball only because so tall.* Ha!

During the five-minute break between the first and second games, May called the girls over and huddled with them while Maddie rested on the bench. May spoke to her teammates with an intensity Maddie had not seen before, once or twice glancing in her direction. Maddie imagined May was giving them a pep talk, telling them to go all out to win the next game for their coach, their best player. When May was done, the other girls glanced at one another and nodded their assent. May stepped over to Maddie.

"I rest this game," she declared firmly. "You rest this game, too."

"What?" Maddie's head jerked back. "Is this a *joke*?"

"No joke. Team agrees," she said, gesturing to the other players. "You are coach, yes. But you follow us this time."

Maddie shot up from her seat and started to pace in front of May, waving her arms in consternation, trying to find the words Dad would have used if his players had told HIM to sit down and let them play the way they wanted. How *dare* they? She was the coach. She had carried them through the tournament to the brink of achieving everything they wanted—victory over Mr. Chung. Payback for his deceit and abuse. And *this* is how they treated her after all she had done for them? She opened her mouth to scream at May. Then she saw her dear friend flinch, expecting to be lashed with words, words she might not understand fully but whose tone would lacerate. Maddie had not hesitated to criticize Mr. Chung, but he deserved it. May did not. Maddie snapped her mouth shut, but shook her head violently.

"Please," May begged, her head bowed. "*Please.*"

May's vulnerability doused the flames of Maddie's anger. May was not just her teammate, she was her best friend.

"Okay," Maddie exhaled. "Okay. I don't understand, but we can start the game on the bench. If we begin to lose, however, we *must* go back in."

May pivoted away without responding and jogged over to tell their teammates who would be playing.

The second game started and Maddie's team quickly fell behind. She started to warm up to go back in the game, but May grabbed her arm and pulled her down on the bench. Maddie yanked her arm away and slouched with her arms folded. She looked over at May, expecting to see her agitated at the prospect of losing. Instead her friend was relaxed and smiling, displaying a carefree attitude that infuriated Maddie even more. The game was close, but their team lagged behind seventeen to fourteen— only four points from losing to Mr. Chung.

"Goddammit, May!" Maddie barked in exasperation. "Don't you understand? We may lose this game."

May swiveled around, fixed her eyes on Maddie's, and replied serenely, "Yes. We know. We lose for *them.*"

May's words stunned her. "*What?*" she gasped and threw her hands out.

"They are friends," May explained. "Mr. Chung is coach. We appreciate your skill, but we not want shame them."

Maddie quickly regained her composure and responded in the only way she knew how—the way her parents had taught her.

"You mean you're not playing to win? You're not playing to *win?*" she screeched incredulously. "What's the point of playing at all unless you play to win? And what if we lose the third game? The whole tournament? The chance to teach Mr. Chung a lesson?"

May did not blink. "You are guest and teammate and coach, yes, but only for summer. Until now we support you. We accept you playing. We practice longer, even when sick. We stay on mats at Y when others go to nice hotel. But now you must support *team's* decision. Tonight you leave for your home but we stay. Must live together in harmony."

Maddie was stunned and didn't notice the second game had ended. Her team had lost.

May shot up. "Okay. Now we go in."

Although Maddie was physically on the court in the third game, May's revelation disoriented her so much she couldn't concentrate. Each time she served, she served into the net. Each time she spiked, she spiked outside the lines. Yet, somehow, her team still won. Her teammates played brilliant, nonstop defense and, astonishingly, the A team started playing terribly, mishitting returns of service, and serving out of bounds at critical moments. When the game was over, the players lined up to shake the hands of the other team. Maddie participated in the ceremony still bewildered by what had happened. Mr. Chung then gathered the players from both Y teams together in the middle of the court and joined the audience in applauding the players as if HE had coached both teams.

Later, as the girls showered and dressed before a celebratory dinner in the cafeteria, Maddie couldn't get out of her mind how badly the A team had played the third game.

"May? Could we talk?" she said, pointing to a quiet corner of the locker room. Looking down at May, she continued, "I'm confused. What happened in the third game? Did . . . did the A team lose on purpose the way we lost the second game?"

May smiled the softest, most subtle smile Maddie had ever seen.

"Sorry. I no understand," she replied and cast her eyes around the room. "Time for dinner," she announced brightly before rushing away. Maddie sensed May did in fact understand perfectly well. That May didn't want to be honest with Maddie confounded her even more.

After dinner, Maddie's departure for the train to Taipei grew near. She desperately wanted May to accompany her so they would have a few more hours together, perhaps even plan to meet again next summer.

"Mr. Chung? I know you probably intended to take me to Taipei, but . . ."

"So sorry," Mr. Chung interjected. "I cannot. Must meet with team to discuss tournament. My secretary go with you. Goodbye and thank you, Maddie Erickson," he said, barely able to keep a triumphant smirk off his face.

"I understand," replied Maddie, delighted he wouldn't accompany her. "If you can't take me, could May come instead of your secretary? She speaks better English."

"Yes, yes. If May want go, no problem." He shrugged and returned to his office.

Maddie ran over to May who was sitting at a table in the cafeteria surrounded by all their friends from both teams.

"May? Mr. Chung says it would be fine if you were to take me to the airport. Isn't that great news?"

May dropped her eyes to the table. She wove her fingers together in front of her and looked up at Maddie. "Sorry, but I stay with coach and team."

Maddie felt as if she had been punched in the stomach. "But May . . ." she begged.

"Please understand," May said. "They are friends, like family. He is coach, like father. You are our guest and we appreciate your ability but now you leave." May rose to go up to the gym with the rest of the girls. "Goodbye, Maddie," she said and bowed slightly. "Thank you for your help."

The other fourteen girls paraded after May each bowing slightly to Maddie and parroted, "Goodbye, Maddie. Thank you for your help."

Afterwards, her teammates disappeared chatting and giggling as they climbed up the stairs to the gym. The stark contrast between the formality of their farewells and their girlish delight in hurrying to practice, in leaving her behind, cut Maddie like a knife.

Maddie rode with the secretary on the train to Taipei in baffled silence. She had been so sure May would want to see her off at the airport. That's what she would have done for a teammate, for a friend. Of course, she had been certain May supported her rebellion against Mr. Chung, that she wanted to win the tournament as much as Maddie did. Had she been wrong about that, as well?

Maddie checked in, passed through immigration, and boarded the plane to Honolulu and San Francisco in a trance. Her parents had instilled in her the belief that you don't play to play the game, you play to *win* the game. Maddie presumed her teammates felt the same way until they intentionally lost the second game. And what to make of May coyly refusing to acknowledge Mr. Chung's team had purposely lost the third. Had the two teams conspired to ensure Maddie's team won the tournament, each by *losing* one game? But, if so, Mr. Chung must have agreed to the ruse. *Mr. Chung!* Why? She didn't have a clue.

As the plane taxied slowly down the runway, Maddie reached down to tuck her carry-on further underneath her seat. Her hand struck two books lying at the bottom of the bag. They were her diary and the book on Taiwan that Skip had given her. She unzipped the bag, took them out, and opened the diary for the first time since Kimberly had interrupted her on the flight from San Francisco. Her black pen still lay where she had placed it between the page agonizing about her parents' marriage and the blank pages where she had planned to describe her experiences in Taiwan.

Maddie picked up the pen and twirled it in her fingers as she considered what she should write about May and her teammates, about her students, and about the most important event of her six weeks, the Taichung City Tournament. Should she write how she introduced her teammates and co-counselors to the Bee Gees and the Swim? How she trained them in American volleyball techniques and strategy? Should she describe how she taught her students American slang and how to converse about American food and clothes and movies? Should she write how well she played at the tournament, motivated by her very American desire to triumph even if it meant—no, precisely because it would mean—badly beating her friends on the other Y team and humiliating their coach?

And then a question struck her, one so excruciating she dropped her pen. She had blithely assumed May and her teammates shared her passion for winning regardless of the consequences. What *else* had she presumed but gotten wrong? Her students' interest in American slang and culture? Her teammates' desire to dance and play volleyball like an American? Their *feelings* for her? What did May call her just before saying goodbye? Their *guest*.

"My God," Maddie uttered to herself as disappointment, frustration, and loss welled up in her. The friendships she had treasured revealed themselves, in the end, to be just daydreams.

Maddie closed her eyes and massaged her temples in disbelief. She had been a complete idiot. She realized now that assuming someone from a different culture will think and act like you is not just foolish, it frustrates developing true attachments. Maddie grieved she had never taken the time to explore how May and her teammates, how her students, even how Mr. Chung might see the world in fundamentally different ways and to consider the possibility that their perspectives might be just as good as hers.

She sighed heavily as she looked down at the words of despair she had written in her diary about her family. Mr. Chung and her teammates chose to lose in order to accomplish something more important than attaining a championship. May had said they were part of a family. Keeping their family together meant more to them than winning. That viewpoint had seemed so foreign to Maddie but now she thought of *her* family. Didn't she hope her parents would come to the same understanding and cease their bickering, their competition for the affection of their only child? Didn't she pray they would realize their life together wasn't a game and their fight to prevail at all costs risked destroying something—their family—more precious than winning?

Staring out the window at the multicolored lights of Taipei receding in the distance, Maddie arrived at a bitter conclusion. She had traveled to Taiwan not with an open mind but with a head full of assumptions. She had physically *existed* in Taichung for six weeks but had never really *lived* there. May was right. She had been their guest and now she was leaving feeling as empty as the pages in her diary. She took a long breath and exhaled slowly. She laid her diary down and opened the book Skip had given her. She set her jaw. She would never make that mistake again.

4 Disillusion

On a late February afternoon of her freshman year, Maddie strolled through a fine drizzle across the verdant Mills College campus toward the career center. She needed to find a summer job, preferably one that would offer her an escape from San Rafael. Skip would be home from UCLA during the summer and he was still dating Maudie McGee. Maddie cringed, recalling the agony she felt over winter break when she turned a corner and saw Skip holding hands with Maudie outside the Rafael Theater.

While she had at first hoped they would remain friends, she told herself she was happier without his pontificating. Her memories of his raving about how he'd made such *wonderful* friends in Mexico made all the more painful her failure to bond with May and her teammates in Taiwan. Nearly a year later, she didn't in the least regret breaking up. As the months passed, she had become even more convinced they had been far too young to sustain a love that would last a lifetime. And, too, she relished the time for self-exploration that separating from Skip allowed her. Still, she knew seeing Maudie and Skip together over the summer would sting.

Maddie's despair—and growing anger—at how her parents were behaving toward each other also spurred her to get away. They had not been fighting as much since she left for college, but they spent little time together. During the day, Dad worked in his office while Mom exercised at her gym or sailed on the bay with her women's sailing club. After work and on weekends, he coached her old high school volleyball team and a college club team for Maddie. The hot war of Maddie's high school years had turned frigid, neither side giving in, neither side communicating, each broadcasting to her—the third "Erickson Musketeer"—the faults of the other. Many times, Maddie wanted to scream at them, *Grow up!* But she held back, fearing that forcing them to acknowledge their rupture would only lead to more recriminations and a wider gulf between them. She prayed her absence over the summer might compel her parents to confront their problems, if not to make love, at least not to make war with each other.

Though Maddie felt more and more alienated from her parents, she remained uncomfortable about confiding her distress to any of her friends. All of them either played with her on her dad's team or had mothers close to her mom. Her longing for a sibling with whom she could freely share her anxiety about the future intensified.

"*Aggh!*" Maddie hissed at one of the many eucalyptus trees dotting the campus, startling two students who were passing by. Sometimes she felt so very alone.

After thirty minutes of leafing through the summer jobs binder in the career center, Maddie stumbled upon a position assisting a tour for a dozen American high school students in Japan. It would take her far away from the Bay Area for three weeks during the middle of the summer, leaving only a few weeks at the beginning and end during which she would have to deal with her parents' childish squabbling.

"May I help you with something?" asked Ms. Williams, a short, sprightly, older woman Maddie had seen ambling around campus. She was Mills Class of 1935, and had served as the head career counselor for more than two decades, earning a reputation for encouraging Mills students to compete for jobs traditionally thought of as exclusive to men.

"Thanks. I'm Maddie Erickson." She held out her hand and hunched over to meet Ms. Williams' eyes. "Do you know anything about this job?"

Ms. Williams perched her glasses just above her eyebrows and squinted.

"It says here, the program is sponsored by the Japanese Ministry of Education and Ministry of Foreign Affairs. It aims to promote understanding of Japan among American youth—certainly a very worthy goal. I know the Association for International Educational Exchange, the organization that screens and selects the American candidate, is a well-regarded nonprofit. It's probably the best organization in the country at promoting international exchanges for students and teachers. Goodness, the compensation is certainly attractive, isn't it? Seven hundred and fifty dollars for three weeks' work in July, room and board, and a round-trip plane ticket to Tokyo."

"Yes, enough money that I won't have to rely on my parents to support me over the summer," Maddie said. "I'm only a freshman. Do you think I qualify?"

"You have to be an American college student with some experience living in an Asian country. Have you ever been to Asia?"

"Last summer. I worked for six weeks at a YMCA in Taiwan."

"Fascinating. Did you enjoy yourself?"

"I was the only American and didn't speak any Chinese. I had some trouble making Taiwanese friends and felt isolated sometimes. But I certainly learned a lot," Maddie replied. "Do you think I should apply?"

"You qualify and you wouldn't be the only American on the program, although the others will be a year or two younger. And you'd work with an English-speaking Japanese college student under the direction of an English-speaking Japanese professor of international relations at Waseda University. Communication shouldn't be a problem, although you should do some reading on Japan and Japanese culture if you're selected. I would be happy to look at your application before you send it in. What do you say?"

"Do I have to make up my mind right away? The position seems interesting, but I'd like to think it over. I'm just not sure I'm ready to go abroad again."

"Well, let's see. The deadline is in eight days. AIEE is in New York so I would guess, to be safe, you'd have to mail your application by tomorrow. Why don't you take a copy back to your dorm tonight?"

"That's a good idea. I'll think about it overnight. Thank you so much for your help."

As Maddie considered the position over the next day, the opportunity to travel far from San Rafael to an exotic place began to excite her. This was Japan, she told herself, a developed country, not Taiwan. The tour hosted American kids, not a group of Chinese girls who didn't speak English. More importantly, Maddie felt she had learned a lot about what *not* to do from her summer in Taiwan and from an Intro to Anthropology course she was taking this term, partly to acquire a better understanding of cross-cultural communication but mostly because the professor was cute, a former Peace Corps volunteer. He reinforced, with many funny, self-deprecating stories—so different in tone from Skip—that presuming someone from a different culture would think and feel the same as you would lead inevitably to confusion, frustration, and disappointment for both people. He stressed that if you wanted to develop a true friendship across cultures, you needed to learn about one another's cultural differences and respect them.

If she were to go to Japan, she vowed she would take his advice to heart and research all she could about Japanese culture and society. Besides, seven hundred and fifty dollars was more than what Maddie could make in *ten* weeks as a salesclerk at the sporting goods store in San Rafael, a job that would trap her indoors for the summer. Being an assistant tour leader would take her outdoors and certainly involve some walking, perhaps even some hiking.

Maddie returned to the career center the next day and handed her completed application to Ms. Williams. "You were kind enough to offer yesterday to review my application for me. Could you take a look?"

"Of course, Maddie. Give me a few minutes to read this in my office and I'll be ready with my thoughts."

After ten minutes, Ms. Williams returned.

"I made a few grammatical suggestions, but I thought the substance of what you wrote and your insights into how to navigate a different culture were splendid."

"Really? Well, thank you. I'm learning so much from my Intro to Anthropology course," Maddie gushed.

Ms. Williams nodded, smiled shyly, and leaned forward to whisper, "He *is* charming, isn't he?"

A month later, Maddie received a letter congratulating her on her selection. That weekend, she drove to San Rafael for Sunday brunch. As she and her parents sat around the kitchen table, she told them about her plans.

"Can you believe I found a job that's interesting *and* pays well?"

"Yes, that's great, but do you really want to spend three weeks in Japan right in the middle of the summer, after being away for nine months?" her dad asked as he spread cream cheese on his bagel. "I could get you a job at Bert's Sporting Goods and you could still practice most evenings with the club . . ."

"We'll certainly miss you, sweetheart," Mom interjected. "But it's only three weeks and the pay is terrific. I think this sounds exciting and you'll need a break from volleyball after playing at Mills *and* on your father's club team for the past nine months," she said, a tight smile creasing her lips.

"You'd make a little less per hour at Bert's, but remember how much you missed your friends last summer? If you were here, you could see your teammates whenever you wanted," Dad said, biting into his bagel.

"Ha! A *little* less?" Mom snapped and dropped her butter knife on her plate. "She'd make a dollar sixty-five an hour at Bert's so about sixty-six a week. This pays almost *four* times more and she could work at Bert's when she gets back. What's your problem? You should be happy. You're the one who's always complaining about money."

"Because you're the one spending it as fast as I can make it!" Dad bellowed and stabbed a finger in his wife's direction.

"Mom! Dad! Wait a second!" Maddie bolted up from the table. "Dad, I wouldn't have applied unless I wanted to go. It's not like I haven't been home for nine months. I've come back almost every week. This is only three weeks. I promise I'll stay in shape and practice with the club as much as you want before and after the trip. I don't understand. I thought you'd be pleased."

Her father ground his teeth and glared at her mother.

"Okay," he finally spat out.

Maddie returned to Mills relieved her father didn't object to her decision, but troubled her parents had opened a new front in their war—how much money Dad thought Mom spent. She had never expected her family to have financial problems. They lived in a nice home in San Rafael and her father was a partner in an accounting firm in the city. She was proud that the volleyball scholarship paid for most of her college costs. The summer jobs in Japan and at Bert's would more than cover her summer expenses. She didn't want to ask for money and give them another reason to fight.

Events that spring persuaded her father that Maddie's trip was not just something to tolerate but embrace. Violent protests had broken out on the UC Berkeley campus and adjacent People's Park. Berkeley lay only a few miles north of Mills and her parents feared the violence might spread to the area around her campus.

Maddie herself paid little attention to the riots. Volleyball, exams, and preparation for Japan occupied all of her time. As the summer of 1969 approached, Governor Reagan declared martial law to quell the protests and newspapers were full of reports of the Zodiac Killer. It seemed to Maddie that the only thing her parents could agree on was the sooner she left the Bay Area the better.

A couple of weeks after school ended in mid-June, Mom drove Maddie to the airport from home, and Dad came from work to meet them at the check-in counter. They walked to the gate in silence, Mom on one side and Dad on the other, neither one looking at the other, the discomfort between them washing over Maddie like a tidal wave. Waiting for the flight, Dad stood with his hands in his pockets and Mom with her arms folded across her chest. Each chatted amiably but only with their daughter. Maddie couldn't wait to escape the smoldering tension. Finally, boarding was announced. First Dad and then Mom hugged her goodbye and quickly strode away.

As she moved in a long line down the gangway toward the Japan Airlines plane for Tokyo, Maddie gulped down several deep breaths and wiggled her shoulders in a vain attempt to release the stress. She put her carry-on into the overhead compartment then collapsed in her aisle seat, bumping her knees against the back of the seat in front of her. For a moment, as the plane taxied and soared into the air, memories of her flight to Taiwan a year earlier swirled in her head. A vision of Kimberly in the seat next to her flashed through her mind but was soon displaced by images from the dozens of books she'd read of the vast Tokyo metropolis, a city more than twenty times larger than San Francisco. She squirmed in her seat. To her surprise, she felt more nervous now than she did last summer even though she was infinitely more prepared. Ignorance really was bliss, she laughed to herself.

Thinking of the adventure ahead, she grabbed her purse and extracted a note she had received two days earlier from the Japanese student who would serve as Maddie's counterpart on the tour.

Dear Miss Erickson,

My name is Emiko Tsuji, a student at Waseda University. I look forward to working with you to assist Professor Fujita on the tour. I wish to inform you I will meet you at the airport in Tokyo. Please have a comfortable flight from California.

Yours truly,

The letter was typed and Emiko Tsuji had signed her name in an artistic hand with looping letters and outsized dots over the *i*'s. What a thoughtful gesture, Maddie mused. She couldn't help but compare it to the brusque welcome she'd received from Mr. Chung and felt comforted that the note was completely consistent with what she'd read about the importance Japanese placed upon courtesy. She reread the message several times and with each reading felt less anxious and more hopeful about the next three weeks. After tucking the letter back into her purse, she folded her hands in her lap, closed her eyes, and felt the muscles in her neck and shoulders begin to loosen.

A loud ring signaled that the pilot had extinguished the *No Smoking* light. Japanese businessmen surrounding Maddie immediately lit up. She crinkled her nose at the stifling smoke. Her eyes watered and the back of her throat burned. Maddie unbuckled and stepped down the aisle to the restroom where she wet a handkerchief and wrapped it around her nose and mouth. Before returning to her seat, she took a moment to examine herself in the tiny mirror. The AIEE letter had instructed her to dress conservatively and for warm, humid weather so she left her maxiskirts at home and wore one of the knee-length cotton dresses she'd picked from the 1968 Sears Christmas Wish Book. She thought the dress made her look older and, somehow, more confident than she felt.

Maddie landed at Haneda International Airport on Sunday evening in the middle of a summer thunderstorm. As the plane taxied to the terminal, she stared out the window through the rain at giant Japanese *kanji*, Chinese characters adopted by the Japanese for their own language, lit up in blood red lights. Suddenly a jagged bolt of lightning flashed across the dark sky. A few moments later, thunder rattled the plane. Maddie grabbed the armrest and giggled nervously.

When she disembarked, her insides began to fizz like a shaken can of Coke. What if Emiko were late? Would her English be good? Would they be able to communicate? Would they be able to form a good working relationship or even a personal one? God, she thought, three weeks suddenly seemed to stretch forever into the future. As she shuffled in a crowded line toward the immigration counter, Maddie extracted Emiko's short message from her purse and recited it like a Buddhist mantra to quiet her apprehensions.

When Maddie stepped out into the arrival hall and saw her name on a sign held up by a young Japanese woman, her insides began to settle. She nodded and the two young women exchanged tentative smiles. All at once, a grinning Emiko began to wave her hand excitedly like a windshield wiper in driving rain. Maddie threaded her way through the crowd.

"Ah, my name is Emiko Tsuji. I am the assistant tour guide from Waseda University. I am so happy to meet you," she said in a light, soft voice and bowed. She held out a card with her name and her Waseda University address. "I am so sorry for your long trip. You must be very tired."

Maddie noticed Emiko didn't waste time apologizing for the flight, even though there's nothing she could have done about it. Maddie had read that the Japanese had many words to say "I'm sorry" and apologized incessantly.

"Thank you for meeting me, Tsuji-san. My name is Madeline Erickson. Please call me Maddie." Maddie half-nodded and half-bowed in what she hoped would be taken as a sign of respect toward her colleague.

"Yes, I will, Maddie-san. Thank you. Please call me Emiko." Emiko lowered her head.

"Thank you, Emiko-san. I apologize I do not have a name card to give you."

Maddie was relieved she had read about Japanese etiquette and knew the proper way to reply. To say just *Emiko* would have been impolite, though Maddie thought Emiko would have forgiven her.

"I had some cards made for you. Here," she said, holding out a tiny box. A sample of Maddie's name card with her name and her address at Mills was pasted on the outside. "You can give one to each of the students."

"Thank you!" Maddie smiled. "That was very kind. And thank you very much for your note introducing yourself and informing me you would meet me here."

Maddie instinctively thought of Emiko as "Emi" even though she would never call her by that nickname. Emiko just looked like an Emi, more than a head shorter than Maddie and petite, with a small roundish face and milky skin, lighter than Maddie's, who had been outside a lot playing beach volleyball. A glossy black bob with bangs framed her large coffee-colored eyes that radiated what Maddie sensed was a generous, gentle nature.

Maddie felt drawn to Emi immediately and her anxiety over whether or not they would work well together melted away. Not because she assumed Emi thought like her. She wouldn't make that mistake again! Maddie understood from her reading that she and Emi wouldn't have the same values, but anticipating their differences no longer troubled her. To the contrary, the knowledge filled her with confidence. As two college-educated women, she believed they would have much to share, not because they overlooked their differences, but because they could recognize and respect their distinct cultural perspectives.

Emi took her by subway to Todaikan, an old Japanese inn near the University of Tokyo campus where they would stay while in the city. They found their room down a dimly lit hallway. Emi removed her shoes in the entryway, set her bag down, and cracked a small window to clear a mildewy stuffiness from the air. Following Emi's lead, Maddie took off her shoes and stepped up into the tiny room. She ducked under a pendant lamp hanging chin-high from the ceiling over a short-legged, forest-green lacquered table surrounded by plush cushions. *How in the world will I get my legs under that?*

After showing Maddie how to store her bags in the closet, Emi accompanied her back to the cramped lobby—a space the size of a small sitting area in an American hotel—to meet Fujita-sensei, the professor of international relations who would lead the trip. She advised Maddie in a whisper to use *sensei* for Fujita-sensei, which Maddie appreciated because it echoed her understanding that *sensei,* not *san,* was used for professors, teachers, and other people respected for their learning.

"Fujita-sensei will wish to exchange business cards with you," Emi advised.

A short, stocky, middle-aged man with a large rectangular head, thinning black hair, and a wrinkled brow lifted himself from an armchair to greet Emi and Maddie. As he rose, he inadvertently knocked his knee against the low table in front of him, jostling a glass of water.

"Ah! *Shitsurei.* I am sorry," Fujita-sensei apologized and emitted a high-pitched, giggly laugh. "Welcome to Japan, Ericksonsan. I am pleased to meet you." He greeted Maddie with a tightlipped smile, offered his business card with two hands, and lowered his head slightly.

"Please call me Maddie, Fujita-sensei." Maddie took one of the new business cards from her purse and exchanged cards with Fujita-sensei, bending forward to return his bow.

"Ah, yes, of course, Maddie-san. Thank you. Forgive me while I speak with Tsuji-san in Japanese."

After speaking at length in Japanese to Emi, he switched back to English.

"I have asked Tsuji-san to explain to you some of our customs. Tomorrow she will discuss with you your duties for the next four days, before the students arrive, and also for their two-week visit." Fujita-sensei glanced at his watch. "Now, forgive me, but I have much work to do. Goodnight. Please have a good rest."

He turned abruptly and hurried down a corridor to his room.

Emi guided Maddie back to their room.

"Please rest here," Emi pointed to a tawny cushion on the floor next to the table. Maddie lowered herself on the cushion and folded her legs in front of her while Emi knelt down opposite Maddie.

"Please allow me to explain how Japanese live. We sleep on a large cushion we call a *futon* on the floor of woven rice straw we call *tatami.* This is *tatami,*" she said and patted the mat beside her. "The *futon* and the quilts are over there in the closet. I have asked for an especially long *futon* and quilt for you. Before we sleep, we go to a separate room to bathe. We wash with soap and rinse completely before entering the *ofuro*, the hot bath. After our bath, we put on a cotton robe we call a *yukata* for sleeping. I apologize if these customs seem inconvenient to you."

Maddie had already learned about these everyday practices, but that Emi's sweet directions dovetailed with what she had read reassured her. With sufficient preparation, she could be comfortable even in a culture as foreign as Japan's.

"Thank you for your very thoughtful explanations," Maddie said to a beaming Emi. "Your customs are not inconvenient at all. I appreciate very much you taking the time to describe them to me. I feel very welcome."

Later, as they lay on their *futon* in the dark, Emi said, "*Oyasumi nasai*, Maddie-san" in her lovely, hushed voice.

Maddie responded, "*Oyasumi nasai*, Emiko-san" and drifted off, delighted at how well the first day had gone.

Monday morning, Emi and Maddie breakfasted on rice, cold cooked vegetables, and a piece of grilled fish in teriyaki sauce.

"Is this food all right with you?" Emi inquired, looking over her rice bowl with raised eyebrows. "I know Americans eat eggs and meat and bread at breakfast."

"I enjoy Japanese food," Maddie declared, lifting a piece of fish into her mouth with her chopsticks and chewing thoughtfully before continuing. "There are Japanese restaurants near my college. When I learned I would be coming here this summer, my friends and I ate there a few times. We liked it because it's so healthy."

"I did not expect the American assistant to be so well prepared!" Emi exclaimed. "And to use chopsticks so skillfully!"

"That's a very nice compliment. Thank you!"

Maddie felt the first glimmer of a possible friendship, but admonished herself not to presume too much too quickly.

"I did try to learn as much as I could in advance. Shall we discuss what is expected of me?"

"Yes. That is our next task. Over the next four days, Fujita-sensei wishes you to read the lectures he intends to give and, if necessary, advise me how to improve the English. In addition, please review with me the Japanese schedule for the tour and assist me in translating it into English for the students. Would that work be acceptable to you?"

"I would be happy to help."

"Thank you very much," Emi replied. "Now, let us move to a small conference room where we can review the schedule for the tour."

Over the next three hours, Emi explained to Maddie in detail each and every item on the twenty-page schedule Fujita-sensei had arranged for the group, occasionally stopping to ask if she had any questions. Maddie tried not to show her concern. She looked forward to creating an English version with Emi as it would involve an interesting exchange about the meaning of Japanese and English words, but she worried the days seemed jammed with activities, visits, and lectures that would overwhelm the typical American teenager.

"Do the students understand the schedule will be so . . . so full?"

"I believe the Association for International Educational Exchange informed the students generally about the content of their visit, but they would not know the details. This trip is the first tour Fujita-sensei has been asked to lead," Emi explained. "He has worked very many hours for several months to organize the activities and prepare his lectures on Japanese history and society and economics and art."

"Did you help him?"

"I assisted him in some ways, but he is the professor and leader and responsible person." Emi leaned forward, her eyes widened, and she spoke with a sudden intensity. "He carries a much heavier burden than I do. I respect him very much for his knowledge and diligence and would do *anything* to help him succeed."

"Well, I hope you will tell me what I can do to help both Fujita-sensei and you."

"Oh, thank you, Maddie-san. I very much look forward to working with you. Once we start the tour, Fujita-sensei would like you to watch over the students and make sure no one is left behind. As I speak Japanese, I will be responsible for such matters as the inns and hotels where we stay, the route of the bus, and the time we spend at each stop. Is that acceptable to you?"

"Of course. I think we will work well together."

Over the next four days, Maddie and Emi settled into a routine. In the mornings and early afternoons, they reviewed the English in Fujita-sensei's forty-odd lectures and translated the schedule for the students. In the late afternoons, they strolled beneath the cherry trees in Ueno Park to refresh their minds and stretch their legs. On these walks, they began to convey bits of information about their lives.

"Fujita-sensei told me you are from a city called San Rafael in California. Is San Rafael near Los Angeles?"

"No. It's in what we call the Bay Area, the region around San Francisco Bay in Northern California. Are you from Tokyo?"

"Oh, no," Emi replied. "I am from Hagi, a town on the southwest coast of Honshu. It is an old castle town, a kind of capitol of one the clans that ruled parts of Japan in the medieval period. Is San Rafael also an old city?"

"Not as old as Hagi, but we have a mission built around a hundred and fifty years ago by Spanish missionaries. San Rafael is a nice place to raise a family, I think. Not too large but close enough to San Francisco to be able to enjoy city life and within an easy drive of the ocean and the mountains. Do your parents still live in Hagi?"

"Oh, yes. I visit them from time to time, but I do not wish to return to live there even though they want me to do so as I am their—how do you say it?—*hitorikko*, their alone child?"

Maddie was momentarily confused then realized what Emi was trying to say. She was stunned. *Alone child* described exactly how she had felt during the past couple of years.

"What a coincidence. I am an only child, too."

"Oh, I am *so* sorry. Please forgive my poor English," Emi exclaimed and clapped her hand over her mouth. "You say *only child?*"

"Yes, we do," Maddie said, but quickly added, "Your English is excellent. And I am embarrassed that I do not speak any Japanese. Perhaps you could teach me a few words, like—what did you say?—*heatowigo?*"

"Very good. Almost perfect. Yes, *hitorikko*. I look forward to our learning from each other."

"I do, too," Maddie said.

After their walks, they dined at a local yakitori or ramen or sushi restaurant, returned to the inn for another hour or two of work, and ended the day with the customary bath. Before they fell asleep on their *futon*, Emi and Maddie discussed and confirmed the plans for the next day.

"Are you tired?" Maddie asked one evening after Emi had turned out the lights.

"Not so much. Why?"

"I was curious what classes you are taking at Waseda. What are they like?"

"I am a student majoring in English language and American history. In each of my classes, a professor lectures in a large room to many hundreds of students," Emi explained.

"Really? You don't have small classes where you can ask questions and get to know the professor?"

"No," Emi replied with a sigh. "Professors do not generally wish to waste their time with students so making a relationship with a professor is quite difficult. That is why I have much gratitude to Fujita-sensei for selecting me to assist him on this tour."

"I see," Maddie replied. "Thank you for telling me about your classes. I feel lucky to have been selected, too, and to work with and learn from you. Goodnight, Emiko-san."

"Goodnight, Maddie-san. I am happy to have the chance to tell you about Japan."

The next night as they were preparing their *futon* for sleep, Maddie wanted to ask Emi about her relationship with Fujita-sensei, but hesitated. She had read Japanese considered it impolite to inquire about personal matters unless you were good friends. Unsure Emi shared her feeling of a nascent friendship, she decided to broach the subject carefully.

"Could I ask you another question about Fujita-sensei?"

"Yes, of course."

"Would you consider him your mentor?"

"Oh, yes," she replied, enthusiasm lifting her voice. "It is a privilege. And also a big opportunity for me. You see, my *dream* is to study in the United States on a Waseda University program and one day to work as a translator."

"Fujita-sensei could help you?"

Emi looked down, a blush of embarrassment reddening her cheeks. Maddie feared her last question had trespassed some invisible border dividing what was welcomed and what was intrusive.

"I'm sorry if my question was rude," she added quickly, hoping to repair whatever damage she may have done. Emi looked up and smiled warmly at Maddie.

"Do not worry, Maddie-san. I know you are American. I think it would be unreasonable to expect you—my very *first* American friend!—to behave always like a Japanese even though you seem to understand many things about our culture."

"You are very kind. Thank you!" Maddie glowed inside. Emi felt a bond growing between them, too! Confidence burgeoned within Maddie. She not only was coping with the complexities of Japanese life; she was experiencing the pleasure of making a friend from a completely different culture.

"You are welcome. To answer your question, yes, you are correct. I have hope he will help me realize my dream, although Fujita-sensei and I would never speak of it directly."

"I hope he will, too," Maddie said as she crawled under the oversized quilt. Remembering the short sheet Mr. Chung had given her in Taiwan made her even more grateful for Emi.

"Goodnight, Emiko-san and thank you again for arranging for the long futon and quilt. They are very comfortable."

"You are very welcome, Maddie-san. Goodnight."

On Friday evening, Maddie and Emi traveled in companionable silence on a tour bus to Haneda to meet the American high school students. Maddie looked back with a mixture of gratitude and regret on the four days she had spent with Emi—thankful to have had the opportunity to begin a friendship and sorry the time alone with her had come to an end. Yet, she also looked forward to meeting the group and working with Emi to make the tour a success. After gathering the students together as they emerged from immigration and customs, Emi led them out to the bus holding a sign with the letters AIEE written on it. Maddie hung back to make sure the one or two stragglers didn't get lost. As the bus rolled away from the curb, Emi stood in the front with a microphone looking back at the students.

"Welcome to Japan. My name is Emiko Tsuji and my colleague is Maddie Erickson."

Maddie rose from her seat and stood next to Emi, crouching down to avoid bumping her head against the ceiling. She waved to the group as Emi continued.

"I apologize for your long and tiring trip, but I would like to explain to you some Japanese customs as we travel to the inn where we will stay in Tokyo."

As Emiko repeated much of what she had said to Maddie five nights before, Maddie studied the teenage faces arrayed before her. To her relief, they all seemed to have followed the AIEE advice about conservative clothes and hair styles. However, instead of seeing heads erect and eyes bright with curiosity, Maddie noticed several of the students dozing from jet lag, three others in a whispered conversation, and a handful more staring blankly out the window. She was tempted to bark them to attention, but felt the interruption might embarrass Emi. She also reminded herself with a chuckle she had fallen fast asleep on the train to Taichung a year ago!

"So," Emi concluded, "breakfast will be served at seven thirty in the morning in the conference room on the first floor. We will meet there at eight thirty to review the day's activities. Copies of the English schedule for Tokyo will be available at breakfast. The weather will be quite warm and humid and we will walk to many places so please wear comfortable clothes and appropriate shoes. Do you have any questions?"

Not one student raised a hand, which didn't surprise Maddie since none of them had paid attention. Did Emi notice how inattentive they were? Their behavior would be unimaginable for a Japanese student. Maybe, Maddie mused, she would have a greater role to play on the tour after all.

"So, you have no questions? Well, we are arriving at the inn now. Thank you for your attention."

The next morning as Maddie entered the conference room, the students had finished breakfast and were so absorbed in grousing with one another they didn't see her come in.

"I had no idea we would sleep on the *floor*. I thought we would be staying at a hotel with a real bed. I couldn't get any rest at all."

"And what is with the raw egg, cold fish, vinegary vegetables, and rice for breakfast? I want eggs and bacon!"

"Did you see the schedule? One shrine, one temple, three museums, the Imperial Palace, Shinjuku Park, and nine lectures in *three* days. And it's like eighty-five degrees and eighty percent humidity outside!"

Maddie wrinkled her nose in annoyance. The students were guests of the Japanese government, after all, and representatives of *her* country. Then she caught herself. She had complained about the very same problems the previous summer in Taiwan. Perhaps she could provide a little perspective that would ease their transition.

"Hi, everyone," she called out.

The voices quieted as heads swiveled toward her.

"Uh, hi, Maddie," a few replied sheepishly.

"We didn't know you'd come in."

"It's okay. I'm glad I overheard you. You guys know I'm the assistant tour leader, but I hope you'll think of me as a friend. Because I'm your *friend*, I'd like to share what I learned in Taiwan last summer."

Several students nodded and a few murmured, "Okay."

"The first few days will be challenging and I know many, many things will seem pretty weird. Be open-minded. Don't *assume*—like I did—that everything and everyone will be the same as back home. I promise you'll be much happier. Got it?"

The students glanced at one another and nodded again. "Thanks, Maddie," they said.

Moments later, Fujita-sensei and Emi walked in the room. After a thirty-minute review of the day's schedule, the group set out to begin the first of three days in Tokyo. They embarked in the steamy Tokyo weather to explore Toshogu Shrine, Kiyomizu Kannon-do Temple, and the Tokyo National Museum in nearby Ueno Park, as well as to the Imperial Palace and Shinjuku Gyoen Park.

Maddie could see the effects of the whirlwind schedule in the dazed expressions on the students' faces. Fujita-sensei expected them to absorb massive amounts of information despite jet lag and the disorientation of being in a radically different culture. While she was pleased that the students mostly remained in good spirits, she worried their attitudes would worsen quickly once the novelty of the tour wore thin and they realized every day would be as demanding as the one before. She wanted the tour to succeed as much as Fujita-sensei and Emi did, but fretted they didn't have a clue how rebellious American teenagers could be if pushed too hard. She resolved to look for an opportunity to raise her concerns with Emi in as gentle a way as possible. She didn't want to jeopardize their budding relationship.

Fujita-sensei spent almost all his time preparing for and delivering lectures. He made little attempt to become acquainted with the students; in fact, Maddie saw him stiffen uncomfortably on more than one occasion when a student would try to start a conversation with him. As Emi had explained, she took responsibility for the logistics of the trip; she dealt with subway tickets, passes to museums and parks, the tour bus driver, and the staff at the inn. Maddie's job was to keep an eye on the students as they moved from one location to another to ensure everyone stayed together. She grew weary of having to count heads over and over and over again, but she understood her task was as critical to the success of the tour as Emi's. Imagine if one of the students got lost in Tokyo!

On the third day, the group toured the Waseda University campus. They ate lunch with a group of Japanese university students and attended a lecture by an elderly Waseda professor on the security treaty between the U.S. and Japan. In a flat monotone, the professor slowly read his hour-long presentation. The subject interested Maddie, but even she struggled to keep her eyes open, pinching herself every few minutes to stay awake. Not surprisingly, some of the high school students fell asleep. As they were leaving the classroom, Fujita-sensei glowered at Emi.

"*Tsuji-san. Karera wa hazukashikunai. Seito ga chanto furumau yoo ni shite kudasai!*" he barked.

Emi massaged the nape of her neck, bobbed her head, and bowed deeply.

"*Kashikomarimashita,* Sensei!"

Maddie didn't understand what Fujita-sensei had said, but the scowl on his face and snap in his voice led her to believe he blamed Emi for the students' behavior. She felt heartsick for her friend, but decided to wait until they were alone that evening to ask what had happened. Maybe then she could broach the subject of trimming the schedule.

"Would you mind telling me what Fujita-sensei said to you this afternoon as we were leaving the classroom? Was he angry with the students or you?"

Maddie sat cross-legged on a *futon* across from Emi. Like Emi, Maddie wore her blue-and-white patterned *yukata* and sipped hot green tea, the bitter taste surprisingly refreshing.

Emi sighed and laid her hands on the table.

"The man who was lecturing today is one of Fujita-sensei's mentors. The students' behavior embarrassed him. He asked me to persuade them to act more appropriately in the future and to appreciate that each aspect of the tour has been carefully designed for their benefit."

"Thank you for confiding in me. I wonder . . ." Maddie began and stopped herself.

Emi had just made it crystal clear that Fujita-sensei wouldn't consider modifying his schedule to accommodate the students, and Emi was responsible for persuading them to adapt to *him*. Should she offer to help her communicate with the students even though Emi hadn't asked? Unsure how to proceed, Maddie changed the subject.

"Do you hope to be a translator for the government or a private company or the United Nations?"

"Oh, no," Emi replied with a shake of her head. "My plan is to be married and have children. Still, I would like to have a part-time job."

"I think you are too smart to be a part-time translator," Maddie exclaimed.

"Thank you, but in Japan, it is very difficult for a woman to have both a full-time job and a family," Emi declared. "For us, family is the most important thing."

Maddie understood from her studies why Emi, as a Japanese woman, would think the way she did about family. If one of her girlfriends back home had said the same thing, however, she would have loudly objected. Since Emi wanted to visit the United States, Maddie decided to share the American view on career and family.

"In America, until recently it *was* difficult for a woman to have a career and a family but my country is changing rapidly. We have what we call the *women's movement*. More and more young women are planning to become doctors, not nurses, lawyers, not legal assistants, and executives not secretaries."

Emi remained still for a long time.

"Hmmmm," she said finally through pursed lips. "A woman in Japan must marry by her mid-twenties. If she does not, the chance of having a family goes down. Japanese men, well, they will not marry a woman who wants a career equal to their own."

"That seems so unfair!" Maddie blurted out.

Emi's eyes widened suddenly.

"I apologize," Maddie hastened to add in a more subdued tone. "I meant to say it would seem unfair in America."

"In Japan, not unfair, I think. I am happy to be a Japanese woman because at least a Japanese woman has control over the family money. We even decide how much of an allowance to give our husband. We also make the decisions important to the family, like where we should live and how the children should be raised. Japanese men must join a company or a government agency out of university and work many hours each day for thirty or forty years. They are told where they must work and what they must do and cannot quit because no other company or agency would hire someone who left another position."

Emi's description did not surprise Maddie. Her reading had explained the different roles of men and women in traditional Japanese society. Still, it *was* 1969!

"I understand why you would prefer being a woman, even without the freedom to pursue a career, to being a man, forced to work for hours each day at the same company for decades, regardless of how badly the company treated him. To Americans, that would seem like a kind of slavery!"

Emi took in a sharp breath at the mention of slavery.

"No, it is not slavery," she replied firmly. "A company is like family, a family whose father has the authority to tell you what to do. A family you cannot leave. But also a family that takes care of you and will give you work and pay your salary as long as you are loyal." Emi dropped her eyes and hesitated a moment before looking up at Maddie. "In America, I understand that companies feel no such obligation to their workers. Can that be true?" she asked sweetly but pointedly, raising her eyebrows.

"That is often true," Maddie admitted, but could not resist adding. "But I would trade the certainty of a paycheck any day for the freedom to work where I please!"

"Oh!" Emi gasped, covered her mouth with one hand, and pointed at Maddie with the other. "I cannot believe it. That is *exactly* what my professor told us Americans would say about work!"

Maddie burst out laughing. "It's not fair. You have learned as much about America as I have about Japan!"

Emi giggled and bowed in mock seriousness. "*Arigatoo gozaimasu,*" she said.

They both laughed again.

"I am so grateful to share ideas about the differences in our cultures," Maddie said. "I . . . I believe recognizing and appreciating such differences is important for true friendship."

"Oh, I think so, too," Emi agreed. "I so very much value your knowledge of Japan and your willingness to speak frankly about American society."

"Well," Maddie said, stretching her arms out and kneading the soreness in her lower back from sleeping on the futon. "No one can know the future. The lives of American men and women are quickly changing. Maybe the situation for Japanese men and women will change just as it has in the United States."

Emi stared at Maddie for a moment, blinked several times, and slowly nodded. Maddie couldn't tell whether Emi's bobbing of the head indicated agreement or just that she was pondering what Maddie had said.

"Let us rest now," Emi breathed finally. "Tomorrow, we board the Shinkansen train for Kyoto."

The bullet train to Kyoto sped through the large cities of Yokohama and Nagoya, crossed sparkling rivers and newly planted rice paddies, and skirted the foothills of Mount Fuji. Maddie chatted across the aisle with two students about their first impressions of Japan.

"Hey, Maddie," called Claire, a petite blonde from Milwaukee, "you don't really *like* raw fish, do you? I think it smells weird." She crumpled her mouth and pinched her nose with her fingers.

"I actually do. It's healthy and good for your skin."

A square-jawed, broad-shouldered Texan named Matt leaned forward in his seat. "Where I come from," he drawled, "we don't eat anything unless it has four legs and hooves."

Maddie and Claire looked at each other and giggled.

"I guess that's why you're constantly hungry here," Claire remarked. "How many of those Morinaga ice cream cones did you eat yesterday?"

"I lost count after six."

"*Six!*" Claire and Maddie both gasped and then guffawed.

"Ah, excuse me please." Emi crept up to the boisterous threesome, her head bent forward, her hands clasped in front. "May I speak with you for a moment Matt-san and Claire-san?"

"Sure," Matt and Claire said.

"I'll see you guys later," Maddie said. She whispered to Emi as she passed her, "Can I help you?"

"No, thank you very much Maddie-san. It is my responsibility."

Maddie moved two rows back and sat down where she could unobtrusively overhear their conversation.

Emi coughed slightly. "Thank you for your attention. I am talking with each student as we go to Kyoto to ask most kindly for your cooperation and understanding during the rest of the tour."

Maddie groaned inwardly. She knew Emi thought she was soliciting the students' agreement to act more politely, as Fujita-sensei had asked her to do, but she needed to be much more specific with American teenagers.

"Well, Tsuji-san"—Claire tilted her head and raised one eyebrow—"of course, we will do our best to cooperate and understand during the rest of the tour," she declared. "Won't we, Matt?"

Matt half shrugged. "Sure enough. We'll do our best."

"Thank you very much." Emi exhaled audibly and untied her hands. "If you have any questions, please do not hesitate to ask me."

Maddie longed to help her communicate better, but worried drawing attention to the likely misunderstanding might fluster Emi. Not wanting to strain their friendship, Maddie kept silent. After all, she reminded herself, Emi had told the students to come to her with questions—*not* to Maddie and her.

After they arrived in Kyoto, the group dropped their bags at another inn, this one larger and more modern than the one in Tokyo; it even had western-style toilets so Maddie didn't have to squat down in a position painful for her tender volleyball knees. While the group waited outside for the tour bus to pick them up, Maddie walked under a hazy sun with two students from Florida down to the Kamo River.

A group of grizzled older men were fishing and a geisha dressed in a salmon-colored kimono strolled on the riverbank with a rotund, sharply-dressed businessman. As the sparkling river babbled along, Maddie's mind flew to the memory of rafting happily on the Russian River with her parents when she was nine or ten years old. She had not thought of them since she'd arrived, let alone had time to write a letter, and doubted she would any time soon. She missed her parents, but hungered even more for the family who had years ago pulled their oars together down that river. She wrapped her arms around herself, heaved a long sigh, and called out to the two students who had wandered away.

"Time to go, you two!"

After they boarded the tour bus and Maddie counted heads, she passed out the English schedule for the next few days.

"Great!" snorted Sam, a wiry, wisecracking student from New York City. "We have fifteen minutes in the morning after breakfast before we leave and thirty minutes in the afternoon after we return before we go to dinner. I *wonder* how I will possibly use *all* that free time!"

"Quiet, Sam," hissed Claudia from North Carolina in a lilting Southern accent. "You are being so very *uncooperative* and *un-understanding.*"

Maddie scowled in their direction to quell the mini-rebellion. She looked over to Emi who was speaking with the driver. Fujita-sensei as usual sat in the front of the bus lost in reviewing his lecture notes. Neither one appeared to have heard Sam or Claudia, but Maddie worried the students would complain again, Fujita-sensei would overhear it, and once more castigate poor Emi.

During the next three days Maddie felt they must have visited a hundred different shrines and temples and castles and museums. They were all lovely and interesting, and Fujita-sensei, otherwise indifferent to the students, came alive during his lectures. Maddie had developed a genuine interest in Japanese history and culture, but after two days even she had trouble telling the difference between the Golden Temple and the Silver Temple and the Heian and Muromachi periods of Japanese history. Many of the students confided in her they felt exhausted physically and overwhelmed mentally, but at least they did not vent their frustration out loud.

On their last day in Kyoto, the group climbed two and a half miles up a steep trail above the Fushimi Inari Shrine. Maddie loved hiking on the stone path as it meandered through one thousand stunning vermillion Shinto *torii* gates, and she lingered at the summit to enjoy the view of the graceful city of Kyoto. After climbing back down, they drove an hour in traffic to visit Sanjusangendo Hall, dedicated to Kannon, the Buddhist goddess of mercy. Maddie was awestruck by the enormous wooden statute of a multi-armed Kannon and by the hall itself, built over eight hundred years before, which stretched more than 120 meters in length.

Back on the bus, Maddie counted heads to make sure all the students had returned.

"The Shinto gates were lovely," Claudia said as she dropped into her seat, "but did we really need to climb all the way to the top in this heat? And why plod through traffic across town to visit Kannon today? Couldn't it have been scheduled for tomorrow? I'm completely worn out."

"I'm bushed, too. I wish Fujita-sensei was more like Kannon and would show us some mercy," Sam griped out of the side of his mouth.

Claudia and three or four other students roared with laughter.

Maddie stifled a giggle with the back of her hand and looked to see whether the outburst was overheard. She cringed when she saw Emi blush and freeze. Fujita-sensei turned around, a broad smile pasted on his face, and glared at the students with ice cold eyes. Then he faced Emi and snarled something in Japanese. Emi's blush turned ashen.

After returning from dinner, Emi knelt down at the low table in their room, folded her hands on her lap, and coughed lightly.

"Fujita-sensei worries some of the American students may be dissatisfied but does not have a clear idea of what they think about the tour," Emi explained, her eyes averting Maddie's gaze. "As you know, the success of the tour is extremely important to his career, so he is seeking your further assistance. He would like to meet us in the lobby."

"What assistance would he like?" Maddie hoped for a hint of what was coming.

"I am not completely certain and do not wish to speak for him," Emi replied, still avoiding Maddie's eyes.

Maddie felt her pulse quicken. "All right. Let's go then."

Emi led her downstairs where Fujita-sensei perched on one of four brown leather armchairs surrounding an ebony-colored lacquer table covered with several Japanese magazines. He raised himself slightly, nodded, and motioned for them to sit down opposite him.

"Thank you for your support during the trip, Maddie-san," he began. "You have been most helpful so far in making sure no student mistakenly leaves the group. Now I was hoping you might assist me in another task during the final days."

"Of course, Sensei," Maddie replied, glancing quickly at Emi who sat stone-still with her eyes fixed on the table. Maddie looked back at the Japanese professor. "How may I help you?"

"Have you heard any of the students criticize the tour?"

Maddie caught her breath for a moment and frowned slightly. She resented the request to divulge what the students may have shared with her in confidence, but wanted to help Emi by reassuring Fujita-sensei. Maddie ran her tongue over her lips as she selected her words carefully.

"Not really criticism, Sensei. The schedule is very full and they become tired occasionally. For many of them, this is their first trip outside the United States, perhaps the first time they have been away from home. The experience can be stressful. I believe you may have overhead them joking about the trip, but I believe their humor is not meant as a complaint, but as a way to relieve the pressure."

"Stressful?" He dismissed the word with a chop of his hand. "They applied to be part of this group. Their selection for this tour is an honor. Do they not understand being here is a privilege?"

Maddie glanced at Emi who had not lifted her eyes from the table. *Come on, Emi! A little help here!* she wanted to whisper, but at the same time understood Emi's reluctance to support Maddie against her mentor.

"Yes, I believe they all do, Sensei," she replied evenly. "But they are also young. I do not believe they mean to offend you."

"I see," he replied after a moment, hunching forward and resting his hands on the table. "Nevertheless, please share with me any criticism or complaints you hear the students make in the future—even if you believe they are made as a joke—so I may understand them better and address them appropriately."

Maddie flinched slightly and sat back in her chair. Demanding she spy on the students distressed her deeply since she had encouraged them to think of her as their friend.

"You're not asking me to *inform* on the students, are you?" Maddie straightened her shoulders and tried to modulate her voice. "I understand my job is to assist you, but I am also here to help them."

"I also wish to help them," he responded curtly and slapped his armrest. "Help them understand the tour is not intended to be for their . . . their amusement, but for their education. By participating they are receiving many benefits, but such rewards do not come without giving up some personal comfort, a sacrifice we are all making." Fujita-san's voice rose a pitch. "Now, I am *sincerely* requesting you report to me *in detail* what the students are saying so I can persuade them of the correctness of my position."

Maddie bit the inside of her lip and folded her arms across her chest. She almost exploded in anger, but gritted her teeth and forced herself to take several breaths. Giving free rein to her wrath would further upset Emi's mentor and might even force

Emi to choose between her loyalty to her professor and her affection for her American friend. She needed to find a solution that would please Fujita-sensei and yet not violate her principles. She unwound her arms.

"I can understand your thinking," Maddie started, trying to defuse the tension. "However, the students would consider it a betrayal if they discovered I was informing on them. They would no longer speak freely in front of me."

"I do not think . . ." Fujita-sensei interrupted, but Maddie held her hand up, something she would never have done a day ago. In her peripheral vision, Maddie saw Emi's mouth drop open in surprise and snap shut. Fujita-sensei's eyes widened as his head jerked back.

"Please let me finish, Sensei. The students would certainly include in their reports to the Japanese ministries that I had spied on them. I am sure you do not wish that to happen, do you?"

"Then . . . then," Fujita-sensei declared in an agitated voice, his face turning bright crimson in disbelief, "you *refuse* my request? I . . . I will report you to the AIEE for your disobedience!"

He turned to face Emi and growled at her in Japanese. Emi's countenance wrinkled. Her shoulders sagged. Maddie struggled once again to conjure up a compromise that would not violate her sense of what was right and yet satisfy Fujita-sensei. She certainly did not want to be sent home.

"I am not refusing your request, Sensei," Maddie clarified. "I am suggesting my doing what you wish could have unfortunate consequences for you and perhaps also for the AIEE. Let me propose I help you in a slightly different way," Maddie offered. "If I hear a student make any *serious* criticism or complaint, I will go to that student and encourage the student to meet with the three of us to discuss their concern. Would that be acceptable?"

Fujita-sensei raised his hand to cut down Maddie's suggestion, but he was interrupted by Emi. She laid her cheek with inches of the table, turned her head, and smiled up at her mentor as she spoke to him at length in a particularly high pitch and lilting tone. Maddie heard Emi begin many words with *"O"* or *"Go,"* which she had learned were used to honor the listener. By her submissive body language and beseeching tone, Maddie surmised that Emi was trying to persuade Fujita-sensei to accept her suggestion. *Thank you, Emi!* When Emi had finished, she cast her eyes downward again.

Fujita-sensei turned to Maddie. His eyes bore into her for a moment. Maddie sat bolt upright, wondering whether she had offended him beyond repair.

His shoulders slumped. "Yes, that will be acceptable," he muttered and jumped up from his chair. "Goodnight," he uttered in English and snarled one more time at Emi in Japanese before striding away up the stairs.

Emi did not mention the incident as they prepared for bed. Before she turned out the light, however, she whispered, *"Ariga-too gozaimashita."* Maddie understood the matter was closed. She felt proud of how she had handled herself and grateful Emi had at last intervened.

Over the next three nights, Maddie and Emi resumed their bedtime conversations. Talking long into the night, they pulled their *futon* together and lay facing each other so they could whisper and giggle softly and catch each other's expressions. They confided more and more, speaking about boys, romance, and, eventually, sex.

"In Japan," Emi explained, "young people are rejecting Western-style 'love matches' popular after the war. We are returning to the traditional belief that we should welcome the assistance of our parents in making a suitable match."

"I wouldn't want my parents deciding who I should marry"—Maddie paused—"but I understand customs and values are different in Japan."

"In most cases, parents do not decide who to marry, but they can arrange or hire a matchmaker to make what we call *omiai*—introductions to suitable people. The couple then considers the possibility of marriage themselves."

"Well, I don't believe it really matters whether a match is approved or even arranged by parents as long as the marriage is happy."

Maddie started to ask Emi whether she had ever dated but halted for a moment. She did not want to upset her friend again and so proceeded tentatively.

"I realize this may be too personal a question so please don't answer if it makes you uncomfortable, but . . . would you mind if I asked whether you have dated a boy?"

Emi's lashes fluttered for a moment. She flushed and put her hand over her mouth.

"I'm sorry if my question offended you. You really don't have to answer," Maddie hastened to add and instinctively reached out to pat Emi's shoulder.

"No, I *wish* to respond," Emi said. "You are my friend, my *first* American friend." Emi paused for a few moments. "I dated one boy who seemed nice. After several dates, however, I learned he, like most Japanese men, considered women to be either a mother or a whore. And he assumed . . ." Her voice rose and her hand shook in anger. ". . . he assumed that since I went to a beer garden with him we would go to a love hotel and sleep together!"

"What's a *love hotel*?"

"A special hotel where couples go to have sex." Emi spat out the words.

"Oh my God," Maddie cried and clapped her hand to her mouth.

She saw the blood drain from Emi's face and could tell she was horribly ashamed. She reached out again to stroke Emi's arm and searched her mind to find a way to show her empathy.

"At my school, there are only girls. We're often invited to attend parties given by male clubs at other universities. I've gone to a few. Sometimes when I danced with a boy, he would run his hands over my body or try to drag me upstairs to his bedroom. I would slap his hands or push them away. Later I would hear he lied to his friends and said we slept together."

"That is shocking behavior!" Emi exclaimed, raising a fist as if to strike a blow for Maddie.

"I agree completely," Maddie said, slapping her *futon*. She was delighted that hearing her story appeared to relieve Emi's embarrassment over how the Japanese boy had treated her.

"May I ask? Have you had a boyfriend?"

"*Of course* you may ask," Maddie whispered, laughing lightly. "You are my friend, my *first* Japanese friend."

Emi giggled at Maddie's mimicry. "Thank you," Emi breathed. "Thank you."

Feeling they had crossed an important bridge, one that separated acquaintances from intimates, Maddie continued. "I had a boyfriend for most of the last year in high school. His name is Skip. We had been friends for many years before dating and I think we loved each other, but in an immature way. I broke up with him because I was going to Taiwan for the summer and afterwards we would be attending different colleges. I hoped we would stay friends, but, well, we drifted apart."

"Did you . . . did you kiss this boyfriend?"

Maddie choked down a laugh. She didn't want to seem to mock Emi's inexperience. "We kissed and gradually began to touch each other's bodies, but we didn't go any further. We both wanted to wait for marriage to have actual intercourse."

Emi's eyes opened like saucers.

"Even kissing would be very risky for a Japanese girl," Emi explained. "If she did, the boy would tell others and the girl might not be able to find a husband."

Maddie rolled her eyes in annoyance at the restrictions Japanese women suffered because of the pressure to marry, but held her tongue. She didn't want her irritation to chill the warmth growing between Emi and her.

"I understand life is very different in Japan but, for me, I would rather live a fulfilling life without a husband than become a servant in an unhappy marriage."

The conversation brought to mind the fragility of Maddie's parents' marriage and her despair that she was not just an only child but increasingly an *alone child*. She wanted more than anything to escape that aloneness, to be able to share with a sibling her anxieties about the future of her family. She felt so *close* to Emi at that moment and for a second considered confiding in her but held back, sensing they needed more time to allow their friendship to deepen. She hoped that soon she might be able to open up to Emi about her fears, the way she would to a sister.

"I wish *so much* to go to the United States on the Waseda exchange program," Emi gushed. "I wish to taste the freedom you have there."

"I would do *anything* to help you," Maddie replied with enthusiasm and reached over to squeeze Emi's hand.

"Thank you, my friend," Emi whispered and grasped Maddie's hand in hers. "Would you mind if we called each other 'Emi' and 'Maddie' like we would in the United States?"

"Not at all. Goodnight, Emi," Maddie replied, deeply moved by her gesture. *Goodnight, dear friend.*

On Tuesday, they rode a local train from Kyoto to Osaka, checked into a small hotel, and visited Osaka Castle. A trip to Kwansei Gakuin University, where Fujita-sensei had been a student, filled Wednesday's schedule. The president of the university, one of Fujita-sensei's former teachers, greeted the young Americans. After the welcome, the group strolled around the campus and attended a lecture about the Tokugawa shogunate.

The professor, a tall, dignified man with a British accent, rarely lifted his eyes from his notes as he spoke. Several students nodded off again. Maddie walked with them out of the hall as Emi led the group to the bus.

"Look you guys," she spoke in a hushed but firm voice. "I know you're tired and staying awake after lunch isn't easy, but you are here to represent our country and falling asleep in the middle of a talk arranged especially for you is not polite. Besides, Emi and I are responsible for you. When you don't behave appropriately we look bad. Okay?"

"Sure, Maddie," both students replied bashfully. "Sorry about that."

Maddie hoped Fujita-sensei hadn't noticed, but on the bus he grumbled to Emi, who seemed to wither in the heat of his criticism.

On Thursday, the students were hoping they might have an easy day, but Fujita-sensei led them on a two-hour train ride to Nara where they visited Nara Park, the huge bronze Buddha statue, and Kasuga, a Shinto shrine of more than three thousand lanterns.

The final stop was Koyasan, a mountain town famous for its Buddhist temples and a huge, ancient cemetery. The *only* way to get to Koyasan from Nara, however, was to go *back* to Osaka and take several trains and a bus from there. On the train, Maddie heard Sam and Claudia grouse about having to backtrack.

"You know," Sam carped to Claudia, "I'm *really* glad we got to spend an extra *three* hours on trains and buses today, aren't you?"

"Thrilled, Sam, absolutely *thrilled*," she replied. "Whoever planned this trip is a logistical *genius*." Matt and Claire overhead Sam and Claudia and chuckled their approval. Maddie, who was sitting just in front of them, whirled around.

"Cut it out!" Maddie scolded. "We're doing the best we can. Besides, we'll be staying at a centuries-old Buddhist temple tonight in the middle of a very scenic, very quiet mountain town. On Friday, you'll have time to explore a cemetery over a thousand years old and enjoy the natural beauty. I've never been there, but I've heard it's one of the most tranquil spots in the world."

The four students sank down into their seats and mumbled, "Sorry, Maddie."

At around six that night, they arrived at the temple. The group planned to stay Friday night, tour the cemetery in the morning, and travel to Tokyo on Saturday evening to pack up for their flight home on Sunday. As they gathered in the lobby waiting to be taken to their rooms, Claire, Matt, Sam, and Claudia approached Maddie.

"We're sorry for what we said on the bus," apologized Sam.

"Yes," agreed Claudia. "This temple is beautiful. We're glad we came."

"Yeah. We will be sure to thank Fujita-sensei for planning a whole morning to relax in this gorgeous place before the long trip back to Tokyo and the flight home," Claire added, and Matt nodded in agreement.

"Thanks for apologizing, you guys," Maddie smiled. "I think we're all a little tired and could use the break tomorrow morning. See you at dinner."

While dinner was being served in the large Japanese-style dining room, Fujita-sensei stood before the group and held his hand up to quiet the students.

"I hope you are enjoying the hospitality of this temple?" he asked raising his eyebrows.

Murmurs of thanks rose from around the room. A few students applauded their tour leader. Fujita-sensei acknowledged the thanks with a nod and held up his hand again.

"Now I wish to explain a tradition of the monks who are our hosts. They humbly request visitors rise at dawn and contribute an hour of work to the maintenance of the temple grounds before participating in their morning service. Accordingly, we will wake everyone at five in the morning to work before we attend the morning service in the temple, which is an hour. Then we will have breakfast and tour the cemetery. Please enjoy your meal."

Fujita-sensei hurried out to join the head monk for dinner in a private room.

Maddie saw Sam and Claudia blanch. She heard Matt, Claire, and a few others groan. As dinner progressed and many of the students drank the *sake* the monks served, she heard their groans became gripes. By the time the dinner ended, most of the students were complaining loudly as they moved along the wooden corridors to their rooms. Maddie and Emi traded nervous glances.

After dinner, Emi met with Fujita-sensei to go over the next day's schedule. When Emi returned to their room at the temple, she was wringing her hands until they glowed scarlet.

"What's wrong, Emi?"

"Fujita-sensei overheard the students protest having to wake up so early in the morning. He is very, very concerned the students are turning against him and will criticize him in the reports they make to the ministries. As you know, any complaints would ruin his future," she declared quietly. Emi's eyes glistened with tears. "He does not believe he can change the morning schedule. It is a custom of the temple and the correct thing to do for the monks who have extended their hospitality."

Emi knelt down at the small table and closed her eyes as if she were praying.

Maddie saw her friend's dream of studying abroad was vanishing.

"I am so sorry." Maddie sat beside Emi and reached out to hug her but then stopped and simply squeezed her hand. "I wish he had told us so we could have put it on the schedule and prepared the students for having to wake up so early.”

“Yes. That would have been much wiser.” She shook her head slowly. “Maddie, you are an American, like them,” Emi whispered, looking sideways at Maddie. “You understand them better than I do. What would you advise me to do?”

Emi seeking her advice thrilled Maddie. Skip had told her many times about the wonderful friendships he had formed with his Mexican baseball brothers. Maddie had hoped to find similar connections among the girls in Taiwan and thought she had before realizing she had failed miserably. Forging a special tie with Emi brought to life a dream of her own. And now Emi was signaling that she also felt a bond between them that transcended language and cultural differences. With time, could she become like the sister Maddie longed for?

“I think I should speak to the students, Emi. Persuade them to accept this one final inconvenience.”

“I appreciate your solution, but to be complete you would have to request the students to not criticize Fujita-sensei in their reports.”

Maddie pressed her fingers to her lips and locked her eyes on Emi’s. “I can’t *tell* them what to think, what to write in their reports,” she declared. “I would destroy the trust they have in me . . . in us. Besides, even if I did ask them to avoid complaining about Fujita-sensei, I doubt they would agree.”

Emi looked away from Maddie and closed her eyes momentarily. “Then, I do not see the purpose in your speaking to the students.”

Maddie sighed. “Then let *me* talk with Fujita-sensei. Let *me* represent the students. I will try to persuade him to allow them to . . . to vote on whether they sleep in or not. That way he would not be responsible for the decision.”

Emi frowned.

"You asked for my advice as an *American*," Maddie rushed to add. "I don't assume a Japanese would make the same recommendation."

"No," Emi replied quietly. "It is not at all the same for us. I do not believe my purpose is to represent the students. My job is to assist Fujita-sensei and, if appropriate, to guide the students to do what he thinks is best."

"I understand, but wouldn't finding a solution for the students help Fujita-sensei?"

Maddie saw Emi's face twist in concentration. Finally, she inhaled deeply and raised herself to her feet.

"I must speak again with Fujita-sensei," she announced, then left their room.

Five minutes later, Emi returned, slid the screen door shut, and knelt down by her futon. Without a word to Maddie, she readied herself for sleep.

"What did Fujita-sensei say?" Maddie inquired.

"He refused to change the schedule. He ordered me to set my alarm for fifteen minutes before five o'clock. I am now responsible for waking everyone."

Maddie examined Emi's face, expecting to see frustration or sadness. Instead she looked calm, like the sea on a windless morning. Emi lay down and pulled her quilt over herself. She switched off the small lamp by her futon without saying a word. Darkness covered them.

As Maddie lay on her *futon* listening to Emi's gentle breathing, she became furious with Fujita-sensei. How could he entangle Emi again in what was *his* problem? Who cared what the monks thought? Was he so foolish to believe the students would blame Emi, not him, for waking them up? But Maddie remained silent. She understood Emi was trapped. In many ways, she admired Emi's intense loyalty to Fujita-sensei. At the same time she abhorred him for taking advantage of Emi's devotion. In the end,

Maddie knew she had to respect Emi's decision, as difficult as it was for her to comprehend.

After many minutes, all Maddie managed to say was, "Are you sure?"

Emi just mumbled, "*Shoo ga nai.* There's no other way."

Maddie could no longer resist comforting her friend. She rolled on her side, draped her arm over Emi, and hugged her.

"Whatever happens, I promise to help you realize your dream of studying abroad. Come to Mills. We could be roommates."

Emi smiled and whispered, "Thank you so much, Maddie. *Oyasumi nasai.*"

"*Oyasumi nasai,*" Maddie replied. As she watched Emi's quilt slowly rise and fall, visions of them together at Mills filled her mind: Emi and Maddie lounging in their room in pajamas giggling and chatting; Emi loudly cheering Maddie at her volleyball games; Maddie guiding Emi around San Francisco; Maddie introducing Emi to her parents, maybe even to Skip. Her parents and Skip. Maddie sighed. Would her parents still be married when Emi came? Would she and Skip ever find their way back together? The prospect of her family breaking apart and a future without Skip terrified Maddie, but seemed somehow more bearable if Emi were in her life. She no longer felt she was an alone child.

A powerful need to express her gratitude for Emi flooded Maddie. "*Oyasumi nasai,* my sister," she whispered finally and fell into a deep, peaceful sleep.

The next thing Maddie knew, Emi was running out of their room. Maddie stared at her watch. *Seven-fifteen.* She could hear the monks chanting in the morning service. Oh my God! Emi overslept!

Maddie threw on her *yukata* and raced after Emi toward Fujita-sensei's room. As Maddie turned the corner, she saw Emi kneeling just outside his door, her arms outstretched to the sides and her body bent completely forward so her cheek pressed against the polished wood floor of the corridor. Fujita-sensei stood above her with arms folded, shaking with anger as he appeared to berate her for having failed to wake him on time. Maddie rushed forward to protect her friend.

Fujita-sensei heard Maddie's footsteps and turned his head to glare at her, teeth bared, his face a purplish red. She stopped abruptly. He looked down to bellow one last time at the prostrate Emi. She put her hands beneath her chest, pushed herself up, and rocked backwards on her legs. Keeping her head lowered and her body turned toward Fujita-sensei, she backed away from him until she reached Maddie. At that moment, she spun around and glanced at Maddie before retreating. Maddie expected to see her eyes filled with tears. Instead there was the same tranquil resolve from the night before. Emi scurried past Maddie to their room.

"Maddie-san! Please wake the students and instruct them to gather in the dining hall in fifteen minutes," Fujita-sensei ordered with a swipe of his hand.

"How could you . . ." Maddie started to rail at Fujita-sensei for humiliating Emi. But she stopped herself and replied through clenched teeth, "Yes, Fujita-sensei."

Maddie wanted desperately to speak with Emi, but she also wanted to avoid making a bad situation worse for her friend by further angering her professor. She dashed from room to room to wake the students.

When Maddie and the students arrived in the dining hall, Fujita-sensei was kneeling next to the head monk at the end of the room. Maddie could see his mouth tighten and his eyes narrow. He raised his hand for silence.

"Good morning. First, I will apologize in Japanese to the head monk for our failing to perform the requested work this morning as well as for missing the morning service."

Fujita-sensei bowed his head and spoke at length to the bald old monk who knelt staring ahead. When Fujita-sensei had finished, the monk nodded his head once but remained silent.

"Now I wish to apologize to you, the students on my tour, for Tsuji-san's failure to wake you as she was instructed to do. As a result, you have missed the opportunity to fulfill your service to the temple and to participate in the morning service. Her failure was inexcusable and unforgiveable. After your breakfast, return to your rooms and prepare to leave for the cemetery tour and the trip to Tokyo."

Fujita-sensei and the head monk raised themselves from their knees and strode out of the room. Some students held their hands up as if to ask, "What just happened?" Others shook their heads in confusion.

"What's going on?" Matt asked Maddie as Sam, Claire, and Claudia surrounded her.

"I'm not sure how, but Emi overslept and didn't wake us all up. Fujita-sensei is furious with her."

"That's an *inexcusable* and *unforgiveable* failure?" Claire asked. "He made it sound like she should be executed."

"Thank God my parents don't feel that way," Sam added. "I oversleep all the time."

"I know. I know," Maddie said. "Look. I want to see how Emi is doing. You guys finish breakfast and get ready to go, okay?"

Maddie yearned to console Emi, who she knew must be profoundly embarrassed. She rushed to their bedroom. She found Emi's quilt and *futon* neatly folded and tucked in a corner. All trace of Emi had disappeared; her dear friend had fled in shame. Maddie dropped to her knees. How could anyone as competent, responsible, and devoted as Emi forget to set an alarm?

Maddie ached to tell Emi that everyone makes mistakes, to assure her that whatever happened would not lessen her love—

and love was what Maddie felt—for Emi. Would she see her in Tokyo before leaving for home?

Emi did not rejoin the group in Tokyo. On the flight home, Maddie struggled to reconcile Emi's serene demeanor on their last morning together with the emotional turbulence that must have been raging within her. As soon as Maddie returned home, she wrote Emi at the Waseda address that was printed on her name card.

I am so sorry for what happened the last morning at the temple and hope you know you are not the only one to blame. I should have offered to set my alarm to help you and did not. I am as responsible as you for what happened. Please write soon, dear Emi. I miss our talks.

The letter was returned ten days later marked "Addressee Unknown." Growing concerned, Maddie called the AIEE. They had no information about an assistant to Professor Fujita and suggested Maddie contact him.

Maddie wanted nothing more to do with Fujita sensei, but her care for her friend's fragile mental state compelled her. She wrote a short, polite note requesting Emi's address. Maddie returned to Mills at the end of the summer but could not stop thinking about Emi. After a month and a half without a response from Fujita-sensei, Maddie's worry turned to anguish. She had read that Japanese students committed suicide at a high rate. Emi had bet her entire future on Fujita-sensei's recommendation and lost. Maddie feared Emi may have sunk into a dark depression and taken her life. She wrote to Fujita-sensei again.

More weeks passed without a reply and Maddie became frantic. Concentrating on her class work was impossible. Why hadn't she offered to set her alarm to help Emi? The note she had received from Emi before leaving for Japan became a talisman whose reading each night evoked warm memories of their time together and lessened, if only temporarily, the dread she felt. Finally, three months after she had first written to him, Fujita-sensei responded in a four-sentence note.

I have been on leave. Waseda University regulations prohibit me from disclosing information about a student. I will, however, convey your request to Emiko Tsuji the next time I meet her. Thank you for your assistance this past summer.

The curt letter lowered the decibel of the bells clanging in Maddie's mind, but did not eliminate her unease. For days she searched her mailbox in vain.

Two weeks later, Emi's reply arrived in the morning mail. Maddie ran to her room clutching the letter and tore it open. She read the message quickly. Her mind clouded in confusion, so she read it again more slowly. When she finished, she laid the new letter on her desk next to the first one whose edges were now smudged and frayed. She sat on her bed, eyes locked on the soft curly-cue letters of Emi's handwriting with the large black circles for dots above the *i*'s that were so like Emi's eyes.

Receiving the letter filled Maddie with joy; reading it broke her heart. For several hours, she examined Emi's letter from a distance as if it were a beautiful stray cat she wanted to pet but feared might scratch her. Finally, she resolved to read it again.

Emi apologized for not writing sooner. She had been in Hagi visiting her parents and did not meet Fujita-sensei until he returned from leave. She explained that when she had gone back to speak with Fujita-sensei that night at the temple, he had worried aloud he would lose face or his reputation or both. The students were turning against him, but he couldn't allow them to sleep in without violating the monks' trust. She said he kept asking, "What can be done? What can be done?"

Emi realized he was communicating with her through *haragei*, the Japanese way of expressing thoughts implicitly. When he tasked her with waking everyone up, she knew Fujita-sensei expected her to provide a way to give the students what they wanted and yet allow him to blame *her* in front of the monks. Her oversleeping, her abject apology to Fujita-sensei in the corridor outside his room, his rage at her mistake, her fleeing the temple were all performances. Their behavior was what Japanese call *mikake-daoshi*, something that appears to be one thing but is really the other.

The letter crushed Maddie. Emi's silence had tormented her for more than three months. Each night grasping her first note, she prayed Emi was happy and safe and begged forgiveness for not offering to set her alarm. And now she realized she had agonized endlessly over her so-called friend's well-being because of a *performance* Fujita-sensei and Emi had staged to deceive her and the other Americans. She even wondered if the monks knew they were part of the elaborate ruse and dutifully acted out their role in the play.

Maddie had spent hours studying Japanese culture and took pains to understand Emi on her own terms. Yet she had *still* failed to understand what happened that day. No, that's not right, Maddie told herself, as she clenched and unclenched her fists in anger. Emi had *manipulated* her into *misunderstanding* what had happened. For all Maddie knew, Fujita-sensei and Emi had secretly laughed at the students and her. How stupid could those Americans be? Ha! Ha! Ha!

Unfortunately, the play hadn't ended at the temple. Emi wrote that when she asked Fujita-sensei in the early fall to recommend her for the Waseda study abroad program, he replied he could not possibly nominate someone who had failed him so miserably. Emi was despondent and yet, *incredibly*, didn't blame him. If he did support her, she understood people would wonder why Fujita-sensei would recommend someone who had acted so irresponsibly. Malicious rumors that their relationship was not what it appeared to be would soon follow.

The last paragraph contained a final surprise.

So, Maddie, I am writing to you with hope you remember your promise to help me fulfill my dream to study in the United States. Please forgive me, but I am asking you most sincerely to help me apply for admission at Mills College next year. If I am successful, my greatest wish would be to share a room with you so our friendship could continue.

Maddie remembered clearly what she had offered when they were in Japan. She had meant every word. But Emi's letter changed everything. She now doubted she knew Emi at all. Emi grew up in a culture where critical information was communicated indirectly, using instincts developed from birth, where what was expressed was often not what was in the mind, where putting on an elaborate performance to mislead others was accepted, even encouraged, as a way to solve problems, and where no one knew when the drama ended and reality began.

Maddie's head throbbed trying to make sense of what had happened and how she should respond. She started to do something she had not done since Taiwan, not even when she despaired about her family. She began to cry. Pain from the loss of her sister—no, her *dream* of a sister—engulfed her. She curled up on the bed, put the pillow over her head, and wept.

A few days later, Maddie still felt deeply wounded. Emi had convinced her that their souls had touched and they would always be truthful with each other, especially concerning their differences. Maddie had cherished that belief and opened herself. Then she received Emi's letter blithely asking for her help without a whisper of an apology! How could Emi fool her without a *clue* as to how betrayed—how *alone*—it would make her feel?

Would she ever be able to comprehend someone from a culture so unlike her own?

When Maddie had received Emi's first note last summer, it filled her with hope such understanding might be possible. Now she doubted she would ever want to try again. When she thought of Emi and looked at her recent letter, Maddie's heart filled with disillusion. Then disillusion turned to rage. She grabbed the letter and carefully folded it with the first note Emi had written. Then she ripped them both to shreds.

5 CONVERSION

"Are you sure you don't wanna come, Mama? The vacation would be good for you."

"Honey, I have work."

"I know you love the kids at the daycare center, but it's San Francisco and, anyways, it's been two years since you had a vacation!"

"Watching you graduate and spending time with you this summer has been my vacation. Besides, an old hag like me couldn't ride on the back of a motorcycle from Kansas all the way to California!" His mama laughed.

Rex loved seeing Mama happy. She was such a good-looking woman for being in her late forties, slim with a short blonde bob, and blue eyes the color of the feathers on the blue-winged teal.

"That's bull! You're *not* old. You're prettier and stronger than any of the girls I know!" Rex objected loudly and stepped over to hug his mother.

"Thanks, honey, but you don't see me with your eyes, you see me with your heart." She chuckled and gently pushed him away. "Are you ready for your adventure? We'll have plenty of time together in a couple of weeks when I bring your things out and help you settle in at Berkeley."

"Okay, Mama. But I'll miss you in the meantime," he said, stroking the stubble on his cheek. He gazed at her with teary eyes. "I worry about you being alone and all."

Rex pawed the asphalt driveway with the toe of his new cowboy boots. He knew any mention of his parents' recent divorce made Mama uncomfortable, but he couldn't help himself. She had always been a puzzle to him, demanding and doting, commanding and cajoling, independent and ingratiating, but always in control. Lately she seemed to want more of his attention and would joke about her appearance or her age knowing he'd compliment her. The thought that Mama needed his approval as much as he craved hers alarmed him.

"Aw, honey, you're sweet, but I'll be fine. Fine." Mama drew him close to her again for a moment and rested her head on his chest. "Now," she said, backing away a step. "Let me take one last look at you."

Rex grinned, spun around, and threw his arms out. "Whaddya think?"

He knew exactly what she would say. After all, Mama had picked out the faded jeans, quilted vest, and tawny long-sleeved shirt he was wearing.

"You look just like James Dean in *Giant,* only more handsome. I just know you'll become a movie star, too," she exclaimed. "Here. One last touch." She reached out to undo the top three buttons of his shirt. "There. You have such a nice chest and, besides, it's going to be hot today. Now, you better get going," she commanded, bringing her hand to her mouth to stifle a sob. "You take care now! Love you, honey."

Rex hugged Mama again and inhaled the rich, sweet, calming smell of her lilac perfume, a scent so constant in his eighteen years of life he didn't have a single memory that didn't also conjure up its fragrance. He wiped his eyes.

"Aw, miss you already," he sighed.

Fighting to hold back his emotions, he mounted the bike, a used 1965 Harley that Mama had bought for him with the money she received for selling her wedding ring.

"See ya soon!" He waved, kick-started the engine, and roared away, the smell of exhaust replacing lilac in his nose.

Rex left white, well-to-do Shawnee Mission, Kansas, without saying goodbye to his father. A standoffish, tight-lipped man consumed by his work, his father had spent little time with him growing up except during boyhood soccer matches. At first, Rex enjoyed the attention from his otherwise distant father. When he developed into a star on the high school varsity team, his father began to analyze his play, delivering cutting post-match critiques. By his junior year, the repeated tongue-lashings had crushed Rex's spirit. His mama pushed back hard.

"You just can't stand seeing Rex become a better athlete than you ever were, can you?" she scolded one night after his father had dressed down Rex in a particularly harsh fashion.

His father had angrily denied Mama's charge and stormed out of the house, but, to Rex's great relief, he never again attended one of his matches.

Heading west to start his freshman year at Cal, Rex thought about his parents and wondered again how his charming, spirited Mama had lasted as long as she had in a marriage with his humorless father. His parents had met nearly twenty years before when his father came from Barcelona to get a graduate degree in business at the University of Kansas. He played on local soccer clubs and met Mama in the last semester of her senior year at KU. His dark good looks, exotic background, and the allure of a life outside Kansas swept her off her feet. They married just after she graduated and made plans to travel around Europe. At the last minute, his father took a well-paying job at a local bank, promising Mama they would go abroad when they had saved a little money. When Rex was born a year later, they put aside any thought of traveling to Europe until he was older. With their travel money they made a down payment on a comfortable home in Shawnee Mission and joined the country club.

Over the years, his parents drifted apart. His father spent most of his time at work and playing golf with clients on the weekends. Because he discouraged Mama from pursuing a fulltime job, she devoted herself to running the childcare center at St. Luke's and raising Rex. In contrast to his father, who rarely offered his help or a word of advice to his son, Mama did not hide her expectations. Rex worked hard for years to become the son she made clear she desired—a straight-A student, high school soccer and track star, leading man in all the school plays, and altar boy at St. Luke's. Even his attending Cal and his trip to San Francisco before school were her ideas.

"The Harley's super, but I can ride it around here. Are you sure you'll be all right if I leave two weeks early?"

"Honey, I love having you around. You know that. But when I was your age, I wasn't brave enough to ride a motorcycle or go far away to school or follow my dream of trying a career in acting. As much as I want to spend time with you, I want even more for you to have all the experiences I missed."

"All right, Mama." After everything Mama had done for him, he would break his back to please her. "I'm not sure I understand, but if that's what you want, I'll do it."

"Good. I know you'll have fun in San Francisco. Everyone's talking about a place called Haight-Ashbury. It sounds exciting! I can't wait to hear about your adventures in a couple of weeks. Meantime, I don't want you ruining your time by calling me every day."

Racing along I-80, the wind on his face and sun on his shoulders, exhilarated him. He spent three nights in ramshackle motels and ate in small-town diners as he sped west. After climbing the Sierra Nevada range, he flew over the Truckee River and raced down into coastal California.

Reaching San Francisco, Rex headed to Haight-Ashbury. He rented a room at the Jeffrey-Haight, giving the unfriendly receptionist a hundred-dollar bill as a deposit and Mama's name as his guarantor. When he closed the door to his tiny room, the excitement of constant motion and changing scenery began to evaporate like the fizz in an open bottle of pop. The three days since he'd spoken with Mama suddenly felt like a lifetime. The eleven days remaining before he arrived at Cal dragged out endlessly. He asked himself what Mama would do to explore a new city and discovered to his horror that he had no idea. Without her to guide him, he felt directionless. Remembering Mama said not to call home too much, he initially fought the urge to speak with her and then gave up. He was on the brink of heading downstairs to look for a pay phone when he heard a rap on the door.

"Who is it?"

"I'm Marie Lace," said a low, raspy voice through the door, "a nursing student at USF. I'm staying across the hall."

Rex opened the door to find a tall woman with long brunette braids and a headband of Indian beads leaning against the door jamb. She smelled of some kind of incense and wore an Indian-print dress, leather sandals, and, as far as Rex could tell, nothing else. In Shawnee Mission, Rex had dated sweet, sunny, Midwestern girls from families his mama approved of, girls who rooted for his teams, went with him to school dances, and later, after perfunctory protests, eagerly wrapped themselves around him, fully clothed, in Mama's station wagon. Marie took his breath away. She was the most exotic looking girl he'd ever met.

"Uh, I'm Rex. Rex Moreno."

"Hey, Rex Moreno." Marie smiled and sashayed into his room. "I saw you come in. Where are you from?"

"Outside of Kansas City," he declared. When he saw Marie frown and her eyes darken, he hastened to add, "But I'm going to Berkeley this fall. I'll be studying political science and drama."

Marie brightened. "Well, I can introduce you to the most beautiful city in the world." She peeked around his room. "You know, it's a little cramped in here. Why don't you come across to mine? I'll put on some music and we can get to know each other."

"Sure," Rex said, surprised at how easily Marie invited a strange man to her room, but intrigued by her airy self-assurance. Thoughts of calling home flew from his mind.

Over the next two hours, Marie introduced him to Janis Joplin and Jimi Hendrix, pot and cheap Napa reds. When she asked if he'd like to have sex, Rex blurted out, "Jeez. I don't have a rubber with me."

"I'll take that as a 'yes.'" She threw her head back and roared with laughter. "You don't have any diseases I should know about, do you? Remember, I'm a nursing student." She explained the magic of the "pill," threw off her cotton dress, and took out a book she called "the Kama Sutra." Pulling him down on to her mattress, she ordered, "Now, take your clothes off and turn to page eighteen."

"Wait," he sputtered. "Do ya want me to turn off the lights?"

"Are you kidding?" she guffawed hoarsely. Rex's face fell. "Aw"—she stopped laughing—"you're serious, aren't you? Well, thanks for asking, but, no, I like the lights on. Nice and bright so I can see every inch of your body and watch your eyes pore over mine."

At first her shameless lust shocked the altar boy in him, but soon he felt freed by it and hungered to prove he enjoyed her body as much as she did his. The next day he offered to take her for a ride on his Harley. Marie examined Rex's vest, jeans, and cowboy boots with a smirk on her face and shook her head.

"You are very beautiful, Rex Moreno. I can definitely see you in the movies. Still, I'd like you even more if you looked less like John Wayne and more like Marlon Brando."

Rex had never considered any man "beautiful." He started to protest. No woman other than Mama had ever told him what to wear. But he stopped himself. The urge to please Marie, to feel her skin against his again and again overwhelmed any desire to preserve his ego. He gave no more thought to shedding his Kansas skin than a timber rattlesnake would to molting. Marie took him to a secondhand clothing store in the Haight where they bought black leather chaps, a tight-fitting black leather jacket, and motorcycle boots. That afternoon they cruised through Golden Gate Park and raced down Highway 1 to Half Moon Bay. The next nine days passed in a haze of pot smoke, incense, and the musky, slightly sour smell radiating from their naked bodies after they made love.

Two nights before he was leaving for Berkeley and Marie for nursing school, she brought some acid over to his room.

"An intern at UCSF hospital gave me a couple of tabs. I think you'll like how LSD expands your mind." She held out a white tablet.

Rex hesitated. His high school civics teacher had handed out an article from *Life* warning that taking the mind drug was a dangerous gamble; some experienced a riot of colors and sounds but others shook in unspeakable terror.

"Couldn't we just smoke some pot and make love again?"

"No deal, Rex. If you won't trip with me, I'll call the intern. He seemed open to exploring the limits of our minds—and our bodies."

"Well . . ." Rex stammered.

"Shit! I guess you can take the boy out of Kansas but not Kansas out of the boy!"

Marie mocking his Midwestern origin cut deeply. Dread of the unknown tugged against his fear of rejection. He knew the old Rex no longer existed and the new Rex would be lost without Marie. Panicking, he stared at the tablet in her hand to steady himself, casually shrugged his shoulders, and reached out to take it from her.

"Cool," she grinned. "I knew you were a fiend at heart."

Rex remembered little of the next day. The hotel manager called his mama and complained of odd smells and childlike weeping and shrieking coming from his room. Terrified, Mama dispatched a male cousin living in Oakland to the hotel. The cousin found Rex naked, balled up on his urine-soaked mattress rocking back and forth and muttering unintelligibly. When the cousin tried to calm him down, Rex screamed and pointed at invisible pythons crawling across the wood floor. Shocked, his cousin dressed Rex quickly, carried him on his back out to a taxi, and sped toward the San Francisco airport and a flight to Kansas City.

Mama burned the stinking black leather clothes she found on her son and nursed him back to health. Rex slipped easily back into the jeans, T-shirts, and cowboy boots Mama preferred. For the next two years, she monitored his every movement until she regained confidence in his judgment. Rex took political science and acting classes at a nearby community college and dated some of the same young women he'd known in high school. His memory of Marie and their time in the Haight died away. In the fall of 1969, he received a letter from his local draft board instructing him to take a physical. Mama took charge. Terrified Rex would be inducted, she paid a friendly Shawnee Mission orthopedist to write a letter justifying Rex's request for a medical exemption based upon an old soccer injury.

"Now that the draft problem has been solved, you're going back to Berkeley in June," Mama announced one morning a few months later. "It's time you left Shawnee Mission for good."

"I feel comfortable here, Mama. What if I go to KU instead?"

"I never left Kansas," she lamented, "and you know I've never stopped regretting it. You are handsome and smart and young. You can be anything you want in California—an actor, a politician, even an actor-politician like Governor Reagan!"

"Nah! You really think I could be like Governor Reagan?"

"Why not? You're more handsome and a lot smarter!"

Rex made arrangements with Berkeley to transfer back. He planned to finish his BA in a year, complete his course work for an MA in political science by the end of 1972, and research and write his thesis the following year.

The week before he left, Mama took him into downtown Kansas City to shop at Brooks Brothers. "Now *these* are the kind of clothes Governor Reagan would wear if he were your age," she murmured approvingly as she ran her hand over a pile of cashmere sweaters in various muted colors. Rex stood before a mirror in a navy blue blazer, gray slacks, and brown loafers.

"Thanks, Mama. I do look pretty swell, don't I?" he said as he straightened his shoulders and turned to one side and then the other to examine how the pants fit his legs.

Just before she put him on the plane to San Francisco, Mama grabbed Rex by the shoulders and hugged him hard. Then she cupped his face in her hands.

"Swear to me you won't take any drugs, you'll stay away from the runaways and hippies in Berkeley, and you'll avoid the antiwar protests. And call me at least once a week to tell me what you've been up to. Promise me!"

The force of Mama's gaze surprised Rex. He took her hands from his face and held them tightly.

"Don't fret over me, Mama. I promise to call you every Sunday evening. Anyways, I learned my lesson for good the last time. No fooling around. Promise."

For the first three months, he circulated methodically from his studio in a university apartment complex to his political science classes then to the same desk in the stacks at the main library and finally back to his apartment at night. He considered auditioning for a play called *Hair* put on by a small theater troupe in Berkeley, but changed his mind when he discovered the role required performing nude. Once a week, he called home to report to Mama on what he was doing.

After four months, he felt as empty and adrift as he had when he first arrived at the Jeffrey-Haight. Rex confessed to Mama that he missed her and wanted to return home.

"You just need to make some friends. I know you've followed my advice and kept away from the troublemakers at Berkeley, but the Reynolds girl, Sarah, just began her freshman year at Mills College. Those Mills girls will be safe—not like the nurse who pumped drugs into you. I'll make sure you're invited to her next house party. I want you to go and I want you to have fun."

"Okay, Mama," Rex grumbled. "I don't know Sarah very well, but I'll try."

"You'll be fine. Everyone's acting at those parties anyway. You're good at acting and telling stories, honey. That's all you have to do."

Rex dutifully went to the fall Mills mixer wearing his navy blazer, a light-yellow button-down dress shirt, and tan slacks. Sarah, a freckled, broad-shouldered, buttermilk blonde, welcomed him at the front door dressed in a sky-blue wool dress with white trim.

"Good to see ya, Rex. Wow, you look even more handsome in your blazer than you did in your soccer uniform." She hugged him, tilted her head to one side, and smiled warmly.

"Thanks, Sarah. That's an awfully pretty dress."

"Gosh! Thank *you*! Come on in."

She walked him through a spacious entry hall with a glistening chandelier into a large living room crowded with young men and women. Taking his hand, she led him through the crowd to the far corner where two young women stood in a sitting area by a marble fireplace.

"These are my good friends. This is Annabelle." A willowy brunette in a gray wool skirt and cashmere sweater shook his hand, widened her eyes, and smiled. "And this is Betty," said Sarah, pointing to a petite woman with short black hair in a crème cotton dress.

"Nice to meet you, Rex," said Betty, who then whispered to Sarah out of the side of her mouth, "Are all the boys in Kansas *this* good-looking?"

Sarah cast a withering glance at Betty. "Girls, Rex and I haven't seen each other since I was a freshman and he was a senior heading out to Berkeley on a motorcycle."

"Really? On a motorcycle? How adventurous!" Betty exclaimed.

"The next thing I heard, you returned home after being drugged by a hippie girl," Sarah continued. "I felt so sorry for you." She squeezed Rex's arm. "What happened?"

"Oh, hey, it's kind of a long tale. Are you really interested?"

"Yes!" All three young women nodded enthusiastically.

"Mills is kind of boring," Annabelle confided, rolling her eyes. "Fewer than a thousand students and *all* girls! You must have had an amazing experience! Please tell us all about it."

"Yeah," Betty chimed in. "Sounds like Peter Fonda and Dennis Hopper in *Easy Rider*."

"Well, jeez, I'll do my best"—he hesitated—"but don't expect too much. I'm no Peter Fonda," Rex said and leaned against the fireplace mantel.

The three young women lowered themselves onto a long rose-colored couch, bent forward, and stared up at Rex with eager eyes. For the next twenty minutes, he stood on a stage performing a version of himself. He recounted with flourishes of his hands an embellished tale of his motorcycle ride across country to Haight-Ashbury, how he had been tricked into taking LSD by an exotic older woman, and how he had struggled to recover but finally prevailed with the help of Mama. As he finished, Sarah and Annabelle clapped loudly. Betty wiped tears from her eyes.

The applause attracted a half dozen other young women who walked over to introduce themselves to the attractive young stranger.

"We couldn't hear what you were saying," one of the newcomers said. "Would you mind starting over for us?"

"We don't want to impose on Rex," Sarah objected.

"The three of *you* don't have to stay, if you don't want to," the newcomer snapped back. "There are some Stanford guys over there who have no one to talk with."

"Oh, no," Sarah said. "*We're* not going anywhere. Would you mind, Rex?"

"Not at all," he said and launched again into the story, adding new details as he spoke. Just as he finished, a voice thundered down the stairwell.

"You know the rules. All men out of the house by ten!"

The few remaining Stanford and Berkeley men began to move toward the door.

"It's the RA," whispered Sarah to Rex.

"Oh, come on, Maddie," she yelled back up the stairs. "It's Saturday night!"

"No exceptions!"

"What about you?" Annabelle yelled. "Your boyfriend was here until eleven last night!"

"Yeah! Skip was in your *room*!" Betty complained.

"You're freshmen!" boomed the voice. "The rules are different for me. Walk your guests to the door, ladies, or I'll do it myself and report you to the dean."

"She's such a ballbuster," Sarah muttered to Rex. "Thinks she's God because she's captain of the volleyball team. Sorry."

"Oh, 'course I understand. Besides all the other guys are leaving," Rex said and took each girl's hand as he said goodbye.

"Look, I had a lot of fun tonight, Sarah," he said at the door and kissed her cheek. "Thanks a bunch for introducing me to your friends. Would you mind giving me their names and the sorority phone number so we all can stay in touch?"

Over the next fifteen months, dinners with a succession of Mills girls followed. They all told him how much he looked like a young Paul Newman. Rex quickly learned to respond that they looked like a young Joanne Woodward, which would lead to acting out love scenes in his apartment, some real and some improvised, from *The Long, Hot Summer.* As usual, Mama had been right. His frequent dates and weekly calls home dispelled any further thought of returning to Kansas. As the months passed, he discovered Tilden Park, inexpensive little restaurants along College Street, and the spectacular views of the water from the Bay Trail running along the eastern edge of the San Francisco Bay.

He took pride in graduating with honors in May of 1971. Mama traveled out to California for the ceremony and gushed over his achievements. He enjoyed showing Mama around the Bay Area and briefly considered returning home with her for a few months until he remembered sweating through the torrid Kansas summers. He decided to begin his graduate studies immediately.

In the fall, he met a lovely senior in the Linguistics Department at Mills and took her to Spenger's Fresh Fish Grotto for steamed clams and beer. When the waitress asked if he wanted another beer, Rex replied, "Nah, thanks. I don't wanna get schnockered."

"That's so cute and *so* Midland!" his date giggled. "Do you mind a little experiment? Would you say the following words for me? We call these minimal pairs because they differ only in one sound."

She wrote down on a napkin *bowl* and *bull* and *pin* and *pen*.

Rex did as he was asked and was shocked when the two words in each pair came out of his mouth sounding exactly the same.

"That's what's called merging vowels," she declared and sipped her beer.

He pretended to laugh at himself, but winced inwardly and never asked her out again. From that day forward, he made a point of eliminating words like *jeez, anyways,* and *schnockered* from his vocabulary and worked to distinguish the vowels in his speech. He had graduated from the University of California and was pursuing his MA for Christ's sake! He was an educated young man, not some Kansas hick.

Despite academic success and a full social calendar, from time to time he missed Mama and the daily direction she had always provided. On those occasions, an unmistakable feeling of aimlessness would well up again. He felt like a compass needle spinning in vain, searching for true north.

A chance encounter in December of 1971 transformed his life. He was striding quickly by Sproul Hall on his way to a class when he noticed a score of shaggy anti-war protesters gathered around a speaker. A woman's voice roared from a small portable platform in the center of the crowd.

"It is long past time that we condemned our bloody government for its criminal bombing of the heroic North Vietnamese people and its support for the repressive regimes of Thieu in Vietnam and Lon Nol in Cambodia."

Rex peered over the heads of the dozen onlookers at a slight, elfin woman with creamy skin, short black hair, and dark eyes that flashed with anger as she railed against the war. He couldn't believe the voice echoing across the plaza came from such a tiny frame.

"Excuse me," he said to an onlooker with John Lennon spectacles who had the dank smell of unwashed laundry. "Who's the speaker?"

"Diana Mittelbach, man. Poli-sci. She's so righteous."

The next day Rex couldn't get Diana out of his head. He wandered over to the political science building to review the classes he might take the next quarter in the hope of running into her in the department's library. As he scanned the list, he couldn't believe what he saw. Diana Mittelbach, who seemed so young, wasn't a graduate student, but an assistant professor. She was teaching Quantitative Empirical Methods, a course he needed to fulfill his masters. Rex squinted at the small print: *Prerequisites: Permission of professor.* Rex started to hum the tune from Al Green's "Tired of Being Alone." He had an excuse to meet Diana and seized it.

"You seem like a smart enough guy," Diana observed from behind her office desk. "Why do you want to take this course?"

"It's required for an MA in poli-sci," Rex replied, wondering if she was testing him already.

"Is that all you do, Rex Moreno from Kansas, what's required by others? Don't you ever think for yourself?" She pointed at his head.

Rex flushed. "Well . . . well . . . what about you? You're *teaching* it!"

"Good. Fight back. But if you take my class, you won't learn a fucking thing about quantitative analysis in a sanitized research setting. What you will do is *act* . . . you will act politically out in the real world and write reports on your experience using quantitative tools. If you're not prepared to do that"—she slapped the desk—"find another section."

Rex stared into her eyes looking for a sign she wanted him to stay. In contrast to the accommodating Mills girls, Diana's expression betrayed nothing, and the nothingness both frightened and aroused him. She was magnetic.

"I'd like to be in your class, but only if I can work with you in the antiwar movement and you'll be my thesis advisor."

Diana fixed her eyes on Rex. He shifted uneasily in his chair.

"Okay, Kansas," she finally said, "but only if you do what you're told and no complaints. Agreed? You can start by handing out leaflets tomorrow afternoon. Come by at three."

She looked down briefly at the papers on her desk and up again at Rex with a smirk. "One more thing."

"What?"

"Lose the button-down shirts and slacks, buy a pair of used jeans, and let your hair grow out."

Rex hesitated a moment, knowing how disappointed Mama would be at the change, but, he quickly assured himself, Mama didn't have to know.

"If that's what you find attractive," he grinned.

"You have no idea what *I* find attractive, but it's obvious *you* think you're pretty hot with your droopy eyes and sly smile. I bet you think you can get into my pants whenever you want."

She gestured with her thumb at her crotch and arched her eyebrows.

Rex opened his mouth to protest.

"Forget it!" Diana cut him off. "It'll never happen. I like men who think with their heads not their dicks," she declared, pointing first at his head and then at the space between his legs. "See you tomorrow. Don't be late."

Rex left wordlessly. He felt lightheaded and entranced. Excited by the challenge of earning Diana's respect, he knew for the first time in months what he wanted. The next day he packed away all of the Brooks Brothers clothes and shopped on Telegraph Avenue for faded jeans, black T-shirts, and an olive-green U.S. Army field jacket.

Over the following nine months, Rex graduated from handing out leaflets to writing them, from drafting Diana's speeches to introducing her at rallies. He still called his mama every week, but the conversations grew shorter and more perfunctory. He knew Mama expected him to become the next Ronald Reagan, so he avoided lying about his anti-war work by saying he was working on a special project with a brilliant professor. Mama seemed content with the explanation and thrilled at his success.

One cool but bright early September afternoon filled with the scent of eucalyptus, Rex hurried across campus to join Diana outside Sproul Hall.

"I've lost my voice, Kansas," she rasped. "You'll have to give my speech today."

"But I . . . I can't whip up a crowd like you. And what if someone challenges me or asks a question? I don't know enough," he protested.

"Look," Diana croaked. "I'm not asking you to *know* anything. I'm just asking you to give my speech and walk off. Christ! You've heard it enough times. Stop being such a dick and fucking do it!"

When Rex stepped in front of the microphone, a hundred pairs of eyes gazed at him, eager to be uplifted, exhorted, incited to act. The sudden urge to please them tempered his anxiety. He began by impersonating Diana. The crowd's shouts of "Right on!" and "Out now!" filled him with confidence. He conjured up sensational details about war atrocities and capitalist exploitation. As his voice boomed through the microphone and his hands chopped the air, the crowd roared. The cheering intoxicated him further. He responded with a more strident tone, which elicited an even greater response. After he finished to thunderous applause, Diana waited several paces away with a half-smile on her face, watching four young women gush their congratulations to Rex.

"Not bad, Kansas. Not bad," she said in a gravelly whisper when the women had left.

She took his hand and led him to her apartment. They made love that night and every night for the next month. Although Diana did not ask him to speak again and continued to critique his work, the unbridled passion with which she made love convinced him she valued him as much as he worshipped her. He began to contemplate staying on at Berkeley after he finished his masters and ultimately moving in with Diana.

Two months after Diana first took him to her apartment, Rex sat in her office editing a speech she was to give that afternoon. Diana walked in, closed the door behind her, and dropped her briefcase on the floor.

"I have something to tell you, Kansas," she said and sat behind her desk. "I'm leaving Berkeley for New York to work for the Debs Caucus, a splinter group from the disbanding Socialist Party of America."

"What!" Rex's head jerked up. "But what about our anti-war work here? And my thesis? If you're not on the faculty, you can't advise me."

"Working for the Debs Caucus means I will be fighting this fucking war, and for social and economic and racial justice, too." She smacked her desk. "And, no, Kansas. I can't be your advisor, but forget your thesis. You need to complete your radical education by working for the poor in a Third World country."

"What?" Rex gasped. "What about us? I want to be with you."

"Stop being a little boy! I'm not your precious Mama! There's a revolution going on. Either go back to Kansas or grow up and do what I say. Maybe you can join me in New York—once you've succeeded in organizing impoverished people to rise up against their oppressors!"

"Where do you want me to go?" he muttered.

Rex had no desire to leave the United States, but Diana had replaced Mama as his lodestar and he was desperate to keep her. Would he ever feel her skin against his again? Ever experience again the exhilaration he felt when she uttered a word of approval?

"The Philippines. Filipinos speak English. The president, Marcos, is an authoritarian bastard. He recently declared martial law, supposedly to suppress the threat of communist-inspired violence, but actually to make himself dictator for life. You'll fit in because you're Episcopalian, which, at least to this daughter of Orthodox Jews"—she cackled—"seems close enough to their Catholicism. And many Filipinos have Spanish blood in their veins, like you."

"Here." She handed Rex a letter. "VSA is a group of cultural imperialists that sends American college graduates to developing countries in Asia to teach English and other subjects useless to the poor."

"VSA?" he asked. What was Diana getting him into?

"Yes. Volunteer Service in Asia, as if America served anything but its own interest in Asia. Anyway, they're asking for recommendations for the Philippines. I'm submitting your name for that job." She pointed to the letter.

Rex saw Diana had circled a six-month teaching position beginning in January in a place called Malabar City.

"Fill out an application and send it to that asshole by the end of the week," she ordered.

She had underlined a name: *Skip Burton, Office Manager and Recruiter, VSA.*

"But . . . but," Rex stammered. "I don't know anything about the Philippines. I don't even know where Malabar City is. Why would they select me?"

"Goddammit, Kansas, you're a Berkeley graduate student. You've got a couple of weeks before the interview, do some reading about the country. Pretend to be earnest, eager, and humble. Talk about how you'll learn from the experience. Don't breathe a word about fomenting revolution. They'll be delighted to find a serious, sober, well-educated young man like yourself. You'll get a couple of days of bullshit cross-cultural sensitivity and awareness training, and then ship out."

"But . . . what do I do once I'm there?" he whined.

"Oh, for Christ's sake! You have good looks, intelligence, and charm, Kansas. And you certainly know how to put on a show. Do what I'd do. Integrate into the local society. Cut your hair short, wear dress slacks and white button-down shirts like an All-American boy. You'll be a volunteer interested in contributing to their economic development, a perfect cover. Then, find a young woman from an influential family, use your charm to seduce her, and persuade her to believe in the revolution. Get her to help start an uprising. You'll figure things out from there."

Do what I'd do? Was Diana manipulating him in the same way she commanded him to use a young Filipina? He remembered the thrill he experienced when his work pleased Diana, and her passion in bed. She may not show it the way Mama does but Diana loved him, he assured himself. The Philippines was another opportunity to work together, to deepen their mutual affection and respect. He would impress her with his accomplishments and reunite with her in six months!

At home over Christmas break, Rex told Mama he was going to the Philippines for six months on the recommendation of his advisor.

"I don't understand, honey," she said, doubt coloring her voice. "What does volunteering in the Philippines have to do with getting your masters?"

Rex stiffened. He hadn't anticipated Mama questioning his decision. The truth would shock his Kansas Republican mother and she would try to stop him. He began to weave a tale.

"I really can't say any more, Mama, but, just between us"— he leaned forward and whispered—"the teaching job's a cover. Professor Mittelbach has asked me to help her gather intelligence on certain political movements in the rural Philippines. We're working under a classified contract for an important government *agency.*"

Mama's mouth dropped open in surprise and then she smiled. "Oh, honey. I am *so* proud of you. But be careful."

"I will, Mama. I will."

Rex was delighted his story had satisfied Mama, but troubled that he had to lie. To quiet his guilt and the nagging concern that Diana might be taking advantage of him, he wrote her a long letter that night. He couldn't wait to join her in New York when his work in the Philippines was done.

"Would Attorney Benito Lazaro please come up to take his seat at the table of honor so we may commence the ceremony?" a shrill voice blared from speakers.

Perched on a folding metal chair at a small table in the back of the Malabar City Auditorium, Rex was waiting for Miranda to arrive. She was the daughter of the most prominent family in the city and he had spent nearly four months charming her and winning her love. However, his failure—so far—to persuade her that the Philippines needed a revolution and the revolution should start in Malabar City deeply frustrated him.

He was even more distressed that Diana hadn't responded to even one of his half-dozen letters seeking advice and encouragement. Her silence confused him. Was she just using him the way she pushed him to exploit someone like Miranda? Or did she still love him and her silence was a test of his resolve, his commitment to her? A nagging fear that he would fail without her guidance sharpened his sense of abandonment.

His simmering anxiety had boiled over in the past week. He felt a conflict coming to a head between his desire to prove himself to Diana and his fondness for the lovely Miranda, affection that had grown despite her stubborn refusal to agree with his political views. He and Miranda had reached an inflection point, he told himself. Tonight, he would stop at nothing to bend her to do what Diana had commanded.

Rex surveyed the stage. A slight, perspiring young man in a starched white *barong tagalog* leaned against a podium to the left of a long rectangular table festooned with tropical flowers and surrounded by a dozen empty chairs. Behind the table, an enormous whitewashed statue of an elderly woman in a chair stood on an illuminated platform. In her left hand she held an open book while her right arm reached toward two young children gazing adoringly up at her. Below the stage, a score of round tables were scattered across the linoleum floor of the auditorium.

"Would Father Angelo Lazaro *please* come up to take his seat at the table of honor so we may commence the ceremony?" the young man pleaded. Rex recognized him as the principal assistant to Mayor Danilo Lazaro. From his seat, he glanced over to where Father Angelo sat, oblivious to the young man's entreaties, engaged in animated conversation with his cousin Benito and his brother Danilo.

Rex looked down at his watch. "Eight thirty," he grunted in disgust.

"Why are you so upset?" Miranda asked in her airy, slightly syncopated voice as she slid onto the chair next to Rex. She smiled and reached underneath the tablecloth to rest her small hand momentarily on his thigh. "Didn't I warn you at least twice not to arrive early?"

"Yes, you did and, no, I didn't," Rex snapped. "I came thirty minutes late. At seven."

Miranda giggled and shook her head. Rex sensed the tightness in his chest fade away. He normally hated being laughed at, but Miranda managed to tease him in such a way he felt loved. He glanced at her. Her fine features, the glow of her skin, the cascade of dark hair falling to her shoulders took his breath away. He massaged the tightness in his neck and ordered himself to concentrate on what he must accomplish.

"Do you remember," Miranda asked, "nearly four months ago? I came up to you at school and asked what part of America you were from? You became irritated and demanded to know how I knew you were from America?"

"Yes," he sighed, recalling the day clearly, but still wanting to hear the song in Miranda's voice as she repeated the story of how they met.

"And I replied that I was sorry to upset you and agreed you might *look* like a Filipino, at least one of Spanish descent like me, but you walked around campus three times *faster* than any Filipino would." Miranda chortled, her light brown eyes flashing at the memory. "Well, you have slowed down in the past four months, but you still came about an hour too early tonight."

"Would School Director Blessica Angela Lazaro please come to the table of honor and be seated so we may start the program?"

"Father Lazaro! Mayor Lazaro! Attorney Lazaro! Director Lazaro!" Rex spat out the names, anxious to shift the conversation onto his terrain. "For months now, we've been discussing the corruption, the cronyism, the concentration of power in the Philippines—in Malabar City! Tell me what the poor get for their backbreaking work and fealty to a feudal system? Certainly not protection against deadly floods or an authoritarian president."

Miranda withdrew her hand from Rex's thigh, wove her delicate fingers together on the table in front of her, and looked away. Then she faced Rex, her lovely dark eyes cold as the night sky. Miranda did not anger easily, but he saw she was furious now. The hairs on the back of his neck stood up.

"Many things in my country are wrong and should change, but we are here to celebrate my great-great grandmother. Her statue will be installed tonight on the grass playground in our city park. She was the foundress of my family and the wellspring of my family's beneficence. *My* namesake. Remember, the school where you and I teach—the Jose *Lazaro* School of Arts and Trades, which trains *hundreds* of young men and women for productive careers—would not exist; the church clinic where I heal the poor would not have been built; the city government, which supplies power and water, paves the roads, and protects the people from murderers and thieves would not have endured . . . without the contributions of generations of *my* family. What you call corruption and cronyism, many call benevolence, philanthropy, even"—she paused for a moment, her voice breaking—"acts of nobility."

Rex could see tears in her eyes as she defended her family, but he would not let her vulnerability restrain him. To the contrary, he saw it as the opening he needed to strike home.

"If your family is so noble, why do they allow the people of Malabar City to celebrate Good Friday with crucifixion rituals, a parade of peasants flogging themselves? My God, the park is already filled with vendors hawking black cloth hoods, rope whips, pieces of glass to tear flesh. How in the world can your family condone such barbaric practices?" Rex drained his glass of San Miguel and clapped it down on the table.

Miranda stared at the empty glass for a moment, unlaced her fingers, and squeezed her hands into fists.

"Neither the Church nor my family approves of the Good Friday rituals. We believe they are contrary to the Church's teaching to treat the body with respect as a part of God's creation. Yet, we also understand the power of the *panata*—the vow the *magdarame* make to suffer as Jesus did—in bearing the pain He endured to seek forgiveness for their sins, to beg humbly for a loved one to be cured. As much as you have tried to learn about our life here, I do not expect you to understand these traditions, nor the ability of these rituals to sustain hope. Some beliefs live in the heart," she said and placed her hand over her left breast. "Not in the head."

"I see that people whose daily lot is to starve, to do without basic necessities, do not believe fasting and abstinence are sufficient proof of their faith, so they must crucify and flog themselves to gain God's favor. If your father, the mayor, and your uncle, the head of the church here, wished to prevent the practice, they would give people better lives so they *could* fast and wouldn't need to whip their backs into a bloody hash to prove their devotion. If you don't approve of the practice, why do you plan to go to watch the poor men torture themselves?"

"I do *not* go to watch. I admire their faith and the fervor with which they seek forgiveness, but I do not go to the plaza to gawk. The cuts on their backs need care. I am a doctor. I go to the plaza where their procession ends to help. What would you have me do? Ignore their suffering?"

"But that's so hypocritical. By caring for their wounds, you encourage the very practice you say your church discourages!"

Miranda opened her mouth to object again when another announcement interrupted her.

"Would Doctor and Professor Miranda Lazaro please come to the table of honor and be seated so we may start the program?"

Miranda glanced up at the young man at the podium and slowly exhaled. Rex noticed the flush on her delicate features had faded. Her rage had passed as quickly as the afternoon thunderstorms that often swept over the Visayas.

"Forgive me, but, as you know, I am the youngest Lazaro so I must go up first otherwise no one else will and we will all be here until midnight." She reached underneath the table to squeeze his thigh. "Meet me by the bench under the *ilang-ilang* tree after the banquet? But not to talk religion or politics!" she scolded gently with a wag of her finger. She smiled and swayed gracefully toward the stage.

No, they would not talk politics. He had done all he could to satisfy Diana. But no more. Miranda and he had indeed reached an inflection point, but it was her will that had bent him toward her and away from Diana. That sudden, surprising realization broke an emotional dam inside and allowed a torrent of relief to run through his body. The muscles in his shoulders and neck relaxed. Miranda would no longer be the object of his propaganda campaign. Admiration for her dedication to family and the tenacity with which she defended tradition coursed through his veins. Those qualities made her even more alluring now, her love even more precious.

Three hours later, Rex lounged in the balmy night air on a wooden bench underneath the *ilang-ilang* tree in the garden of Miranda's family home. The rich, floral fragrance of the tree's flowers filled his nose. Three nights ago, he had sat with Miranda for an hour in the same place as their tongues danced together. For the first time, she had allowed him to touch her breasts through her blouse and, moaning, she stroked the inside of his thigh until he ached. Even now the memory aroused him. Tonight, they would finally throw off their clothes and make love on the blanket she always brought to ward off the chilly night air but never used once she was in his arms. He stared through the palms dotting the Bermuda-grass lawn at the illuminated top floor of her family's home. He knew she waited until her parents went to bed and they often stayed up well past midnight. Goddamn!

Gazing at the front of the two-story stucco structure with mahogany trim, covered balconies outside all three upstairs bedrooms, and a fountain burbling by the front door, he thought of his tiny one-room apartment. Each morning he awoke underneath the whirring fan with a groan, rolled off the foam cushion of his metal-framed bed, stepped around the small pine table that served as his writing desk, nightstand, and bookshelf, and stumbled sleepily to make himself instant coffee with boiling water from an electric kettle. The first few weeks, he had reveled in the austerity of his room and scorned the elegance of Miranda's family home as conspicuous consumption and criminal extravagance in the face of so much poverty. Gradually, as he spent more time in the lush garden with Miranda, envy, even respect, had grown. To create something so beautiful out of what had been acres of impassable jungle only a hundred years before required the determination and courage of several generations of her family.

A motorbike buzzed on the street outside the gate. He looked through the palms again; the upstairs lights shone brightly as if warning him: *Your wait will be long tonight.* He sighed, leaned back against the bench, and closed his eyes.

Rex felt something soft graze his lips and stirred. He inhaled the sweet, slightly spicy scent of Miranda's perfume and opened his eyes. She was leaning over him, head cocked to one side, a wide smile on her lips. A blanket lay folded over her left arm.

"If you are so tired, perhaps you should go back to your apartment," she teased.

"Only if you come with me," Rex replied and reached out to pull her down onto him. "Tomorrow is a holiday after all."

"Oh, Rex," she protested and pushed his hands away. "How many times must I tell you? I cannot."

"Then spread out the blanket here on the grass and lie down with me," he persisted. "You know you want to." He reached up for the blanket, but Miranda clasped it to her chest.

"Stop, Rex! Do you think what would be a sin in your apartment would not be a sin here? It is against my faith and . . . and would violate my vow to follow my family's traditions and the commandments of the Church to give myself solely to the man I marry."

"Why am I not that man?" he surprised himself by demanding. "You have said many times I look and sound more Filipino than many Filipinos. I've told you I would gladly become Catholic to please you. Besides," he quipped, "your faith doesn't prevent you from meeting me here at night, allowing my hands to run over your body, gasping when I caress your neck, climbing on my lap, pressing your hips against mine. You've said many times you loved me."

Miranda took a deep breath, looked back at her home for a long moment, and lowered herself beside him. A slight breeze ruffled the leaves of the *ilang-ilang* tree. Rex could feel her body strain to control her emotions. Finally, Miranda turned to face Rex and grasped his hands in hers.

"What my heart wants . . . what my body yearns for . . . I will not deny, but I also will not . . . cannot allow those temptations to overcome my faith in God, my devotion to my family. I know you have tried so very hard to act and talk and think like a Filipino and would even become Catholic to please me. I . . . I have appreciated your efforts and loved you for them. I even fooled myself that you could miraculously become a man with whom I grew up, a Filipino who feels in his soul what you have struggled to learn. I have dreamed of our wedding day." Miranda stopped and released Rex's hands. "Still, I am troubled. You have remade yourself so easily. You are eager to give up your own culture, tradition, and religion for me—and we have known each other less than four months!"

"But that's what love is, Miranda!" Rex exclaimed.

"No!" Miranda jumped to her feet her eyes flashing alarm. "No. No. No. Love is not *losing* yourself in another. It is *giving* yourself, as you *are,* to another," Miranda said, clutching the blanket to her chest. "I am so very, very sorry. It . . . it would not be fair to you if we continued to meet like this. I realize now, I cannot give what you want, and what you wish to give, I cannot take. I must let you go."

She raised her hand to her mouth and began to sway from side to side, sobbing. "I have much to atone for this Holy Week. Much to confess."

"Miranda! Please! Please don't leave me." Rex reached for her arm.

Miranda jerked it away and wiped tears from her eyes.

"I did love you, Rex Moreno. I truly did," she cried, wheeled around, and ran back toward the house.

"Here's to God and her fucking family," Rex hissed and took another gulp from the bottle of Tanduay he'd purchased on his way back to his apartment. He lurched over to the open window. In the dark, he could see none of Malabar City Park, but in the morning, he would look out over its grassy expanse to watch hawkers setting up their stands. He would raise his eyes to the miles of emerald sugar cane fields on the city's outskirts, and gaze out beyond them toward the mahogany and palm forests of the Malakili Highlands, verdant hills that rose steeply at the horizon to the crest of Mount Dalagang. The view, at once exotic and familiar, always stirred his spirit at the start of his day. Tonight, however, he stared out and saw only the black night. The smooth sweetness of the sugar cane liquor turned sticky and sour in his mouth. He poured more rum down his throat, the fiery liquid burning its way down to his stomach.

"I love her," he whispered to himself and suddenly realized, as often as he had repeated those words to Miranda, he felt it in his soul for the first time. "And I love living here," he admitted out loud, sweeping his hand out toward the city. The tightly knit web of family, church, and tradition had become second nature to him, no longer stifling but warming, nourishing. The prospect of losing Miranda and with her their scores of friends and his profound sense of belonging in Malabar City rocked him.

"Damn . . . damn . . . damn," he swore. "I have tried so fucking hard. Shit, what *more* do I have to do?" Rage flared inside him. "Goddammit! What more do I have to *do*?" he bellowed out the window.

"Why are you shouting at this time of night?" yelled a man from the apartment just below his. "Close your window and go to sleep!"

Rex heard the window below slam shut. He guzzled down the rest of the rum.

"Fuck her!" he hissed and flung the bottle as hard as he could out the window toward the park.

Wiping his mouth with the back of his hand, Rex began to turn from the window when he heard a loud *CRACK* and the shattering of glass. *What the hell?* He swung around. He couldn't have missed. The grass was too large, too close. A terrible thought suddenly took shape through the fog of rum. The statue of Miranda's great-great-grandmother! They were moving it to the park tonight. He slammed the window shut, pulled the curtains, and staggered to his bed. He began to shake. Sweat poured from his body, soaking his shirt. A vision of the bottle smashing the outstretched right arm of the statue flashed across his mind. His stomach convulsed. He jumped to the wash basin and retched. What had he done?

For two days, Rex hid in his apartment eating little and drinking only water. After a peek out his window on Wednesday morning, he could not bear another look at the statue, cordoned off and protected from further vandalism by thick plastic sheets. Behind closed curtains, he passed hours listening to radio broadcasts of homilies about Judas's betrayal of Jesus, Christ's washing of his disciples' feet, and the Last Supper, when Jesus foretold his suffering and death.

On Thursday evening, he walked quickly to the church as the Mass of the Lord's Supper began, stopping briefly at one of the stalls set up in the park. He slumped in a back pew, let the music and Latin chants meander through his mind, and hurried out before the Eucharist, making sure no one recognized him. Back in his apartment, he turned off the light. After putting flame to a candle and fixing his eyes on the picture of Miranda standing on his bedside table, he did something he had not done since he met Diana. He bent over to pray. He asked for forgiveness and begged to be cleansed of his sins, to be reborn.

The next morning, Rex knelt in the stifling heat on the grass with a score of other barefoot men. All wore black hoods garlanded with a crown of leaves and shirts whose backs had been torn away below the shoulders. He peered out through the slits in his hood at the statue of Miranda's great-great grandmother, still covered in thick plastic, and gazed at his surroundings.

A boisterous crowd had gathered around the men; hawkers sold fruit juice and young-coconut *samalamigs* and sticks of grilled chicken and pork; children screamed and scampered around the kneeling men. One of the *penitentes* in front shouted an order. Rex watched as the men unleashed their *burilyos* and began to flog their backs. He hesitated for a moment before unfurling his whip. The first few lashes stung sharply. He gasped for air and winced behind his mask with pain. With each stroke of the whip, he felt his back swell from the trauma. Another command rang out. The other *magdarame* paired off and started to make small cuts in each other's backs with razor blades. Rex had no partner so he removed the *panabad* he had purchased the night before from his belt, reached behind his back, and pressed the glass shards into his skin just above his pants. The glass felt cool, the way he had imagined Miranda's fingertips would feel when they at last caressed his skin. Rex gritted his teeth and scraped the *panabad* across his back in one slow motion. The pain seared. He gulped for air, felt faint, and lurched forward briefly. Forcing himself to imagine Miranda's fingernails digging into his back as they embraced under the *ilang-ilang* tree, he drew the broken glass twice more across his back, each time a little higher until the wounds reached just below his shoulder blades. He could feel blood ooze from the cuts and trickle down his back.

Rex replaced the *panabad* in his belt and closed his eyes, waiting for the other men to stand. When he heard them rise, Rex staggered to his feet and, like the others, held the rope end of the whip in two hands and began to swing the *burilyos* back and forth metronomically across his chest. The fourteen sharp bamboo sticks at the end of the whip, one for each station of the cross, flayed his bloody back. At first, Rex flinched as the bamboo cut into his wounds. After a short time the burning pain subsided to tingling and then to numbness.

Still whipping themselves, the *penitentes* marched barefoot out of the park. Rex followed as they moved in a steady beat of one lash for each step. Children ran through the procession, ducking in and out to avoid the *burilyos* while gawkers on motorbikes cruised along the side urging the hooded men onward. The flagellants stopped from time to time to pray at shrines, each signifying one of the fourteen stations. After a few minutes of worship, they continued winding through the streets of Malabar City to successive shrines until they reached the plaza where the church stood.

The crowd in the plaza parted, allowing the *penitentes* to pass through to an area just in front of the church portico. The odors of burning incense, smoke from grilled meat, and vomit from the *penitentes* swirled around Rex. The flagellants continued in silence to whip themselves as they stood in the plaza. The boisterous crowd grew quiet, observing in silent awe the gory spectacle of faith and devotion. Suddenly, one man fell to his knees with a groan, dropped the *burilyos* by his side, and lay prone on the cobblestone plaza, ankles crossed and arms outstretched to the side as if crucified. Several more men fell and prostrated themselves.

A few more lashes and Rex's eyes blurred. He sank to his knees and swayed from side to side for a few seconds. At last, he lay himself flat on his chest embracing the warm ground with his arms as he had once held Miranda. Rex closed his eyes and whispered, "Please forgive me. Please forgive me. Please forgive me." As his mind began to swim, he saw a vision of Miranda dressed in her white doctor's coat moving slowly among the *magdarame*, tending to wounds with a saint-like gentleness. He imagined her kneeling by his side, her hands cleaning the gashes on his back as she wept. He felt her tears spilling on his bloody back, salve to heal his wounds, balm to soothe his soul, and, he prayed, an elixir to be reborn as Filipino.

6 ROMANTICISM

Rex had no place to go. The air around him reeked of sweat, dust, and the metallic odor of dried blood. His room was a jail cell, closed in, stifling. He wanted to flee somewhere, anywhere, to escape the nothingness inside. He had given up Mama's devotion for the intoxication of striving to fulfill Diana's ideals and filled the void Diana left with the dream of a life with Miranda— only to be forsaken again. The lacerations on Rex's back burned, but not as intensely as the memory of Miranda recoiling in horror when she removed his black hood.

"Oh, dear God! Not you! Not *you*." Miranda cringed, covered her nose and mouth, and turned away in disgust. "Nurse!" she cried out. "Nurse, please help this . . . this poor soul." She pointed to Rex and, without a glance, bolted from the plaza.

Rex splashed water on his face and flinched as he washed his torso with a wet towel. He threw a few clothes in a small bag and staggered out of his room. Dazed, he roamed the streets of Malabar City, avoiding anywhere Miranda or her friends might walk. A shift in the direction of the breeze brought the briny smell of the ocean. He followed the scent down to the town's ramshackle fishing wharf. A muscular young man in shorts and sandals was helping an old woman with a bulky bag wobble down a ladder into a large outrigger canoe. A large mainsail and a smaller triangular foresail dangled in the air.

"Where are you going?" Rex called out.

"To Buaya, sir. A most beautiful island just over there."

The sailor pointed out toward the west and jumped down into the boat. Rex shaded his eyes from the sun and looked out, but could see only some haze on the horizon.

"How far is it?"

"It depends on the wind, sir. In this *paraw*, two hours is the usual."

"And you say it's beautiful? Peaceful?"

"A paradise, but you should see for yourself. I will give you a special rate. Only two *pisos* for the trip." He grinned and swept his hand over the boat, inviting Rex to board.

Rex had nothing left in Malabar. Taking refuge on a tropical island for a couple of days would give him time to rest and think about his past. Why had he allowed Diana and Miranda to misuse him so cruelly? Why had he not realized neither one understood love required sacrificing yourself for the sake of another, the way his mama always had for him and he had for her? He no longer believed Diana had loved him at all, but used him as a tool to further some ideological objective. And while Miranda said she loved him, she refused to abandon her family and her faith for the sake of that love, even after witnessing in the plaza the depth of his devotion to her.

"Excuse me," Rex called to the old woman. "Do you live on Buaya?"

"Yes, young man."

"Do you mind if I join you?"

"I'm bringing some books and supplies for a teacher in our school," she shrugged. "There is plenty of room."

Rex walked to the ladder, handed his bag down to the young man, and clambered down into the boat, grimacing at the sting from the wounds on his back.

"My name is Rex. I'm a teacher, too. Your package looks heavy. Let me help you when we arrive."

"You are very kind, sir."

Rex sailed from the Malabar City dock across serene, azure seas. As they approached the island, he spied the dark green of a rainforest lying just beyond the graceful curve of a gleaming white sand beach and breathed in a rich, earthy aroma. The smell was of dead trees rotting, but also of saplings reaching for the sun and the fruit and flowers of mature trees. The scent of the cycle of life itself, he thought. An omen of hope?

The boatman tied up the *paraw* at a wooden pier that extended out over shallow turquoise waters toward a series of rock breakwaters. Although he winced as he jumped onto the planks of the landing, Rex immediately sensed something changing inside himself: the months of stress from living in Malabar City and trying to please first Diana and then Miranda began to evaporate. He felt lighter, almost able to soar with the seabirds circling overhead. From that moment he knew he wanted to stay longer than a few days. A week or two respite in this tropical Eden would restore him physically and mentally.

"Where would you like me to put your package?" he asked the old woman as they walked off the pier.

"Right here on the sand. The schoolteacher will arrive in a moment."

Rex grunted in pain as he lowered the books onto the ground.

"Do you know a place I can rent for a few weeks?"

"The schoolteacher has a grandmother who owns the cottage over there," she pointed to a coconut-wood structure about two hundred yards down the beach. "I am certain she would be happy to rent it to you."

The old woman squinted past Rex and shaded her eyes with her hand.

"*Kamusta*, Joy." The old woman waved. "Here she comes now. I will introduce you to her."

Rex stared at the lissome figure of a young woman strolling down the dirt path toward them. The throbbing from the lacerations on his back eased.

"Mama? Mama?" Rex shouted into the telephone. A burst of static exploded in his ear. He jerked the handset away from his head briefly. "Are you there?"

"Oh my God! Honey! It really *is* you! *How* are you? *Where* are you?"

"I'm in a phone booth in Cebu City. Sorry I had to call collect again. I know it's not cheap."

"Don't worry. It is *so* good to hear your voice. Did you ever receive my letter?"

"Yes. Yes. I finally received it three days ago. Thank you for wiring money for airfare!"

"But I sent the letter more than two weeks ago. Aren't you in Malabar City anymore?"

"I was . . . but . . . well, I wanted to hear your voice, Mama. There's no reliable international service in Malabar."

"Oh, Rex. I have been just *beside* myself with worry. Why haven't you responded to the telegrams I sent you?"

"I'm sorry, Mama. I never received the telegrams. I wasn't in Malabar. When the letter was forwarded to me and I realized I had to go to the bank in Cebu, I decided to call you from here. Listen, I have some wonderful news."

"I'm confused. A couple of days ago a young man named Scott—or was it Skip?—called from Tokyo, of all places. He said he needed to talk with you. He was upset. What's going on? Did you stop teaching?"

"Yes. You remember the attack in Malabar I wrote you about?"

"Of *course* I do, honey."

"I needed time to recover from my injuries. The school gave me administrative leave and released me from my contract. The man you talked with is just a paper-pusher, drunk on his thimbleful of authority. My obligation was to the Lazaro School and they let me go a month ago."

"But what about . . . you know," Mama whispered into the phone, "your other work . . . with your professor . . . for the *agency*?"

He had completely forgotten the lie he'd told Mama about a secret project for the U.S. government. "Oh, I had actually finished just before the assault," Rex quickly replied.

"I am *so* glad. You can come home!" Mama gushed.

"No, I can't go home now."

"Honey, you have no reason to stay and I could help you recover more quickly."

"But I *do* have a reason to stay, Mama," Rex insisted.

Joy flashed in his mind—her large, milk-chocolate eyes, satiny *morena* skin, and a wide, sensuous mouth. Peace filled his heart, a profound calm he had never experienced with Diana or Miranda.

"That's my news. I . . . I've fallen in love with a woman who lives on a small island called Buaya. It's heaven, Mama. So different than the dirt and noise and stench of Malabar City with its oppressive Catholicism and its corrupt, feudal politics." As different, he thought, as Joy's natural grace and innate goodness was from the pompous pretense of Miranda and her family.

"That's why you didn't receive my telegrams? You've been on . . . where? Buaya? With a *woman*? How long?"

Mama's incessant questions began to erode his sense of well-being, but he held his irritation in check.

"Yes, Buaya. For the past month. Her name is Joy. And she's lovely."

"I thought you said you were in Cebu . . ."

"Mama!" Rex interjected loudly. "I'm in Cebu *now*. But I'm returning to Buaya as soon as we finish talking. The reason I called was to thank you for wiring me money for airfare and tell you I would be staying on Buaya for a while."

"Rex, listen to me. I want you to come *home*," Mama ordered.

Rex gritted his teeth. He didn't recall his mother being so demanding. But he would need her financial support to stay on Buaya, so he ruled out confronting her directly.

"Mama, you told me for years you wanted me to have the adventures you never experienced. I was always so grateful for that wise advice. I thought you'd be delighted . . ."

"Well, I am . . ."

"Mama," he interrupted her again. "Let me tell you about Joy. You'll understand why I want to stay."

His mother took a sharp breath that hissed over the line. "I'll bet she doesn't even speak English," she huffed.

"Of course she does!" Rex stifled a snort. "Joy is Ilonggo and speaks *three* languages: Hiligaynon, a regional language, Tagalog, the Philippines' national tongue, and English! She was raised on Buaya by her grandmother, her *lola*, but she graduated from a college in Malabar City."

Mama hesitated a moment. "You must care a great deal about her. Is she . . . well, is she *Christian*?"

"Oh, Mama," Rex snickered. "She's *Catholic*. But it's not like being Catholic in America or even Malabar City. Hers is a cheerful, unrepressed, almost ecstatic faith, intertwined with Hiligaynon folk traditions."

"But what do you talk about? I'll bet you don't have a *thing* in common." Mama's voice trailed into a whine.

"She has little interest in politics—a welcome contrast to *some* women I've known—and she cares deeply about her family and friends. She's the most genuine, giving person I've ever met." Rex hastened to add, "After you, of course, Mama."

Mama remained silent for a long time. "All right, honey. I guess a couple more months of vacation would be good for you," she finally exhaled. "But on one condition—you write me once a week to let me know how you are."

"Of course, Mama. Thank you! Love you, Mama!" Rex shouted into the receiver, then hung up and set out immediately to return to Buaya.

Gazing out over the water from his perch on the *paraw* headed to Buaya, he pictured the dark brown wooden bungalow he now called home—a word that he could never use in describing it to Mama. It wasn't spacious, just a tiny bedroom with a foam mattress pad and a sturdy bamboo nightstand, and a larger living area with a square teak table and a couple of teak chairs. Yet the building had a charming balcony overlooking the cerulean waters of the bay. Joy's *lola* had located the home close enough to the sea for a soothing breeze, yet near enough to a grove of coconut trees to benefit from their shade in the torrid afternoons. A smaller structure a few steps away had a metal tank on its corrugated plastic roof and contained two enclosures, one for an outdoor toilet and the other for a gravity shower. He knew in Mama's eyes it wouldn't compare to the houses in Shawnee Mission, but it had everything he needed. He couldn't wait to get back.

The morning after he returned from Cebu, he awoke at dawn as he had for the past month to the sound of jungle birds cawing and whooping. After a swim, he washed off the salt in the shower. While he showered, Joy stopped by on her way to school to prepare his breakfast—mangoes and papaya on rice made with sweetened coconut milk.

"Rex," she squealed when he sneaked up behind her and kissed her neck. "You know I cannot stay this morning. Please stop." She turned to stroke his cheek and rose up on her toes to kiss him lightly on the lips. "See you at dinner!" She waved and ran away up the dirt road that led to the small town of Dagaya about a mile away.

His eyes followed her up the path. He marveled at her beauty, an inborn elegance made all the more alluring because she seemed so oblivious of it.

After breakfast, Rex strolled into town, a scattering of one- and two-story wooden buildings with corrugated roofs and a handful of traditional stilt homes with thatched roofs. He chatted amiably with the old men and women selling fresh produce, eggs, and meat from nearby farms and glistening fish from local waters, haggled happily with the two or three shopkeepers in town over the few canned goods he needed, and played hide-and-seek with the small children.

"Rex! Rex!" everyone called out to him. "How are you this morning?"

"Well! Thank you," he responded over and over again. "How are you?"

"Come join us for lunch," one of the shopkeepers said with a wave of her hand.

"No, come join *us* for lunch," a fruit vendor interrupted.

"Perhaps another day," he replied to both, not wanting to accept one and offend the other. He basked in the warm smiles and genuine affection displayed by the people of Buaya, so unlike the shallow, deceptive game-playing nonsense in Malabar. He felt embraced by all as part of a large extended family.

As he steered toward home, he stopped by the elementary school, a worn coconut-timber and bamboo building, to catch a glimpse of Joy. He watched through a side window as she taught an English class. When a student answered correctly, she clapped her hands and beamed. She had graduated with honors from a Catholic women's college in Malabar City and could have stayed, but she returned to Buaya to teach, out of love for her community and her frail *lola.* To Rex, she embodied the two ideas essential to life on Buaya: *pakikisama,* getting along well with others, and *utang na loob,* reciprocity in life, repaying those who have treated you well.

Because it looked like rain, he had planned to read in his hammock that afternoon. When the sky suddenly cleared, he set out to explore the interior of Buaya, a pristine tropical forest crisscrossed by foot trails and dotted with waterfalls pouring into coruscating crystal pools. Birds in vibrant scarlet, jade, sapphire, and lemon colors swooped and cried overhead as he hiked. After returning home, he looked out from his balcony over the calm waters of his cove past emerald islets and enjoyed the zephyrs rustling through the trees. He thought back to the day he had flogged himself bloody and asked to be forgiven. Miranda had not heard his prayer, but he believed more strongly than ever that finding Buaya and Joy meant God had.

Joy walked from school to his cottage just after sunset to cook a simple meal of fried fish, cabbage, and rice, the salt of the fish complementing the sweet and sour cabbage. For dessert, she brought from a shop in town a *suman,* a luscious cake made of glutinous rice and coconut milk wrapped in banana leaves. Rex missed his mother's cooking from time to time, but loved being cared for by Joy. No longer the shy girl he first met, who cast her eyes down when she spoke and answered his questions with "sir," Joy exuded confidence. Her eyes twinkled as she told him about her day. No truer name was ever bestowed than hers, he thought. The sheer delight of being with her moved him to wax poetic.

"Will you stay tonight and look up with me at the great wheel of stars circling the heavens?" he asked as they finished their meal.

"My goodness! Such beautiful words. Are they for me?" she teased him.

"Inspired by you!"

"Ah, yes. Thank you. But no matter how lovely your words, I have to care for my *lola* tonight. She's not feeling well and needs me to massage her back and feet. I must assist her with the housework, too, and prepare my lessons for tomorrow. The mothers are coming to help the children plant vegetables in the school garden. I'm teaching them how we depend on plants for oxygen and how they absorb carbon dioxide for us, to show them how humans are part of the natural world, too. But tomorrow is Friday and I will be happy to stay with you tomorrow night and Saturday."

"I will miss you," Rex said and kissed her.

That night as he stared up at a night sky blanketed with stars, he thought back to the conversation with Mama and her inability—unwillingness?—to understand his decision to stay. The emotional gap between them on the call would have distressed him in the past. Why not now? As soon as he asked himself the question, he knew the answer: Joy. Hers was the most brilliant smile of the many smiles that surrounded him each day, but her determination to better herself and be kind to others endeared her to him even more. He knew in his bones that she loved him without reservation, as he was, for who he was. The emptiness he had felt the day he first came to Buaya had vanished. In its place, the assurance of her love filled him with peace.

Two months passed since Rex visited Cebu, with each day more perfect than the last—and all due to Joy. She taught him to live from his heart not his head. She helped him find his identity on Buaya and take pride in his place in the community. And she showed him the delight of living in harmony with nature without the glut of material possessions that life in Kansas and California seemed to demand. His love for Joy and for the life they lived crowded out his memories of Diana and Berkeley, Miranda and Malabar City, and even Mama and Shawnee Mission. Only when Joy's obligations to her *lola* kept her away from his side did visions of Mama, Diana, and Miranda flicker in his mind. As the days passed, however, they grew fainter and fainter.

"Are you excited about the *paraw* race and the celebration for Saint Mary Magdalene this week? It's the most important festival of the summer."

Joy gazed down at Rex, who was lying on his back, eyes half closed, his hands behind his head. Even half asleep, she thought, he was such a handsome man. Would he also be a kind one?

"Will you wear the woven *tampi* I gave you around your waist like a true Ilonggo?" Joy asked in her soft, songlike voice, as she slid next to Rex and snuggled up against him.

Rex inhaled her loamy scent and rolled over to admire her umber eyes, her glowing skin, and her lovely mouth—a mouth that could emit a cackle as loud as her grandmother's.

"Of course I will wear the *tampi*. You and your family and friends have accepted me as Ilonggo so I will dress as one. You know, I've missed you terribly the past four nights," Rex sighed, then lifted a strand of her dense, silky black hair away from her forehead and kissed her brow. He reached down to cup her left breast and felt himself stiffen.

"I have something to tell you, Rex," she whispered and placed her hand on his.

"Can't it wait?" he asked and ran his hand over the flat of her stomach. Joy grasped his hand and brought it to her face.

"No, it cannot," she replied, the nostrils of her small, wide nose flaring, tears falling from her eyes. "Do you remember when we became lovers in May how I told you I hoped to have your child one day?"

"Yes. And I replied several times I could not imagine a more beautiful existence than the one we already led and absolutely did not want a child—"

"—because you felt one would ruin our carefree life together," Joy interjected, searching Rex's face for a sign that his mind had changed.

"Yes, I remember," Rex said, his eyes narrowing. "Why? What's happened?"

Joy looked away for a second, swallowed hard, and pursed her lips. "I am with child," she murmured and began to whimper like a wounded animal. She raised her hand to her mouth. Her whole body trembled as she sobbed uncontrollably.

Rex reflexively stared down at Joy's stomach, expecting a small bulge, but saw nothing. He cupped her chin with his palm, brought her eyes up to meet his, and searched in vain for the spark of life she said lay within her.

"Are you sure? Perhaps you are just late this month."

Joy wiped her eyes and took a long, slow breath.

"I am now three weeks late. Four or five days ago I woke up with an awful feeling in my stomach and could not eat anything. My grandmother immediately asked me if my monthly bleeding was late. When I confessed it was, she took me to a *hilot* in the town, a kind of midwife, who examined me down here." Joy pointed to her vagina. "She said I was swollen and my skin had darkened. Then she looked at the color of my pee. The *hilot* is certain I am pregnant."

"Jesus, this is a surprise." Rex exhaled, flipped on his back, and stared up at the wooden ceiling. She felt his body shudder. He turned on his side to face her. "How could this happen?" he demanded. "You said you knew your cycle and it never varied. We were so *careful.*"

"I am very sorry. You are mad at me. It's my fault," Joy cried out, slapping her fist against her chest and casting down her reddened eyes. She was terrified he would ask her to choose between losing him and losing her unborn child.

Rex sat up and gazed at Joy. She had covered her eyes with her hands. Her body shook. In May, he could not conceive of a life with Joy and a baby. Still . . . confronted with the life growing inside her, a being as much his as hers, a desire to protect Joy, to safeguard their child and its mother cascaded through him, submerging his anxiety. Visions of the future tumbled across his mind: a smiling Joy ripe with their child, a sleepy Joy singing their baby asleep, a laughing Joy mimicking the waddle of their toddler, a proud Joy watching their son scamper across the sand to his father, to him, to Rex.

"No," Rex murmured. He lifted her hands from her face and wiped the tears from her cheek. "It's not your fault. I was . . . shocked at the news and upset, but no longer. I had worried a child would change our life together, a life that delighted me beyond words. But, I see now, a child—*our* child—will bring even more happiness to us. Your news fills me with . . . with you, with Joy." He wrapped her in his arms.

"Oh, I am *so* glad," she sighed and ran her hands along his back, over the scars she had never found the courage to ask about. "I worried you might not want me anymore."

"No, no!" replied Rex immediately. "The news has made a difficult decision much easier for me," he continued. "I have been struggling to decide if I should return to the United States, to please my mother, or stay here, knowing my soul had found a home with you. Now that I know you carry our baby, my mind is clear. My heart is calm. I belong here."

"What? What about your mother?" Joy began to mewl. "She will be angry with you, and me, too. That will not be good for our child. We will need her help in Kansas."

"Kansas? Dear Joy, don't you understand? I will invite her to come meet you and experience Buaya for herself. She won't be mad. She'll see the tranquil beauty of life here. She'll feel the glow of your family's humanity and the warmth of our friends in Dagaya. She'll see why we want to raise our child surrounded by natural beauty; why Buaya is so much better than the United States."

"You are right. I don't understand," Joy declared and wiggled free from Rex's arms. "You don't want our child to be born in the United States, to enjoy the childhood your mama gave to you in Kansas, to attend good schools, to be cared for by good doctors, to be an American citizen?"

"Look, I . . . I haven't had a chance to think everything through. Still, I *love* our life here. I think I would want our child to live a simple, uncomplicated life in tune with nature and supported by loving people, to have all the wonderful things that brought you back here from Malabar."

"Now, *you* do not understand." Joy closed her eyes momentarily. "I didn't come back because I *wanted* to. I dreamed of traveling to Manila and someday working in the United States. *Utang na loob* made me return. My *lola* had raised me. She was aging and needed help. She begged me to return so I had no choice. In America, life would be so much easier for our child, for *lola*, for us."

"I . . . I don't know," Rex stammered, momentarily struck dumb by a vision of Joy's grandmother wandering around his mother's Shawnee Mission home. "Your grandmother would miss her family and friends here and would certainly suffer in the hot, dry summers and freezing winters."

"Hmm," Joy murmured. She reached out to play with the hair on his chest. "Perhaps you are right. We can send her money from the United States. She can pay a girl to do the work I do. It would be very little in U.S. dollars. And we can return here every summer so our child will know Buaya as we do. That's a good plan, don't you think?" she asked brightly.

"Joy, why aren't you listening to me?" Rex clutched her hand. "I cherish our life here. I have never experienced such serenity. You have made me feel accepted. You have taught me the bliss of a simple existence at one with nature."

Joy stared at Rex. How could he want to trade the advantages of Kansas for the hardships of Buaya?

"Life here is simple but only because we are so poor. Look at my *lola*," she cried and waved in the direction of her grandmother's shack. "She is only thirty-nine years older than me and she is wrinkled and bent from enduring your *simple* life!" Joy's mouth twisted in sarcasm.

Rex's head jerked back. Joy had never before raised her voice, never before ridiculed him.

"Enough," he yelled, thrusting his chin out. "I would be miserable in Kansas! Forced to wear a suit and tie at some crummy desk job just to pay for possessions we don't need, settling in a city of asphalt and concrete cut off from nature's splendor, feeling my face flush at the subtle and not-so-subtle slights our child and you will suffer from the racism endemic in American society, slowly suffocating without the sense of belonging, the peace that is in the air we breathe here. No, Joy. *No.* This is my home now. *Our* home. Our *family's* home. We are *not* going to the United States. That's final." Rex struck the mattress with his fist.

Joy sat up and stared for several moments into Rex's eyes. His sudden rage startled and frightened her. She stiffened as though an electric shock had traveled up her spine. She opened her mouth to protest, but swallowed her words when she saw his jaw set with determination. She collapsed against him, wailing.

"Okay, Rex," she murmured after she had calmed herself. "Now I understand you."

Joy slogged in the torrential monsoon rain up a muddy path from her *lola*'s house. She had spent much of the morning ankle-deep in stinking filth shoveling muck to clean out the drain from the pig pen and nailing down a plastic tarp over the chicken run so the typhoon winds wouldn't tear it away again. Her *lola* was only sixty-one years old, but she could not manage physical labor; arthritis had gnarled her hands and decades of carrying heavy packs on her back had begun to buckle her backbone.

As Joy trudged up through a stream of water flowing down the trail, she ruminated on her decision and concluded again she had no choice. Even without a child, she could no longer teach and take care of her aging *lola* whose memory seem to evaporate like the morning mist and who often didn't know where she had put her sewing or the kitchen utensils or the oil for the lamp. Joy covered her mouth with a hand to stifle a sob.

And she could no longer rely on Rex. Fantasies of an ideal life on Buaya fluttered in his head like butterflies, and she knew his smooth, soft hands, while pleasurable on her skin, could not tolerate planting or plowing or fishing to support a family. A few months of grueling labor and he would desert her and her child. Joy could teach in Iloilo for more money than on Buaya and afford, just barely, to live there and pay a young Dagaya girl to care for her grandmother. She silenced the voice shouting *Shame, shame!* in her head by swearing to herself she would say a thousand Acts of Contrition and visit her *lola* every weekend. Her soul brimmed with pain and remorse, but she had chosen the only path that would ensure the well-being of her *lola* and preserve a glimmer of hope for her own future.

She arrived at her destination, a wooden shack on the side of a corn field about a mile outside of Dagaya. Inside, the *hilot*, a lively woman with a round, flat face and a nearly toothless grin, gave Joy an empty pint-sized rum bottle that had been filled with a dark purple concoction.

"Drink this," she commanded.

Joy unscrewed the cap and peered inside at a frothy liquid with a pungent, tart smell.

"What is this?"

"It is a tea brewed from RC Cola, the root of the *makabuhay* plant, and a handful of dried skins from the *lanzones* fruit. Drink it."

Joy gulped down half the bottle and gagged at the chalky, foul taste.

"You must drink it all. When you have, take off your clothes and lie down here for the massage," the *hilot* said, pointing to a cot in the middle of the room.

Joy forced herself to swallow the rest of the tea, then stripped away her blouse and skirt and lay down on the bed, staring at the ceiling. The *hilot* moved below Joy, leaning forward and gripping her lower abdomen with both hands in a pincer-like hold. Then she thrust her hands together crushing Joy's stomach and released, crushed and released, crushed and released. After a few minutes, sweat covered Joy's entire body. She felt nauseated and began to moan. The *hilot* stepped to Joy's side, raised her right fist, and started to strike Joy rhythmically just above the vagina as if Joy's abdomen were a single-headed gimbal drum. Joy's sobs turned to howls of pain as the *hilot* pounded her abdomen over and over and over again.

Joy did not return the next evening to prepare his dinner, but Rex didn't worry. They had reconciled after their brief disagreement, and she had embraced him fiercely before leaving in the morning. Besides, one of the occasional summer typhoons heading northwest across the Philippines had brought strong winds and rain to Buaya. Rex assured himself she was caring for her *lola*. He prepared a dinner of rice and cut-up carrots, okra, and squash boiled with ginger and scallions on his two-burner propane stove. After his meal, the winds died down. He lay back on his cot in the dim light of a kerosene lamp, listening to the rain drumming against his roof. An exquisite contentment swelled inside of him. He had at last found his place in the universe and a meaning to his life. He was Joy's lover and protector and soon, the father of their child. He fell asleep dreaming of Joy cradling their baby while he wrapped his arms around them both.

The following morning dawned fresh and clear. Rex swam, showered, and consumed his favorite breakfast of mangoes, rice, and sweetened coconut milk. Since the rain had stopped, he expected Joy to come by so they could walk around the island to view the *paraw* race and afterwards stroll hand-in-hand into Dagaya for lunch and to shop for dinner. To please her, he wrapped around his waist the red and white checked *tampi* she had given him. When he heard footsteps at his door, a broad smile split his face. He flung the door open, ready to embrace his love, the mother of his child, the woman who had given him new life as surely as she would give life to their baby. When he saw Joy's *lola*, he dropped his arms and stepped out. Her unexpected presence alarmed him.

"Why are you here? Where is Joy?" he asked, speaking slowly so her *lola* would understand.

"Joy gone," her grandmother declared, resting her left hand on her arthritic hip and waving her right hand up in the air as if it were smoke from a fire disappearing into the night sky.

"What do you mean?" Rex demanded, struggling to talk evenly. "Where has Joy gone?"

"Joy gone Iloilo."

"Why?" Rex exclaimed. "Is she sick?"

"No. Joy okay. Look for job in Iloilo."

Rex recoiled in shock. Acid rose up his esophagus and singed the back of his throat. He fought to keep his mind from careening out of control.

"No . . . wait. That . . . that cannot be!" he shouted.

Joy's *lola* shrugged and turned to leave. Panicked, Rex reached out, grabbed the old woman by the shoulders, and spun her around. She screamed with pain.

"*Ahhh!* Stop, mister. Stop!" she begged.

Rex released her and she backed away with her hand held up to fend off the enraged American.

"Wait!" he cried. "Wait. Please. Joy is carrying our child."

"No." She shook her head vigorously.

"What do you mean, *no*? She told me she was pregnant."

"No. No baby, Mister. Sorry."

"*What?*" Rex bellowed in agony.

"Sorry. No baby."

"*Nooooooooooooo*," he roared and dropped to his knees. His dream of an idyllic life on Buaya vanished. His vision of a future with Joy, with their baby, so vibrant last night, faded in a moment. He could not believe Joy—lovely, kindhearted, guileless Joy—had lied to him. Why? The answer thundered in his brain. She never loved him! She was never pregnant! She misled him thinking he would take her to America! Once there, she would have faked a miscarriage and abandoned him. His insistence on their living on Buaya surprised her and thwarted her scheme.

Rather than admit her duplicity and ask his forgiveness, she fled to Iloilo. She pursued her dreams, not giving a damn that her selfishness obliterated his. He saw himself now as she must have: a quixotic fool. Pain shot through his temples. How could he have been duped again?

"Goodbye, Mister Rex. You go home now," the old woman said, pointing out over the sea. "To States. Goodbye. Goodbye."

Rex gazed up at Joy's *lola* and watched her limp away. He glanced back at what had been his home only a few minutes before. A mud-splattered, dilapidated shack stood in its place. He looked out at what had this morning been the pure white sand and turquoise waters of the bay and saw now water cloudy with silt and a beach covered with debris from the typhoon. He felt the earth sway beneath him as if he were crouched on a *paraw*. His stomach churned and tightened. He retched violently. His favorite breakfast, acidified into a stinking mash, spewed out, soaking the *tampi* Joy had given him to wear.

The hollowness he felt the first day he sailed to Buaya swamped him again. Without Joy, what was he to do? Where was he to go? Only one answer rose to mind. He would do what Joy's *lola* had told him to do. He would go home. Home to the one true constant in his life. Home to Mama.

7 Isolation

Rex stared in astonishment at Miranda across the crowded, dimly lit cafeteria of Les Villages Internationaux, which had been converted into a *discothèque* for a Friday night party. The Stones' "Jumpin' Jack Flash" blared from speakers. The funky smell of sweaty bodies hung over the dance floor. He had descended in a preoccupied haze minutes before from his tiny room on the fourth floor of La Résidence des États-Unis, one of the dormitories in the mammoth residential complex for foreigners studying in Paris. Avoiding the polyglot throng pulsing to the beat, he intended to forage quickly for something to eat and return to his reading about Wilson at the Paris Peace Conference. But the sight of Miranda talking animatedly with two Nordic-looking young men confounded him. What was she doing here? Had she tracked him over the last eight months to Paris? Had she finally realized how much he had sacrificed for her? How much she loved him for his devotion? How her revulsion at his bloodstained back had devastated him? His heartbeat quickened at the thought of holding her again. As he threaded his way toward her through the multinational swarm, she vanished behind the two enormous men and reappeared with her back toward him.

"Miranda! What are you doing here?" he called, but she didn't hear him over the thumping bass and the cacophony of voices. He moved closer and reached out to touch her shoulder.

"Miranda! It's me. Rex!" he shouted.

She whipped around and stared at him. Her lips snarled. She raised her arms as if holding a machine gun and pumped imaginary bullets into his chest.

"*Ne me touchez pas, salaud Américain!*"

Rex jumped back in shock. The young Asian woman who looked so much like Miranda from across the room wasn't Miranda at all. She had Miranda's lovely frame and luminous complexion, but her face, while beautiful, was moon-shaped and her skin a shade lighter.

"I'm sorry," he mumbled. "I don't speak French. I . . . I thought you were a friend of mine."

"Do not touch me, American bastard!" the young woman hissed in French-accented English, her almond eyes flaring. "My name is not Miranda. I am Tran Kim-Ly and I am no friend of yours or any American. You have destroyed my country, murdered my people."

"You're Vietnamese? I'm . . . I'm so sorry . . ." Rex stammered.

"Sorry?" She spat out the words like spoiled milk. "Did you march in Washington to bring down your bloody government? No? Then you are guilty of killing my friends. Get away from me now!" she commanded, raising her imaginary machine gun again and firing point blank at his chest.

"I'm sorry, so sorry," Rex said, thrusting his palms out as he staggered back.

He spun unsteadily around, his shoulder grazing the arm of a tall, blonde woman with sky-blue eyes who looked at him with alarm. Stumbling through the crowd and across the courtyard of Les Villages Internationaux, he hurried back to the sanctuary of his room. He sat on his bed, his hands shaking, and struggled to push from his mind the image of bullets pouring into his body.

Several days later, Rex sat alone in a chilly, musty corner of the Sorbonne library engrossed in his reading. A stack of books stood on his desk. As he pored over the memoir of an assistant secretary to the American delegation to the Paris Peace Conference, he scribbled notes on index cards. From time to time, the memory of Tran Kim-Ly shooting at him would break his concentration and send a chill down his spine. He forced himself to focus.

Maddie had just returned a volume on the Lost Generation of expatriate writers in 1920s Paris when she saw the American, the one from the party whom Tran Kim-Ly had yelled at a few nights before. He was bent over a book with his head resting in his hand. She turned to walk out of the library into the damp fall air, then stopped and gazed back. She remembered the hurt and confusion she had seen in his eyes as he fled the party. No one defended him. No one left with him. Perhaps he was as alone in this cold, dark city as she was? She stepped over to his desk.

"Mind if I disturb you for a moment?" she whispered.

Rex looked up from his seat into the face of the tall, athletic young woman he had nearly run over as he fled the party at Les Villages Internationaux. She had an unmistakable girl-next-door allure.

"Not at all. I'm Rex Moreno."

"I'm Maddie, Maddie Erickson. I saw you at the party last Friday night. I . . . I thought what Kim-Ly did to you was awful. You didn't deserve to be treated that way."

She slid on to the chair facing Rex.

"Nice of you to say. I saw you, too. But she's right, you know, to be furious with us Americans," Rex said. "Our actions in Vietnam have been criminal."

Maddie felt her nose crinkle. "Not *our* actions. Perhaps some of the acts of our government have been misguided, but the Viet Cong haven't been saints either."

"What do you mean?" he demanded. How could she challenge his perspective on the war? His views had been fortified over the course of two years by reading Marcuse, Halberstam, Mailer, and Kahin. He launched into the speech he had given fourteen months before at Berkeley.

"When our military assistance couldn't save the colonial French from defeat, we invaded their country on the pretext of stopping an aggressive global communist movement before it took over all of Asia. The Viet Cong are in fact *agrarian* revolutionaries fighting to save their country from American imperialism, from the grasp of our *rapacious* capitalist system, from our murderous military industrial complex," he thumped his fist on the table.

He imagined the crowd outside Sproul Hall cheering him as they did last October and raised his eyebrows, anticipating Maddie's admiration.

"Maybe some Vietnamese believe that, but not all of them," Maddie insisted. "The South Vietnamese certainly don't."

"The South Vietnamese government is an *illegitimate* puppet regime financed, armed, and *manipulated* by our bloody government," Rex snorted. "How can you cite them as representing the views of the Vietnamese people?"

"Look—" Maddie stood up scraping her chair against the floor. She didn't appreciate being lectured to, especially by someone she had gone out of her way to comfort. "You obviously have studied this a lot more than I have. See you around."

"No, *wait*. I'm sorry," Rex said, suddenly realizing how starved he was for human connection. "Please don't go. I . . . I haven't had a lot of contact with people recently and my social skills are rusty. You were kind enough to offer me support and I ended up haranguing you about the war. Occupational hazard, I guess. I spent a year doing almost nothing else. Typical know-it-all poly-sci major," he apologized. "Please sit down."

"Thanks, but you've obviously got a lot of work to do and so do I," Maddie replied and shoved her chair in. "I just wanted to tell you how badly I felt you were treated. That's all. Goodbye." She pivoted to walk away.

"And I really appreciate it. I do," Rex shot up from his seat and gestured to the chair across from him. "*Please* sit down, Maddie. I'm so sorry."

Maddie turned and examined Rex. He was holding out his hands and staring at her with wide eyes. He seemed to have shed the condescending attitude and sincerely wanted her company. She had been pretty isolated in Paris, too.

"Maybe just for a few minutes," Maddie pulled out her chair and sat down. "I admit I haven't studied the war the way you have. All I'm saying is that nothing justifies some of the things the Viet Cong did."

"Like what?" Rex asked, leaned forward, and wove his fingers together on the desk.

"A friend of mine was in the army over there a couple of years ago. He told me about a deeply religious boy from Virginia—raised a Mennonite—who was a conscientious objector. Because of his faith, he refused to kill, but he loved America and wanted to support his country, so he went to Vietnam as an unarmed medic. He was captured in a battle and taken prisoner. My friend said they found him hanging from a tree with his genitals stuffed in his mouth."

"My God!" Rex jerked back. Diana had cursed the massacre at My Lai and loudly condemned atrocities committed by American soldiers, but she had never suggested the Viet Cong could be as depraved. She painted them as heroic fighters against imperialism and any reports to the contrary she dismissed as government lies.

"Are you . . . are you sure the story isn't U.S. government propaganda?"

"My friend was there. He saw what they did to that poor boy."

Rex scrutinized Maddie to see if she was exaggerating. Her eyes had dropped to the desk and her shoulders sagged as if the effort to report such cruelty drained her. She was either an accomplished actress or completely sincere.

"I guess both sides have committed immoral acts. Still, that Mennonite medic would be alive today if our government hadn't sent him to fight an unjust war."

"You're right about that." Maddie nodded, looking up. "We have no business fighting wars thousands of miles away, wasting money that could be better spent at home. I'm glad we signed the Paris Peace Accords and withdrew our troops in March. But I don't believe America is evil. What use could a backward, agricultural country like Vietnam be to American capitalism? We were fighting against communism, to help the Vietnamese be free. I think our intentions were good even if we made mistakes."

"The road to hell is—" Rex began when Maddie interrupted.

"—paved with good intentions."

"Samuel Johnson," Rex couldn't resist adding smugly.

"Actually, St. Bernard de Clairvaux," Maddie corrected him with a sly smile and raised eyebrows, delighted to have taken a little wind out of Rex's sails. When she saw his face fall, she decided to reciprocate with an apology. "Sorry. I major in literature. I guess I suffer from the same occupational hazard."

Rex laughed lightly and inspected Maddie's face. Perhaps he had misjudged her.

"Don't apologize," he insisted, happy to move the conversation to common ground. "It's December 1973, after all, and any sensible man enjoys being around a smart, strong woman like you."

Maddie's mouth opened slightly in surprise. Rex's personality had morphed from contemptuous to apologetic and from insecure to sweet. She was perplexed but also curious about this intelligent and attractive man with an air of melancholy even more intense than her own.

"That's nice of you to say. But you *are* right, Rex. We were bound to screw up over there." She threw her hands out in frustration. "Understanding people—*really understanding* people—from a different country and culture is impossible."

"I couldn't agree more . . ."

"*Silence, s'il vous plaît!*" hissed an owlish old woman from behind the information desk.

"Would you like to get a coffee?" Rex leaned forward and whispered. "There's a café around the corner where a lot of American expats hang out. Not much cigarette smoke and they don't mind speaking English."

Maddie smiled warmly. "Sure. Let's go."

Rex stuffed his books into his briefcase and slung the strap over his shoulder. Ten minutes later they were sitting at a small, round marble table in the back of Le Café Américain, sipping their coffee.

"How long have you been here?" Maddie blew on her coffee. "I don't remember seeing you before the party."

"Three very long months," Rex replied. "I spend almost all of my time in my room or at the Sorbonne library doing research for my master's thesis in political science. I've hardly spoken to another person in weeks, which is probably why I ranted at you.

Sorry again . . . Do you live in La Résidence des États-Unis? I haven't seen you before either."

"For the past two and a half months, but I'm barely there other than to sleep. I spend most of my time at ACIP."

"ACIP?"

"The American College in Paris, near the American Church in the seventh district. The food's much better than the cafeteria at Les Villages Internationaux."

"Yeah, it couldn't be worse. I usually cook something in my room on a hot plate. You know, oatmeal for breakfast and soup or stew for lunch and dinner. I don't like the cafeteria food either. Too saucy, and I can't stomach eating a vinegary salad after the meal."

"I think they wait to serve it on the same plate as the main dish to disguise how old the lettuce is."

"That would be funny if it weren't so true." Rex laughed.

"What's your thesis on?"

"Wilson's attempt to build an international order at Versailles. I contend he was not just idealistic but almost criminally credulous; therefore, doomed to fail. He spent so much time and political capital on the League of Nations, he neglected more important domestic problems to America's detriment. Just like we were saying."

"The road to hell . . . ?"

"Yeah. What are you studying?"

"I'm getting a masters in American literature at Stanford. The professor supervising my work is teaching this quarter at ACIP. Why I'm here. My thesis is on how F. Scott Fitzgerald's work suffered because of his frequent visits to Paris and his friendships with Hemingway and others in the expat community here. He was a great writer, of course, but I argue he could have accomplished so much more had he stayed in New York."

Rex stirred a spoonful of sugar into his coffee. "So . . . you said you think understanding foreigners is impossible. Why?"

"Because of my experience living in Taiwan and Japan . . ." Maddie said, biting the inside of her lip. She laid her hands on the marble tabletop.

"I went to Taiwan pretty naive, thinking girls there would more or less be like girls in America. They weren't at all, of course, and learning that lesson was excruciatingly painful. The next summer—after my freshman year in college—I traveled to Japan determined not to make the same mistake. I educated myself about the culture and thought I understood the differences between their society and ours. I became really close to a Japanese girl; like she was a sister. I believed in my heart we respected and trusted and even loved each other, notwithstanding our differences." Maddie sighed. "In the end, I discovered no amount of study or hours spent sharing feelings with her gave me any *real* insight into how this Japanese girl would react in important situations, or how she felt about life. She deceived me and didn't realize how foolish she made me feel."

Maddie peered down into her coffee.

"We can't really grasp why foreigners behave the way they do, so going overseas, even with the best intentions, is fraught with risk. We make mistakes and get hurt and become disillusioned," she sniffed. "Not that they understand us. I don't think they even try! They expect us to be like them and, if we're not— and how could we be?—they reject us or, worse, take advantage of us."

Rex nodded sympathetically.

"I spent some time in the Philippines. I thought I understood the people—English is widely spoken, they're Catholic like a lot of Americans, and they often have family or friends in America. I discovered I didn't know them at all, not really. They didn't appreciate me, either. Like you said, they expected me to behave like them. I bent over backwards to fit in. I struggled to gain their approval, but failed miserably. It was like an invisible cultural force-field repulsed me whenever I attempted to get close to people."

Rex stared out the window of the café for a moment. A light rain was falling, making the afternoon light dusky. He turned back to face Maddie.

"They thought I was a fool for trying so hard to understand them . . ." Rex squeezed his eyes for a second trying to shut out memories of the Philippines. He balled his hand into a fist.

"I know exactly how you feel," Maddie said, placing her hand briefly on his fist. "Really, I do."

"I *never* wanted to go abroad again, but my advisor insisted I see the papers of the U.S. delegation held at the Sorbonne," Rex continued. "So, here I am. I spend all my time working through the research as quickly as I can. I feel so . . . cut off. I can't wait to go home."

"Me neither. I thought living in France would be easier than Asia. You know, the French are Western and their culture and language are so similar to ours. They look and talk and dress more or less like us, which makes the inability to connect with them even more frustrating. I didn't expect them to be so different, but they are!"

"The same with Filipinos and why I've kept away as much as possible from the French. Besides, they smoke like chimneys, even indoors."

"I wish I could avoid them. When I arrived in mid-October, there were a few sunny, warm days. I would stroll through the Luxembourg Gardens, smiling and happy, dressed in shorts or jeans, like I would in California. French guys would hoot and whistle and even try to talk with me. I don't speak French, but I would tell them to get lost in English. They'd just laugh and keep following me until I had to call a taxi. They made me feel like a whore."

"I'm so sorry, Maddie. It isn't still happening, I hope?"

"No, I complained about it to an American girl I met at ACIP. She said they would leave me alone if I stopped dressing like an American from California and wore clothes like a French girl. You know, fancy dresses and pants and an ankle-length coat all in a dark color. She also warned me to stop smiling and keep my eyes lowered when I walked in public. Can you believe it?"

"It worked?"

"Sure, but at what *cost*?" Maddie demanded hands outstretched. "I hate pretending to be someone I'm not . . . just so I can walk through a park without being mistreated? I sacrificed a part of who I am. The whole experience made me feel even lonelier here. I . . . I told a friend from home, who's in Japan, I wanted to spend all my time at ACIP. He said not to judge French guys by American standards or take their conduct personally. He said I shouldn't *define* myself by my clothes, I should try to blend in. He made me so mad."

"What about your smile? That's a pretty important part of who you are."

"Exactly!" Maddie's eyes flashed and she slapped the tabletop.

"Anyway, it's easy for him to say," Rex snickered. "He doesn't have to deal with the hassles a beautiful woman like you does."

"Oh." Maddie blinked in surprise. "Thank you." She smiled and touched Rex's arm lightly again. "A lot of handsome guys like you don't find tall, athletic girls attractive."

"A lot of guys are pretty dumb!" Rex exclaimed and studied Maddie's eyes. He smiled and looked down for a moment. "I hope you don't mind my asking . . ." he said, folding his hands on the table and leaning forward. "Is your friend in Japan a boyfriend type of friend?"

"Oh, we've known each other forever, dated in high school, and . . . well . . . began to see each other a lot junior year; he was at UCLA while I was at Mills College. We even talked about living together after graduation. He surprised me by taking a position in Japan."

"Mills!" Rex cried out. He was about to add that he had visited many times, but choked back his words. His instincts told him Maddie wouldn't appreciate hearing about his experiences with Mills girls.

"I'm getting my masters at Berkeley, just down the road." Rex stood up. "Excuse me for a second. Strong coffee shoots through me pretty quickly. I need *les toilettes*." He stepped by Maddie, allowing his palm to graze her shoulder. "Be right back."

"Sure," Maddie sighed.

She closed her eyes and thought back to the last time she'd seen Skip. The pale blue of San Francisco Bay came to mind. Oakland harbor shimmered in the foreground and the Bay Bridge and city skyline rose in the background. Pines framed the view. She could almost smell their sharp, sweet scent. She had roused Skip from their motel room on a sunny, early May morning to hike the Sequoia Bayview Trail before it became too crowded with small children, dogs, and mountain bikes. She wanted them to be able to talk without distraction.

"It's beautiful, isn't it?" Maddie reached out to wrap her arm around Skip.

"Yes. I didn't know the Oakland hills had so many parks and trails."

"I can't wait to show them all to you. After graduation, when you've moved back from LA, we'll have so much more time together," Maddie enthused. "I saw an ad for a guest house in the Berkeley Hills. It looks perfect for us."

Maddie felt Skip's muscles tense. She cocked her head and examined him. He looked away, avoiding her eyes.

"I know we haven't decided to live together yet, but it doesn't hurt to look, does it?" She laughed lightly, stepped in front of Skip, and kissed him softly on the lips. He didn't respond. "Does it?"

Skip gazed out toward the west, past the city to where the Pacific wrapped the horizon like a pale blue ribbon. And beyond, to where his mind often wandered.

"Maddie, I told you I wasn't sure what I wanted to do after graduation."

"I know, but we've been together every other weekend or so for almost a year and a half now. And it feels so damn good, so easy, so . . . well, complete. I just . . . oh, I just thought the next step would be to live together."

Skip rubbed the tension from his shoulder, took a deep breath, and exhaled loudly like air released a balloon.

"What if I wanted to travel, to live abroad before settling down? Would you understand? Would you consider coming with me? Please say you would."

"What do you mean?"

"I've . . . I've decided I want to take the VSA job. If I work in their San Francisco office for six months after graduation, I can direct the Japan program in Tokyo. It's a great opportunity and the Japan part is only a two-and-a-half-year commitment."

"What?" Maddie erupted. "What do you mean ONLY a two-and-a-half-year commitment? I can't believe it! You know how I feel about Japan. I will never go back there."

"I thought you might look at it differently if I was there with you. We couldn't live together, not being married, but we could stay in the same building, spend just as much time with each other as if we were living together. On break we could travel around Asia. It would be fun, an adventure, something we'd remember for the rest of our lives."

"I am NOT following you to Japan. I've told you a hundred times what happened to me there. I can't trust any of them. Besides, what would I do? I wouldn't have any friends. I can't speak the language. I would be totally dependent on you!"

"There's a large expat community. I'm sure we'd make lots of friends. You could earn a ton of money teaching English to Japanese businessmen. Besides, my job recruiting and training volunteers would bring us back to the Bay Area for a couple of months each year so we could see our families and friends. Please, Maddie, think about it."

"I won't go and that's final." Maddie stomped her foot and crossed her arms.

"Maddie, please," he begged and grabbed her shoulders. "Can't you compromise just this once? For Christ's sake, I waited TWO AND A HALF years for you!"

Maddie spun away and glared back at him. "You know we were too young to have a mature relationship in high school. You know we BOTH were going away for the summer and we BOTH had decided to go to different schools. You made THIS choice by yourself, for yourself."

"You were the one who decided to break up four years ago, not me," Skip shot back. "What you did hurt me terribly. It took me months to recover."

"Really?" Maddie rolled her eyes. "You started dating Maude right away, took her to the prom, and continued seeing her the summer after freshman year! Is that what you mean by recovering?"

"You know I never stopped loving you! I need to do this, Maddie. If I don't, I'll always regret it and I don't want to end up resenting you. Can't you change your life plan just this once? For me? For us?"

Maddie stared at Skip. She couldn't believe what she was hearing. She felt sick to her stomach and weak, like she had food poisoning.

"I thought you loved me, truly loved me. My parents are on the verge of separating, my family is in tatters, and you do THIS to me? When my heart has been shredded already? When my dreams of our future together are what gets me through the day? Do you realize how incredibly selfish you're being?"

"I do love you, always have, always will, and I'm deeply sorry about your parents, you know that. Still, we can't let the choices they've made affect how we live our lives. For God's sake, Maddie, don't force me to choose between my dreams and us."

Maddie shook her head, tears flooding her eyes.

"There is no choice because you have made US impossible!" she shouted and sprinted down the trail.

"Are you okay?" Rex asked as he sat back down. "The way you just scowled scared the shit out of me."

"I was thinking about how pissed I was when Skip—that's his name—took the job. We fought about his decision *a lot* and decided to break up. That's when I committed to Stanford."

And hadn't felt whole since.

"What's he doing in Japan?"

"He's the director of the Japanese program for Volunteer Service in Asia."

"Really?" Rex grunted. "VSA arranged for my teaching job in the Philippines."

"When?"

"Last fall. I was there the first six months of this year."

"He was office manager in San Francisco last fall. Did you meet him? His name is Skip Burton."

"No kidding," Rex responded, fearful that Maddie might have heard about his experience in Malabar. "Small world. You were broken up by then?"

"Yes, and I wasn't in any mood to stay in touch. But . . . we've been friends most of our lives and he seems to thrive abroad. That's why I wrote to ask him about Paris."

"I talked with him several times"—Rex breathed more easily—"but we never met. Now I understand why he gave you such crazy advice. VSA is full of sanctimonious jerks like him. They think they can save the world by helping young Americans learn about Asia through service in Asian countries."

Maddie giggled, brought her hand to her mouth, and nodded emphatically. "He *can* be pretty full of himself."

Rex looked into Maddie's eyes and laughed along with her. This unexpected connection lightened the weight of solitude he had struggled to bear since arriving in Paris. He didn't want the afternoon to end.

"It's almost four," he said, glancing at his watch. "I'm pretty much done for the day. I was thinking about picking up a pizza on my way home and I have a bottle of wine in my room. Would you like to share them with me?"

The invitation caught Maddie by surprise. She enjoyed Rex's company, but she wasn't going back to the room of a man she'd just met.

"Thanks, but I need to go back to ACIP for my leather satchel. It has all my books in it."

Rex's shoulders slumped.

"But," Maddie hurried to add, "the weather is supposed to be pretty nice tomorrow. Maybe we could go for a late afternoon walk and grab a bite to eat?"

"A walk and dinner tomorrow would be great, but are you sure about tonight?" Rex raised his eyebrows and smiled. "I'd be happy to wait for you. This place I know is near the residence and makes wonderful pizza."

"Sorry. I can't," she replied. "What time tomorrow? Five or so? In the courtyard?"

"Five would be fine. Fine," Rex sighed and looked down for a moment.

"Wonderful!" Maddie gushed, trying to reassure him. "You know, I'm so glad we ran into each today. I . . . I've led a pretty secluded life here until now." Maddie laid her hand on the table. Rex nodded and placed his hand briefly over hers.

"I feel the same way, Maddie. See you tomorrow."

Maddie mounted the damp concrete stairs of the subway station as the clock in a nearby church struck five. She stopped to wrap her gray cashmere scarf around her neck, cinch up her long charcoal wool princess coat, and sling her chestnut leather satchel over her shoulder. Passing through the swinging doors, she noticed the rain had stopped, leaving a layer of wispy silver clouds through which shone an incandescent setting sun.

She crossed the street toward La Résidence des États-Unis. To avoid the exhaust-spewing evening traffic, she decided to leave the sidewalk and stroll through the elegant public park that stood between her and her dormitory. The park closed at five thirty, but she knew she could reach the exit nearest her residence in fifteen minutes along its serpentine asphalt path.

As she walked, she inhaled the heady, earthy aroma rising up from the wet grounds and glanced up occasionally at the sky. Evening had turned the silver clouds a more somber gray, but Maddie's heart glowed with anticipation. The more she thought of Rex, the more he intrigued her and the possibility of a friendship—or, with time, more—excited her. She had not experienced this dizzy light-headedness since she had broken up with Skip. Footsteps sounded behind her. Startled, she glanced over her shoulder and spied two young men walking quickly in her direction, one waving a lit cigarette as he talked. "*Shit!*" she muttered to herself and picked up her pace. In a few seconds, the *thump, thump, thump* of the men trotting behind her drowned out the scrape of her boots on the pavement.

"*Allo, mademoiselle!*" one called in a nasal voice. "*FWEET!*" the other whistled.

Fright flowed through Maddie's veins. How could she have been so dumb to walk alone at night in a park? She grabbed her satchel with one arm and began to jog on the balls of her feet.

"*Oh, non! Ne cours pas, ma belle!*" called a high-pitched voice.

"*Deux pour le prix d'un, ma petite?*" laughed the other.

Maddie did not dare look back, but she could hear their footsteps quicken. After a minute, she could smell the stink of tobacco as they gained on her. Another pathway connected ahead at a sharp angle to hers, but it led back into the park and offered no escape. The exit was about a quarter mile away. She started to run but forgot she was wearing a tightly belted coat and nearly tripped when she tried to raise her knees. *Damn!* She felt a hand reach for her satchel and jerked the bag away. *Enough!* She whirled around to confront the two men, her breath billowing out in the cold air.

"Leave me the *fuck* alone, you bastards!" she screamed and raised her fist.

"*Ma belle, ma petite. Sois gentille.*" He puckered his lips and made kissing sounds as he circled Maddie to the left.

"*Pas besoin de se battre.*" The other smiled and circled to the right.

"Maddie? Is that you?" called a familiar voice from the trees to her right.

"Yes! Help me, Rex. Please!" A moment later, she heard Rex's boots pound the pavement behind her and watched the two men back away.

"Leave her alone, you assholes!" Rex bellowed and, panting hard, planted himself in front of Maddie. She glared at the two assailants over Rex's shoulder and watched them laugh and shrink away.

Rex and Maddie sat cross-legged facing each other on Rex's bed, an empty pizza box and a few crumpled paper napkins between them. The smell of bacon and mushrooms hung in the air. They each held a glass tumbler with only a gulp of red wine left at the very bottom.

"I can't believe you happened to be passing nearby just as I screamed."

"I'm glad I decided to walk back from the café. If I'd taken the Métro, I would have been in the residence when you needed help. What do you think of the pizza?" He wiped his mouth with the last of the napkins.

"It is pretty great and tastes especially good with the wine. Thanks again for chasing those jerks away," Maddie said, raising her glass to salute Rex.

"Cheers." Rex toasted Maddie and drained his glass. "From what I saw they were lucky I came along before you knocked their lights out."

Maddie smiled. "Maybe," she said and emptied hers. "But I felt pretty relieved when you came out of nowhere to defend me. So glad we met by chance at the library. Best thing to happen to me in Paris."

"Thanks. I feel the same way."

"So . . ." Maddie looked away briefly. "Your parents are divorced, too?"

"Yeah. Separated just after I finished high school. When did your parents break up?"

"A few weeks after I graduated from Mills. They divorced soon after. They told me they hadn't been happy for years but wanted to keep the family together until I graduated. They were completely oblivious to the decade of acrimony and tension between them that had already destroyed my sense of family."

Maddie gazed out the single, grated window in the room. The loss of her family was still hard to bear. She looked around to collect herself. The space was spare with a desk and a chair, a small wooden chest of drawers, a tiny bathroom with a shower, and a closet. Exactly like her room but without the 1969 Monterey Jazz Festival poster on the wall and flowers in a vase.

Rex noticed the sides of Maddie's mouth curl downward and her eyes crunch in despair.

"My situation was different than yours. I never spent a lot of time with my father growing up and haven't seen him much since the separation. The occasional holiday when I'm home. He's remarried to his old secretary if you can believe it. Laughably cliché if it didn't hurt my mother so much. My mother and I are extremely close. She's my family, the one who raised me. She writes me every week and I try to do the same."

"It speaks well that you have a strong relationship with your mother. Men who don't . . . well, I'm not sure what kind of husbands they make. I'm sure Skip loves his mother, but he could be condescending, even contemptuous toward her. He complained she was overprotective, but never realized how his resistance to her bled into his relationships with other women, making him insensitive and unwilling to compromise."

"I can understand why my parents broke up," Rex offered. "My father's nice enough but distant, detached—maybe like your old boyfriend—a real numbers guy, committed to his bank job. My mother couldn't be more different; she's demonstrative, opinionated, and passionate. She makes enough to get by, but doesn't get any money from my father because she traded support from him for the house, and he paid for my education."

"Do you have a picture of her?"

"Sure." Rex reached across to his desk drawer and pulled out the mini photo album Mama had given to him before he left for Paris. "Here."

"Oh, she's lovely," Maddie murmured. "Never remarried?"

She began to leaf through the pictures.

"Remarried? No . . ."

Rex recalled the day last summer he returned from the Philippines.

"Welcome home, honey!" Mama shouted as Rex walked up the driveway where the taxi had dropped him. "It is so good to see you." She ran up, grabbed Rex, and hugged him hard. "How was your trip back? Your visit to Berkeley?"

"I slept most of the flight to San Francisco. Berkeley was good. I've found a new advisor. I had to re-enroll in the MA program, but I should be able to finish next May."

"That's great. Come on in out of the sun."

Rex walked arm in arm with Mama into the spacious entry hall of her two-story traditional wood-shingle home.

"Let me look at you," Mama said. "You've lost weight, haven't you? I'll put those pounds back on you in no time." She patted his shoulders.

"Thanks, Mama. I have missed your cooking." Rex put his suitcase down on the tiled floor. "Tell me the surprise you said you had for me."

"Well, I . . . I've been seeing a man I met at St. Luke's. His name is Clay. Clay Martin. He's a lawyer and a widower with two grown daughters, both married and living outside Chicago. He's a really wonderful man, Rex," Mama bubbled with girlish enthusiasm.

Rex had never heard her speak like this before; he felt slightly nauseated.

"That's nice, Mama. I . . . I'm happy you have a friend to keep you company from time to time . . ." He heard himself say in a strangely disembodied voice.

"Oh, Rex. Clay is much more than just a friend! I don't know how to explain it. It's all happened so quickly," she enthused. *"His daughters and their families have driven all the way from Chicago for dinner with me tonight. And, of course, when he heard you were coming today, he insisted that I bring you, too. We plan, well, we plan to announce we're going to be married. I am so very happy, honey, and just thrilled you're here to share this with us."*

Rex's mouth went chalk dry. He never imagined Mama would desert him, too.

"Excuse me, Mama. I don't feel so well," he gasped and rushed to the guest bathroom off the entry hall. Feeling a fever flash through his body, he stripped off his T-shirt and threw water on his face and neck. Mama knocked once and without waiting entered to see what was wrong with her son.

"Rex? Are you . . . Good God, what happened to you?" Mama exclaimed running her hands over the scars on his back.

On his flight home, Rex realized the scars would shock Mama and he began to weave a story that would please her. In the same way he embodied a character he acted in a play, he gave himself over to a fantasy so complete he couldn't distinguish fact from filigree by the time he arrived in Kansas.

"Remember the beating I got from three thugs who attacked my friend, Miranda?"

"I thought it was a fistfight. They whipped you?"

"The wounds don't hurt that much anymore, but when they do, I remind myself that Miranda escaped unharmed, which makes me feel better."

"You saved Miranda from robbery or worse, honey. What you did was heroic! I'm so proud of you, but why in the world would they lash your back like this?"

"I'm not a hero, Mama. As soon as I knew Miranda was safe, I tried to run away. I thought I had broken free when one of the muggers reached out and tripped me with his bamboo cane. I tumbled to the ground, they jumped on me, and flogged me until I lost consciousness. Luckily, a passerby found me and drove me to the local hospital. The doctors and nurses took good care of me. I know the scars look awful, but the doctors say they will fade. They do burn and throb terribly from time to time—like just now. I'm really sorry. I . . . I want to meet Clay and his family, but I'd rather skip the dinner tonight. I hope you don't mind. Go ahead without me."

"I absolutely will not! I will call Clay right now to tell him you're not feeling well and I'm staying home to take care of you. He'll understand."

"These are really great pictures," Maddie said as she placed the album on the desk. "Too bad your mom hasn't found someone nice."

"Yeah," Rex replied. "I know. I encourage her to meet people but she still devotes more time to me than she should."

"You're such a good man to worry about your mother's happiness," Maddie sighed. "I felt close to my mother until I was about twelve or thirteen. She's not very domestic. We didn't cook or sew or do girly crafts together, but she's a remarkable athlete. When I was young, she took me for long hikes up Mount Tamalpais and coached my grade school soccer team. As I got older, she'd run or bike with me around the Bay Area."

"What happened?"

"I sprouted up and started playing volleyball. I got really good and wanted to focus on just one sport. My dad played volleyball in college and loved the game. He coached all my volleyball teams, so I spent more time with him and less with her. I sensed a gap opening between us but didn't know what it was about. Looking back, I think she resented my success and the time and attention Dad gave me. Before my senior year at Mills, it all changed. I told him I didn't want to play volleyball over the summer with his club—I was burned out. He was furious. Told me I was ungrateful, a traitor. He apologized afterwards, but something between us changed. We spent less and less time together."

Maddie stopped and ran her finger along the rim of her glass.

"I used to think my parents loved me. Now I wonder whether either really did at all, at least how they're supposed to, unconditionally. When I ask myself that question, I get headaches and feel terribly depressed, like I have a rain cloud perpetually hovering over my head. The truth is I've avoided spending time with either of them for the past year."

"It's so hard to know what goes on in your parents' minds. I'm lucky my mother is open and supportive. She knew how to adapt to the changes in our relationship that came as I grew older. There's no question she's my anchor, but I think it's rare. Most guys are like your old boyfriend. Not that finding love is all that easy with someone our age."

"Yeah, I know what you mean about people our age. Skip . . ." Maddie hesitated. "I . . . I'm certain he loved me, in his way. But when a hug was all I wanted, he would insist on cramming advice down my throat. What is that all about? Is that really love?"

"I don't know." Rex stopped for a moment and locked his eyes on Maddie's. "I can tell you this. You are a strong, resilient, caring person. Someone who deserves to be loved."

"How sweet, Rex. Thank you. It's so nice to meet someone so . . . so open and empathetic rather than preachy and . . . and patronizing."

"Like your old boyfriend?"

"Yes." She chuckled. "I guess. At least he can be that way. But he's *not* my boyfriend anymore. You know, I wish we'd met earlier, but I'm glad I ran into you at the Sorbonne today—and you were miraculously around to rescue me from those hooligans. Fate, I suppose."

Maddie raised her empty glass toward Rex. "Here's to going home. If you ever come down to the Peninsula, I'd really enjoy seeing you." Maddie cocked her head and smiled.

"I'll be across the Bay beginning in January. Maybe, it *is* fate we met. Here's to home," Rex said, reaching over the pizza box and clinking his glass lightly against Maddie's. "I would love to see you again, too."

"Hmmm," Maddie murmured. "The pizza and wine were perfect. The cold air had chilled me to my bones."

"I'm sorry," Rex said and instinctively reached over to rub warmth into Maddie's shoulders. "I hope that helps. Or I can turn up the heat if you'd like."

Rex swung his legs over the side of the bed to get up.

"Oh, I am a little chilled, but no need to get up."

Maddie bounced off the bed, tossing the pizza box and wine bottle in the trash can and placing the empty glasses on the desk.

"There. We wouldn't want to spill anything on your bed." Maddie lowered herself next to Rex and leaned ever so slightly against him. "Now, about my being a little cold still."

Maddie swiveled her torso toward Rex, put her arms around his neck, and brushed her lips across his. Rex felt desire rush through his body. He wrapped his arms around her and kissed her hard.

"You taste like pizza, and I really like pizza." Maddie laughed lightly. She unwrapped herself from Rex, kicked off her shoes, and lay back on the bed. Rex shifted his weight and started to lie on top of her.

"Wait a minute." She put a hand on his chest. "I *would* like it if you took your shoes off and came over by me for a little, but only if we keep our clothes on. We're both leaving next week and may never see each other again."

"Oh, we will. I guarantee it," Rex declared, aware more than ever that the hermetic confines of his Paris life had cut him off from any emotional connection. He had not held a woman for six months and now yearned to feel Maddie's body pressed into his. "I won't let someone as kind, as smart, and as beautiful as you get away."

"Oh, you are so lovely," she cooed and looked into his eyes. "I'm not used to a man—especially one as attractive as you—being this attentive. And . . . I'm embarrassed to admit it, but I love being with a man who's taller than me. Still, I . . . I like to go slow. Is that okay?"

"Sure." Rex unlaced his shoes and slid next to Maddie, anxious to please her.

They kissed again, playing with each other's tongue and lips. Rex wrapped a leg over her lower body and began to play with her hair. They kissed more deeply. Rex felt himself becoming aroused, pulled her close to him, and ran his hand down her side, over her legs. Maddie's breathing quickened.

"This feels so good," she whispered. "If we agree to keep our clothes on, I'd love to feel the weight of your body on mine. Okay?"

"Of course," he said and swung himself on top of Maddie. He nuzzled her neck and nibbled her ear lobe. "How's that?"

"Good. Very good," she replied and ran her hands down the back of his shirt. Suddenly, her body went rigid. Her fingers probed more deeply over what felt like beads sown into his skin.

"What happened? Your back is covered with welts, or scars of some kind? Did you fall on something?"

"Oh . . ." Rex stammered. "They're just a few scars," he muttered and leaned forward to kiss her again, hoping to end the conversation quickly.

"A *few* scars? Whatever it was must have hurt like hell. I'm *so* sorry for you."

Rex felt Maddie's concern wash over him, but it didn't calm the panic rising in his chest. Joy had never said a word about his wounds. Maddie's noticing them immediately stunned him. He feared she would be as revolted as Miranda if he told her the truth.

"It hurt a lot at first, but the pain is gone now," he replied as casually as possible.

"But what . . . *who* did this to you?" When Rex did not respond immediately, Maddie insisted, "Please tell me what happened."

"It has nothing to do with you, Maddie. Can't we just forget it?"

"Why can't you tell me? Something traumatic happened to you. It's clear. But if you don't want to open up to me about it, that's fine."

Maddie pushed Rex off of her, sat up beside him, and began to reach for her shoes.

"No, wait!" Rex pleaded. The vision of this strong, bright, attractive woman walking out of his life, leaving him alone again, terrified him.

"You don't trust me. You're happy to run your hands over my body but have no interest in sharing anything more. Frankly, it feels like rejection, and I've had enough of *that* from men."

She grabbed one shoe and began to pull it on.

"No! Of course I trust you," Rex objected.

"Let's call it a night. Okay? Maybe we'll run into each other again before we leave."

Maddie reached down for the other shoe.

Rex saw determination tighten her jaw. Maddie was not as charismatic as Diana, as alluring as Miranda, or as naturally beautiful as Joy, but she was pretty and thoughtful and intelligent. Being with her today made Rex realize how forlorn he had felt. He ached to be close to her again, to see the flash of desire he had glimpsed in her eyes. The thought of her deserting him was unbearable.

"A whipping with a bamboo cane," Rex finally admitted, not wanting to lie to Maddie but afraid to be completely truthful.

"A bamboo cane!" Maddie's eyes widened in horror. Her shoe fell out of her hand. "Who in the world whipped you?"

"Remember I said I tried really hard not to disappoint my friends in the Philippines?"

"Yes, but what does that have to do with the scars on your back? Oh my God, you didn't allow your friends to whip you? Are you *crazy*? What kind of sadistic game were you playing?"

"No! No, I didn't allow anyone to whip me," Rex interjected, seeing revulsion crumple Maddie's face. "Let me explain . . ."

Rex hesitated. Maddie's persistence gave him no choice. He could tell her the truth and watch her disappear forever or he could perform for Maddie the same play he put on for Mama.

"Last Easter, I was really depressed. I had tried so hard to fit in, but I didn't understand how society worked there, made some mistakes, hurt my friends' feelings."

"Intentionally?"

"No, of course not. I still felt awful though. Easter night I was walking back from a fiesta and I saw a friend—someone I had let down—ahead of me. Three guys with canes jumped out from the shadows and assaulted her. I shouted at them and ran to her as fast as I could."

"Just like you did tonight for me!"

"I guess so. Anyway, I knocked one of them over. The other two let her go and turned to face me. I saw she had escaped, so

I tried to run for it. One guy tripped me with his cane. I fell hard on my chest. The three of them jumped on my back and lashed me pretty good until a car came along and they ran off. Luckily the driver stopped and took me to the hospital."

"You sacrificed yourself to save her! Just like you protected me this evening."

"I was actually kind of embarrassed I didn't outrun those guys," Rex demurred, but could not help swelling with pride.

"But you saved your friend. Was . . . is . . . she your girl-friend?"

"I liked her a lot, but she couldn't accept me because I wasn't Filipino or Catholic, and never would be. I really tried to please her, but I kept screwing up."

"I'm so very sorry," Maddie said. "So, no Filipina girlfriend? I've heard there are some really beautiful women there, women who would go crazy for a guy like you."

"I don't know about that, but I *do* know you're gorgeous," Rex declared, seeing warmth return to Maddie's expression.

"People have always said I'm 'cute' . . ." Maddie said, making a quote sign with her fingers. "I know there's an unspoken '*but*' though, as if I'm too muscular or too competitive or too tall for a girl."

"There's no *but* after mine, Maddie." Rex put his arm around Maddie and kissed her again.

"You're wonderful," Maddie whispered and kissed him back. "She rejected you and yet you saved her at great cost. I know how awful it feels to be cast aside by people you love."

"That's not the worst. I was pretty vulnerable and should have gone straight home, but I escaped to a small tropical island to recover. I . . . I met a girl there and convinced myself we loved each other. Turns out, she lied to me about being pregnant. She just wanted a ticket to the States."

"You dear man. You were rejected again? That's awful." Maddie cupped his head in her hands. Her eyes glistened.

Eager to win Maddie over, Rex couldn't resist embellishing the story of Joy's mysterious disappearance.

"I accepted responsibility for the baby, but I wouldn't take her home to Kansas until we went to see a real doctor to make sure she and the baby were healthy. She disappeared the next day. Her grandmother told me she wasn't pregnant after all." Rex looked away, his eyes misting. "I was pretty devastated."

Maddie ran her hands over his back again. "After your body was literally flogged, this horrific woman flays your heart." She leaned forward and kissed Rex again. "I'm so, so sorry. How many times were you lashed?"

"I don't really remember," Rex shook his head. "I passed out. Maybe a hundred . . ."

"A hundred!" Maddie gasped. "You're such a brave, kindhearted, humble person, Rex. Trying so hard to fit in, you suffered so much to save a friend, and then were betrayed by someone you loved. How your soul must have ached!"

"Yes, I was scared then, but even more frightened now . . . to lose you. Stay a little while longer? *Please* don't leave me," he begged.

"I won't," she purred and stroked his cheek. "I know being thrown aside by the one you love wounds deeply. I have no intention of doing that to you."

Maddie reached up and began to unbutton Rex's shirt.

"What are you doing?" He put his hand over hers. "I thought you wanted us to keep our clothes on."

"I did, but now I want to feel your skin against mine and . . . and I want to kiss your scars."

An hour later, Maddie lay in Rex's arms listening to his heartbeat, unconsciously timing her breathing to the rise and fall of his chest. The flame of a large candle bathed their bodies in a golden glow.

"I was thinking about seeing each other in California . . ."

"Yeah," Rex murmured sleepily.

"I'll be in Palo Alto and you'll be in Berkeley . . ."

"But we'll be writing our theses, not taking classes. We can do that from anywhere."

"That's right," she breathed. "Still . . ."

"Oh, Maddie," Rex sighed and stroked her hair. "Do you know the hymn 'Amazing Grace'? I learned it in Sunday school."

"Sure. Judy Collins sang it a couple of years ago with a male choir backing her up. Beautiful song. Why?"

"There's a line that goes *I once was lost, but now I am found.* That's the way I feel after three bitter months of agonizing isolation here. I feel found . . . found by you."

She nestled into his chest and whispered, "I've felt lost and alone, too. Here especially, but not just here . . . for months, maybe years before."

"You know, I would be happy to visit you in Palo Alto every other weekend. Maybe you could come to Berkeley once in a while?"

"I would love to spend more time together over the next few months. If that goes well, we can talk about longer visits. How does that sound?"

"It sounds great. In fact, maybe we can save money by splitting rent. The way I feel now—finally found—I would be willing to live with you in Palo Alto, if you'd have me."

8 Relativism

A gentle knock on the door shattered Skip's concentration on his Japanese *kanji* flashcards.

"*Chotto matte kudasai,*" he called out, rose from his desk chair, and responded in English, too, in case the visitor was one of the VSA Japan volunteers. "Just a second."

He opened his door to find Jenny's candescent eyes smiling up at him.

"Do you mind if I come in?" she asked, her head lowered slightly, a tinge of hesitation in her voice.

"Of course not. Welcome to Tokyo!"

Jenny stepped past him and sat down on the twin bed in his dorm-style room at the International House of Japan. As she slid by him, he marveled at how her thick black hair fell to embrace her shoulders, how her skin had an inner glow like a lantern, and how her petite frame moved with such grace she seemed to float rather than walk. She was *sansei*, a third generation Japanese-American, who combined a sunny, almost bubbly, Californian personality with the tranquil beauty and innate elegance of her forebears.

They had met six months before when she applied for a teaching position with the Japan program of Volunteer Service in Asia. Skip had been director for a year and was visiting San Francisco from Tokyo over the New Year holiday when Jenny first came into VSA's cramped Japantown office. As she inquired about the organization and asked for an application, her quiet strength and musical laugh enchanted him. He'd broken up with Maddie more than eighteen months before, and since that emotional earthquake no one he'd met had sent electricity running through his veins the way Jenny did. At first, he planned to create a pretext to become better acquainted with her. When she submitted her application for his program, however, he cautioned himself against approaching her until the selection process was completed. Two months later, the day after the VSA selection committee unanimously accepted her, he was in San Francisco again and invited her for a Friday lunch to talk about the upcoming trip to Japan. Soup and a sandwich turned into an afternoon walk along the Embarcadero, dinner in North Beach, and a bottle of wine in her apartment in Oakland. They spent the weekend talking, laughing, sharing the stories of their lives, and making love, their touching sometimes fierce and frenetic, sometimes so languid they both ached before fulfilling their desires.

When they parted on Monday morning, Skip realized he had never felt such immediate ease with a woman. He had loved Maddie for more years than he could remember and knew she had loved him. Still, he always sensed that Maddie competed with him as much as, if not more than, she supported him; that Maddie—pretty, talented, driven Maddie—always felt somehow diminished by his successes at the same time she celebrated them. They had even joked over the years that Maddie—taller, faster, stronger than Skip—was his Annie Oakley, a woman who could, in fact, do almost anything better than he could—and could not resist the urge to prove it. Being with Maddie was like rafting on a raging river, exhilarating, challenging, and . . . exhausting. He realized her constant striving to succeed was innate. He loved that part of her nature and the way she pushed him to excel, too. Over time, however, he realized her relentless drive ignited insecurities in him that he would try to douse with a cool, self-assured intellectualism. He knew he used this ploy to shift their relationship onto more comfortable footing. Though it often enraged Maddie, he couldn't stop himself.

By contrast, being with Jenny was like gliding across a glassy forest lake on a cool summer morning: calming, soothing, restorative. She seemed to intuit his anxieties, still them in a way that settled his soul and freed him to just *be* rather than strain to outdo.

Skip could not wait until he saw Jenny again the following weekend. Still, as the days passed, he began to worry their relationship might create the appearance of favoritism and undermine his ability to counsel the other dozen volunteers going to Japan. He could not bear the thought of giving her up, so he begged Jenny to agree to hide their relationship from everyone in the program. Jenny pursed her lips in irritation at the notion, but quietly acquiesced.

Whenever Skip could travel from Tokyo to San Francisco for orientation, they secretly reveled in feigning indifference to each other during weekday training sessions, disinterest belied only by the occasional slight brush of one hand over the other. Their clandestine weekday conspiracy intensified their weekend passion.

The summer and the start of Jenny's volunteer assignment had approached more quickly than either wished. Skip was to leave for Tokyo three days before Jenny to finalize preparations for the arrival of the VSA Japan group. The morning of his departure from San Francisco, they had wept as they made love for what Skip insisted would be the last time until Jenny finished her assignment in Kyoto nine months later.

Jenny's reply to his welcome roused Skip from his memories.

"Thanks," she said. "I'm so happy to be in Japan finally. Sit here with me?" She patted the bed beside her.

Skip lowered himself carefully to avoid brushing against her body. He inhaled her light scent, a rich fragrance of ripe figs tempered slightly by black tea smokiness. She seemed to radiate heat across the space between them. He felt aroused and took a deep breath.

"How was your flight over?" he asked in the hope that conversation would dampen his desire.

"Long," she giggled. "But it gave me time to finish Reischauer's history of Japan. Great book. Thanks for recommending it." Jenny glanced out of the corner of her eye at Skip and draped her hand on his leg.

Skip shifted his body away from Jenny and faced her. "Jenny, please. Do you know how you touching me makes me feel?"

"No," she smiled disingenuously and cocked her head. "How?"

Skip sighed. "Jenny, please."

"All right," she said and lifted her hand from his thigh. "I stopped by to tell you my parents and grandparents—my father's parents—all came to the airport to see me off. You told me they would be proud of me, and you were so right. I had never seen my grandparents cry before, but everyone, even my father, teared up. I am the first in my family to return to Japan since my grandparents left Fukuoka seventy years ago. And I will work as a teacher, which you know is a position of great respect in Japan."

Her excitement caused her voice to rise a pitch as she continued. "I hope to visit Fukuoka while I'm here and take pictures for my grandparents. My parents have never been to Japan and always claimed to have no interest in traveling here. Now they might come visit me in Kyoto this summer! It's thrilling and so . . . so immensely fulfilling. And all because of you. I can't thank you enough, Skip." She looked up at him with lustrous eyes.

"Because of the program, Jenny, not because of me."

"As far as I can see, you *are* the program. You recruited us, arranged the selection process, found our assignments, trained us, and organized our travel, our host families, two weeks of cross-cultural training, everything."

"I hope I didn't overdo the preparation. I wanted to avoid problems we've had in the past, like the issues we had in the Philippines last year."

"I can't believe your training was to blame."

"It was a host of bad decisions. VSA had a teaching assignment to fill at the last moment and selected someone who seemed perfect on paper. I was instructed to rush him through orientation to get him to his assignment on time. After we found out he left his post, we received conflicting reports from the school. The principal insisted the volunteer took off before fulfilling his assignment. He was quite upset. A doctor, who was on the faculty, believed he suffered an injury at a local festival that made teaching difficult, if not impossible. We tried to get his side of the story, but he never responded."

"Nothing like that will happen in our program, Skip. You've done a great, great job and you've made *me* very, very happy!" Jenny leaned toward Skip, put her hand behind his neck, and kissed him.

Skip tensed momentarily and then relaxed, allowing their tongues to flirt while fighting off the urge to wrap his arms around her.

"Sorry. I just couldn't resist," she whispered.

"God, how I want you!" Skip leaned forward and whispered in her ear.

"And I want you. I know we agreed we wouldn't make love again until I finished my assignment, but"—she stopped to stroke the inside of his thigh—"why not tonight, one last time? What harm would it do?"

"I would love to, Jenny, more than anything, but I have an early meeting with Shimizu-san tomorrow and you have a tour of Tokyo. Besides, the floor is full of volunteers, including your roommate. How would it look if someone saw you sneak out of my room late at night?"

Jenny pouted briefly and moved her hand from Skip's thigh.

"Then how about when you visit Kyoto in a month? There won't be any other volunteers around then."

"Jenny," Skip sighed. "We discussed this, remember? I'll be visiting as the director of the program, not as your boyfriend. You'll be living with your host family. They will think of you as their daughter, someone whom they are responsible for while you're living with them!"

Jenny frowned and looked away. Suddenly, she turned to Skip, enthusiasm widening her eyes. "I know. What if we met over that weekend at an *onsen*? No other volunteers and no host family. No one would have to know. I would tell my family I wanted to do some sightseeing."

"Jenny, dear Jenny." Skip exhaled and shook his head briefly. "I can't encourage you to lie to your host family simply to spend a weekend with me, behavior they would consider shockingly immoral."

"It's not immoral! We love each other!"

"Remember your cultural sensitivity training? The importance of understanding the differences between Japanese culture and ours without judging them? Respecting the Japanese as they are and not as we might want them to be? To do otherwise risks imposing our own values and becoming the worst kind of cultural imperialists. Besides, you agreed when you signed the contract that you would follow Japanese cultural prescriptions, especially those of your host family, and do nothing that would hurt the reputation of our Japanese partner organization."

"But I'm NOT Japanese! I'm American and I don't see how being with the man I love would hurt my host family or anyone's reputation. They wouldn't *know*!"

"I know you're American inside and I *love* the woman inside. I'm not Japanese either; but for the next nine months *we* must try to abide by Japanese social expectations. You know how they view a woman who sleeps with a man before marriage. Please understand, as the man who loves you completely, I want nothing more than to spend a weekend together at a hot spring. As the director of the program, I can't."

"You sound so clinical, so detached. Like you don't even care."

"You know I care about you. Deeply. But I learned long ago that letting your emotions go when you're overseas leads to disaster."

Skip paused for a second and cleared his throat.

"During my first trip to Mexico, years ago, I was furious at how unfairly I felt some Mexican boys were treating me. I said and did some things I will always regret. I learned later they were afraid of me, as likely to misunderstand my behavior as I was theirs. I screamed at them, even tried to injure them, and yet later they became some of my best friends. That's when I learned to use my head, not my heart, to govern my behavior in a foreign culture."

"I know. I know," Jenny grumbled and shook her head. "But it's so unreasonable!"

"You mean from *our* cultural perspective it seems unreasonable. Nothing I know of in Japanese culture would allow a young, unmarried woman—a teacher, a guest in her host family's home—to have a lover, especially not the director of her program!"

Jenny turned away from Skip, inhaled slowly, and exhaled her anger in a whoosh of resignation.

"I don't know what to say. I feel so empty inside now."

"Oh, Jenny," Skip said and wrapped his arms around her. "I love you so much. You make me feel so . . . whole. If . . . if it makes the next nine months any easier for you, know I want to spend my life with you. Will you, Jenny? Will you marry me when all this is done?"

Jenny looked up at Skip with tears in her eyes.

"Oh my God! Oh, Skip! Yes, yes! I will marry you."

She threw her arms around his neck and drew him to her. After a moment, she released him and stared into his eyes.

"I will marry you, but . . . well, I don't want to tell my parents, yet. They . . . they don't even know we've been dating."

"What? You haven't told your parents we've been seeing each other? Why not? They're second-generation *American*, for Christ's sake!"

"I know. I know." Jenny avoided Skip's gaze. "But you're only the second man and the first non-Japanese American I've ever dated. Since we agreed not to see each other while I was volunteering, I didn't think it mattered."

"You didn't want to share with them that you'd fallen in love with an Anglo? Would they object?"

"No, but I told you my old boyfriend was the son of friends, someone they knew from childhood, someone they loved and felt comfortable with. I think they assumed we would get married and our breakup last year upset them terribly. When I decided I wanted to spend almost a year in Japan, they began to worry about me. I thought telling them about us on top of all that would be a lot for them to absorb. Besides, I figured they would meet you when they came to visit me and see what a wonderful man you are. I thought that would make it easier to tell them. Are you angry with me?"

"You mean for being sensitive to your parents' cultural expectations?" Skip chuckled. "No, of course, not. I'm Mr. Cultural Sensitivity, remember?"

"Oh, Skip. I can't wait to introduce you to my parents!" Jenny kissed Skip fiercely. "I love you *so* very much and so will they," she said and embraced him. Then she rose quickly, blew a kiss to him, and left, closing the door quietly behind her.

Jiro Shimizu sighed loudly. A tall, elegant man who had spent a couple of years in England and spoke excellent English, Shimizu led the High School Native English Instruction Program within the Japanese Ministry of Education. Skip had been sitting across from him for the past three hours in a small, stuffy conference room reviewing the details of each of the assignments and host families for the VSA teachers. Skip found Shimizu pompous and occasionally haughty, but nonetheless appreciated his meticulousness.

"The last assignment is for Jennifer Nonaka," Shimizu said.

Skip straightened himself, trying to stretch out his back muscles, sore from sitting so long.

"Yes. I believe her placement with the Kyoto Nishiyama High School for Girls and her host family, the"—Skip hesitated as he looked through Jenny's file—"Hasegawa family appear to be excellent choices. Thank you for your arrangements."

Skip bowed slightly toward Shimizu, hoping to end their meeting on an especially cordial note.

"Yes. I also *believed* the arrangements were quite good, but *saaaaa* . . ." Shimizu exhaled heavily, then continued, "most regrettably, the principal of Kyoto Nishiyama called me yesterday to inform me they could not, after all, accept Nonaka-san as a teacher in their school."

"*What?*" Skip gasped and rocked forward in his chair.

Shimizu's eyes narrowed.

Skip told himself to calm down. He didn't want to offend his Japanese counterpart. Perhaps there was a miscommunication.

"I don't understand," he said as evenly as he could. "You told me they were excited to have her teach at their school. I saw the letter—two months ago—confirming they had accepted her. What happened?"

Shimizu shifted uneasily in his seat, took out a handkerchief, and dabbed perspiration from his upper lip. "The principal informed me, with regret, they had miscalculated the number of students who were interested in English conversation classes. He apologized for the error but concluded their current staff was more than sufficient."

"Their current staff? Older Japanese nationals? Non-native speakers? I thought the whole point of the ministry's initiative was to engage Japanese students with a native speaker who was closer to their own age to encourage students to learn to speak English."

"Yes, that is the purpose. The principal, however, indicated there wasn't sufficient interest."

"How could there be? The school has never had a native speaker before. Did you suggest Jennifer could teach alongside one of their Japanese teachers? To small groups? We've used that formula before and it worked well."

"No. I didn't feel it was appropriate to question his decision." Shimizu sniffed dismissively, closed the file in front of him, and folded his hands on top of it.

"*Appropriate?*" Skip barked, his face flushed with anger. Skip saw Shimizu flinch at his outburst. He took a deep breath and reminded himself he would need Shimizu's help to find a solution.

"Appropriate?" he asked again more mildly. "Well, at the very least, she can stay with her host family until you find her another school in the area."

"I am most sorry," Shimizu replied and turned his eyes from Skip to stare down at Jenny's file. "The host family has also indicated they can no longer, unfortunately, welcome Nonaka-san. Their oldest child is preparing for the university entrance exams and has unexpectedly struggled with the pressure. Besides, finding another school at this point . . . well, it is simply not possible. Because of this most lamentable situation, however, the ministry is prepared to pay for her flight home this week rather than in nine months."

Skip shook his head in disbelief. He had lived long enough in Japan to know two last minute cancellations were highly unlikely. Something was going on below the surface. Shimizu was hiding the real reason for these stunning changes.

"Your ministry values its relationship with my program, does it not?" Skip demanded, an edge creeping into his voice.

"Yes, of course."

"You are responsible for maintaining that relationship and would be accountable if the relationship were terminated, right?"

Shimizu's face reddened and he nodded stiffly.

"Then stop giving me the *tatemae*, the surface story. What is the *honne*? What is really going on?"

"*Saaaaa*," Shimizu emitted a loud hissing sound again and dabbed sweat from his brow. "Are you familiar with what we call the *burakumin*, the village people?"

"The outcast group dating back to the feudal era, the lowest group in the class system? They are sometimes called *eta*, which means something like 'polluted.' They belonged to segregated communities, or *buraku*, made up of laborers working at jobs considered impure or tainted by death, such as butchers, undertakers, tanners, and executioners. They were subjected to severe discrimination, ostracized by other classes. But the government *abolished* the caste designation in 1871." Skip rattled off facts, emphasizing the archaic nature of Japan's *burakumin* designation, trying to bolster his leverage for what he feared was coming.

"What does an outlawed feudal practice have to do more than a hundred years later with Jennifer Nonaka, a *third*-generation *American?*"

And, Skip wanted to cry out, *the woman I love.*

"Her grandparents were *burakumin* and so, unfortunately, is she," Shimizu declared quietly.

"What?" Skip blurted out. "How could anyone possibly know that for a fact?"

"In her application she wrote that her grandparents came from a section of Fukuoka called Ootoo. There is a list of communities where *burakumin* used to live and in some cases still do. Ootoo is on that list."

"It can't be that every family who lived in Ootoo seventy years ago was *burakumin,*" Skip countered.

"No, you are correct. Only about half the families were, but someone in Kyoto had an investigative firm check the Nonaka family registry in Ootoo. There is an 1871 entry in the family registry for her great-grandfather that reads *kyu-eta,* or former *eta.*"

Skip's eyes bore into Shimizu.

"But Nonaka is a very common family name in Japan," Skip objected trying to hold back his fury. "There must be other Nonaka families in Ootoo who were not *eta* in the past."

"I am sorry to say the family registry system is very precise. When her grandfather left Japan for Hawaii in the early 1900s, an entry in the registry was made indicating that, because of his emigration, he no longer was part of the *kyu-eta* Nonaka family in Ootoo. Besides, you are familiar enough with Japan to know what matters is not what *is* true, but what people *believe* is true.

The principal of Kyoto Nishiyama and the Hasegawa family and many others in that school's community are now convinced Nonaka-san is *burakumin*."

"But that's completely unjust!" Skip shrieked and jumped up from his seat. "Your ministry cannot really accept such . . . such prejudice. It's 1974. We are talking about a practice that was outlawed in Japan more than a *century* ago," he yelled and slapped the table.

Shimizu blinked rapidly but remained impassive.

"Please sit down and calm yourself." Shimizu gestured to Skip's chair after a few seconds.

Skip lowered himself, but glowered at Shimizu.

"We neither accept nor reject the beliefs of schools and communities that host *gaijin* English teachers. We do, however, acknowledge we cannot force them to accept someone they do not wish to welcome. Please understand there would have been no problem if Jennifer Nonaka had not mentioned Ootoo on her application, but she did. Someone in Kyoto very recently noticed that unfortunate fact and raised a question that forced the principal to investigate."

"But this is unadulterated bigotry against someone who has *never* done anything to harm these people. What are they afraid of?"

"Like most human beings," Shimizu replied with a shrug, "they are afraid of the strange, of that which they do not know, and they wish to protect their children from such things. To be fair to them, it is common knowledge that young *burakumin* men have recently joined our criminal syndicates, our *yakuza*; if that were not the case, perhaps attitudes would not be so severe. As it is . . ." Shimizu's voice trailed away. He tucked his handkerchief into his jacket pocket and laid his hands on Jenny's file.

"I cannot accept this." Skip cut the air with his right hand. "I will talk tonight with the VSA executive director. He will wish to speak with you and with your superiors in the ministry. We will go to our embassy, take this to the press, if we need to."

"Burton-san." Shimizu's eyes grew cold. "In your organization's contract with our ministry, VSA agrees to respect and adhere to Japanese cultural norms, does it not? To train its teachers to refrain from judging, for better or worse, the social and cultural expectations of their host community and to adapt their behavior and communication accordingly? To avoid interjecting the emotions that often trouble young Americans in their encounters with Japanese? This is what your executive director and you yourself as head of the Japan program have called 'cultural sensitivity,' I believe. This philosophy is what you have argued makes your organization different than others that seek to arrange work-abroad programs for Americans in Japan under our auspices. Am I not correct?"

"Yes," Skip murmured. He clenched his teeth.

"We would view any attempt to bring political or public relations pressure upon us to act in a way inconsistent with Japanese cultural standards as incompatible with your stated philosophy and with the terms of our agreement. And," Shimizu continued, clearly mocking Skip's lecture minutes before, "since you are responsible for maintaining the relationship with my ministry, you would be held accountable if the contract between us were terminated and *all* of your volunteers, not just Nonaka-san, were sent home. Am I making myself clear?"

Skip felt nauseated and remained silent for a long time. Finally, he uttered, "Yes."

"What do you mean my assignment's been canceled?" Jenny demanded.

She pressed her temples as if trying to squeeze out the pain she felt, then dropped her hands and locked eyes with Skip.

"How the *hell* did this happen?" she cried, raising her fist to strike out at whoever had dashed her dreams, the hopes of her family.

Desperate to spare Jenny the agony that the truth would cause and keep the *honne* from threatening their future together, Skip recounted Shimizu's *tatemae* story of a principal's terrible mistake and an older Hasegawa child suddenly collapsing under the pressure of preparation for university entrance exams.

"I am so very sorry, Jenny," he said and reached out to touch her hand across a low-slung table in a quiet corner of the lobby lounge.

"I know how much coming to Japan meant to you, but"—he forced his voice to brighten as he continued—"I have some good news. I spoke with VSA's executive director. He has an unfilled teaching position at a girls' high school in Incheon, in South Korea, and a wonderful family there who would love to host you. I know you haven't prepared to live and work in Korea, but we're confident you would transition quickly. The position is for almost a year, a little longer than here in Japan, but we could announce our engagement next summer when we both return to the States. You could be on a flight there tomorrow. What do you say?"

Jenny withdrew her hand from his and wiped the tears from her eyes. She gazed out a large floor-to-ceiling window over a manicured Zen rock garden. A light rain had fallen earlier that morning and darkened the color of the rocks, gravel, and sand. Skip watched her look out over the garden and realized again how much he adored Jenny, how much he longed to share his life with her.

"It's true, isn't it?" she asked in a whisper without taking her eyes from the garden.

"What's true?"

"That time grinds rocks to gravel and gravel to sand until finally the finest grains of sand are blown away by the wind or washed away by the rain. But the process takes time, more than a hundred years, doesn't it?"

"Jenny . . ."

She shifted her body abruptly to face him. "Please, don't!" she hissed and thrust a quivering hand in his face to silence him.

"You have told me a story," she said, lowering her voice. "Now let me tell you one. Mine is not *tatemae*, it is *honne*, literally the sound of truth. Around ninety years ago, a man lived in northern Kyushu. He amassed a fortune working as a tanner due to his skill and the monopoly his family had enjoyed in his area for generations before the so-called emancipation of 1871. He and his wife had a baby son in 1886 whom they loved above all else. So great was their love that when he reached the age of twenty, they offered to buy him a marriage into the family of an impoverished samurai from a nearby town. The samurai, though poor, was a member of the highest class in feudal Japan, just below the nobility. There was only one condition: the son would have to take the samurai's family name and never again see or even mention his real parents."

"Jenny, please . . ."

"Quiet," she commanded. "I am *not* finished." She paused to collect herself then continued.

"The son refused out of loyalty to his parents and also because he had fallen in love with the fifteen-year-old daughter of a butcher in his village and could not bear to part from her. When word of the son's refusal reached him, the samurai became enraged at the insult. He vowed to kill the son, something the samurai could do with impunity, given his class. So the son and his bride hurriedly sailed for Hawaii to labor in the sugar plantations there. They worked hard and saved enough money to migrate to the Central Coast of California. After trying for many years, they were overjoyed when they gave birth to a son. The new parents purchased a fruit farm just outside of San Luis Obispo in the name of their son who, as an American citizen, could own agricultural land, something forbidden to the parents under California's alien land laws. A sordid piece of American history you probably didn't know about, did you?"

"No," Skip mumbled. "No, I didn't."

"I didn't think so. So busy studying Japanese history you don't know your own?"

"I never said America was without blame in its treatment of Japanese immigrants," Skip objected. "The internment was horrific."

"Yes, it was. But this is the first time I've heard you speak of it. You didn't even think to ask what my family endured!"

"I thought about it. I . . . well, I just felt it would be prying to ask."

"Prying? You said you loved me. How in the world would learning about the discrimination my family suffered be *prying*?"

"Wait a minute, Jenny. It's not like I spent a lot of time with your family. You didn't even tell them about me!"

"No. And now I'm glad I didn't."

Skip opened his mouth to protest, but Jenny cut him off.

"Here's some more family history you didn't care enough to learn. Despite being treated as less than fully human by the white society around them, the family prospered over the next two decades. The boy excelled at school and graduated from UCLA in 1941. Although his parents and he were unjustly relocated to an internment camp in early 1942, the son answered the army's call for Japanese-American volunteers and fought in Europe with a regiment made up mainly of other Nisei. After the war ended, he returned to graduate with honors from USC dental school and married a lovely Japanese-American woman from Los Angeles.

They gave birth to a girl, whom they named Jennifer, and raised her in West Los Angeles."

"Jenny, I don't know what to say," Skip declared in a hushed tone.

"I'm surprised," she responded bitterly. "You always seem to have something sensible, something *fucking* rational to say, but, if you don't now, shut up! Just shut up! I have listened to you for months; you can listen to me for a few more minutes."

Jenny took a deep breath, choked back a sob, and continued.

"The little girl was raised to be thoroughly American, but, curious about her family's country of origin, she studied Japanese language, history, and culture at Berkeley. After graduation, she applied to go to Japan to teach English with a program based in San Francisco. As she learned more about Japan's feudal era and the caste system and patched together what she had heard over the years from her grandparents about their lives, she began to wonder if her grandparents had been born outcasts. She never asked, not wanting to meddle and embarrass her family, but also because she was terrified . . . frightened in her bones to learn the *honne*."

Jenny stopped for a moment, lowered her head, and covered her face with her hands. Skip watched as her shoulders heaved with sobs. After several minutes, she uncovered her face and composed herself, her swollen, reddened eyes cutting into Skip.

"And now," she declared numbly. "And now, she doesn't have to be afraid any longer. Because she knows. I will tell my family the pretty *tatemae* story you told me, but they will *know* the truth just as I do. The joy they experienced at my returning to Japan will die because no matter how many decades have passed, time has not yet worn the rocks of superstition into gravel and the gravel of prejudice into sand and the sands of suspicion into grains finally insignificant enough to be blown away forever."

"Jenny . . ." Skip begged, his hands outstretched toward her.

"Wait," she snapped. "You asked me a question. My answer is: '*No.*' I will not go to South Korea. I will return home to Los Angeles on the ministry's ticket. I'm tired of hiding behind *tatemae.* I would not be a good representative of VSA anymore. I do *not* believe in cultural sensitivity, if that means repressing anger at what is so obviously immoral, standing silent, hands in your pockets in the face of injustice."

"I didn't ignore the injustice!" Skip objected. "I argued against it. I fought for *you.* But it's not my right to judge people for making choices driven by a culture I only partly understand. That's what *they* are doing to *you*, judging you without knowing you. Reacting irrationally. Besides, even if I were to judge them, what would it change? What good would it do you? I don't have the power to force them to accept you."

"Yes, they have tried and convicted me without knowing me, but that's not judging. Judging means to decide based upon evidence. That's where you're wrong. It is your right to *judge* them for their choices; their choices are *proof* of their bigotry. As for what power you have, you could go to the US embassy and complain or to the press, at least the American press, since I doubt the Japanese press would concern itself."

"I threatened to do exactly that! But Shimizu said the ministry would terminate its contract with VSA, send everyone home, and destroy the program for anyone involved now and in the future. Is that what you want?"

Jenny's eyes flared with rage. "Perhaps you can't act for VSA, but you can act for yourself. You can quit!"

Her words tugged at his soul, but his shoulders sagged.

"You know I can't do that," he exhaled. "Not just because of my contract with VSA, but I promised the volunteers, *your* friends and colleagues, to see them through their assignments. You said yourself I *was* the program here. If I left, I would be abandoning everyone else. But . . . I won't renew my contract for another year, I promise. We can be married as we planned, assuming . . ." Skip understood Jenny's suffering and outrage, but also felt unfairly attacked for an impossible situation he did not create. "Assuming your parents won't *object* to your marrying an Anglo."

As soon as the words escaped his lips, he regretted them.

Jenny's head snapped back. Her face blanched.

"How *could* you say something like that? I never said they would object. I said I wanted them to meet you first before telling them we were in love. I believed they would have loved you—or at least the man I thought you were—and I was willing to fight if necessary for the person I thought I loved. And you, what are you willing to *do* for me? *What?*"

Jenny closed her eyes and took a deep breath.

"I'm sorry, Skip. I don't want or need your *promise* to *someday*, when it's *convenient,* act on your conscience."

Jenny rose abruptly. Skip jumped up and reached for her arm.

"Don't touch me!" She jerked her arm free, spun around, and slapped Skip on the face.

"Jesus, Jenny." Skip rubbed the red blotch on his cheek. "Please be just a little reasonable. You're demanding I choose between your love and the promise I made to the others."

"Yes! That's exactly what I'm asking you to do! And, yes, it may be completely irrational, but emotions are what make us human, what it means to be alive—and to love. So, choose Skip. Choose!"

"I don't want to lose your love, Jenny."

"Lose my love? Ha! You have a bigger problem: You've lost my respect. You told me you wanted to spend the rest of your life with me, didn't you?"

"Yes, I did and I do," he whispered, holding both hands over his heart.

"Well, I don't. I want a man I can respect, someone who knows right from wrong *today*, in *any* culture. Someone who is willing to fight for my love, the way my grandfather fought for my grandmother's. Goodbye, Skip. Don't worry about taking me to the airport. I can find my own way."

Jenny whirled around and rushed away.

Skip took two steps to follow and stopped. One more and stopped himself again. He stood paralyzed, his heart urging him forward, his head holding him back, unable to move, unable to choose, until he collapsed into his chair, dazed at how his dreams of a life with Jenny had turned to dust so quickly.

9 Exploitation

When the burgeoning tension rising within her reached a crescendo, Maddie uttered a long "*Aaahh*" and felt her stomach muscles shudder and release. A moment later, she pulled Rex up from between her legs and drew him into her, moving her hips furiously in rhythm with his until he cried out, drove himself deep into her, and collapsed. She gathered him into her arms, kissed him gently on the lips, and lay his head against her shoulder. She inhaled his heady, leathery scent and smiled.

"Well," she sighed, "six months was a long, long time but I think we're doing a good job of making up for it. How many times in two weeks?"

"I lost count," Rex replied. "God, it's so good to feel you against me. How did we ever let ourselves be separated?"

She gazed down at him and marveled at the mystery of why a gorgeous, magnetic man like Rex would love her—too tall, more than slightly gawky, overly-competitive Maddie.

"We didn't choose to be apart, love. It just happened. Skip did what he could."

"Fuck your old boyfriend!" Rex yelled and flipped over, his arms outstretched toward the fan whirring above their bed at the Tong Ah International Hostel and Hotel in Singapore's Chinatown. "We wanted to be in Bali, remember?"

"VSA didn't have any positions on Bali. Bandung and Sukabumi were the closest cities with openings."

"Right!" Rex snapped. "He said Bandung and Sukabumi were only fifty miles apart. I thought we'd be together at least every weekend like when you lived in Palo Alto and I lived in Berkeley. Shit! He didn't mention it takes four hours by bus on a good day, eight when it rains, and we'd only have Sundays off from teaching."

"Rex," Maddie pleaded, anxious to avoid another argument over Skip. "He did his best on short notice. Remember we refused to take assignments outside Indonesia? We wanted to be able to travel cheaply to Bali after we finished?"

"There was an opening at Lembaga Ilmu Bandung for another English teacher! Did he mention that? We could have been in the same city."

"He probably didn't know."

Maddie hated lying to Rex, but wanted desperately for their vacation to end as happily as it had begun. She feared he would grow even more agitated if he knew the truth.

"I'm sorry, Maddie," Skip raised his voice above the static on the phone line. "I've done everything I can. Frankly, the executive director doesn't trust Rex after what happened in the Philippines and neither does our Indonesia program director. The only reason they've agreed to send you both to Indonesia is because I vouched for you, and you promised you would make sure Rex fulfills his contract and follows VSA rules."

"That's so unfair!" Maddie objected. "Rex left his post early because of his injuries. You know he saved a woman from being raped. How can you hold that against him?"

"I told you. The information we received said nothing about rescuing someone, only that he sustained an injury during a local festival."

"Exactly," Maddie insisted. "The rescue happened after the festival."

"Then why didn't he contact someone at VSA? He took off and sent a letter of resignation to the principal."

"I'm not sure he was thinking straight. Have a little compassion."

"Maddie, please," Skip begged. "I trust your judgment, but the Indonesia head only agreed to the placement if you are in different cities. He's your boyfriend and they don't want to risk offending cultural sensitivities. I'm sorry, Maddie. It's the best we can do."

"Oh, yeah? I don't believe you," Maddie snorted. "You're still angry I broke up with you and keeping Rex and me apart is your revenge."

"Oh, come on, Maddie. We broke up two years ago. We've both moved on."

"Okay, if you've moved on, tell me this: Would you be happy living away from your girlfriend?"

"As a matter of fact," Skip declared, "we will be living apart for nine months in order to comply with VSA rules. So I don't see why Rex and you can't."

"I THOUGHT we were close friends," Maddie retorted, irritated by Skip's condescending tone. "This is how you treat me after all the years we've known—and loved—each other?"

"Come on, Maddie! Give me a break! We hadn't SEEN each other for almost TWO years when you called. We didn't communicate except for a couple of letters complaining about living in Paris. Then, out of the blue, you telephone two weeks ago asking for help securing VSA posts in Indonesia—a much more challenging country than France—for you and Rex, someone who

abandoned his VSA post a year before. Christ! Under the circum-
stances, I think I've done everything and more to help you both."

"Still, I don't see why . . ."

"I'm sorry you're not satisfied with what VSA is offering,"
Skip interrupted. "But there's nothing more I can do. Take it or
leave it, Maddie."

Skip's tone on the call nearly eight months ago still rankled
her, but she couldn't dwell on it; she had to turn her energy to
Rex.

"Even if we *were* in the same city, we couldn't live together,"
Maddie stroked his shoulder, hoping to soothe him. "We're not
married and neither one of us wants to get married. You know
the rules. It's probably easier to be physically apart than to see
each other constantly and not be able to touch."

"And the *two* times in *six* months that I was able to visit,"
Rex interjected, "we couldn't stay together even for one night.
How fucked up is that? Huh?"

"What was I supposed to do?" Maddie demanded, holding up
her hands in frustration. "Sneak out of my host family's house?
Pak Wibowo is the rector of LIB for Christ's sake and Bu Wibowo runs the English-language program for the entire institute.
They are prominent people in Bandung and, more importantly, I
have come to like and respect them. They are the kindest, most
thoughtful, and most compassionate couple I've ever known."

"But not *understanding* enough to allow us to sleep together?"
he bleated.

"Of course they wouldn't understand! They're conservative
Muslims. Do you know they have scrimped and saved for years
to put down a deposit for a trip to Mecca for the *hajj* later this
year? It's been their *dream* to make the pilgrimage before they
get too old. They think this year might be their last chance. Yet
they're spending money every week on me—not just my meals,

but they've bought me clothes, too, and taken me on day trips around Java."

"You teach them English they can use during their *hajj*, right? Lessons they don't pay for!"

"I'm *happy* to. They've been so sweet. Remember, they invited you over for dinner when you were in Bandung."

"A couple of dinners don't justify their keeping us apart!"

"Oh, come on. Lighten up, sweetheart," Maddie begged and playfully punched his arm. "It's our last day of vacation and we've had such a great time. It's 1975. A new year."

"I know. I know," he groused and jerked his head back against the pillow. "That's what makes it so damned hard to go back to Sukabumi alone. What right does some asshole in the ministry or Pak Wibowo or anyone else for that matter have to dictate how we define our relationship? We lived together in California after Paris. We're just as committed to each other as any married couple. A scrap of paper with a gold seal on it has no meaning for *us*," Rex growled and slapped the mattress.

"I know it doesn't, babe."

"How did we allow one of the most important expressions of who we truly are to be throttled by the nonsensical rules of a sexually repressed culture? Not only can't we sleep together, but I had to shave my beard and cut my hair. And you can't go outside unless your shoulders, arms, and legs are covered. We should have fucking stayed in California."

"Take a deep breath, sweetheart, and remember where we were when we decided to come." Maddie knew from experience Rex could let his emotions run wild, and with them his judgment. "We graduated in the midst of a stagflation recession and neither one of us could find a job worth anything. If we'd stayed in California, you'd probably be working at a gas station and I'd be waiting tables. We're making more money here, earning credit toward a teaching credential, and in only five months we'll be able to live together on Bali, one of the most beautiful tropical islands in the world."

"We swore to each other we would only go abroad if we had a refuge where *we* could be ourselves, remember? What happened to *that* promise?"

Maddie remembered the promise. She also remembered the dinner with her Stanford classmate, Shirley, a demure, shapely woman of mixed American and Filipino blood, when her feelings changed. As they shared a pizza and a couple of pitchers of beer at the Oasis, Rex held forth on the recent indictment of seven former White House officials for obstruction of justice in connection with Watergate. Shirley raved about his *brilliant* analysis and implored Rex to share his thoughts on the oil embargo. Maddie watched Rex beam at Shirley. When they were walking out, Shirley coyly suggested they should all get together more often to talk politics and Rex eagerly agreed. Alarm bells sounded in Maddie's head.

"In two months," Maddie said later that night as they lay like spoons in bed, "I'll have a masters in American literature and you'll have your MA in poly-sci. We have to support ourselves in a raging recession. Maybe there'd be more opportunities in the short run outside the United States to find interesting work, to save some money."

"We agreed never to go abroad again. You said you couldn't be happy outside the States. Remember?"

"I know . . . but I received a letter from Skip . . ."

"What?" Rex interrupted. "You're still in touch with that jerk?"

"It's a form letter. I'm sure he sent it out to scores of people. VSA is actively recruiting for positions beginning in July—four hundred dollars a month, room and board, and plane tickets all included. They've arranged with the University of San Francisco

to give volunteers credit toward a teaching credential. I wonder if we should think about it."

"Why in God's name?"

"If I'm with you, someone I love, someone I really trust, we could create a refuge from all the crazy foreignness, a haven where we could recharge and relax, where we would be accepted as our old American selves . . . I don't know. It might be okay."

"We'd still be living among people who would expect us to be like them."

"Not if we went to a place like Bali, in Indonesia. It has a young expat community, gorgeous beaches and tropical forests, a thriving local arts scene, and a pretty tolerant culture based on Hinduism. Don't you think we could be happy living in our own American cocoon in a place like that?"

"Perhaps . . . It would be nice to save some money," Rex replied, then rolled over to face Maddie and began to stroke the inside of her thigh.

"Oh, that feels so good." Maddie reached for Rex and pulled him toward her. After they made love, Maddie held Rex in her arms and caressed his cheek.

"What do you think about Bali?" she asked.

"Bali!" Rex exhaled. "Exotic Bali would be wonderful."

"Be reasonable," Maddie implored again. "When we're finished in June, we can travel to Bali with enough money to live on the beach at Kuta for six months, no rules, just tropical fruit, coconut trees, beautiful sunsets, and a laid-back community of travelers and surfers. You can grow your hair out again, and I'll be able to wear shorts, even a bathing suit. It's supposed to be paradise, the haven we dreamed about."

"It's still a fucked-up situation," Rex griped and slammed his fist down on the bed again. "Being together these past two weeks has been great, but it's made me realize how painfully lonely I am in Sukabumi. Frankly, I would rather go home than rot by myself in my claustrophobic bedroom for another five months."

Maddie tried to quiet the fears fluttering inside. She loved Rex, and when Rex, handsome, captivating, charismatic Rex, was by her side, her insecurities seemed to evaporate. Still, during the six months they lived together in California, she couldn't help but notice his compliments—which had been so effusive in Paris—had waned and he seemed not just to notice but revel in the envious glances cast at Maddie by other young women. She had suggested Bali to keep women like Shirley away from him, having convinced herself that more time together would deepen their love. If they returned to California now, she had little doubt that another woman would capture his attention sooner rather than later. Losing her family to divorce and Skip to his stubborn selfishness had deadened her zest for life. When she met Rex in Paris, he magically revived it. She couldn't bear to lose him— and that part of herself he brought to life.

"And miss our chance to live on Bali? Be practical. If we left now, we'd lose the salaries we make teaching and VSA wouldn't pay for our return ticket. It would take all the money we've saved and more just to get home."

"So, we're fucking screwed?" He shook his head in disgust.

"I'm sorry, sweetheart." She kissed his salty cheek. "The only exception to VSA's rules is for married couples, and that's not us."

"Hey." He turned and laid his leg on Maddie's stomach. "Maybe we could get married in Singapore. I could take the open teaching position in Bandung, we could live together until June, and get divorced in Bali. What do you think?"

Rex had a tendency to be overly dramatic, as if he were the leading man in a daytime soap. She loved his passionate temperament, so different from Skip. But his hot blood scared her when it led to grandiose claims and impulsive choices with disastrous consequences.

"Now, *that's* a crazy idea." Maddie rolled her eyes. "I haven't a clue what the legal consequences of being married and divorced would be and don't want to find out! Besides, what would I tell my mom and dad? They'd be apoplectic if I didn't say anything and then discovered I'd misled them. And would you lie to your mama?"

"All right," he grumbled. "Too bad we can't *pretend* to be married for six months, you know, like we were in a movie showing only in Indonesia."

Now, Maddie thought, she did agree with Rex. Certain situations would be so much easier if they were only scenes in a play that could be forgotten once the final curtain came down.

"Wait! Wait!" She bolted up. "You've given me an idea. Let's talk to Old Wang at the desk. Come on." Maddie leapt from the bed and began to throw on her clothes.

Fifteen minutes later, Maddie and Rex were meandering through the warren of streets in Chinatown. They darted in and out of the narrow paved road, trying to hide from the sweltering midday sun in the shade of storefront awnings and canvas canopies suspended over street hawkers. The air was thick with the pungent, sweet-sour smell of ripe fruit and vegetables mixed with the dank, putrid stench of human sweat and dog shit.

Maddie held a slip of paper with a crude map penciled on one side and the address and name of a man scrawled on the other. They stepped by a street market filled with old women in cotton *samfu* and black slippers, each with a single plait of black hair down her back. The women squatted behind woven baskets piled high with *gai lan*, bok choy, Chinese cabbage, and red and yellow lantern chilis as they bellowed in Chinese, begging the passing crowd to buy their wares. The vegetable market gave way to men in shorts, loose-fitting T-shirts, and plastic sandals standing behind makeshift street stands and hacking with cleavers at carcasses of ducks, chickens, and cows. Customers elbowed to the front of the stalls, yelling out the precise portion they wished to buy. Dogs scurried around the throngs, hunting for dinner. Rickshaws and bicycles wove their way down the crammed street, their drivers barking at pedestrians who failed to move quickly out of their way.

"We make a left here," Maddie said looking up from the map and pointing to a narrow opening between two shops. They walked single file down the alley, passed a man in a tiny room beheading and skinning a large snake and a woman wearing a *cheongsam* behind a counter stacked with jars of herbs, plants, and animal parts sold for use in traditional Chinese medicine.

"What's that?" Rex exclaimed, pointing to a rack behind the woman where long, slender animal parts with a pink, meaty color hung.

"Well, the basket below them is full of deer antlers," Maddie gestured. "So I'd guess from their shape those are deer penises."

"Good God!" Rex shuddered.

"Come on," she giggled. "Just another block."

In a few minutes, Maddie stopped before a faded concrete building and checked the address. "This is it," she whispered and pointed to a tiny enclosure where an elderly man lounged behind a table reading a Chinese newspaper and smoking the stub of a cigarette. Brushes, ink, paper, and an abacus rested in front of him. "He's a professional letter writer," Maddie whispered. "We want his son, Hu Chien-ping."

"Excuse me." Maddie moved into the doorway. "We would like to speak with your son, Hu Chien-ping."

She enunciated each syllable of the name slowly and clearly as if talking to a child. The letter writer looked up from his reading, stared with glassy eyes at Maddie for a moment, and shouted in Chinese toward a door in the back of the room. The door opened and a chunky young man with short hair and a pencil-thin moustache stepped out.

"My name is Chien," he said in a clipped, British accent, smiling mischievously. "How may I be of service?"

Maddie explained briefly what they needed and Chien nodded.

"Easily done. Please write down your names here exactly as they appear in your passports. The cost of the service is fifty Singapore dollars. In advance."

Chien handed Rex and Maddie a notebook and a pen. After they each had written their names in the book, Rex handed Chien a fifty dollar note.

"Excellent. I'll be back shortly."

Fifteen minutes later, a grinning Chien gave Maddie a manila envelope. "Congratulations to you both and sincerest wishes for a long life of happiness."

Maddie and Rex nodded and stepped outside. A few paces down the alley, Maddie reached into the envelope. She extracted a square piece of parchment with their names on it, the typed Indian-sounding name of a solemnizer, the typed Chinese names of two witnesses, a handwritten signature in the lower left-hand corner of a Malay Deputy Registrar, the printed official initials of the Registry of Marriage at the bottom, the gold and cardinal red coat of arms of the Republic of Singapore embossed at the very top and, just below the state crest, large, red cursive letters inscribing the words *Certificate of Marriage*.

"Hooray!" Maddie cried and threw her arms around Rex. "We're married! Now, give me a week to talk to Pak Wibowo and Bu Wibowo about our thrilling announcement. I'll try to persuade them to arrange for LIB to take you on. I hate to deceive such goodhearted people, but it's only a little white lie," she said, holding her thumb and index finger slightly apart. "They will never know the truth."

"You're a genius, Maddie!" Rex exclaimed and then kissed her.

"It was your idea, really," she responded, knowing how much he appreciated praise. "I don't expect a problem. After all, if I move out, they'll no longer have to feed me and they'll be able to save a little more for their *hajj* later this year. I'll send you a telegram after I've arranged everything with Pak and Bu. Explain to Pak Suprato and Bu Sinta what happened in Singapore and apologize deeply to Rector Susilo at the Institut Teknologi for leaving your position halfway through the year. Tell them that you are sorely needed in Bandung in a couple of weeks . . . by your wife!"

"Wait! What about VSA? Rector Susilo will certainly contact VSA in Jakarta to ask for a replacement."

Damn, Maddie thought. Rex was right. Rector Susilo would inform Alan Black, the Indonesia director. Alan would be enraged when he heard their marriage had disrupted his program. Yet, what could Alan do other than whine they should have waited until their teaching obligations were fulfilled? He would realize VSA's Indonesian partners would expect a married woman to live with her husband and would look critically at VSA if he objected. Alan would surely complain to Skip. And Skip, punctilious Skip, Skip who wore his pride in always doing the *right* thing on his sleeve, would be outraged. But no less furious than Maddie had been with him for separating Rex and her in the first place. Maddie smiled. Fuck him, she snorted to herself. Serves him right.

"Yes, you're right," Maddie replied. "Rector Susilo will tell Alan and Alan will be angry. But, love, we're married! What God has joined together not even VSA can tear asunder!"

"*Selamat pagi*, Bu Wibowo. *Selamat pagi*, Pak Wibowo," Maddie greeted her Indonesian mother and father as she walked into their kitchen and inhaled the scents of coconut, coriander, and lemongrass. Bu Wibowo—a short, bustling woman, with a round face creased by a brilliant smile and long black hair tied in a bun—was making breakfast. Pak, tall for an Indonesian man, sat waiting. His long face, graying hair, and a thin moustache whose ends drooped at the corners of his mouth reflected his taciturn nature.

"*Pagi*, Maddie," replied Pak from his seat at the square wooden table. He took a sip of his *kopi tubruk*. Maddie loved the earthy, slightly acidic aroma of strong Indonesian coffee poured directly into a glass, residue and all, and sweetened with sugar.

"*Pagi. Apa kabar*, Maddie?" asked Bu as she set down two platters, one filled with a pile of *nasi kuning*, rice flavored with turmeric, lemongrass, and *pandan* leaves and cooked in coconut milk, surrounded by sliced cucumbers and tomatoes, and another with *enche kabin*, chicken pieces marinated overnight in coconut milk and spices and then pan-fried.

"*Aku baik. Kalau kamu?*" Maddie replied, sitting in the chair opposite Pak Wibowo. She could smell the spicy scent of *kretek*, the clove cigarettes beloved by Indonesians, carried by his clothes. She scanned the two large platters. Bu had made her favorite breakfast on her first morning back from Singapore.

"*Baik, terima kasih,*" replied Bu Wibowo, who lowered herself onto the chair between Pak and Maddie. Knowing they had exhausted Maddie's limited store of Indonesian phrases, Bu inquired, "How was your trip to Singapore? You arrived so late last night we didn't have a chance to talk."

"It was wonderful," she gushed, her eyes shining. "In fact, I have some happy news. May I . . . may I share it with you?" Maddie asked knowing it would be impolite to blurt out the story Rex and she had devised.

Bu Wibowo put her glass of sweet tea down on the table and faced Maddie. Pak, who had just served himself some *nasi kuning*, set the serving spoon down on the platter.

"Please tell us," Pak said, lacing his hands together on the table in front of him. "You know we consider you to be the child we were never blessed to have. Of course, we wish to hear what has made you so happy."

"Thank you, Pak. Do you remember the teacher from Sukabumi who visited me last year? Rex Moreno?"

"Yes. He seemed like a nice young man," Bu offered and tilted her head forward slightly.

"We met in Singapore and spent a great deal of time together. On the day before we were to return, he asked me to marry him and . . . and I said, *yes!*"

"So you are engaged?" Bu asked. "How exciting!" She beamed at Maddie.

"No, I mean, yes; we were engaged, but . . . we couldn't wait so we went to the Registry of Marriage and were married that day!" Maddie exclaimed.

Pak's mouth dropped and Bu's eyes grew large as a full moon. Maddie quickly removed the marriage certificate from her canvas bag.

"Look!" She placed the certificate on the table before Pak and Bu.

They stared down at the parchment. Pak reached out to touch the Coat of Arms of the Republic of Singapore, as if to assure himself he wasn't dreaming.

"He will come to Bandung in about three weeks and we . . . we were hoping we could stay in one of the LIB cottages for married faculty and he could take up the vacant English teaching position."

"But," Pak sputtered, looking up from the certificate, "what . . . what about your parents? Do they know this Rex? Did they not wish a proper marriage ceremony? A reception with family and friends? They must be very troubled."

"Oh," Maddie responded. Why hadn't she realized Pak and Bu would react with concern for her parents? "Ah, well, they met Rex before we left for Indonesia and they . . . I mean, my mom, knew how much I liked him." Maggie tried her best to allay their anxiety, embarrassed to lie to such dear people, but certain the truth would distress them more.

"We called my mom first and then my dad—you remember they are divorced? They were a little startled, but when they heard the delight in our voices, they were thrilled for us. We'll have a ceremony and a reception when we return to California."

"This seems quite unusual, even for young Americans," Pak declared sternly, shaking his head. "How could you marry someone you've known for less than a year? How could you do this without . . . without *rasa bersalah*! Marriage is not . . . not something to be done without serious thought! And how could you do this while you are living in our house and we are responsible for you?"

Pak's rebuke pricked the bubble of confidence Maddie felt. Her eyes dropped like stones to the table.

"Pak," Bu interjected, turning toward her husband. "It is not our place to judge Maddie, to expect she have the same sense of shame, of *malu*, we do. She is an adult and a foreigner free to do as she wishes."

Bu rose, embraced Maddie, and cupped her face with her hands. Maddie gazed up into Bu's eyes, begging her to understand.

"Look at her eyes! Look how joy lights them up! Do you not remember my eyes on our wedding day?"

Pak pursed his lips and stared at Maddie. After stroking his chin for a few moments, he let out a long breath.

"Yes," he muttered as he nodded his head slowly. "I remember your eyes on our wedding day, and I see how happy she is."

"So you will arrange their housing and permit me to hire Rex for the English teaching position?"

"Yes." Pak exhaled audibly. "Of course."

"Oh, thank you, Pak," Maddie enthused, the weight of deception lifted off her shoulders. "Thank you so much. *Saya gembira.*"

"We are truly happy, too," Bu said. "Still, I am a little worried."

"What about, Bu?" Maddie asked as she helped herself to some fruit.

"Well, we have only three weeks to prepare."

"Prepare what?" Maddie set the serving fork down on the platter.

Bu did not respond. Her eyes stared out the kitchen window; her brow furrowed in concentration.

"I will call upon Ibu Sardjono," Bu muttered to herself. "She is a famous *dukun manten.* She will know what ceremonies are appropriate for such an unusual situation. Some combination of wedding rites and a reception, perhaps . . ." Her voice faded away into thought.

"Bu?" Maddie asked. "I thought a *dukun* was a shaman, a healer with magical powers to predict the future and communicate with spirits. Why would my marriage require a sorceress?"

"Oh, there are many kinds of *dukun*, Maddie." Bu laughed. "A *dukun manten* is a female *dukun* who uses her training and her spiritual knowledge to help organize wedding ceremonies, make the appropriate offerings to the spirits, and recite the correct prayers. Most of all, she conducts the rituals necessary to prepare a bride for the ceremony, to make her not just lovely on the outside, but to reveal her inner beauty, the sanctity of her soul. If you do not wish to use the word *dukun*, we also call such people *Pemaes.*"

"Okay," Maddie replied with a nervous laugh. "I'm glad you don't think I need to seek advice from the spirits—or a psychic—about marrying Rex."

"No, not about marrying Rex. That you have done. However, we must still ask Ibu Sardjono for her advice."

"I'm already married; why do you need to consult a *Pemaes*?"

"As I said," Bu explained patiently, "a *Pemaes* is a woman who helps a bride undergo the traditional rites before a marriage and also organizes the wedding and wedding reception. You are our daughter here in Bandung. Although we missed your wedding in Singapore, we must nonetheless celebrate your marriage."

"Oh, no!" Maddie bit the inside of her lip. "Please. We don't want to cause Pak and you any trouble."

"It is not a matter of trouble," interrupted Pak. "It is a matter of *bangga diri*. We would lose our sense of pride before others in the community if we did not commemorate an event as momentous as your marriage."

"But I don't want you to spend any of your money on a celebration for Rex and me," Maddie protested. "Please, we're just happy to be together."

"Maddie," Pak declared firmly. "We have accepted your choice to marry in your way. Now you, as our daughter here, must accept our decision to honor it in our way."

"But . . ."

"Pak is right, Maddie. Please allow us to do this according to our customs," Bu pleaded. "It is not just for you, but also for us as your Indonesian parents."

Maddie wanted to insist a celebration wasn't necessary, declare herself unworthy of such generosity of spirit. Seeing the determination in Bu's face, however, tears filled her eyes and a wave of gratitude washed over her. Improbably, Bu and Pak loved her, cared for her happiness without condition or complaint, even if it meant spending a small part of their own precious resources. If she was the daughter they were never blessed to have, they were becoming the family she had lost and longed for again. To refuse their offer would be ungracious and demean the affection they felt for each other.

"Of course. Thank you, Pak and Bu," Maddie acquiesced. "A little celebration would be wonderful, but please, please don't do anything special for us."

"We will consult with Ibu Sardjono and do what she advises, dear daughter. Do not worry. Because you are already married, I am quite sure the event will take the form of a reception that will be modest compared to the ceremonies surrounding a wedding."

"Oh, I'm glad it won't be too much trouble. Thank you again," Maddie smiled at Pak and Bu. Perhaps, she mused, a small party would be fun.

A couple of days after her conversation over breakfast with Bu and Pak, Maddie sent Rex a telegram saying they had agreed to hire him as an English teacher and would arrange for them to live in an apartment for married faculty. And, they had also sweetly insisted on hosting a small party to celebrate their marriage in three weeks. She couldn't wait to see him!

As the day of the party approached, Maddie slept fitfully at night and struggled during the day to remain focused on her teaching. She pestered Bu and Ibu Sardjono, a slender woman with an aura of mystery about her, a hundred times to tell her what they planned. Ibu Sardjono's English, however, seemed to be limited to a single phrase, "Do not bother, daughter," while Bu kept repeating that she had no time and Maddie should not fret because Bu would guide her through the whole day. *A whole day?* What modest reception could possibly take an entire day?

The day before the event, Bu refused to serve Maddie her usual breakfast and instructed her to fast.

"Why can't I have at least a little fruit, Bu?" Maddie complained.

"Because fasting cleanses the body and purifies the soul," Bu explained. "And tomorrow you must be as pure as rainwater both inside and out."

"But I'm already married," Maddie objected. With her high metabolism, she feared she would crash if she didn't eat.

"Yes, you are married, but this is what Ibu Sardjono has recommended to celebrate your marriage and ensure you live together in harmony."

"Will Rex fast as well?" Maddie asked anxiously, knowing Rex would likely rebel against what he would see as a silly superstition.

"Rex will fast from the time he arrives this afternoon. Pak and Ibu Sardjono will meet him at the bus station and take care of him until you see him tomorrow."

"Tomorrow?" Maddie rolled her eyes. "Why can't I see him today? Goodness, Bu. He's my husband!"

"It would be ill fortune to meet him tonight," Bu decreed. "Now, I have many things to attend to. I will see you this evening."

Maddie opened her mouth to protest but Bu hurried out of the kitchen before she could utter a word. *Goddammit!* she muttered to herself.

Just after midday, Maddie was meandering home, light-headed, hungry, and preoccupied with what the next day might hold. Suddenly, a man reached out from an alley and grabbed her arm.

Shocked a mugger would be so brazen in peaceful Bandung, she shouted, "Let go!" Spinning around, she raised her hand to slap him.

"Whoa! It's me, love." Rex took a step back and held up his hands to protect himself.

"Rex! What are you doing here?" Maddie hissed. "Bu said you were arriving this afternoon."

"Come over here out of the sun."

He stepped into a narrow passageway running between the tall concrete walls of two residential compounds. Maddie looked around to make sure no one would see them and followed Rex. Ten steps away from the road, Rex wrapped his arms around Maddie, and began to caress her neck.

"After making love every day on vacation, the last three weeks have been agony. I've missed you so much," he sighed, then squeezed her body against his and kissed her deeply.

"Rex," Maddie gently pushed him away. "I don't understand. Bu said Pak would meet you this afternoon at the bus station."

"I know," Rex snorted. "They are such fools. When I heard they planned to meet me at the station and sequester me until tomorrow, I boarded an earlier bus so I could meet you without anyone knowing. We have about three hours until I have to meet Pak at the station and there's a small hotel about five minutes from here. Come on, we can spend the afternoon together before they lock us away for the night."

Rex took Maddie's hand and began to walk back to the road.

"Wait!" Maddie freed her hand from his. "I . . . I can't."

"What?" Rex turned to face Maddie. "Why the hell not?"

"Because . . ." Maddie started to explain and stopped.

"Maddie!" he yelled. "Let's go. No one will find out."

Why not? She longed for the intimacy they shared in Singapore and Rex was right, no one would know. And yet, she hesitated. Why?

"I do want to make love with you this afternoon, and I know you'll think I'm being stupid," she declared finally. "Still, I would feel terribly guilty if we did. I realize we don't share all or even most of Bu and Pak's beliefs, but I love them. They are such good, decent people and all they're asking is that we wait another day. I . . . I don't want to disobey them, not on the last day I will be living with them."

"I don't believe this!" Rex shrieked, spinning around and clapping his hands over his head. "We're married, remember? What *right* do they have to tell us how to live our lives?"

"It's not about rights, Rex. I'm not doing it because I feel compelled but because I *want* to do it . . . because of everything they've done for me, because of how I feel about them."

"Even if they won't have any idea what you've given up?"

"Yes," Maddie sighed, "even if they won't have any idea."

"I can't believe you're choosing some antiquated notion of obligation to them over a romantic afternoon with me. Your husband!"

"I'm not choosing them over you at all," Maddie insisted. "I agreed to fake our marriage, to *lie* to them, so we could be together. Come on, love. It's only one day."

Rex turned away for a moment and then abruptly pivoted to confront Maddie. "This feels an awful lot like rejection, Maddie. Have your feelings for me changed during the last three weeks?"

"Oh, Rex," she replied, then stepped forward and kissed him. "*Nothing's* happened that affects how I feel about *you,* about us. It's just, well, the prospect of moving out of Pak and Bu's home has made me appreciate them even more. I want to be, for at least one more day, the daughter they say I am to them."

"I think you're crazy," he finally replied. "But, okay, for today. After tomorrow, we're free to do as we please. Agreed?"

"Yes, agreed," Maddie said and threw her arms around his neck. "And thank you."

Maddie walked the remaining mile home feeling proud she had obeyed Pak and Bu's wishes. She was anxious, too, knowing Rex did not react well when he felt rejected, even for a day. She passed through the gate to the backyard in a haze, still grappling with her conflicting emotions. To her astonishment, she looked up to find a graceful canopy of diaphanous blood-red and milk-white cloth on a wooden stage that workmen had elevated in the backyard. Behind the stage, they had constructed a luxuriant backdrop of emerald banana leaves. Hanging from the poles supporting the canopy were long strings of jasmine blossoms, garlands of white lilies, and ornaments made from plaited coconut leaves. Maddie walked over to stroke the fragrant decorations and, a smile parting her lips, inhaled the sweet, rich scent of the flowers. Almost immediately, she felt her neck muscles loosen and, for the first time in days, a sense of peace filled her. She had worried what a reception would entail, but saw now the party would take place at Pak and Bu's unpretentious home, a place where Rex had visited twice, and which could accommodate only a small group of familiar faces from the Institute. Rex loved parties and being the center of attention. She felt sure he would quickly forget their quarrel. Exhausted from fasting, she moved to her bedroom and lay down for a nap in the sultry afternoon air.

Maddie awoke at twilight just as Ibu Sardjono arrived in a brightly colored horse-drawn cart filled with plants. After unloading the *dokar*, Ibu Sardjono directed two workmen to festoon the canopied stage with gigantic stems of ripe bananas, pots of deep green palm fronds, and baskets of young yellow coconuts. In the center of the platform, she placed a gracefully curved polished teak stool.

Surveying the stage, Maddie was amazed. In less than a day, the *Pemaes* had transformed Pak and Bu's backyard into a dreamscape of the elegance and bounty of nature, as if Maddie had stumbled upon a wondrous clearing in a magical forest. She felt grateful but also a little guilty. Were they using part of the funds set aside for their *hajj*?

"Daughter, you must retire shortly after sunset," Bu commanded. "You will need your strength tomorrow."

Irritation at Bu's new directive immediately supplanted her concern for their finances. "If I will need strength, why can't I have just a small bowl of rice?" Maddie whined. "I'm *starving*."

"Maddie," Bu said sternly. "I explained to you this morning why you cannot eat until tomorrow. Now I must go. I will wake you at dawn."

Maddie wanted to scream in defiance of Bu's officiousness. She began to regret her decision not to spend the afternoon in Rex's arms and worried again she had offended him. Fatigued by sleepless nights and weak from fasting, she stifled any protest against what she hoped would be Bu's last order. As she walked to her tiny room, she assured herself that Pak and Bu must have an expense account at LIB to cover the cost of a small party that would be, after all, as much for their colleagues as for Rex and her.

Despite her weariness, sleep did not come easily. She fidgeted in the stifling night air until midnight.

"Time to begin, daughter," Bu whispered in her ear.

Maddie groaned and rolled over. "It's pitch dark. Please let me rest a little more, Bu," she begged.

"There is no time. We need the morning to make you beautiful like a queen, like a goddess," she purred and stroked her shoulder. Maddie sat up and rubbed her eyes. Shadows cast by Bu's candle danced on the wall of her bedroom, mesmerizing her.

"What did you say?"

"Today you will become a queen, daughter."

Visions swirled in Maddie's head of her grass-stained-jeans, dirt-under-the-fingernails, bruises-on-the-knees childhood playing soccer and riding bikes and the hours spent as a young woman straining on weight machines, sprinting and jumping and drilling until she dripped with sweat. Skip's joking complaint, so painful at the time, echoed like a soundtrack over her memories: *Jesus, Maddie, sometimes you make love as if you're competing to win a wrestling match rather than expressing your affection.*

"I've never been treated like a queen or goddess before," she murmured, half to Bu and half to herself. Tears flooded her eyes. "I never wanted to be, or, maybe, I was too afraid to want to. I don't know what it feels like to be . . . adored."

"Today you shall be, dear daughter. Come, stand up tall and let me help you with this," Bu insisted quietly.

Maddie rose and gave herself over to Bu's gentle hands. Soon Bu had wrapped around Maddie a gossamer ivory *sarong* dotted with crimson stars. Bu led Maddie outside into the warm air as the sky began to lighten and the first calls of songbirds greeted the dawn. Approaching the stage, the scent of jasmine filled her nose and made her head swim. From somewhere in the house the shimmering, meditative chimes of bronze *gamelan* metallophones echoed. Entranced, Maddie was sleepwalking through a lush, verdant dream. Ibu Sardjono stood beside the curved teak stool and gestured for Maddie to sit down. When Maddie had lowered herself onto the flowers and blossoms scattered on the polished wood, Ibu Sardjono ran a comb several times through her thick blonde hair, drawing it backward from her forehead. She set a band of jasmine blossoms on Maddie's head and draped a shawl of jasmine blossoms over her shoulders. Maddie stared down at the flowery cloak and inhaled the ambrosial scent.

"This is the *siraman* ceremony," Bu explained as she took up a metal ladle and dipped it into a large bronze pot filled with warm spring water and floating jasmine, magnolia, and rose petals. "Please close your eyes and fold your hands on your lap. Now take a sip, wash your mouth with the water, but do not spit it out. Let the water fall slowly from your lips."

Maddie opened her mouth slightly to allow a rivulet of water to run down her chin onto the jasmine shawl. As the moisture soaked through to her skin, Maddie felt as though she were being baptized again, reborn.

"Excellent. Now, we shower you with water to purify your soul and cleanse your body."

Bu poured water over Maddie's head and gently massaged the perfumed liquid into her hair. Maddie closed her eyes, relishing Bu's touch. Bu repeated the dipping and showering three times before handing the ladle to Ibu Sardjono. The *Pemaes* streamed water slowly three times over Maddie's shoulders, legs, and feet. Maddie slipped in and out of consciousness, luxuriating in the caress of the water on her skin. When Ibu finished, she patted Maddie dry with cotton towels.

"*Wis pecah pamore*," whispered Bu. "Your beauty is revealed. You are ready for marriage. Now come with us to your room."

Maddie opened her eyes but could not focus, languishing in a half dream state in which her senses were strangely heightened. The two women took her by the arm and led her to her room. Once they had stripped Maddie of the damp *sarong* and gently dried her, Ibu Sardjono motioned for Maddie to lie face down on a fresh white cotton cloth that Bu had spread on her bed. Over the next two hours, the *Pemaes* massaged Maddie with flower-scented coconut oil and rubbed her skin smooth with a blend of rice, turmeric, sandalwood, jasmine flowers, and a hint of jasmine oil. Maddie felt her muscles soften and her skin luminesce.

Ibu Sardjono led Maddie to her bathtub. Lukewarm water laced with petals of jasmine blossoms awaited her. During the bath, Bu brought Maddie a wooden cup.

"We call this *jamu*. It is a special drink made with turmeric, ginger, egg yolk, and herbs. It will purge your blood as Ibu Sardjono has cleansed your body."

Maddie lifted the cup and inhaled a sweet, woody aroma. She sipped the brew and felt the warm, spice-ladened liquid course through her veins. She lay back against the bathtub and dozed and dreamed for she did not know how long. At some point, Ibu Sardjono tenderly lifted her from the embrace of the water and patted her dry with cotton towels. Maddie, still groggy but glowing inside and out, held her arms over her head and swayed into Ibu's touch, savoring the tenderness of her fingers. When Maddie was dry, Ibu rubbed a moisturizer scented with jasmine and frangipani over her body while Maddie swayed from side to side in rhythm with the tintinnabulation of the *gamelan*.

"Now, sit here, daughter," Bu said softly.

Maddie lowered herself again onto the teak stool, which had magically been transported from the stage to Maddie's tiny bedroom. She closed her eyes. Her mind moved in and out of consciousness as Ibu Sardjono dried Maddie's hair with a clean towel, occasionally massaging Maddie's scalp and temples until her head tingled.

"We call this special incense powder *ratus*," Bu explained, swinging an ornate bronze incense burner that poured fragrant smoke around Maddie's head. Once her hair had thoroughly dried and been perfumed by the incense, the *Pemaes* combed her hair straight back and tied it tightly into a bun. Over the next hour, Ibu Sardjono cleaned Maddie's neck and face, skillfully shaving off any tiny hairs that marred her satiny skin. Afterwards, the *Pemaes* massaged foundation makeup on to Maddie's face by pressing and smoothing the cosmetic with her fingers, accented Maddie's eyebrows and lashes with eyeliner and mascara, and carefully applied lipstick using lip balm, a lip liner, and finally a lip brush.

"Now," Bu said as she came back into the room. "One last thing and you will truly have become a queen. Please close your eyes again."

She handed the *Pemaes* a tiara-like silver hair comb studded with diamonds and decorated with tiny flowers made of gold. The *Pemaes* carefully laid it on Maddie's hair and fastened it with bamboo hair pins. When she had finished, Bu stepped in front of Maddie. She held up the oval hand-carved *suar* wood mirror Bu had brought from her room.

"Now open your eyes, daughter, and behold, you have become a goddess."

Maddie opened her eyes and gasped. She touched her lips and then, trembling, reached out to the image in the mirror. The young woman who stared out from the glass was an exotic, alluring, blond Javanese beauty, a queen, a goddess to be not just admired, but worshipped. Maddie felt dizzy for a moment in disbelief. She stared into the mirror and smiled tentatively. The vision smiled back. *You are beautiful, Maddie. You are a goddess.*

Ibu Sardjono and Bu helped Maddie into her undergarments, a lushly decorated night-blue and silver batik skirt, and finally a lace overlay wedding dress that sparkled with beads.

"Come, Maddie," said Bu a few moments later. "The *andong* is here. It is time to meet your Rex."

"Oh," Maddie said vacantly, her mind still intoxicated by the picture she had seen of herself. "When will Rex arrive?"

"No"—Bu giggled softly—"he is not coming here. We are going to the Savoy Homann."

Bu took Maddie's hand and led her outside where a multi-colored, four-wheeled, horse-drawn carriage waited. The driver helped them into the carriage and drove slowly off, the bells on the horse's harness jingling. As the carriage rocked and swayed down the street, Bu reached over to take Maddie's hand in hers.

"When we arrive at the Savoy, you will see your Rex standing by the entrance with Pak. Please do not be startled. Rex will be dressed as a Javanese king just as you have become a queen. You will approach him until you are about three meters away. At that moment, you will engage in what we call *Balangan Suruh*, a ceremony where you will throw to each other seven small bundles of betel leaves wrapped around limes. Betel leaves have the power to chase away evil spirits. It is to show that you are Maddie and he is Rex, real persons, not demons. Do you understand?"

Maddie felt as if she were riding on a magical carriage floating somewhere on a cloud high above Bandung. She heard Bu's voice from somewhere far below.

"Do you understand?" Bu asked again.

Maddie shook her head trying to regain focus. "Yes, I think so."

"Good. Next Rex will crush a chicken egg with his right foot and you will wash his foot with water scented with flower petals. This is the ritual of *Wiji Dadi,* which shows that Rex is ready to assume his responsibility as a husband and you are ready to serve him faithfully. Afterwards, Ibu Sardjono will accompany you into the reception hall. A *cucuk lampah,* a man in traditional Javanese dress, together with several other dancers, will parade before you, leading you through the guests to your throne on the stage. There Ibu Sardjono will hand each of you some food and you are to feed each other and drink sweet tea. This symbolizes your desire to share your food and property in marriage. Please eat and drink slowly even though your fasting has made you hungry."

"Yes, Bu. I will," Maddie muttered, still in a trance.

"Good. Pak and I will sit to your right on the stage. When you have finished eating, guests will come to the stage to congratulate Rex and you and to greet Pak and me. Afterwards food and drink will be served to the guests, there will be *gamelan* music, and the performers will celebrate your marriage with classical Javanese dances near the stage. When the performance has ended, Ibu Sardjono will lead Rex and you to Pak and me for the last ritual, *Sungkeman,* when we will give you our blessing."

As Bu recited the various ceremonies and rites, Maddie's mind gradually cleared. She gazed down at her dress and remembered her image in Bu's mirror. The spell cast by the morning, however, was broken. She looked like a Javanese queen, but she had no idea how to act like one. She was, after all, still Maddie, impulsive, insecure Maddie, who towered awkwardly over most Indonesians. Anxiety shot through her veins.

"Oh, Bu." Maddie turned to her Javanese mother. "I don't want to make any mistakes. I don't want to embarrass Pak and you or myself. Will you help me, please?" Maddie grasped Bu's hand.

"I will be there, but Ibu Sardjono will assist Rex and you." Bu squeezed Maddie's hand. "You are not the first young person to be frightened by having to observe these rites," she assured Maddie. "When Pak and I were married, he tried to crush the chicken egg three times but was so nervous he kept knocking it aside. Finally, the *Pemaes* knelt down to hold it for him." She cackled at the memory.

"How many guests will there be?" Maddie asked. "Fifty or sixty? All friends from the Institute?"

"Oh, no, Maddie," Bu replied and laughed in surprise. "Five or six hundred."

"Five or six hundred!" Maddie exclaimed, alarmed at what the reception must cost and fearful how she would behave before so many friends of Bu and Pak.

"Yes. We *must* invite the whole community to join in the celebration," Bu said. "It is our custom."

"But how could you pay—" Maddie began before Bu interrupted her.

"Here we are," Bu gestured toward the entrance of the hotel. "There is your Rex and Pak. Now is the time of the *Balangan Suruh*. I will step down first. Follow me, daughter, and remember to walk with your spine straight and your head high like the beautiful goddess you have become."

For the next four hours, Ibu Sardjono guided Rex and Maddie through the various ceremonies and processions. She made sure they thanked each of the hundreds of smiling guests—"*Terima kasih banyak*"—who greeted them in return with "*Selamat menempuh hidup baru,*" wishing them much happiness in their new life.

Even with Ibu Sardjono's guidance at every moment, Maddie felt terribly unsettled. She agonized over each step, whether she was acting appropriately or had unintentionally committed some offense that would bring shame to dear Bu and Pak, who had obviously gone to great expense to celebrate their marriage.

Maddie could not help but notice that Rex, by contrast, reveled in his role, grandly accepting the guests' goodwill and congratulations and loudly expressing his gratitude with a flourish of his hands. The effortlessness with which he assumed the character of Javanese royalty made her feel even more inadequate.

"You are remarkable, you play the role of a Javanese king—and a very handsome one—so well," she said out of the side of her mouth conscious of the crowd in front of her.

"Thank you. Sweet of you to say," he replied. He gestured out toward the hordes of guests, the elaborately decorated hall, the *gamelan* orchestra, and the dancers who were gathering in front of them. "I never thought anything could make up for how much I've suffered since we came to Indonesia—long hours teaching, living in an oppressive culture, separated from you—and then you made me feel miserable when you turned me away yesterday. But this is incredible. We must be the first foreigners to be honored like this. This is the most fun I've had since we left California."

"Fun?" Maddie replied incredulously.

"Sure! Haven't you loved being pampered and dressed and honored and allowed to act monarch for a day? We should have gotten married sooner!"

She knew by the beaming smile on Rex's face that he wouldn't understand the emotions bubbling inside her. The adulation seemed to have intensified what she had always dismissed as his occasional self-absorption. Bu and Ibu Sardjono had made her more beautiful than she could have ever imagined and yet he neglected to return her compliment. Did self-regard blind him— or did he simply not care? His failure to utter one word of praise cut her to the bone. In the past, she had disregarded his egotism as the part of his personality that loved to perform and had sympathized when he described how someone or something had victimized him. Now an unfamiliar unease flowed through her mind. She took a deep breath and forced herself to concentrate on the dancers to show appreciation for the celebration Pak and Bu had arranged.

When the last dancer had finished, Ibu Sardjono led them to where Pak and Bu were sitting. The *Pemaes* reached up to their shoulders and gently but firmly pushed them to their knees. Bu and Pak placed their hands lightly on the young Americans' heads.

"Rex and I ask for your blessings," Maddie said to Pak and Bu, her head bowed, her voice breaking. She gazed up and saw joy radiate from their faces. "And we wish to thank you *so* very much for arranging this wonderful day, a day we will never forget."

She peered sideways at Rex, hoping he would join her in expressing gratitude. To her distress, he added nothing except an ostentatious nod and a patronizing, entitled smile. Her previous agitation flooded back. Was he still performing the role of a Javanese king worshipped by his undeserving subjects? Or was this Indonesian lord Rex at his core, and the man she loved only a character he played for her?

"You have our blessing," Pak responded, withdrew his hands, and turned toward Bu.

"Yes, you have our blessing," Bu said, lifting her hands. "Now, the *Pemaes* will lead you in a procession through the hall, to the elevators, and to your wedding room here. On Sunday, Pak's assistant will help you move into your new cottage. Maddie will have her usual teaching schedule beginning on Monday. I apologize, but it will take me two weeks more to arrange for classes for you, Rex. In the meantime, return to Sukabumi to pay your final respects to your family and friends there."

"Thank you again, Pak and Bu, for everything you have done for us. We are overjoyed," Maddie said, gratitude welling up in her. "And . . . and we hope to repay your kindness. Although it is a small thing, I wish you would allow me to continue to give you English lessons for your *hajj* later this year."

Bu looked down at Maddie. Her face shone with pride.

"You are so kind, daughter. We would be glad to accept because we still hope to do the *hajj* in the future."

"In the future? But . . . but I thought going on the *hajj* this year was your *dream*." Maddie's voice caught in her throat.

"Yes, it was a dream of ours, but only one. Today has been another. Now, go with our blessings, dear daughter. With our love."

Maddie looked up at Bu and Pak and felt her heart break open.

"No!" she cried out. What was she forsaking? Her body started to tremble. Tears streaked her makeup. She reached out for Bu's hands and kissed them. She grasped Pak's hands in hers and clasped them to her cheek. "No! Please no," she implored them. "I don't want to leave you!"

"Maddie," Rex hissed and raised himself up. "It's time to go."

Maddie glanced over her shoulder at Rex, whose face contorted in annoyance. She turned and cast her eyes up at Bu and Pak who were now standing. They exchanged glances, leaned forward, and together gently lifted a sobbing Maddie to her feet.

"You are not the first daughter to be afraid to leave your parents for a new life." Bu smiled and softly wiped the tears from Maddie's face. "Now go, knowing you take our love with you."

Bu nodded to Ibu Sardjono, who took firm hold of Maddie's arm and led Rex and her away.

10 REALIZATION

A round golden moon rose in the sky above Sukabumi. Its bright beams cascaded through the sole window in Rex's bedroom and penetrated his eyelids. He groaned, cursed the sheer, translucent curtains, and wrapped the pillow over his head. He would, at last, leave Sukabumi tomorrow for Bandung. His body craved rest after a frenetic few days of apologies and goodbyes to Pak Suprato, to Bu Sinta, to Rector Susilo, to his students, and, most difficult of all, to lovely Wulan.

The inexorable moonlight flooded his small room. It illuminated the dark wood walls and floor with an eerie luminescence so palpable that Rex sensed it creeping across the floor toward him. The hairs on his neck tingled. He wrapped the pillow even more tightly around his head. CRACK! A plank in the wooden floor snapped under the weight of . . . what? Rex tossed the pillow aside, flipped over, and sat up, sweating in the muggy night air. He rubbed his eyes in disbelief. On the floor about five feet from the end of his bed a Javanese langur squatted in a gleaming pond of moonlight. The long-tailed monkey had a ghost-white face and ebony eyes that glared accusingly at Rex. It's musky, pungent smell suddenly pervaded the room.

Rex's eyes darted to the window. It was closed. His heart began to race.

"Wulan has sent me," the langur announced and leapt onto the foot of the bed.

Rex jumped backward in terror, his shoulders banging against the wall at the head of the bed.

"You have hurt her deeply and now she will repay your cruelty."

"Wulan? Why?" Rex cried. "Wait! No!"

The langur bounded onto Rex's lap, opened his mouth, and spewed a stream of putrid, viscous liquid into his face.

"Agh!" Rex shrieked and tried to wipe away the fetid, sticky spittle.

The langur leaned back and howled with laughter. Abruptly the monkey turned, jumped into the hole of incandescence on the floor, and sank slowly, silently below its surface.

Rex's head began to ache furiously. His insides churned and he retched several times. He tried to get up to call for help but the room spun around him. He slumped over and collapsed.

When Rex woke at dawn, a treacly substance covered his face and hands. He remembered the langur and examined his fingers. They were coated in blood. He instinctively reached for his nose. Blood seeped from his nostrils. He touched his ears and felt blood in his hair. Propping himself up, he looked down at his pillow. It was soaked with blood. He panicked and bolted upright. The early morning sunshine shone through the closed window. What happened?

His head exploded in excruciating pain. He squeezed his temples with the palms of his hands, trying to force out the knife-like sensation. His stomach convulsed. The light receded rapidly from his eyes. As he lost consciousness, he fell backward, sinking into a black pool.

Maddie sprinted along the dilapidated concrete platform of the Sukabumi train station and threw her arms around Skip. She inhaled his scent, surprisingly familiar, a mix of his citrusy cologne and the musty smell of his sweat. His wiry body, which she had once known so well, felt different somehow. She looked up into his eyes and realized with a start he'd grown a couple of inches and put on ten pounds of muscle in the two and a half years since they had last been together. He was now taller than she was.

"Oh, I am *so* glad you're here!" she exclaimed and hugged him hard again before releasing him. "Thank you for coming so quickly. I know it's not an easy trip from Tokyo."

"No, it's not," Skip replied more brusquely than he intended, fatigue permeating his body. "I was leaving for Hong Kong on holiday when your telegram arrived. Luckily, I was able to get a cheap ticket on short notice from Hong Kong to Jakarta."

"You made good time, Skip, but I'm not surprised. You've always been so efficient about everything."

"Well, I'm not sure about that. I feel pretty beat-up right now; it's almost twenty-four hours since I left Tokyo and I haven't had much sleep," he said, wiping sweat from his face. "God, it's a sauna out here."

"Yes"—Maddie laughed—"but you get used to it. Come on. Let's walk to the station. No air conditioning but at least we'll be out of the sun."

They walked into the worn, one-room depot, and Skip dropped his carry-on bag to the floor.

"So, I'm confused," Skip said. "You telegrammed you were in trouble. That it was a matter of life or death, but you seem fine. Are you okay? What's going on?"

"It's Rex," Maddie began.

"Rex?" He cut her off. "I thought *you* were in danger."

"I know. I know. I'm sorry, but I knew you wouldn't come for Rex."

"So you *lied* to me?" Skip bellowed.

"No, not exactly. It *is* a matter of life or death and I *am* in trouble. Would you let me explain? Please?"

Skip gritted his teeth. "Has Rex taken off again? Done something to offend his host family? And why couldn't Alan handle it? He's the head of VSA here."

"No, nothing like that. Rex is very sick. Severe, migraine-like headaches, vomiting, bloody diarrhea, abdominal pain, and bleeding from his nose and ears. He can hardly move he's so weak."

"That's awful. I'm sorry," Skip said, taken aback. "What does the doctor say?"

Maddie stopped and looked at Skip with teary eyes.

"Doktor Suyono says, well, Suyono says he may die if he can't keep anything down and the bleeding doesn't stop. He's been in the hospital, or what passes for a hospital here, for four days. Just a bed with a saline drip to try to keep him hydrated and a fan overhead. They've given him an antibiotic to deal with what might be some kind of parasitic intestinal infection or amebic dysentery, and an injection of vitamin K to try to stop the bleeding. Nothing's helping. The healthcare system in Indonesia is pretty primitive, especially in a place like Sukabumi. There's also the problem of his blood type."

"Why?"

"It's O negative, very rare among Indonesians, so blood transfusions are not an option until we find a source and neither the hospital nor the Indonesian Red Cross has a record of any Rh-negative donors. I'm AB positive. You're not O negative are you?"

"No, A positive. I can see you're terrified, Maddie." Skip reached out to squeeze her arm. "I'm sorry for him and . . . I apologize for snapping at you just now."

"Don't apologize. I knew I was misleading you, but I'm scared to death. Suyono insists the antibiotic and the vitamin K should have worked. He examined Rex thoroughly and couldn't find any medical reason for his symptoms. People with his blood type are more prone to bleeding, but nothing like what's happening."

"What does Rex say?"

"Rex has been sleeping most of the time, but when he's conscious he hallucinates and rambles on about a monkey from *bulan* coming into his room and spitting poison in his face."

"What is *bulan*?"

"It means 'moon' in Indonesian."

"Goddamn, he's sick, isn't he? Still, if he's so ill he might die, how can there be no medical cause?"

Maddie bit the inside of her lip and murmured, "Nothing a *doctor* can find, anyway."

"What? I'm sorry. My mind is numb from travel. I don't understand."

"It's . . . not easy to understand. Do you know what a *dukun* is?"

"I picked up a book on Indonesian culture at the Hong Kong airport. If I remember correctly, it said a *dukun* holds himself out as a shaman who can communicate with the spirit world—a traditional healer and a soothsayer, right? The book gave me the impression they're all charlatans taking advantage of ignorant people."

"Yes," Maddie replied slowly, "some are scammers, but others help people solve real problems."

"You don't actually believe a *dukun* has supernatural powers, do you?" Skip snorted.

"No, well . . . I don't know. I know one who helped my Indonesian family and . . . me a great deal. But," Maddie continued, anxious to keep the focus on Rex, "not every *dukun* tries to help people. Some practice *santet*, black magic to harm people. Suyono says that's the only explanation for what's happening to Rex."

"Jesus Christ, Maddie! What am *I* supposed to do? I don't know Indonesia very well at all. We need to contact Alan immediately. We should be able to call the VSA office or at least send a telegram from Rector Susilo's office. Let's go."

"*No!* I mean, yes, we could send a telegram from here, but we can't involve Alan."

"Why not?"

"Because he's furious with Rex."

"What aren't you telling me, Maddie?" Skip roared and threw up his hands. "Why would Alan be angry at Rex? You said this had nothing to do with Rex breaking VSA rules again."

Maddie took a deep breath and closed her eyes for a moment. Ever since she begged Skip to fly to Indonesia, she agonized over how to explain her fake marriage. Now the time had come. She could hardly breathe, as if the stress of the moment had locked her lungs in a vise.

"It doesn't. Not with the rules you mentioned anyway. Rex was about to leave Sukabumi to . . . to live with me in Bandung. Alan doesn't want anything more to do with Rex or, frankly, with me."

"You can't be serious!" Skip roared. "You know the policy against unmarried VSA volunteers living together. That's precisely why they posted you in separate cities. Why you *agreed* to live apart. Besides, VSA or not, I can't imagine anyone in the Bandung host institution would allow it either. Indonesia is an incredibly conservative country."

"Yes, it is. That's why we . . . well . . . we were married."

Maddie waited for the volcanic reaction she knew would erupt.

"*WHAT?* You're *married?*"

"Well, we are, kind of . . . but . . . only on Java," she muttered and looked away, her voice fading off into a whisper.

"How on earth can you be married only on *Java?*"

Maddie pawed the station's dusty concrete floor with her foot.

"We . . . we obtained a fake marriage certificate in Singapore and used it to convince my host parents we were married." She raised her eyes to meet Skip's.

His eyes widened in disbelief and then narrowed with rage.

"And *this* is how you repay me?" Skip exploded. "I persuaded VSA to send you to Indonesia despite everyone's misgivings about Rex. You gave me your *word* that you would live apart, follow VSA rules, and fulfill your contracts! I put *my* reputation on the line for you! What *were* you thinking?"

"We do take our work seriously and . . . and I love, truly adore, my family," Maddie objected. "They are *so* nice. They don't have a child of their own so they've practically adopted me. I am incredibly grateful to them," she said, her voice cracking as tears filled her eyes. "You know how depressed I was after my summers in Taiwan and Japan. I never thought I could feel close to someone from a different culture. I certainly didn't expect to develop deep bonds here in Indonesia. We are so different in many ways, but my Indonesian parents care profoundly for me and . . . and I cherish them. Please, *please* don't tell them or Alan or anyone else what I've told you."

Skip clenched and unclenched his teeth and dropped his head to his chest. "All right," he looked up and agreed finally. "I won't tell anyone. I'm glad you have a good relationship with your family here. But that makes your duplicity even worse. How could you deceive them? Just so you and Rex could live together for a few months?"

"We were impulsive and screwed up. We didn't give a thought to how my host family would react. I realize now I should have." Maddie's eyes pleaded for understanding.

"Yes, you fucking well should have," Skip swore under his breath and looked away.

Maddie had heard Skip curse only a handful of times before and never at her. She glared at him.

"I *already* said you were right and we were wrong," she barked. "Rex may be *dying*, Skip. What we did was foolhardy and dishonest, okay? But how can you let your goddamned moral purity stand in the way of helping to save his life?"

Skip opened his mouth to assail Maddie again, but just as quickly closed it. He exhaled, turned his back to her, and started to step away.

"*Please*," Maddie implored him as she grabbed Skip's arm and spun him around. "Look at me!" She pointed to her face. "All I'm asking is that you meet Doktor Widiyanto. Alan won't help and besides, I *trust* you, Skip. You're so damned sensible and smart. You're the only person within a thousand miles who can figure this out. We've been friends forever and we . . . we really loved each other once, remember? Meet Widiyanto; if not for Rex, then for me. If not for who we are now, then for who we once were. *Please.*"

"*Ahhhh*," Skip bellowed and threw his hands up in the air again. After several shakes of his head, he locked his eyes on Maddie and cleared his throat.

"Okay. That's why I came, and that's why I'll try to help Rex. Once I've done what I can, I will leave as quickly as possible because I don't want to participate in misleading anyone about your *marriage*."

"Oh, thank you!" Maddie gushed. "Thank you so much," she said and wrapped her arms around him.

"Sure. Sure," Skip replied, unwound himself from Maddie, and kneaded the stiffness from his neck. "Now, tell me why my meeting with the doctor is important when he's already concluded he can't do anything for Rex."

"That was Doktor Suyono. Widiyanto is a kind of specialist. Suyono suggested he might help Rex."

"A specialist? What kind of doctor is he and why would my meeting him be useful?"

Maddie hesitated and pursed her lips searching for the right words.

"Widiyanto isn't . . . a doctor. Not of medicine, anyway. He studied at the University of Indonesia and went to Cornell University for a PhD in agricultural sciences."

"Agricultural sciences? Maddie, I'm totally confused again. How is an agronomist supposed to cure Rex?"

Maddie faltered a moment. "By using white magic . . . Widiyanto is a *dukun* . . ." She quickly added, "The *good* kind."

"What? You've got to be joking. Maddie, what's *really* going on?"

"I'm telling you everything I know, goddammit! Indonesia isn't San Rafael, Skip. It isn't even Japan. Most Indonesians believe spirits exist all around them, not just causing sickness but also helping solve family problems and a lot more."

"I realize Indonesia isn't California or Japan—though some Japanese believe that humans can be possessed by a dog-spirit called *inugami*; perhaps it's similar that way—but why haven't *you* met with Widiyanto?"

"When Suyono met with him this morning, he told Suyono he wouldn't meet with me. Only with you."

"Oh, come on," Skip wiped his hand across his face. "That's not possible. Widiyanto can't know me!"

"You're right, you're right. He can't know me, either. But Suyono told me that, before he breathed a word about Rex or me, Widiyanto seemed to know everything about us, that Rex was sick, that we were married, and . . . well . . . about my old boyfriend who lived in Japan."

A shudder ran down Skip's spine. What was he getting into? What if he screwed up and made a mistake that caused Rex's death? His stomach began to churn.

"I need to think for a moment," Skip gasped, "and get out of the heat. Is the hotel nearby?"

They walked in silence to the Losmen Asri, a modest inn on a busy commercial street that ran about a hundred yards behind the train station, parallel to the tracks.

"Here are directions to Widiyanto's home." Maddie handed Skip a smudged piece of paper. "Widiyanto is expecting you this afternoon around five thirty. It's a thirty-minute ride on a motorcycle south of here. One of Rex's students, his name is Amat, is an *ojek* driver. He will pick you up here at five, take you out there, and bring you back when you've finished."

"What's an *ojek*?"

"A motorcycle taxi."

"Will he have a helmet for me? You know VSA prohibits volunteers from riding motorcycles without a helmet."

"For Christ's sake!" Maddie waved her arms in exasperation. "Same old Skip. So risk-averse, so rational, so rule-abiding about *everything*."

"Sorry to be so rule-abiding," Skip snarled. "Perhaps you might try it sometime. Could save everyone *else* a lot of trouble."

"Look." Maddie held out her hands. "Amat won't wear a helmet and he won't have one for you. It's not *keren* to wear a helmet, not cool. You'll be safe with him, don't worry. I've ridden with him a couple of times already and he's a careful driver."

"Oh, I apologize. I'd forgotten how important it was to you that I be *keren*. By the way, how's married life? I suppose that's *cool*, too?"

Maddie glowered at Skip, her arms folded across her chest. She *had* in fact been wondering whether one of the tectonic plates supporting her relationship with Rex had shifted. The vibrations she sensed had something to do with their wedding reception. Rex had too easily metamorphosed into a Javanese king who did not deign to trouble himself with the impact of the wedding on Pak and Bu's finances. And his failure to utter even one small compliment on her transformation into a gorgeous Javanese goddess had wounded her deeply. When Rex returned to Sukabumi, Maddie had had a few days to think. For the first time, she felt fissures in her love for him and wondered whether living together in Bandung would close them.

When she received the message that Rex was sick and needed her in Sukabumi, she had locked her doubts away. Skip's caustic question reawakened her concerns. But she wouldn't share her worries with Skip, not with his mocking tone—a stinging, taunting sarcasm she remembered too well from their time together. Whatever disquiet she felt about Rex, she had to focus on saving him. There would be time in Bandung to sort out what might be troubling her.

"Great," she declared brightly, swallowing her urge to bark at Skip. "Marriage is great. Thanks for asking. How's *your* relationship? Excited now that your nine months apart is almost over?"

"We . . . we broke up," Skip replied curtly and pressed his lips together.

"Ah, I . . . I am so sorry," Maddie said and, to her surprise, meant every word. "You seemed so happy on the phone in April." Maddie reached out to squeeze Skip's hand.

"Thanks," he sighed. "I guess I'm discovering that working for VSA is not conducive to being in a relationship."

Was he referring to their relationship, too, she wondered? Did he regret choosing VSA over her, after all?

"Look," Maddie said after a few seconds. "I apologize about the helmet, but there's nothing I can do and I've already paid Amat. Please persuade Widiyanto to see Rex," she pleaded.

"Okay, okay. I said I would try, Maddie," Skip replied in a voice weighed down by fatigue and exasperation. "I'll do my best."

"Thank you!" Maddie hugged him once more. "Get some rest. Amat will come to the lobby when he arrives."

At five, a coffee-colored, scarecrow-thin young man in tattered shorts and leather sandals, pulled up with a screech in front of the hotel. Skip was waiting in the lobby and walked out with a wave of his hand.

"Amat?"

"*Ya*. Amat," he replied, bowing his head slightly and placing his palm over his heart.

Skip handed Amat the paper with directions to Widiyanto's home. Amat read them quickly, nodded, and said, "*Silakan*. Please." He patted the seat behind him. Skip mounted behind Amat, who smelled of clove and gasoline, and they roared off on a paved road heading southwest.

Amat wove his way through a maze of pedicabs, motorcycles, and the occasional battered compact car crowding a commercial area of one-story shops selling textiles, plastic kitchenware, and motorcycle parts. Skip held his breath as long as he could to avoid inhaling the gassy, sooty exhaust spewed by the traffic. When he gasped for air, he immediately gagged on the fumes. The ear-splitting buzz of the bike made Skip's head ache.

As they left the town behind them, the pavement became a hard-packed dirt road bordered by rice paddies. Tucked here and there were tiny villages, each consisting of a few ramshackle wooden dwellings constructed with thatched, gabled roofs and woven bamboo walls perched on wooden stilts a few feet above ground. A small porch fronted each structure. Gardens of tomatoes and beans and the occasional papaya, pineapple, or apple tree bordered most homes. On the road by the villages, old women hawked fruit and vegetables to passersby from makeshift tables while grimy children raced around the houses, laughing and playing. In the dry paddies outside the villages, gray, leathery water buffalo transported sheaves of newly harvested rice to areas for threshing by hand. Beyond the rice fields, Skip could make out stands of banana, cassava, and coconut trees and the occasional patch of corn before the cultivated area faded toward the horizon into dense, verdant forest. The scenery was nothing like the well-tended, intensively farmed rural areas of Japan where small vehicles and farming equipment dotted a landscape crisscrossed by asphalt roads. In the filtered light of the late afternoon, Skip had the sensation he was riding back centuries in time.

Amat slowed the bike and yelled, "*Di sana!* There."

He gestured with his head toward a path on the left and steered onto a muddy, narrow trail. They slowly climbed a grassy incline to a large home with two gabled roofs perpendicular to each other, dark hardwood walls, and a floor raised off the ground by stone columns. A graceful, spacious veranda jutted out from the front. About thirty feet to the right of the porch stood an immense banyan tree. Its aerial roots descended down like the tentacles of some giant insect, embedding themselves in the soil below.

Amat stopped a hundred feet short of the front steps that climbed to the veranda and switched off the engine.

"Amat no go there," he said, shaking his head vigorously and gesturing toward the house. "Amat wait here," he stomped the ground and pointed to his feet.

"Okay," Skip replied and hopped off the bike. He rubbed some of the soreness from his backside and strode up to the house. At the foot of the steps, he waited for a moment to peer into the darkening deck above. The astringent smell of burning tobacco wafted over him. Out of the corner of his right eye, he noticed four odd-looking objects hanging from branches of the banyan tree. He squinted through the dusky light at the peculiar forms. A round piece of black plastic sat at the top and a large tin funnel was suspended on wires about a foot below. A long net draped from the funnel like an oversized fish net. He turned to take a closer look.

"Do not move!" a deep, gravelly voice commanded from the porch.

Skip heard the sound of a mallet striking a *gamelan* metallophone, which chimed and reverberated from the porch. A flock of some type of creature dropped from their perches in the banyan and flapped their wings furiously. Skip crouched and covered his head. His heart pounded violently. He glanced up to see what had darted from the tree and whether they were flying toward him. The creatures rose in the air and took flight over the forest behind the house.

"Welcome, Skip Burton. I am sorry to startle you. Most visitors do not appreciate having bat guano squirted on their heads. It is better to warn my guests to stay away from the beautiful banyan and, as a precaution, encourage my little friends to leave. Please come up now."

Skip straightened himself and calmed his breathing.

"They . . . they don't bite, do they?" he called out.

"No, no," responded the deep voice, followed immediately by a hoarse laugh like the cawing of a crow, only more guttural. "Hah. Hah. Haaah . . . Hah. Hah. Haaah. Bats are actually quite harmless, unless, of course, you are a mosquito, moth, or other insect or, in the case of fruit bats, a piece of fruit."

"Really? I thought they fed on blood. A friend of mine told me a bat swooped down to attack her and almost got tangled in her hair."

"Hah. Hah. Haaah . . . Hah. Hah. Haaah." The odd laugh resounded again. "Only three species of bat feed on blood and all live in South America. I am certain the bat did not intend to bother your friend. It is much more likely her scent attracted a number of mosquitos and the bat dove to feed on them. Bats do not attack humans unless the humans attack them first. Then they will defend themselves quite aggressively and bite back. Now, please, come up so we can talk in comfort."

Skip climbed up the wooden staircase and stepped onto the deck. He peered through the fading light to his right where two cushioned teak chairs and a low teak table covered with a batik runner stood. A slight, middle-aged man hovered by the table. A thin moustache wound around his lips to form a sparse goatee. A squashed *kretek* cigarette emitted fumes from a ceramic ashtray. Skip noticed Widiyanto wore a mixture of Western and Indonesian clothes all in colors of the night—and of wizardry: jet-black pants, a night-blue batik shirt festooned with white stars, and a black velvet *peci* on his head. He lit a kerosene lamp hanging overhead and several mosquito coils, which he placed on the table.

"There," he said as he sat down. "I do not normally need the coils because of the mosquito traps hanging from the banyan tree. Because you are a Westerner, however, I thought I should have additional protection. Please—" He motioned with long, bony fingers for Skip to sit.

Skip settled himself in the chair and examined Widiyanto's face in the light of the lamp. Deep furrows ran down his cheeks and amber eyes sparkled beneath bushy eyebrows. Widiyanto cocked his head and smiled broadly, inviting Skip to speak.

"Thank you for seeing me," Skip offered, then stopped in the hope that silence would induce his host to reveal why he had been summoned. Widiyanto, however, continued to smile and bobbed his head, indicating he expected Skip to make the first move in their game of conversational chess. Skip cleared his throat.

"I'm curious," Skip began, asking a tangential question he considered a safe opening gambit. "Where did you buy the mosquito traps?"

"I did not buy them, but obtained the separate parts and constructed them myself. Those are my homemade mosquito-collection devices," Widiyanto replied proudly. "The black plastic cover serves as a rain guard, the funnel acts to prevent mosquitos who enter from escaping, and the netting below collects them."

"But why would they fly into the funnel?"

"Because I have inserted in the bottom of each net two very sweaty socks whose smell seems to attract them. Capturing the mosquitos keeps them away from my home and consequently the bats from flying close to the deck. Every couple of days when they are full, I pull one of those strings to open the bottom of the nets." Widiyanto pointed to long threads that ran from the bottom of each net to the deck post nearest the banyan tree. "The mosquitos fly out and provide a feast for my bat friends."

Skip imagined a swarm of frenzied bats diving through the air a few feet from the deck devouring the mosquitoes like flying piranha. The vision sent chills running down his back.

"Well, thank you again," Skip said, reflexively relying on the politeness he used in Japan to establish goodwill before broaching a sensitive subject. He had no idea whether it had worked with Widiyanto, but felt it was time to engage with the *dukun*. "May I ask? How do you know my name?"

"Ah," Widiyanto rasped, betraying his smoking habit. "An Indonesian from Sukabumi would attribute such knowledge to my power to communicate in ancient Javanese with the spirits who inhabit our world but are invisible to all but a *dukun*." Widiyanto intoned with a dramatic sweep of his surprisingly graceful hands. "Hah. Hah. Haaah . . . Hah. Hah. Haaah." Staring into Skip's eyes, he continued with a thin smile. "On the other hand, a Westerner, like yourself, might reason that someone in the Indonesian family Rex Moreno lived with heard often about his girlfriend, or, should I say, wife? Hah. Hah. Haaah . . . Hah. Hah. Haaah." Widiyanto guffawed at the idea of Rex and Maddie's marriage so boisterously that afterwards he had to hack twice to clear his throat. "Her name is Madeleine but everyone calls her Maddie, am I not correct? And Rex did not hide his anger at her former boyfriend for not allowing them to be in Bandung together."

"Why would they communicate that information to you?"

"One of the advantages of being a *dukun* is that many people consult me to solve their problems if they believe those difficulties have a connection to forces beyond the natural world. It would not necessarily be wrong to deduce that among those people were members of Rex's family in Sukabumi looking for help with an issue involving Rex."

"What problem concerning Rex? And what does that have to do with knowing my name?"

"I apologize but I have a strict rule. Like a medical doctor or psychotherapist or lawyer, I do not disclose the nature of my work for others, although you may surmise in time why they were concerned and sought my help. As for your name, Skip Burton, rather than bore you with another contrast between a Western and an Eastern exegesis, I have a single, simple explanation. Maddie told Doktor Suyono you would arrive today. When Suyono and I met, he gave me your name . . ." Widiyanto's voice trailed away and he shrugged his shoulders.

"So, when you met Dr. Suyono, you already knew about Rex, Maddie, and me? And you allowed Dr. Suyono to think you knew all of that from spirits? How is that ethical? I thought you considered yourself the equivalent of a doctor or therapist or lawyer."

"Suyono came to *me*," Widiyanto emphasized, pointing his index finger at his chest. "He contacted me because he faced a conundrum his Western medicine could not resolve. I do not need to enhance my reputation with him. Like a doctor or therapist or lawyer, I also do not need to disclose the source of everything I know. Suyono is a Western-trained medical doctor, but he is also a Javanese. He accepts I have an ability to commune with spirits; it is as natural to him as believing in the Pythagorean theorem."

"All right," Skip said hesitantly. He accepted without question irrational beliefs could be part of a Javanese's cultural background, but wouldn't training in Western medicine have forced Dr. Suyono to question and ultimately disregard such convictions? The idea that someone could simultaneously hold two diametrically contradictory views of life disquieted Skip, but he wanted to get to the end game. "Why did you wish to see *me*? Why wouldn't you meet with Maddie?"

"Ah," Widiyanto sighed deeply and closed his eyes for a moment. "Suyono is a good medical doctor. I trust him when he says there is nothing more he can do to help Rex and does not know the cause of Rex's sickness. Because we have worked together before, he respects my approach to problems afflicting the mind or body, the consideration of other, less straightforward explanations. Suyono and I both fear someone has paid a *dukun santet*, a *dukun* who practices black magic, to make Rex suffer. I do not wish Maddie to know what Rex did to enrage this person so I asked to see you when I heard you were coming."

"How do you know Rex has done something to cause this? Who would be angry enough to want to make Rex suffer?"

"I need to see Rex and hear from Suyono again; there may be further information on Rex's medical condition. But if the situation is unchanged, let us agree I have reason to *suspect* what has happened, though without the evidence a rational Westerner would require."

"Why not tell Maddie?" Skip persisted. "She's his girlfriend after all," he added, noting Widiyanto had already ridiculed the idea she was Rex's wife.

"Because she will soon come to a fork in the road of her life and I wish her to choose a path for herself, not—as would be her impetuous nature, a character you know well—in reaction to what Rex has done. By contrast, I wish *you* to know the cause of Rex's sickness. You see, you also will be presented with a choice. Your decision must be informed by that knowledge."

"How could you possibly know what choice I have to make in the future?" Skip snorted skeptically.

"You do not need to understand everything now, Skip Burton. What *is* necessary, at this time, is to tell me what you wish from me."

How can I tell you what I want from you without you telling me first everything you know about the situation? he wanted to bark, but instead swallowed his irritation.

Skip had promised Maddie he would try to persuade the *dukun* to visit Rex and snapping at him would likely be counterproductive. Gathering his thoughts, Skip paused for a moment. He stared out at the banyan tree, whose huge form was vanishing quickly into the dark shadows of the night.

"I have a few questions first."

"Excellent. Very careful. Very reasonable. I expected no less. Please proceed."

"Who are you? How do I know that you're really a *dukun*, a shaman of some kind, someone with special powers?"

"You are skeptical with good reason. Many who call themselves *dukun* are in fact imposters seeking to fool simple folk into giving them money or property or even sexual favors for fake cures. In my case, my father's father was a *dukun*, as were both my father and my mother. All three were kind, generous, insight-ful people. They raised me to follow my own path, to become a *dukun* only if I chose to do so once I had learned enough to decide wisely. They taught me what they knew—and their learning and experience were prodigious—about herbalism, natural medicine, and the nature of human beings. In time I combined their knowledge with what I learned from my Jakarta University stud-ies in biology and psychology, and later at Cornell in agricultural science. Like them, I consider myself primarily a healer, someone whose calling is to cure human sickness whether of the body or the mind."

"So you heal by using herbal medicine?"

"Yes, sometimes. Occasionally by chanting mantra or *jampi*, what you would call an incantation, and sometimes by prophesy or by communicating with spirits."

"Do you really believe you can cure someone by casting a spell?" Skip snickered. "You can predict the future? You can communicate with spirits?"

"Hah. Hah. Haaah . . ." Widiyanto's laugh reverberated again. "A question only a Westerner would ask, and you are, undoubt-edly, a Westerner, Skip Burton. Perhaps I could respond by ask-ing whether *you* really believe in the power of what you call hypnosis and meditation and whether *you* believe some people, like my mother above all I have ever known, by training, experi-ence, and emotional intelligence have developed uncommon wis-dom and perceptiveness?"

"I have read some therapists use hypnosis and meditation to help people. I believe it's possible some people have innate per-ceptiveness or develop uncommon wisdom," Skip replied, think-ing of Francisco, who had introduced Skip to his baseball brothers.

"Good. Now ask yourself what is the difference between a Ja-vanese spell and Western hypnosis, between a Javanese communicating with spirits and an American psychologist encouraging meditation to commune with the unconscious mind, and between a Javanese predicting the future and an especially insightful Westerner using experience and intuition to assess what will likely transpire?" Widiyanto raised his bushy eyebrows, tilted his head, and spread his hands out. "Is your way of describing the same phenomena any better than a Javanese's?"

"If what you do can be explained scientifically, rationally, why do you hold yourself out as a *dukun*, as a person with supernatural powers? Isn't that deceptive?"

"Don't *you* respect our traditions?"

"Of course, I respect your traditions. I believe Indonesians have every right to follow the customs they wish. I don't think it's ethical to impose my cultural values, which may be no better than yours, on you," Skip declared. "However, *I'm* not seeking to judge; I am asking why *you*—with your Western training and education—pretend to be something you know you're not."

"Hah. Hah. Haaah . . . but I am not dissembling, Skip Burton. I simply do not see the world through only one eye. If I explained to a Javanese what I do in terms of science it would be like speaking English to him instead of *Bahasa*; he would not understand and, more importantly, he would not accept my advice. My goal is to help people, not to change their way of thinking. Curing an ailment may require guiding a person's thoughts in the right direction, but many times existing beliefs should be left undisturbed and instead used to facilitate relief."

"All right," Skip exhaled slowly and massaged his temples. "You asked me what I want you to do. Suyono informed Maddie that Rex may die but his sickness has no medical cause. She wants you to see Rex, to save him, if you can. I am here to ask you to do so. It's pretty simple."

"Nothing is simple when a *dukun santet* is involved."

"So you know for a fact that a *dukun santet* has caused Rex's illness? What has Rex done to the person who paid the *dukun santet*?"

"Based on what Suyono has told me, I am fairly certain a *dukun*, or at least someone who calls herself a *dukun*, has been asked to make him suffer and she is using what she holds out as *santet*. Why has someone paid to make Rex suffer? I will explain this as you ask, but on the condition that you must not share the information with Maddie." Widiyanto's eyes went cold and bored into Skip. "Do I have your pledge?"

"Yes," Skip replied uneasily. He didn't like withholding information from Maddie, but she had begged him to persuade Widiyanto to see Rex and the *dukun* seemed to condition his help on Skip's promise.

"Good. I will explain what I know. Rex apparently spent a great deal of time with a young woman named Wulan, a student in one of his classes who is very beautiful. She is also very intelligent and speaks exceptional English. There are rumors she was walking along a path in the forest outside Sukabumi when he appeared on the trail heading in the opposite direction. They decided to walk together. They reached a small grassy clearing where they agreed to rest. Their hands grazed, they began to kiss and caress each other, and they exchanged words of love. The next day Rex left for Bandung. When he returned, Wulan learned he had married Maddie. She became delirious with rage at having been betrayed and consulted a *dukun santet* whom she paid to punish Rex."

"You say there are 'rumors.' Is there proof they are true?"

"Hah. Hah. Haaah . . . Hah. Hah. Haaah . . ." Widiyanto cawed even louder than before and wheezed for air. "You are quite perfect! Just like a Westerner to ask for proof as if this were a trial. Given the circumstances, there is little question she is the source of the story. Perhaps what she believes really took place.

Perhaps she had become infatuated with her teacher and dreamed she met him along a forest path where he acted exactly as she desired. Perhaps it was some combination of the two."

"She would know it wasn't real, if it were only a dream, wouldn't she?"

"If she had been raised in your country, she would distinguish between what she fantasizes and what she actually experiences. Javanese, on the other hand, grow up believing their dreams are *part* of the same world as their real life. Their visions are just as real as if they actually happened. In Java, it matters little what actually took place because it is certain she *feels* Rex was unfaithful. However, the truth would matter if *you* would not want me to help Rex if what Wulan claims actually transpired."

"I . . . I don't want to judge her or Rex. I acknowledge my instincts as to what is real and true here on Java are based upon my Western cultural biases. It isn't rational for me to believe my response to a situation here would be any better than yours."

"So you will accept whatever I decide, Skip Burton?"

"I consider myself a guest in your country. I believe the situation should be evaluated according to Indonesian or Javanese cultural norms and values. I . . . I don't believe I have any right to interfere. If I did intervene, I would be more likely than you to make a bad decision. So, you should do whatever you would do according to your own cultural prescriptions."

"Hmmm. Well then, if Rex were Indonesian and the rumors were accurate, I would not allow black magic to kill him. He would deserve some punishment for taking advantage of Wulan when he was already committed to Maddie, but he has suffered enough already to atone for his betrayal. I will see him tonight and try to help in my way. You are content with that?"

"Yes. I am here to ask for your assistance as you see fit to give it."

"All right, Skip Burton. Before you go, there is something else you should know: Wulan is the daughter of a powerful army general in command of the region around Sukabumi. Helping Rex will inevitably anger the *dukun santet* and Wulan herself. If she goes to her father, there may be danger along our journey."

"I understand she feels wronged, but what could she say to her father that would lead him to endanger us? Is a young couple kissing or holding each other viewed as so immoral here?"

"They are frowned upon, but she would not go to her father with a tale of a few, now regretted, kisses or a heart broken by an impulsive, unfaithful man. No, she would enrage him by alleging something much more serious, for example, that Rex attacked her physically and tried to rape her."

"My God!" Skip exclaimed.

"We have to understand she feels deeply abused and could say anything to enlist her father's help in seeking revenge."

Skip took a deep breath. Rex and Maddie's fake marriage had begun as little more than an elaborate prank. Now it threatened Rex's life and endangered Maddie's, Widiyanto's, and his.

"Thank you for warning me. I would suspect the risk is even greater to you than to Maddie or me—or even Rex."

"Yes." He gave a half shrug. "If I help Rex, they will realize they must deal with me first before turning their attention to you. In any event, I will meet you in an hour at the hospital where Rex Moreno is being treated."

"Should I bring Maddie with me?"

"Yes, but tell her she must stay outside the hospital room until I call her."

"She won't like that," Skip muttered to himself and rose from the chair.

"Hah. Hah. Haaah . . . You see, Skip Burton, you, too, are capable of predicting the future!"

"I don't understand why I have to stay out here," Maddie growled at Widiyanto. "I've visited Rex many times since he was hospitalized four days ago."

"If you wish me to help Rex, you must do as I say," Widiyanto sighed.

Maddie bit the inside of her lip. Skip could see she was trying to keep her temper from erupting.

"Okay," she uttered, exasperated. "I'll be over there." She pivoted abruptly and strode toward a wooden bench in the dimly lit hallway of the hospital.

Skip walked with Widiyanto and Suyono through the swinging doors leading to the ward. Four painted metal cots with guardrails and black foam mattresses stood on each side of the center aisle. A movable wall of light-blue plastic curtains separated each of the beds giving a little privacy to the patients. Fluorescent lights flickered from the ceiling. Despite four fans squeaking as they turned overhead, the humid air reeked of excrement, bleach, and sweat.

"Rex is on the right at the end," Suyono gestured with his right hand. They moved down the aisle and stepped around the curtain shield.

Although he had never seen Rex before, Skip immediately recoiled at the sight of him. He was sleeping propped up on two pillows in a bleached white cotton hospital gown. His head was tilted to one side mouth agape, his face was pale and glistened with sweat, and his hairy legs sprawled out under a thin white sheet toward the foot of the bed. Something that looked like gauze protruded from both his ears and his nostrils. An IV ran from his arm inside the elbow to a saline drip hung on a metal stand behind the bed.

"Could you tell us again what you've concluded?" Widiyanto asked Suyono.

"Yes. Initially, we thought amebic dysentery or an infection of some kind was causing the abdominal pain, diarrhea, and bloody stool. Accordingly, we gave him the antibiotic flagyl and a saline solution to keep him hydrated while we performed tests on his blood samples and feces. Those tests unexpectedly came back negative and he has not responded to the flagyl. As for the bleeding from his nose and ears, we could not find evidence of a blow to his head so we ruled out trauma and assumed the bleeding would stop on its own. Naturally, we gave him vitamin K to promote clotting, as well as iron supplements," Suyono explained. "Yet his bleeding continues. Though he has type O, the bleeding is excessive even for his blood type. We would give him a transfusion, but he is O negative and we have no supplies available. As I told you this morning, we can think of no medical reason why the dysentery, vomiting, and bleeding continue. His youth and general good health are favorable factors. Still, he has grown very weak. We do not know how much blood he has lost, but I worry he may go into hemorrhagic shock if we cannot find a solution within a day or two."

"Could I examine him?" Widiyanto asked.

"Of course."

Widiyanto moved to the side of Rex's cot and stared down at his face for a moment. He yanked down the sheet and pulled up the gown to expose his midsection. Widiyanto peered down at something on Rex's side.

"Look at this," he said and pointed to a large splotch of dark purple. "This is a bruise indicating internal bleeding, isn't it?"

"Yes," Suyono said, leaning over to peer at the patch on Rex's side. "It wasn't there when I examined him in his bedroom. He may have been unintentionally hurt when he was transported here."

"But that was four days ago and the color remains deep purple, not green or yellow as would normally be the case for a bruise of that age."

"I can ask the nurse whether he has fallen from the cot more recently."

"Good idea. We'll wait here."

Dr. Suyono swiveled around and marched through the swinging doors.

"What do you think?" Skip asked as he stared at Rex. His dark features and black hair stood in sharp contrast to his pale skin. Even though Rex was extremely ill, Skip could see he was strikingly handsome. Widiyanto did not respond. His eyes were turned toward the window. He seemed to entreat the night sky to reveal its secrets.

"I believe," Widiyanto responded finally, "he is the victim of a powerful *dukun santet* whose work I've heard of several times in the past. She specializes in causing a person to bleed suddenly and uncontrollably, often to death"

"But what about the abdominal pain and vomiting?"

"They could be the result of the same substance that is causing him to bleed, rather than dysentery or an infection."

"Can you be sure?"

"I am not certain, at least not in the way a Westerner would understand. But because of the bleeding, I believe this *dukun santet* is responsible. My father first told me of her. She has special knowledge of how to harvest the most potent bark from a cassia cinnamon tree and to mix that with tonka beans imported from South America and water. She allows mold to form on the mixture. She bribes or blackmails a servant or someone else to place a concentrate of the moldy mixture in the victim's food. The victim's blood becomes so thin they bleed profusely even with only a slight injury."

"So there *is* a medical explanation for the bleeding?"

"For a Javanese, this would be an example of her black magic. When I was at Cornell, I undertook to investigate some of the more intriguing phenomena my grandfather and parents had told me about, including the work of this *dukun santet*. My research disclosed that cassia cinnamon and tonka beans share a natural substance called coumarin. I also learned a fungus in the mold could react with coumarin to produce a chemical called dicoumarol. That chemical can prevent the clotting of people's blood."

"Can you neutralize dicoumarol?"

"That is what is mysterious in this case. Usually an infusion of vitamin K counteracts the dicoumarol and clotting begins again. I suspect, however, the *dukun santet* realized Rex would have access to a doctor, which many of her victims do not, and so fortified the dicoumarol with a similar manufactured blood thinner called warfarin."

"What's that?"

"A stronger version of dicoumarol developed to kill rats by causing them to bleed to death."

"Rat poison?"

"Yes."

"Good God! Can you cure Rex?"

"I believe so . . . this time. I also suspect the antibiotic flagyl, far from helping with the nonexistent infection, may have exacerbated the bleeding."

"How?"

"When I was researching coumarin, I came across several studies at Cornell where farm animals, pigs and cows primarily, who had been fed antibiotics died of internal bleeding. The autopsies showed the animals had eaten substances that may have produced dicoumarol, or something like it, in their bodies and the antibiotics likely heightened the effect."

"So taking him off the antibiotic and giving him even more vitamin K should stop the bleeding? Once that stops, he will recover?"

"That is my belief and I will suggest to Suyono those steps. You should remember, however, the *dukun santet* will try again and again to make Rex suffer, even to kill him, and may take action against those who have helped him survive," Widiyanto declared with a shrug. "Her client is the daughter of a powerful man. At some point, she may succeed unless . . ."

"Unless what?"

"I apologize," Widiyanto said and turned to face Skip. "I thought you said you didn't wish to interfere, that I should do what I would do if Rex were a Javanese. Is that not right?"

"Yes, of course."

"Then you have no need to know what I plan, do you?"

"I don't. But I *am* curious. I believe knowing about other cultures helps me understand my own and therefore myself."

"Ah, you are a cultural anthropologist at heart, Skip Burton. I see. To satisfy your curiosity, then, I plan to have the *dukun santet* killed."

"WHAT?"

"That is what our social norms would prescribe in order to protect a Javanese from being killed by her."

"But you said you were the kind of *dukun* who only helped people, who didn't practice black magic."

"Oh, I would not kill her myself. I would not want anyone to know of my involvement. I would simply whisper to those who know people she has harmed before—and there are reportedly many—that she is the one who has made them suffer."

"They would kill her? Without a trial?"

"Yes, they would, together with their friends. Others who have suffered some unexplained harm and need to cast blame on someone, would also join in murdering the *dukun santet*. Rumors have incited mobs to commit such killings in the past. It would not be difficult to stir up the emotions of such people."

"But . . . but . . . can you be sure it is this woman?" Skip stammered in alarm.

"I am not as certain as a Western court would require. You told *me*, however, to act as if Rex were Javanese. I am convinced enough to take action in this case."

"But you can't just *murder* someone!"

"I already explained," Widiyanto snapped. "*I* will not murder anyone."

"Can't you just threaten her?"

"Yes, I could. But even if she agreed to meet and listen to what I say, which she would almost certainly not, she would scoff at my threats. She is well aware of who her client is and knows the client's father would not hesitate to kill her if she failed his daughter."

"I still don't think it is right to have her *killed*," Skip insisted.

"I'm sorry. Did you say *right*? As if you know what *we* Javanese consider good and evil. And speaking of what is right, you declared before you didn't have any *right* to interfere. You admitted it would be irrational to believe you wouldn't make a mistake in a context completely foreign to you. Yet, aren't you meddling now, imposing your Western values? Aren't you arguing implicitly that your beliefs, your ethics, your principles are superior to mine?"

"No, but . . ." the American tried to interrupt.

"Are you calling me immoral? Uncivilized? Less than human, even?"

"No! No, I am not saying anything like that. I don't believe my values are better than yours; of course, they aren't. They . . . they *are* just different. Still, this isn't a question of respecting what type of clothes others wear or the food they eat or how they express friendship or respect or love or even what God they worship. This concerns the taking of a human life!"

"From a person who has done great harm to many, including your friend, Rex."

"I still can't bring myself to acquiesce in *murder*."

"I see. So where does your emotional obtruding in other people's customs and traditions stop? Only to prevent a killing? What about to prevent a person from inflicting severe bodily harm?"

"Perhaps, I don't know," Skip mumbled in confusion. He had never considered that the cultural relativism he enthusiastically preached could lead him to accede tacitly to murder or grave injury.

"To obstruct a person from enslaving another? To block a person from kidnapping a child?"

"I . . . I said I don't know. *Maybe*."

For two and a half years, he had convinced himself—and others—of the sanctity of the principle that no person from one culture could truly understand a person from another, so the only rational response was to withhold judgment. Now, he found his mind treading water in a whirlpool of uncertainty.

"What about to forestall a person from inflicting serious emotional distress, the kind of mental trauma someone might suffer as a result of being openly and unfairly discriminated against for reasons beyond their control, on account of race, sex, or religion, a psychological injury that could afflict someone for the rest of their life?"

"No physical harm? I . . . I don't think so . . . but I don't know . . . it would depend," Skip replied and then stopped. His mind leapt back seven months to the last time he saw Jenny. He had been so sure at the time, but now . . . was the vile discrimination he had countenanced being perpetrated against Jenny, innocent, vulnerable Jenny, any less evil than inciting the murder of someone who might kill Rex? Did it warrant any less intervention, no matter how irrational?

"Well?" Widiyanto demanded.

Skip lowered his head and mumbled, as much to Widiyanto as to himself, "I . . . I don't know any more what I would do."

Maddie jumped up from her bench when Suyono burst through the doors. Her irritation had swelled when Suyono first appeared and dismissed her with a short wave of his hand before dashing away. She decided to tackle him if necessary to get an update on Rex. To her relief, Suyono approached her with a wide grin.

"Please wait here for Widiyanto and Skip. They will explain the situation, but we have good news. Rex will live, I believe, though he is extremely weak and will need time to recover fully. Now I must give instructions to the nurses without further delay."

He bowed stiffly and hurried down the stairway to the ground floor.

Maddie slumped down on the bench and closed her eyes in a silent prayer of thanks. She took a deep breath and slowly blew the air out, allowing her shoulder muscles to loosen for the first time since she heard Rex was sick. She choked back a couple of joyful sobs as relief surged through her body. A few more gulps of air and, spontaneously, her mind flew off like a bird freed from its cage, the cage of caring for Rex, back to Bandung. She saw herself sitting in Bu and Pak's kitchen, chatting in their own familiar jumble of English and *Bahasa*, and feeling their affection warm her soul, the glow of her devotion to them radiate from within. So strange, she thought, that people different in every way had discovered an ineffable connection deep in their souls.

As she imagined the scene, she realized what she must do. No, what she *wanted* to do with every cell in her body. She would continue to teach Bu and Pak English to repay them for their kindness and generosity and she would persuade Rex to postpone their trip to Bali so they could teach private lessons in Bandung for four or five months. They would make enough money to replenish Bu and Pak's *hajj* fund. The clarity with which she saw the future brought a broad smile to her face. She could not wait to see Bu and Pak's reaction when she shared her intention to repay them for their extraordinary kindness.

"Thank you for waiting so patiently," Widiyanto said, startling Maddie out of her daydream. She shot up from the bench and glanced at Skip who stood beside Widiyanto.

"What's happened?"

"The good news is Rex will recover now we have identified the reason for the bleeding, vomiting, and dysentery."

"I am *so* glad. Thank you, Doktor Widiyanto! What made him so ill? Was it really some type of black magic?"

"Some might call it black magic. A *dukun santet* is almost certainly responsible."

"But why would the *dukun santet* want to harm Rex and, even if he did, how could he do it?"

"She. The *dukun santet* is a woman. Let us say someone paid her to prepare a powerful potion to hurt, perhaps even kill, Rex and then mixed it in food or drink that Rex consumed, or paid someone else to do so. Revenge is always a likely suspect in these cases, but motive is irrelevant at this point. In any event, you must take him out of Indonesia as soon as possible."

"What!" Maddie cried and looked at Skip who nodded his agreement. "If he's going to recover, why does he need to leave Indonesia? Why isn't leaving Sukabumi enough?"

"Because your husband has obviously made a dangerous enemy here, someone who might try to harm him again wherever he is on Java, perhaps in the whole of Indonesia. Don't you see that? As his *wife*, surely you would not want him to suffer again, you would want to do *anything* to make sure he is safe," Widiyanto demanded, his tone signaling he expected a quick affirmative reply.

"I don't want to see him suffer again. But . . . I . . . I can't leave Indonesia now. I have . . . I have to stay here for a while longer . . . to repay . . . a debt."

"I am quite sure those whom you owe would understand saving your husband is more urgent than any repayment. Besides, you could work to repay the debt from the States. You have no choice. You must go with him, because he cannot travel by himself, not in his condition."

"But I . . . I have a responsibility to VSA, don't I, Skip? I can't just leave."

"Well . . ." Skip started to reply when Widiyanto interjected.

"I have heard from Skip that VSA believes its volunteers should respect and obey the local culture. In this case, your family and friends and colleagues in Bandung would be shocked if you, his wife, did not go with your sick husband. VSA would certainly understand your decision. Am I not correct?" Widiyanto asked Skip.

"You're right, of course."

Skip turned to Maddie and grabbed her arm. "You don't seem to understand. It's not just Rex who's in danger. If he stays in Bandung with you, you'll be at risk. And Widiyanto for helping you. I'm leaving the country as soon as I can and so should you!"

Maddie looked away down the hall toward the doors leading to the ward where Rex lay. She returned her gaze to Widiyanto.

"I'm not his wife," Maddie confessed in a whisper and threw her hand over her eyes, choking back sobs. "Not really. He is . . . or maybe was . . . my boyfriend. I'm not sure anymore, but he's not my husband. I made Skip promise not to tell anyone."

"Then you have a choice, Madeleine," Widiyanto declared solemnly. "But before I ask for your decision, let me first inquire: Is it true your travels outside the United States, in Taiwan, Japan, and even France, were, shall we say, less than satisfying?"

"How do you know that?" Maddie bristled and swiveled to confront Skip.

"How dare you share my secrets with a *complete* stranger?" she barked, jerking her thumb at Widiyanto.

"What? No, of course I didn't say anything to him."

"Then how in the world do you know?" Maddie demanded of Widiyanto.

"I do not *know* it, Madeleine. I have heard from those in Sukabumi about conversations in which Rex described your experiences. Would it be fair to say you failed to forge a lasting connection to anyone in those countries?"

"Yes," Maddie grudgingly admitted. "But not because I didn't try!"

"By naively assuming everyone in Taiwan would think and act like you, presupposing you could learn from books all you needed to know about Japan, and, in despair at your failures, cloistering yourself in an American enclave in Paris?" Widiyanto inquired.

Maddie's face crumpled.

"I'm sorry to be so blunt. I do not mean to blame you for mistakes that most commit when they encounter a foreign culture. I have made the same errors myself. My goal is to assist you in making the choice that now confronts you by casting your past experiences in relief."

"What is my choice?" Maddie asked quietly.

"You could, on the one hand, maintain your lie, refrain from further hurting your friends and family in Bandung, and leave with Rex. Given your unhappy experiences living abroad, no one would be surprised, perhaps least of all yourself, if you returned home and added Indonesian culture to the list of those that have frustrated and disappointed you."

"Or?"

"Or?" Widiyanto snapped. "I think you know very well what the alternative is. You find someone else to accompany Rex to Kansas while you return to Bandung. You confess your deceit, wreaking great pain on those who care deeply for you, and stay to make amends, if they accept your apology. In other words, you do not run from the foreignness of your family and friends in Bandung. You run toward it with open arms. You do not blame the strangeness of their language and customs for your actions. You accept complete responsibility for your behavior and for having caused great anguish, in the hope you will be forgiven and, with time, loved again."

"They will hate me for what I've done," she simpered and slumped forward. "Why wouldn't they? I despise myself."

"They will almost certainly abhor what you have done, and you are right that there is no guarantee of forgiveness. You must act without any expectation, knowing you may be spurned. However, if you seek unconditional love, Madeleine, you must be prepared to give it. Which path do you choose?"

After a few moments, Maddie wiped the moisture from her eyes and faced Skip. "Skip? Could I talk with you for a second?"

They walked across the hallway to a corner near a window looking out at the busy street below.

"Rex was still a VSA volunteer when he became ill, and Suyono said it will take time for him to recover fully. VSA has insurance to pay for his airfare home in the case of medical emergencies, doesn't it?"

"I believe so, yes . . ."

"Skip? Could *you* take him home? If the doctor says Rex is too ill to return to teaching and must be accompanied back to the States, the insurance will pay for your airfare, too."

"You've got to be kidding!" Skip's face flushed in anger. "I traveled day and night to come here only to discover you had lied to me and VSA. Despite that, I did what you asked and persuaded Widiyanto to help Rex, only to learn your marriage scheme had endangered yourself, Rex, Widiyanto, and me. And now you're asking me to give up my vacation to do what is *your* responsibility? Really, Maddie, your gall takes my breath away."

"I know it will screw up your vacation, but . . . you could stop in San Francisco on your way back to see your parents. *Please*, Skip," she pleaded, reaching for his hand.

Skip ripped his hand away and stomped a few paces from her. He glared back at Maddie, balling and unballing his fists. "Why have you decided to stay?" he growled. "If this has something to do with feeling guilty, my advice would be to leave and do no more harm to your Indonesian family and friends."

"No! No, it isn't guilt. I've had a lot of time to think and want to tell you what I've realized about myself. My parents' divorce and . . . and our break-up put me in a terribly dark place for months."

"Well, I'm sorry, Maddie, but . . . ."

"I'm not asking for an apology, Skip. I'm not telling you to make you feel guilty or to make excuses, but to explain my emotional state when I met Rex in Paris. Being with him made me feel alive again, and so when we returned to California it felt natural to live together. The more I relied on him to make me feel good about myself, the more insecure I became when other women flirted with him. That's why I pushed him to come to Indonesia."

"My God! Just to get him away from other women?"

"Yes. I know. It's a terrible reason to go abroad, but it's the truth. When I arrived in Bandung, something completely unanticipated happened. I became attached to my Bu and Pak. It's so . . . thrilling because it's so unexpected. Oh, Skip, I heard you describe how your friendships abroad have been some of the most mysterious and fulfilling experiences of your life. Developing those bonds made you feel *good* about yourself and optimistic for our future on this planet. I never understood what you meant. I . . . I frankly resented you for having found something I hadn't. But now I have or, at least, I feel close to it."

"Well, I'm glad for you, but still . . ."

"*Please*, Skip. Give me the chance to really know those people, to beg their forgiveness, to open my heart to them, to care for them, and to let them care for me, if they will after what I've done. It isn't guilt, I promise. It's . . ."

She stopped for a moment to sift through her emotions. What she was feeling was so unlike anything she'd been taught by her parents. *Her parents* . . . she hadn't thought of them in weeks. Suddenly, she came to a stunning conclusion.

"It's . . . the joy of discovering love where it's least expected and so preserving the hope that it may be found with anyone, even with those who are completely different, even with those you've treated terribly," she whispered. Yes, if she could find love with Bu and Pak, an elderly, conservative Muslim couple who lived a world away from California and whom she selfishly mistreated, perhaps she might discover it again with her parents.

"Preserving the hope love may be found even with those . . ." Skip murmured to himself.

Maddie grabbed Skip by the shoulders and stared fiercely into his eyes. "Please! I need you to do this for me!"

All right, Maddie," Skip exhaled. "A visit to California might be good for me."

"Good morning, Rex. I am pleased to see you doing better," Widiyanto said as he set a metal chair down next to the bed. "We were quite worried about you last night. However, now it is time to wake up."

Now it is time to wake up. Rex heard a voice call to him from above the bottomless lake into which he'd fallen. *Now it is time to wake up.* He felt himself float upwards until he broke the surface. He opened his eyes and blinked twice to focus. A doctor stood over him. He instinctively touched his nose, then his ears. The bleeding had stopped.

"Who . . . who are you?" he asked, then coughed roughly. "Is Maddie here?"

"My name is Widiyanto. I am a colleague of Dr. Suyono, the physician whom your family in Sukabumi called and who ordered you brought to this hospital. Maddie is here but she is asleep. It is five thirty in the morning. We were up quite late last night. She was kind enough to tell me what she knew of you to help me with my diagnosis."

"Could I have some water? And . . . you know, I'm suddenly starved. Something to eat."

"I'll ask a nurse to bring you water to sip in a moment. As for eating, my guess is some chicken broth might be appropriate, but Suyono will have to order that. He will be here in an hour to check on you. In the meantime, I thought we might talk about how you came to be so sick."

Rex closed his eyes. He remembered the monkey who spewed the sticky, putrid substance in his face and declared it was revenge for hurting Wulan. Was that a dream? It felt so real at the time, but he had no desire to sound like a lunatic. He had probably eaten something rotten, been poisoned, and hallucinated.

"I don't know. Probably ate or drank something I shouldn't have. How long have I been here?"

"I believe this morning is the beginning of the fifth day. And, yes, I agree you probably consumed something that caused a severe reaction . . . bleeding, vomiting, diarrhea, abdominal pain. How do you feel now?"

"Weak, very weak, and hungry, but no pain," Rex replied hoarsely.

"Excellent. You know, when I examined you, I noticed the scars on your back. Maddie told me you were beaten in the Philippines saving a young woman friend of yours, whose approval and perhaps love you desired above all. Maddie also related the story of how another young Filipina you had subsequently fallen in love with traumatized you by lying about carrying your child in order to persuade you to take her to the United States."

"Oh," Rex hesitated, not sure how or whether to respond. "Something like that happened, yes."

"Ah, having heard those stories from Maddie, I wondered how those encounters related to the rumors here in Sukabumi. The story being told is that you enticed a young woman student of yours with promises of love into kissing, touching, and perhaps more."

"We did NOT do anything more than kiss and hold each other," Rex rasped and tried to stop his head from spinning so he could think. "That's totally false!"

"I believe you, Rex Moreno. But I suspect your false promises of love hurt the young woman's feelings enough that she paid someone to poison you."

"*What!* Why? I told you. Wulan and I were just good friends. We met by chance, and I was just . . . just trying to be nice to her."

"Of course. Of course. You know, you remind me of myself many years ago," Widiyanto looked out the window and shook his head as if embarrassed by the memory of his youth.

"Really?" Rex coughed in disbelief. The older Indonesian doctor didn't seem in any way like him.

"Yes. I struggled as a young man to assert myself with strong, attractive women on whom I had become emotionally dependent. I'm not saying they took advantage of my affections in an evil way. No, they sincerely believed they knew what was best for me and naturally they encouraged me to think the same. I realized after much time and reflection, however, that I had become so deeply attached to these women—profoundly afraid they would reject me—that I unconsciously valued them and their opinions more than I respected myself. Does that resonate with you?"

"I don't understand," Rex said uneasily. "You seem so well-educated."

"Oh," Widiyanto chortled. "Even well-educated people can lose their sense of self by relying too much on another person whose affection they crave. I had some vague idea of the problem when I graduated from university in Jakarta. At the time, I felt deeply exploited because a beautiful young woman—whose arresting personality I could not resist—had abruptly ended our relationship despite my herculean efforts to preserve it. I believed traveling for graduate study in the United States, being in a different culture, would solve my issue with women. How wrong I was! Hah. Hah. Haaah . . ."

"I've never thought of Indonesian women as commanding," Rex grunted to Widiyanto.

"No? Well, to be sure, Indonesian women learn to exert their influence subtly, indirectly, one might almost say unconsciously, but nonetheless in a way that is palpable to their male friends. You mentioned Wulan, whom I have heard is lovely and, also, strong-willed. Did you not experience the exquisite sensation of being Wulan's marionette, a puppet who, in order to win her attention, enthusiastically tied his hands and feet to her strings while believing *he* was the dominant force in the relationship?" Widiyanto's eyes widened as he waited for a response.

Rex offered none. Instead, his mind raced to recall how he had felt with Miranda, with Joy, and with Wulan. He *had* always believed he was the one in control. Now . . . he was suddenly less sure.

"In any event, when I went to Cornell, I became involved with a Western woman. She was alluring, a charismatic Chilean whose culture encouraged her to be much more outspoken and forthright than I was accustomed to. I found being with her thrilling and the possibility of her casting me off unbearably painful. As a consequence, I scurried to do anything she wanted me to do all the while deluding myself into thinking *I* was the master. Have you ever felt that way?"

Rex felt his heart pound and face redden. He thought back to Diana, who threatened to withhold her love if he didn't go to the Philippines to start a revolution he had no interest in, and even to Maddie, who insisted on living and working in Indonesia despite his foreboding about living abroad again. He started to sweat. His breathing quickened.

"I'm not sure . . . I really don't know," he finally mumbled.

"My last year at Cornell, the Chilean woman crushed me and again I felt grievously ill-treated. I tried to extinguish the rage and agony with cheap wine. A friend of mine became worried. He urged me to talk with a college psychologist who had done some field work in Indonesia. By talking with this therapist over many months, I realized the core difficulty lay not with the women whom I adored and whose affection and approval meant everything." Widiyanto waved his hand in a circle. "But with me!" He pointed his long, bony index finger at his chest and paused for a moment.

"With you?" Rex demanded out loud. *With me?*

"Yes, with me. You see, my mother was passionate, headstrong, and devoted to me above all else. Needless to say . . . well, I found being with her compelling and returned her love with equal fervor. So much more so because my father, while quite learned and intelligent, was reserved and showed little interest in my upbringing. I loved my mother, but I came to realize after months of therapy that my unfortunate emotional dependence on women—whether Western or Indonesian—had its primal origin in the powerful, intimate bond with her. She was my sun. Her warmth provided life at the same time her immense gravity held me in her orbit.

"You blame your mother for loving you?" Rex asked, doubts about Mama swirling in his mind.

"I do not fault her in the least for loving me the way she did. *I* was the one who had failed to accomplish the arduous but necessary task of outgrowing my reliance on her. I did not develop a sense of self even when I left home and physically separated from her. Instead, I unconsciously sought out women like her, headstrong, intense, attractive women whom I valued more for how they made me feel than for who they were themselves. When these women threw me aside precisely because they tired of my dependence on them, I felt abused rather than recognizing that it was *I* who needed to take responsibility for my problems."

"And did you . . . did you take responsibility?" Rex asked in a whisper.

"Yes, finally. I faced up to my failings and did my best to understand myself. When I returned to Indonesia, I had several long talks with my mother. She listened to me intently and, while the adjustment took some time and caused us both some painful moments, we endeavored to change. Like lost pieces from two old puzzles that miraculously fit together in a new one, we became closer than ever."

Rex felt his chest heave with relief and tears flow down his cheek.

Widiyanto gazed down at him for a moment.

"I am glad my story may have helped you in some way, Rex Moreno." Widiyanto patted the sheet covering Rex's leg. "I can see you will recover with time and effort not only physically but psychologically. For now, let me get the water for you. I have one or two more questions to ask and then I must say goodbye. I have to prepare for some guests who will be arriving this evening."

"There's the bus to Bandung." Skip pointed about two-hundred yards down the road where a dusty red bus was letting passengers off. "It'll be here in a couple of minutes."

"I'm scared, Skip, really scared. What if Pak and Bu won't forgive me?" Maddie asked, her voice breaking.

"If they are the people you say they are, they will forgive you. But whatever happens, I know you'll get through it. You've always been one of the strongest, most determined people I know. I admire your willingness to atone for your mistakes. I . . . I know you've groused in the past that I think I'm perfect—know everything and never screw up. I can assure you that risk-averse, rational, rule-abiding Skip Burton has made plenty of mistakes and has a lot to learn. I'm sorry I've never been good at acknowledging my failings. I want to change, Maddie. You've shown me how and I can never thank you enough."

"Wow!" Maddie gasped, her eyes misting. "You saying that means the world to me."

Maddie stepped toward Skip. They embraced for a long time, neither one wishing the moment to pass.

"Give my love to your family," Maddie said finally. She took a step away, stopped, and faced Skip. "Love you . . . Always will," she whispered, her eyes glowing.

"Love you back. Always will."

They waved one last time and Maddie boarded the bus to Bandung.

A few minutes later, Amat drove up in a minibus with Rex in the back seat. Skip climbed in beside him and shut the door. Amat roared off, weaving the rented vehicle through the cacophonous streets of Sukabumi. Rex, who was still pale and weak, sat up and faced Skip.

"I'm so glad she decided to stay," Rex said. "She belongs in Bandung."

"So you're not upset she chose to stay rather than return with you? I'm astonished you would say that after everything you two did to be together."

"I'm still very fond of her, but when she told me her decision this morning, I didn't feel angry or abandoned the way I would have before. I thought back to how she looked at the wedding reception, beaming with delight dressed as a Javanese princess, and realized she found part of herself in Bandung, a part of herself I can never touch. I'm happy for her because I know she belongs here just as clearly as I know I do not."

"Could I ask you a personal question?"

"Sure."

"Wait a minute!" Skip called out to Amat. The road they were on was the one they had taken to Widiyanto's home. "Amat, why are we taking this road rather than the highway to Jakarta?"

"Big water on highway. This road no problem. We go Cimanggu then other Jakarta highway. Airplane, no problem," Amat assured Skip.

"Okay," Skip replied and shifted to face Rex. "Were you and Wulan just friends or . . . did something more happen?"

"Widiyanto told you about Wulan? Did you tell Maddie?"

"No, he made me promise not to. He wanted her to choose her way forward without knowing about Wulan and you."

"Really? God, he's an interesting man. He visited me early this morning. Told me all about his complicated relationship with his beautiful, strong-willed, devoted mother. He said he became dependent on how she made him feel emotionally and continued that pattern with women like her."

Skip recalled Widiyanto had described his *dukun* mother very differently, but said nothing.

"The more I thought about it, the more I realized I might suffer from the same problem. Strange, huh?"

"Yeah," Skip answered, wondering whether Widiyanto had misled Rex . . . or him?

"He also told me I had to leave Java now but could possibly return in six months to meet Maddie on Bali. I didn't say whether I would, but before he left he congratulated me on the decision I had made and said I had started on the lifelong path to wisdom. I have no idea what he meant. Do you?"

"No. No, I don't. But you didn't answer my question about Wulan."

Rex took a deep breath. "We spent a lot of time together. We flirted, felt attracted to each other, but nothing happened for months until we met by chance—at least at the time I thought it was by chance—on a trail she knew I liked to hike in the early evenings."

"She just happened to appear? Right before you left for your wedding reception in Bandung?"

"Yes, but she didn't know anything about my moving to Bandung. We met and began to walk together. Our shoulders grazed. We sat down in the shade of a clearing and, you know how it happens sometimes, our hands touched and we kissed."

"That's all?"

"She is smart, charming, and very beautiful, Skip."

"You made love? Are you sure that's what she wanted?"

"No! No, we didn't make love. After we kissed, she said she loved me and asked me whether I loved her. Being with her intoxicated me. I wanted desperately to kiss her again, to hold her so I . . . well, I told her I was falling in love with her. Maybe in that one moment I meant it, I don't know. Anyway, we kissed and held each other a little more and then she suddenly announced it was time to walk back. I have to admit I felt kind of rejected. Turns out so did she when she learned about my moving to Bandung."

"But you would have made love with her if she had been willing? Even though you were leaving to see Maddie the next day for your *wedding reception*?"

"I don't know," Rex said as he shook his head. "No," he continued after a moment, "I *do* know. I wouldn't have made love with her. Holding hands and kissing seemed . . . well . . . somehow innocent, playful. Making love the day before the wedding reception would have been depraved, a betrayal of both Maddie and Wulan. I . . . I know I don't always act wisely, but I'm not evil."

"Still, do you understand how angry your actions made Wulan?"

"Yes," Rex sighed. "I'm not proud of it. I seem to have trouble controlling myself, especially in foreign cultures. My impulsiveness has caused a lot of pain to myself, to others. Jesus, can you believe Wulan was angry enough to have me *killed*? People like Maddie seem to learn about themselves by being overseas. I drift into trouble the way Widiyanto said he did, seeking out strong, attractive women not for themselves but because being with them made him feel better about himself. I need to work through that before ever thinking about going overseas again."

"So that's what Widiyanto meant? You won't be meeting Maddie in Bali when she's finished?" Skip asked.

"No. She doesn't know that yet, or maybe she does."

"Then you have learned something about yourself from Widiyanto."

"That I need to deal with my relationship with my mama and my tendency to become overly dependent on women, terrified they will reject me, and furious when they do?"

Skip nodded.

"I know I have to go home to get better but it frightens me, Skip. I don't know what I will find there." Rex closed his eyes briefly and shook his head. "Do you think it's possible to completely change your relationship with the most important person in your life?"

"I don't know," Skip muttered to himself. "I've been asking myself that same question."

"Look, I'm exhausted," Rex wheezed. "I should get some sleep before we arrive at the airport. Wake me when we're almost there."

Rex leaned back, tipped his baseball cap over his eyes, and folded his arms in his lap. Soon, his breathing slowed and his head tipped slightly to one side.

Skip took out the book on Indonesia culture he had bought in Hong Kong, but couldn't concentrate. He put it down and stared out the window at the villages he had passed on his trip to visit Widiyanto. He marveled at how the *dukun* had helped Maddie and Rex. Skip wished he had a chance to talk with Widiyanto. He had been wrestling with a problem ever since their discussion in the hospital.

"Amat," Skip called softly to not wake Rex. "I'd like to say goodbye to Widiyanto. We're on the road that passes by his home. Please stop when we get there."

Amat nodded, smiled, and thrust his thumb up.

Thirty minutes later, Amat turned up the dirt trail to Widiyanto's home. A dozen or more villagers stood outside shouting and gesturing at his house. He was nowhere to be seen.

"Amat, come with me. Ask the men what happened."

Amat approached the crowd and spoke with them for several minutes. As the Indonesians gestured and talked, Skip surveyed Widiyanto's house. The four mosquito nets lay on the ground under the banyan tree. Strewn nearby were four or five large pieces of wood that looked like truncheons. The bloody bodies of a couple of dozen bats lay motionless. *Caw. Caw. Caaaw . . . Caw. Caw. Caaaw . . .* A forest bird's call reverberated from the treetops sounding so much like Widiyanto's raucous laugh that Skip instinctively searched the sky for the *dukun*. Stop it! His Western mind commanded. It *couldn't* be.

"Some man from village hear big noise last night and run here," Amat reported, snapping Skip back into focus. "He see many strange man with big stick. They come to hurt *dukun*. But *dukun* see strange man and use his power to call spirit. Spirit become many, many bat. Bat fly down and bite strange man. Strange man hit bat but too many, too many bat so strange man run away."

"No, that isn't . . ." Skip started to object. He knew Widiyanto had not summoned spirits but had loosened the mosquito nets, allowing the insects to swarm around the attackers and provoke a bat feeding frenzy. The facts were obvious. Yet the Javanese would never believe that explanation. More importantly, allowing everyone to think the *dukun* had summoned spirits would protect Widiyanto from further attacks.

"Amat?"

"Yes."

"I want the villagers to tell everyone they know about the *dukun*'s great power. And you should tell everyone you know, as well what you learned today."

"Okay. No problem."

"Does anyone know where Widiyanto is?"

"Man from village say Widiyanto go after strange man leave."

"Did he say where Widiyanto went?"

"He say *dukun* fly to forest to live as a bird."

Skip's mind again balked at the absurdity of the statement. "But . . ."

Amat held his hand up to interrupt. "He give paper to man from village for young Western man who visit today."

"He knew I would come? How . . . Oh, all right." Skip shook his head in wonder. "Let me see the paper."

Amat handed him a dirt-stained piece of paper on which Widiyanto had scrawled a short note.

Thank you for helping me guide Maddie and Rex onto the right paths. I wish you a safe journey to Kansas, Skip Burton, and afterwards on your own path to Los Angeles. I am sorry not to have the chance to meet your Jenny.

Skip's hand began to tremble as he read and re-read the note. How could Widiyanto have known he was going to Los Angeles to beg Jenny to forgive him? Had Maddie said something? But what? Maddie didn't know why Jenny had left him or why Skip would be desperate to seek her forgiveness. Maddie didn't know Jenny's name or where she lived.

The unanswered questions filling Skip's mind clamored for a rational response. None came. Suddenly, a familiar sound rolled across the sky above the forest behind the home. Skip turned toward the trees where the villagers said Widiyanto had flown. The call of a forest bird echoed in the distance.

Skip stared at the note in his hand. For years he had clung to the belief that rational thinking was the pinnacle of human achievement and that withholding judgment about other cultures was one of the highest expressions of human rationality in its battle against man's primitive instincts. When Jenny asked him to choose between VSA and her, she had insisted emotions played an equal role in defining the human condition. Widiyanto understood how to use reason but also how to avoid being trapped by it. How did he put it? He saw the world *through more than one eye.* Skip laughed. He had wanted to ask Widiyanto's help and here it was for the taking.

Skip did not know how Jenny would respond to his begging forgiveness. He did know that now he had the strength to ask and the courage to change. He wanted to understand better how manhandling emotions in the service of reason was just as harmful as giving sentiment free rein. He wanted to see the world through more than one eye.

Skip turned to walk back to the van. Just before he opened the door, the cry of a jungle crow resounded again behind him. *Caw. Caw. Caaaw . . . Caw. Caw. Caaaw . . .* Skip looked back over his shoulder, shaded his eyes from the glare of the sun, and scanned the treetops. He thought he spied something perched on the highest branch of the tallest tree. He squinted. Nothing. Had he perceived something or imagined it? He couldn't be sure.

Skip laughed at himself. He conjured Widiyanto and heard him sigh with exasperation. *Still searching for certainty in an uncertain world, Skip Burton?*

No, or, at least, not always. Thanks to you. He returned to the minibus and closed the door behind him. He was about to slip Widiyanto's note in the book on Indonesian culture when he stopped himself. For a moment, he looked from the note in one hand to the book in the other and back again. Then in one motion he tossed the book onto the carry-on in back. After carefully folding the note, Skip tucked it in his shirt pocket over his heart.

Epilogue

"So," Jen exhaled after a long silence, "you took Rex to Kansas, went to L.A. to beg Mom to forgive you, and you got together and married? Is that what happened?"

"Well, not exactly," Skip laughed quietly and shook his head, reaching up to touch his cheek where Jenny had slapped him so many years before. "Your mom—you know you're so much alike—was pretty strong-willed. She didn't answer my letters for a month and, when she did, told me she never wanted to see me again. But I wouldn't give up. I resigned from VSA, entered law school at UCLA, and continued to write her letters every few days. It took me a year to persuade her just to meet me and another year before she introduced me to your L.A. grandparents. By that time, I was in the last year of law school and I asked her to marry me again. She agreed but on two conditions."

"What were they?"

"That we live in Los Angeles near her family and never go overseas. She said she could deal with the subtle discrimination in California as long as she had her family close by, but had no desire to suffer the prejudice a mixed-race couple would face in a foreign culture."

"And you agreed even though you loved living and traveling abroad? You never went overseas again after Indonesia twenty—what?—twenty-seven years ago?"

"I loved her very much, Jen. I would make the same decision all over again in a heartbeat."

"And Maddie? I think I've seen holiday cards from her. What happened to her?"

"Maddie? She returned to Bandung, begged Pak and Bu to forgive her, and ultimately reconciled with them. She started an English as a Second Language school there, repaid her Indonesian parents, and made sure they went on their *hajj*. A few years later she met her old anthropology professor at a Mills reunion. They fell in love, married, and have two teenagers. Around a decade and a half ago she wrote me that she had decided to try to contact Emi. She realized if her Indonesia parents could accept her after all she had done, she could forgive Emi."

"And did she find Emi?"

"Yeah," Skip smiled. "They now run an organization that brings young Japanese women to Mills each summer for cross-cultural training and English language instruction. Maddie bounces back and forth every few months between the Bay Area and Asia."

"So someone who swore she would never go abroad again has the life you wanted?"

"No!" Skip snapped then added more softly, "I had your mother and then we had you. *That's* the life I wanted."

"Okay, Dad. Okay. And Rex? Do you know what happened to him?"

"A little. We exchange letters every couple of years. He earned a doctorate in cross-cultural psychology at the University of Kansas and started a practice in St. Louis specializing in helping international students at Washington University adjust to American culture. About twenty years ago, a few years after his mama passed away, he married a French graduate student—a former patient of his, if you can believe it. They spend every July and August in a cottage in Normandy not far from Le Havre where I first set foot outside the United States."

"Widiyanto? Francisco?"

"Maddie wrote about ten years ago to say she'd been in Sukabumi and asked about Widiyanto. She was told he never reappeared after the attack by the general's men. No one knew where he went or whether he was still alive. Many villagers still believed he lived in the trees behind his home as a forest bird. And Francisco . . . I received a letter about a dozen years ago from his grandson. Francisco suffered a heart attack while coaching a youth baseball team and passed away shortly thereafter."

Skip fought to keep himself from sobbing, tilted his head back, and gulped for air. A single tear slid down his cheek, as he continued. "Like your mom, they're both gone. And yet I remember them as clearly now as when I first met them. I thank them over and over again in my mind for what they taught me about myself."

Jen sat in the darkness with her father for several minutes. Then she placed the box down, stepped over to the door, and switched on the room light.

Skip shielded his eyes from the sudden glare.

"What are you doing?"

"You kept the box for a reason, didn't you?"

"What? No, I just forgot it was there."

"Come on, Dad! I'm your daughter. You can't bullshit me. The leaflet, the glove, the note, the picture all reminded you of a life you loved. Having them around was painful, but throwing them out—which you could easily have done—was even more so. You boxed them up and stored them away, just as you've hidden one of the most important parts of yourself for years. I'm right, aren't I?"

She folded her arms against her chest.

Skip examined the spots on the back of his hands.

"Look at me! I'm right, aren't I?"

"And so what if you are?" he said, looking up. "You're so young. You don't realize life is made up of choices, often excruciating ones. I decided your mom was the most important thing in my life and never regretted it."

"I loved Mom, too. Just as much as you. And I believe you had no regrets while she was alive, but she's not anymore. We have the rest of our lives to live and what you told me today convinced me we need to start now. I'm taking a gap semester to travel overseas."

"What? No, I don't think that's a good idea. Traveling alone for the first time . . ."

"It's *not* your decision. It's mine. And I'm not traveling alone. *You're* coming with me. We'll go to France first, visit Rex, then travel overland to Asia and meet up with Maddie in Indonesia and Japan. It's perfect timing. You have a sabbatical semester at the law school so you're free."

"Just like that?" Skip said and felt his heart begin to race. "Pick up and go for a half a year? Be reasonable, Jen. Besides, it's been too long and I'm too old. I'm . . . I'm not sure I have the strength for it anymore."

Jen threw her hands up in the air, then strode over and reached down to grasp Skip's head in her hands. He felt her eyes bore into his.

"Yes, it's impulsive, but what did Widiyanto teach you?"

Look at the world through more than one eye. As Skip mouthed the words, the cry of a forest bird resounded in his head.

"Yes, it's risky, but what did you learn from Francisco?"

Don't be afraid to fail, mi amigo, he heard Francisco laugh.

"You said I'm just as strong-willed as Mom was, but at least she gave you a choice. *I'm* not. You've been in that chair long enough. Get up, Dad! Get the *fuck* up!" She grabbed his arms and tried to pull him up.

"You have no right . . ." he protested and tried to free himself.

"Oh, I have every right," she interjected and yanked Skip to his feet. He felt her hands clasp his shoulders. "I'm your daughter and that gives me the right to learn about myself like you did by experiencing different cultures, even if that means getting hurt sometimes. And I'm mom's daughter, too, and that gives me the right to ask—no demand—that *you* start living again. You said you never felt more alive than when you were overseas, right? You know that's what she would want for you."

"Do I?" Skip murmured as Jenny appeared in his mind. *Do you? Do you forgive me, my love?*

You know I forgave you long ago. Now it's finally time you forgave yourself. Take care of our girl. Take care of yourself. Now go, my love. Go.

Skip took his daughter's hands from his shoulders and kissed them.

"All right, Jen. I guess it's time to put that box of memories away and go make some new ones."

ACKNOWLEDGEMENTS

First of all, I wish to thank the hundreds and hundreds of people whom I have met abroad during my more than six decades of wandering across cultures. People of all races, religions, and ethnicities welcomed me into their lives despite my foreignness, forgave my transgressions, and helped me become a better human being. These stories would not have been possible without them.

I am deeply grateful to my editor and publisher, Katharine Cluverius, for her insightful comments helping me to turn a series of interconnected short stories into a novel and for her unwavering belief in my ability to realize her vision.

I am indebted to screenwriter, author, and consultant, Richard Kletter, educator, literary critic, and poet, Tim Gillespie, author, Jerry Boak, and my friend, M.E. Malone, for their thoughtful notes on earlier drafts of the manuscript.

My thanks also go to Sasha Tropp, copyeditor, and Rebecca Lown, who designed the cover, for their outstanding work.

Finally, I am thankful today as I am every day for the love, encouragement, and support of my wife, Katie.

Q&A with Greyson Bryan

1) Where was your first trip abroad? Where was your most recent trip?

In 1958, when I was eight, my family of six children aged one-and-a-half to ten travelled by train from Los Angeles to New York and then by ship from New York to Le Havre, France. From there, all eight of us drove in a Volkswagen bus to Munich where my mother's sister lived, working for Radio Free Europe.

This year—sixty-four years later—my wife and I travelled to Berlin, where she ran the marathon, and then to Paris for ten days.

2) What is the funniest thing that ever happened to you while traveling overseas?

In the summer of 1973, I had arranged to stay with a family in Kyushu, Japan to improve my Japanese. On the first night, my Japanese mother prepared an especially elaborate sashimi and sushi dinner for me. I popped what looked like a beautifully carved flower in my mouth only to discover it was actually wasabi—spicy Japanese horseradish. My eyes overflowed with water, sweat soaked my body, and my face turned bright red, but I didn't say anything lest I embarrass my new family. Weeks later, when my language skills had improved, my Japanese mother told me she had noticed my reaction but didn't say anything to avoid embarrassing me! We laughed at our mutual, cultural discombobulation.

3) Which trip abroad is your favorite?

It's impossible to select a favorite out of hundreds of trips over sixty-plus years, but certainly one of the most memorable was my first trip to Asia, in 1969, when I travelled with a Stanford student group to Japan, Taiwan, and Hong Kong. It was in Hong Kong where I played on a local Y volleyball team and we won the city tournament.

4) What was your worst overseas trip?

I traveled from France to Japan in the summer of 1977 stopping in many locations, including Afghanistan. I was not allowed to check my small bag on an Indian Airlines flight out of Kabul. The bag was lost and I ended up spending three days in New Delhi sick with only one set of clothes.

5) Did any of what happened in the book actually happen to you?

Many of the stories reflect my own experience. The family trip to Europe in 1958, for one. I played baseball with a group of local boys in Mexico in 1962. I also competed on a volleyball team in Hong Kong in 1969 and travelled with a student group across Japan in 1971. These trips all led to chapters in the book.

6) Why do you think it is difficult for people to relate across cultures?

Most people learn their home culture at a very early age like their native language. Their home culture and native language become so ingrained that it is difficult to imagine relating to other cultures or speaking differently. Even if they desire to have the skills, it is daunting to learn them.

Some people grow up from an early age in bi-cultural and/or bilingual environments and seem to develop a flexibility of mind and spirit that allows them to relate more easily across cultures and languages. I have always admired that flexibility and sought through working and living abroad to develop it.

7) Do you miss living overseas?

During the pandemic, I did not travel abroad for nearly three years—the longest period of time I had stayed in the United States in more than five decades. That experience made me realize how lucky I had been to work and live overseas for much of my life and how much I missed the challenge and also the thrill of moving across cultures. Working on ABROAD undoubtedly helped me relive my time overseas through my characters.

8) When and how did you decide to write ABROAD?

I am fascinated by the range of reactions to living and working in a different culture—from the "we're not in Kansas anymore" shock of the first trip through ignoring and embracing, rejecting and relativizing, romanticizing and exploiting cultural differences. I suppose the idea of writing a novel that would explore this tension crystalized for me about four years ago, after the BIG series was finished. As I drafted the first pages, I decided to try to answer two questions: can we ever truly understand someone from another culture and can we ever truly understand ourselves if we don't try?

9) Who is your favorite character?

I like Maddie the best because I think she travelled the furthest in the book, that is, her character grew the most.

10) Did you really meet a *dukun?*

In 1972 when I was in Indonesia, I was told that a Javanese man whom I was to visit was a *dukun* or shaman, as we would call him. I was surprised to discover he had an extensive Western education and spoke at least four languages: Javanese, Indonesian, Dutch, and English. I did not spend much time with him, but fifty years later I needed a catalyst to help Skip, Maddie, and Rex realize themselves, and he formed the basis for the wise, sometimes Delphic Widiyanto.

ABOUT THE AUTHOR

GREYSON BRYAN is an international lawyer with a B.A. from Stanford and a J.D. from Harvard, who lived and worked for many years in Europe and Asia. A longtime L.A. resident, he is the author of the *BIG* financial thriller series, *BIG: Beginnings, BIG: Crisis* and *Ending BIG. Abroad* is his fourth novel.